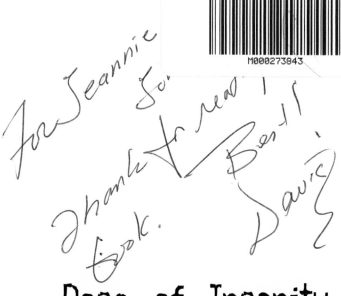
Dose of Insanity

Davis L. Temple, Jr.

"All things are poison and nothing is without poison, only the dose permits something not to be a poison."

—Paracelsus (1493–1541), widely recognized as the Father of Therapeutics

Dose of Insanity

Published by Wheatmark®
610 East Delano Street, Suite 104, Tucson, Arizona 85705 U.S.A.
www.wheatmark.com

ISBN: 978-1-60494-487-7
LCCN: 2010929978

Notes and Acknowledgements

My first three novels were about the South and featured a tatter-demalion array of characters that might have been inspired by William Faulkner. However, I had suffered a long and pressing need to write about another aspect of my life—the pharmaceutical industry and drug research and discovery. I had a marvelous career that spanned decades and involved either conducting or managing almost every phase of drug discovery and development. While the technical aspects of this book are accurate, the characters and their misadventures are pure fiction. They are, however, loosely based on real experiences encountered over my long career. I worked for the good guys; however, this story is about a battle of biblical proportions between a small biotechnology company and a giant pharmaceutical company that endeavors to squash them like a bug for their block-buster drug. This, after their own miracle drug goes wrong, really wrong and provides the dark core of this story.

Like Arthur Hailey's best seller, "Strong Medicine (1986), "A Dose of Insanity" is a thrilling presentation of the pressures, pitfalls, and risks encountered in the high pressure, billion dollar world of the pharmaceutical industry, but seasoned with a modern day dose of murder and mayhem. I wanted my antagonists to be amazingly evil and relentless and my protagonists to never yield; I wanted the winner to go undecided to the end. I believe I achieved those objectives and I hope my readers agree.

This story could not have been completed without the help and support of my friends and family. I would like to thank Shirley Briggs and Butch Mixon for reading and commenting on the manuscript, Chuck Wilcox for input regarding clinical trials, Adele Hailey and Alan Mendelson for consultation regarding Wall Street aspects, and Les Riblet for his knowledge of all things pharmacological. I would especially like to thank my wife Patty for her calculus teacher's eagle eye. Without her, there would be too many errors to count. Those that remain are my own. I also appreciate the inspiration and support provided by the Greensboro Georgia Writers Guild, especially Kathy Wright. Neither this book nor much of my life could have happened without the inspiration of the late John Shelton, my high school science teacher, or Joe Sam, my graduate school advisor, who passed away this past year.

1

How It All Began

The young scientist blinked. The data that was spread out before him on his laboratory bench could shock the scientific and medical community to its very core and revolutionize the discovery of drugs to treat diseases of the human brain. Perhaps coming to Germany had not been such a bad idea after all, though it had seemed so until this moment. He looked up at the knock on the door.

Steven Lewis was well into his second post-doctoral year in Wolfgang Schmidt's molecular biology laboratory at the Ludwig Maximilian University of Munich, known as LMU by faculty and students. The precocious student had come to Munich after achieving near superstar status at Stanford for his molecular biology doctorate research. Steve had ignored the pleas of his father in Kansas, who still held World War II against the modern day Germans. He had arrived at the fabled institution, founded in 1472, eager to make his mark. Steve wanted to walk in the footprints of Max Planck, the founder of quantum physics and Nobel laureate in Physics in 1918. So many great scientists had worked there and thirty-six of them had won Nobel Prizes. Sure, America had great universities, but he wanted to be a part of something old, a great lineage, and America hadn't even been officially discovered in 1472.

Steve's first disappointment had been the building that contained his laboratory. The LMU Gene Center was a modern glass and steel edifice that stood apart from the old university. The building contained excellent core facilities and scientists from all over the world worked on genetic studies of fundamental importance. The Gene Center was a great laboratory, but Max Planck had never worked there.

His second disappointment was the sheer size of Wolfgang Schmidt's research group. He had come to feel ignored, even slighted, but the simple truth was that the famous professor commanded a scientific army that was so large and bureaucratic that only a chosen few

1

students received any real guidance from their high powered mentor. Steve had never met the man! Herr Professor Wolfgang Schmidt was a leading contender for a Nobel Prize in Physiology or Medicine and spent most of his time on the lecture circuit trying to influence the Nobel Prize Selection Committee while his associates were left to the direction of lesser scholars. Really, the man was an empty suit, a dilettante, but Steve had reasoned that the scientist's fame could still serve him well.

Unaccustomed to such nonsense at Stanford, Steve had soon assigned his own priority to his pedestrian research problem involving the memory of roundworms. Steve's supervisor, Yan Ishikawa, was one of Schmidt's many laboratory directors, and Steve considered the man both incompetent and untrustworthy. The diligent post-doc easily generated enough data on his assignment to keep the man happy while frying his own fish.

Initially, it had been more of a hunch than anything else; he had no real data to support his theory, but little bits and pieces of anecdotal evidence had continued to point to the presence of an unknown factor—a peptide or protein—that had important effects on the health and function of the mammalian brain. Lewis had become driven by the concept and had foregone the nightly drinking bouts with his fellow lab mates at the local *biergartens*. Steve extracted proteins and studied gels while his friends threw up in deserted parking lots.

However, most Sundays found Steve enjoying the sights, food, and drink of the great European city that was Munich. Sunday mornings he visited museums and historic sites, but in the same afternoons he often retreated to *Das Englischer Garten*, a lush park near LMU, with an armload of scientific journals. The beautiful park was a quiet place for academic study, but as winter transitioned into spring, there was an explosion of life of all kinds.

One warm Sunday afternoon the naïve American found himself surrounded by unclothed young girls and was pleased to learn that would be the status quo for the summer. Steve would soon forget his conservative upbringing and join the group of happy nudists, who worshiped every ray of the rare Bavarian sun. There, he met a pretty, blond girl named Ana Weingarten. Ana immediately captured Steve's attention when he learned she was from Kiel, Germany. Kiel is a seaport to the north on the Baltic and is the birthplace of Max Planck, Steve's hero. Not only did Ana know a great deal more about Max Planck than he did, but she was a fellow graduate student in biology at LMU and could follow Steve's excited descriptions of his work up to a point.

Eventually, he fell hopelessly in love with the beautiful girl. She taught Steve the joys of swimming naked in the icy Isar River whose clear waters flowed from snowmelt in the Alps and rushed gurgling through the park. The two lovers would raft together with their nude friends and enjoy the trees and bridges and towers of the Deutsches Museum. Ana was his lover, best friend, and only confidant. Without Ana, it would have been a lonely existence.

The warm Bavarian sun sparkled in Ana's eyes as she sipped her morning tea. She stood out as a singular beauty among the young, German women who filled the café that morning. "So," Ana said with a smile, "why do you trust this boss of yours, Doctor …"

"Ishikawa," Steve supplied.

"Yes, Ishikawa. I worry about him figuring out what you are up to."

"I'm not hiding anything; I just report progress on my assignment when he shows up, which is infrequently. The silly project is going well, leaving me plenty of time—Saturdays, evenings—to work on my idea. At least until you came along," he added with a laugh.

Ana was very Germanic and direct in her way of speaking. "You *wunderbare Mann*, I love you, but I have to say that you are not thinking clearly! You have not considered what you will do if your idea comes to fruition. If you are correct, this could be of great importance. How could you publish your findings without the blessing of this Ishikawa and his *fuehrer*, Herr Schmidt?"

Steve looked at the smart girl for a long moment and responded, "You are correct; I have not thought this through entirely. I have been trying to dream up a story that makes sense and lets everyone off the hook. It is true that it was some of my observations on the behavior of the worms that got me thinking, and I went on from there …"

"You Americans! So a little worm got you thinking and you have almost completed a major piece of science without even bothering to discuss it with your research director? How nice. Ishikawa will probably chop you up with his Samaria sword and make sushi out of you for the Friday afternoon research meeting."

Steve grinned at her and waved at the waitress for a check. He had no fear of the cocky, little Japanese scientist. "My Dear, you are busting my balls, but you're right; I have to refine my story. Now, seeing you're feeling so frisky this morning, maybe we should adjourn to my apartment for a romp?"

2

The Price of Science

Despite Steve's long hours in the laboratory and Ana's rigorous academic schedule, their relationship matured and prospered. Ana spent her evenings in Steve's laboratory immersed in her graduate studies but would drop her books at a moment's notice to assist Steve with a particularly difficult experiment.

Eventually, Lewis isolated and purified a previously unknown, small protein from rat brain. It had not been easy—as is so often the case, complex isolation and purification procedures had yielded nothing at the end of the day—yet he persisted until he had *his* protein. Although his excitement was justified, he was at the beginning of a long process that would be required to provide the myriad of data needed to disclose his discovery to the world and have the scientific community embrace it. Surely, he could get his work published in *Science* or *Nature*.

Ana was assisting Steve with an experiment late one evening when Ishikawa walked into the laboratory unannounced after he had noticed Steve's laboratory light still burning. He smelled of alcohol and raw fish. Steve's heart sank as he watched his supervisor scan the laboratory, missing little. Eventually, his bloodshot eyes settled on Ana. "Do I know you?" he asked rudely.

Steve silenced the quick-tempered girl with a hard look. "Oh, this is Ana Weingarten. She's a biology graduate student here who occasionally assists me and learns new procedures in return. Ana is very good, I might add."

Ishikawa obviously didn't like this surprise but moved on to more pressing matters. "I here because I no understand your monthly laboratory charges. You work on roundworms, yet big rat bill. What you do with all these rats?"

Steve pretended to be surprised and examined the bill. "Hmm;

yes, I have been using some rats, but this seems a bit excessive. An overcharge, perhaps."

"Dr. Lewis, I asked you what you do all these rats—any rats, for that matter?"

Steve knew that the jig was up if he didn't manage this situation effectively, "Sir, we haven't talked in some time, and with all due respect, I felt free to follow up on whatever novel observations or ideas our project generated." Steve continued though no immediate affirmation was given. "Based on my findings with worms, I came to believe that there had to be an important mammalian brain factor that had not been discovered, and yes, I have been looking for it. This work is being done on my own time." Steve nodded to the clock on the wall which indicated it was well past midnight.

Ishikawa shrugged; he liked students who were willing to go the extra step, but he was a product of the old boys' club system in Japan and would not tolerate disobedience. Extra work was to be dedicated to *his* brilliant ideas, not the hair-brained ones of some green student. On the other hand, if this kid had somehow stumbled onto something important, he would take full credit for it and his own vainglorious, Nobel Prize-seeking boss would love him all the more for it. Besides, Ishikawa had felt his relationship with the future Nobel Prize Laureate slipping almost daily and he would do almost *anything* to restore it and keep his position at LMU.

"I no tolerate disobedience, but what is done is done. You be in my office first thing in the morning and show me what you have so far. If it looks important, you can continue with my close supervision. If not, you will do as I say."

The little man nodded to Ana and strutted out of Steve's lab without another word. "What an arrogant *esel*," Ana exclaimed as soon as Ishikawa was gone. "You should resign your position and find someone reasonable to work for."

Steve laughed. "Not yet; not just yet."

Steve was waiting in Ishikawa's outer office when his supervisor's secretary arrived the following morning. "Dr. Lewis?"

"Yes, Dr. Ishikawa requested that I meet with him in his office first thing this morning and here I am ..."

"I'm so sorry; Dr. Ishikawa was unexpectedly called out of the country. He will not be back from Japan for at least six weeks. Family matters, you know. His directions to you are to continue to work on the projects you discussed last night and then to meet with him as soon as he returns."

✑

Steve had been given a reprieve and had ample time to fully characterize his protein with Ana's help. Cloning and expressing the substance provided the scientist with sufficient material for study, and eventually he was able to generate antibodies specific to that protein so that he could light up areas of the brain where the substance resided and exerted its actions. Once Lewis had discovered a human brain protein with close homology, he could no longer remain silent. The world needed to know about the new brain factor he named *promodulin*. But he dared not even think about preparing a manuscript describing his discovery without Ishikawa's permission. He would wait.

Eight weeks after Ishikawa departed for Japan, Steve's telephone rang. It was the man's secretary requesting that he have all his data laid out in his laboratory the following morning for convenient review. The bastard was back, and it was show-and-tell time. The remainder of the day was spent in preparation for the meeting and the following morning he felt his confidence soaring. The gestalt of his careful work was clear—promodulin was an important brain factor previously not known to the scientific community and it would undoubtedly attract attention and open up many new avenues for investigation. He might even become the most cited scientific investigator ever.

There was a light rap on the door and Steve nodded politely to his supervisor. "Hello, Dr. Ishikawa; welcome back from Japan."

Ishikawa managed a grunt and picked up a gel without saying a word. Apparently the trip had gone badly. The man looked even more angry and emaciated than before. He now bore the weight of family financial difficulties in addition to his concerns about his position at LMU. Steve became agitated as the man carelessly handled key pieces of data that had taken endless hours to prepare. Eventually, Ishikawa withdrew a notebook from his case and directed Steve to walk him through the entire process. Steve nodded his agreement and waded in while Ishikawa scratched furiously in his notebook. However, Steve was no one's fool and left out several key steps.

Steve talked with few interruptions for over two hours. He kept his conclusion simple, knowing better than to make outrageous claims about his discovery. Best to let the data do the bragging, he considered, assuming the bastard understood any of it.

Ishikawa stared at Steve, slowly moving his head from side to side. He looked for all the world like a cat contemplating its next meal while watching a bird flit about a cage. Finally, he mustered the courage to state his dismal opinions.

"Many problems; I see many problems with this work. You no ready to go off on your own with such an ambitious project. I no give you permission either; you also violate many regulations. Where animal welfare approval of your rat experiments? You ignore me and you ignore LMU committees and requirements."

Ishikawa stood silently before Steve with his arms crossed and a sardonic smile on his face, waiting for his student's response. The only complaint the man had waged that was even vaguely true was the one regarding the necessity to obtain permission from the animal welfare committee. Steve had simply forgotten in his enthusiasm.

"Dr. Ishikawa, as I said before, you are never to be found, so I assumed, and wrongly perhaps, that it was my decision to follow the project wherever it took me. You are wrong when you doubt my work; I was recognized for research excellence at Stanford and I get better every day. I have left no loose ends or shaky findings—period! All experiments have been repeated many times and are fully reproducible. promodulin, as I have named the protein, will create a major stir when this discovery is published and besides, could be worth millions to the university. This is no time to punt the ball!"

Punt ball? What's this punt business? Ishikawa wondered. The angry man closed his eyes and took a deep breath. Americans! God, why couldn't they just dance in lockstep with their superiors like Japanese and German students did. Americans were both insolent and entrepreneurial—a dangerous combination.

"You no tell *me* whose work to question—you challenge my honor as a professor. Now on, you are on probation with the LMU Gene Center and will do exactly what I say. You mess up again, and you are out of here!"

Steve bristled; he had had enough of the arrogant, little prick who had no ground to stand on. He had studied Ishikawa's resume and knew he had accomplished far more at Stanford than the poorly trained Japanese scientist had in his entire freaking career. That's why he still hung around LMU as a glorified post-doc. He probably couldn't snag a real job if his life depended upon it.

"Dr. Ishikawa, it is true that you hold power over me at this moment in time. It also remains true that I did not come to this respected university to serve time under you. Why would I do such a stupid thing? You are an unknown scientist with a thin resume and are a very poor supervisor to boot. I traveled all the way to Munich to work for Wolfgang Schmidt and only him. Now, I am going to demand a meeting with Schmidt, and either he will address my situation in some favorable way, or I, *and my findings* , are history. Do you understand me, Ishikawa?"

Ishikawa realized that he couldn't afford to have this happen. His relationship with Wolfgang Schmidt became more tenuous by the

: was bright red and shaking with anger. "Ahh, big mistake
et with Schmidt; he respect what I say—big man eat you for
breakfast and destroy your career."

Steve's face hardened and he clenched his fists and walked slowly
toward his adversary. The insulted supervisor raised an accusing finger at Steve and his mouth made little Os, like a goldfish in a bowl,
but no words formed. Ishikawa, having lost face and boiling with anger, turned and hurried out the door. Ishikawa couldn't let this ride;
he would get to Schmidt first. Besides, the shamed supervisor gloated, he had contacts—dangerous contacts. This American would soon
understand how things worked in Germany.

Steve turned to the sound of clapping behind him just as Ana
stepped out from the darkness of the adjacent laboratory.

"Bravo, you silly goose; I think you just dropped the atomic bomb
on Hiroshima again. I was worried about you and did not want you to
meet with the bastard without a witness, but I did not expect you to
threaten him with your fists. You might as well start packing."

"Ana, wow, you never cease to amaze me. And you are right, I
should not have embarrassed Ishikawa and made him lose face in his
own territory—he is just ignorant."

"Ignorant maybe, dangerous definitely. The rumor around LMU
is that he has some connection to the Yakuza—the Japanese Mafia.
Something was said about a brother. I don't recall what, exactly. And,
Schmidt may not be much better; at one time he was a greatly loved
faculty member at the university, but now he is a driven man and sees
only the Nobel Prize, dangling there, waiting for *him*. He has become
ruthless and would stop at nothing, especially not some American
post-doc who has something he could use. I believe he was a Hitler
Youth, whatever that's worth."

Steve made a clumsy attempt at the *Heil Hitler* salute and em-
braced the girl and said, "Yakuza in Germany sounds a stretch, but
I agree; we do in fact have a risky situation here. No matter, what's
done is done, and I'm getting on the phone right now to try to get to
Schmidt before Ishikawa does. I know he's in town at the moment."

♀

"Professor Schmidt, I am sorry to interrupt your meeting but one
of your post-doctoral students, Steven Lewis, is on the line, and he
said that it is extremely urgent that he speak to you."

Schmidt rose to address his secretary. The man stood ramrod
straight with steel gray hair and chiseled features. He towered over
both his assistant and his troublesome guest and looked more like a
World War II U-Boat captain than a university professor.

"*Danka*, Marta. Please tell him that I am not available, but someone will contact him in the near future."

"So, Dr. Ishikawa, you can wipe that smirk off your face. I understand the situation perfectly, but remind me once again who this Lewis is; I have never had the pleasure of meeting the man."

"The difficult case is an American post-doc from Stanford who has been with us for about two years. He big problem; both arrogant and entrepreneurial. Do much work on his own behind my back with LMU resources and is threatening to walk away with some pretty interesting discoveries. He had the nerve to menace me with his fists."

Schmidt touched a match to his pipe and sucked on it vigorously for a moment, thinking that it was too bad Lewis didn't use them on this slimy bastard that stood before him whining like an infant. Ishikawa and his unhappy students were a never ending source of problems he didn't need, particularly at this critical moment in his career. He made a mental note not to renew Ishikawa's contract, when that opportunity arose. Before Ishikawa, he had so many good Japanese researchers.

The professor took a few more puffs on his pipe and then said, "Ishikawa, you are a poor research director and don't know how to manage young scientists, particularly Americans. This is an issue we must deal with, and soon. However, you were right to come to me in this case. First of all, I cannot afford trouble of any kind in my group. Do you understand that?"

Ishikawa understood.

"Then, I have a couple of questions to ask. First, is this ... Dr. Lewis a good and believable scientist?"

Ishikawa nodded grudgingly.

"So he is a good scientist, likely well trained at Stanford. Well then, do you believe that this protein he has cloned—threatens to steal—is legitimate and that it really is a novel factor that regulates brain function?"

Ishikawa replied, "Yes, I have seen all data, and it could be ... very valuable to LMU or *ourselves*, depending on how we handle this. This novel discovery might be the basis whole new avenue brain research and drug discovery."

Schmidt frowned; what was this lunatic thinking? "Doctor, I need not remind you that we are LMU! But I do believe that Dr. Lewis has something of great value that cannot be allowed to walk out the door of LMU Gene Center. You and I shall derive one hell of a lot of publicity by publishing this work in *our* names only. Can you simply make him go away? Perhaps seize all his data and then fire him?"

"No, big mouth and at least one nosy girlfriend on campus. Accident only way."

Schmidt, though a former Hitler Youth was aghast. "You mean kill him?"

"Yes; accident. I have ... *connections,* you see. My brother, Shan-Ti, big man in Yakuza in Germany. Make many people go away, no problem."

Schmidt assumed a look of disbelief. "Japanese Mafia, tattoo covered criminals, in Germany. Why?"

Ishikawa smiled smugly. "Easy. German automobiles in big demand among fellow Yakuza in Japan. Think BMW and Mercedes automobiles are like *Panzers* make Yakuza invincible. Shan-Ti's men steal cars and he arrange for illegal transport to Japan. Scam easy business and big money, but Yakuza descendents of the *Samurai warriors* and kill people on side just because can. For one-half million euros, Steve Lewis have bad accident."

Schmidt knew that he had done some questionable things in his time, but kill an innocent student in cold blood, never. Besides, that was a lot of money he didn't have at the moment. But maybe, just maybe, he knew where to get it. promodulin could easily clinch the Nobel Prize for him. And what's a troublesome, little American shit compared to that?

"Ishikawa, why don't you go tend to your business. I'll get back to you on this after I have made some phone calls; *verstehen?*"

Schmidt watched the small man slink out of his office and then considered his options. They could simply impound his office and fire Lewis, but based on what Ishikawa had said, that seemed risky. There was also the mouthy girlfriend to consider; she was obviously dangerous to him as well. Perhaps they both had to go. He glanced at his watch and noted that business offices in Connecticut would be open. A quick scan of his computer file located the number he was seeking and he dialed it on a secure line.

"May I speak to Maxwell Hall, please?" He took several puffs from his pipe before the President and CEO of Apex Pharmaceuticals, the largest pharmaceutical conglomerate in the world, came on line. Apex had supported Schmidt's laboratory with big bucks in the past.

"Hello, Wolfgang, how are you?"

"I am fine, thanks. You?"

"Also fine and the business is keeping me hopping; that's for certain. Always looking for new drugs, but it's getting more difficult all the time. Seems the low-hanging fruit has all been picked."

"Look, Maxwell, I am calling you in regard to a very important and confidential matter. The gestalt is that I believe that you and I can be of great value to one another. I need the Nobel Prize, you need new drugs, and I very well may hold the key to both."

"I'm all ears, Wolfgang."

"My laboratory has made a major discovery that will rock the biomedical community. We have characterized a previously unidentified protein that regulates behavior in laboratory animals; we call the substance promodulin. Once these findings are published, every drug company in the world will jump on this approach as an entirely new way to develop drugs for the treatment of psychiatric disorders. However, if one company had a heads-up on the data, they could blow the competition away and capture new markets worth billions."

Hall laughed, "And you would receive the Nobel Prize for your contribution; so what do you need me for?"

"Let's not mince words, Maxwell. I need additional funding to ... to expedite the project. I think about one million U.S. dollars would do the job. This would be under-the-table, you understand?"

Hall understood under-the-table deals very well since that was his preferred way of doing business. "And for this, I own the patent," he said, probing for position and value for dollar.

"No, what you will get for your money is all the data required for you to develop a drug screen several months before the publication appears—and my consultation, of course. You will soon find your drug but never mention how you discovered it. Sooner or later the LMU patent attorneys will sue you, but you can deal with that. Agreed?"

"All right, I trust you, Wolfgang, but I need to know how you intend to use the money"

℘

Although Steve had never heard another word from Schmidt or Ishikawa, he had continued to extend his findings, and he became more excited by the day. However, he knew he was still in hot water and one day the axe would fall, so he tried to cover himself as best he could by removing certain data from his laboratory and hiding it in his home. Although promodulin had held up as the mother of all brain proteins in terms of its beneficial effects, Steve learned that there were other closely related substances in the brain that opposed the positive effects of promodulin. Any drug that affected these unknown brain modulators could have devastating effects. All data related to these new *promodulin-killers*, as he had come to call them, were hidden in his apartment and remained unknown to his supervisors. If push came to shove and he had to leave Germany, this provocative data would leave with him.

Exactly six weeks after Steve's war of words with Ishikawa, things changed very quickly. It was a dark, rainy day and Ana had just left his laboratory for class. Big rain drops spattered on the massive glass windows of the Gene Center, not improving Steve's uncomfortable, depressed feeling. That morning it was back to the round worms, which added to his melancholic feelings. There was a light rap on the door and Steve was almost happy for a reason to leave the silly worms which encoded little of interest in their genome.

It was Ishikawa and he was accompanied by two LMU security guards. "Ah, so, Dr. Lewis working hard on his *last day* at the Gene Center. Very impressive, must be near the cure for death," he quipped.

"What do you want, Ishikawa?"

Ishikawa nodded at Steve's clenched fists. "Oh, that very bad idea, today. I come tell you, you fired, Dr. Lewis. I think you understand why, so no need to discuss. Now, please relinquish your security pass to these gentlemen and clean out your desk. Guards will watch, so take only what belongs to you. No data!"

Ishikawa waited outside humming an irritating Japanese children's song about Samurai warriors. Eventually, the two guards emerged with their ward and Ishikawa said, "Now for good news!" He handed Steve two envelopes; the first one contained a check for one month's pay plus a document promising five more months severance if he agreed to be out of Germany by the following day. The second envelope contained a first class, nonrefundable Lufthansa ticket to New York's JFK with a flight departure time of 8:00 p.m. the following evening. There was also five hundred dollars.

"One more thing, Professor Schmidt has made the most generous offer to write you a positive recommendation if you require that to land a new job in America." It made Ishikawa sick to even tell that lie. "You have nothing to complain about."

Steve's face was red and his pulse was racing. "Yes, I do. What about promodulin and all the work I did? It is *my* discovery, after all!"

"Professor Schmidt will deal with promodulin now. You will be awarded whatever credit is due when we publish this work. That all! Guards, escort him off the campus!"

It was raining even harder as they exited the building, and once the guards found he had no car, they drove him the few blocks to his apartment. Fortunately, they were embarrassed by the firing, a rare event in Germany, and wanted to help. For that, at least, Steve was grateful. As soon as his few things were safely inside his apartment, he called Ana on his cell phone.

"Ana, it has happened; Ishikawa fired me this morning. I ... I don't know what to do.

"Oh, Steve, don't say one more thing. I am between classes and will be right over."

Though it was painful, Steve explained exactly what had happened to Ana, not forgetting that he had to be out of Germany by 8:00 p.m. the following evening. Predictably, Ana exploded.

"Those ungrateful bastards! How could they have done this to you after all the work you did? Only one reason! They have stolen promoduln because it is the key to ... to the great Wolfgang Schmidt's Nobel Prize. They pay you off for a *pfennig* and then take full credit for the discovery."

Steve looked at Ana in amazement. She was right; he was being robbed of his lifetime discovery. End of story. "They can't get away with that; they have to at least credit me on the paper. I'll sue them— I'll sue them all."

Ana took on a sarcastic tone. "Poor darling—broke, unemployed American is going to sue Herr Professor Schmidt and the great big LMU? *I don't think so.*"

"Well, what then?" Steve retorted.

Ana glanced up as the thunder shook the old apartment building. "You will be gone, but I will be here, and I will think of something."

It was Steve's time to be unconvinced. "I can't imagine what, but that brings up another issue, doesn't it? What are we going to do about our relationship? I have to get out of Germany, and you have to finish your studies. My thinking is: I will put this behind me and get a good job back in the States. You have another year at LMU, and it will take me that long to find a job and get established. I am leaning toward Southern California; there are hundreds of biotech companies there, and I can easily find a job, as can you when you come to join me. I love you, Ana, and I want to marry you, but we have to get over this bump in the road first."

She ran to him and held him close, brushing away rare tears. "Steve, you are a strong and practical man. And, yes, I will move to California when the time comes. I know that you will never be able to return safely to Germany, but my family has some money and I can visit you whenever I have a break. I have never been to California but I know it is beautiful and we can make a *wunderbare Leibbish* there. I will stay with you and help you pack and clear out your business. When the time comes tomorrow evening, I will drive you to the airport in my car. Tonight, you and I have some very personal business to tend to ... *Ich liebe dich.*"

♀

Ana skillfully merged her little Volkswagen with the rush hour traffic on Saurbrushstrasse and then accelerated, on her way to deliver Steve to the Munich airport. She was an expert driver of the Germanic variety and scared Steve to death with her frantic maneuvering among the much larger BMW and Mercedes Benz automobiles. Ana laughed when she noted his white-knuckle grip on the dash.

"It's OK, Steve; you only have to survive another twenty minutes, and we'll be at the Lufthansa terminal." But her broad smile faded as she realized that a large, black Mercedes tailed her closely through every lane change.

Steve said, "What are you doing?" as she accelerated to over 150 kilometers per hour.

There was real fear in her voice when she answered, "Someone is ... following us, more like *chasing* us."

Ana swerved onto the U6 and the Mercedes momentarily lost ground, but its powerful V-12 engine regained the loss in seconds. By now, Ana was in the far outside lane and was rapidly approaching slower traffic ahead.

Steve screamed, "Watch out!" just as the Mercedes pulled alongside the speeding Volkswagen. For a brief moment, the passengers of the two automobiles, separated by a few feet, were staring at one another. The set expressions on the faces of the two Asian men in the Mercedes belied their intent. Ana screamed as the other driver jerked his steering wheel hard to the left and collided with her old Beetle with a grinding screech. The lighter car hit the divider, flipped over the concrete edifice, and then collided head-on with an oncoming gasoline transport truck. There was a blinding flash followed by a thunderous explosion. Other speeding traffic joined in the melee, and whatever was left of the Volkswagen and its passengers was reduced to bits of charred flesh and searing hot metal.

The Mercedes had served its lethal purpose and had suffered only a crumpled, left front fender in the attack. It and its murderous passengers were soon lost in the flow of rush hour traffic. Within days, the fender would be replaced in a carefully hidden Yakuza shop a few miles away, and the like-new Mercedes would soon thereafter be on its way to Japan to meet the pressing needs of the Japanese Mafia.

The loss went far beyond the promising lives of Steve Lewis and Ana Weingarten. The last surviving sheet of Steve's report describing the dark side and risks associated with the promodulin system burned brightly as it soared in the breeze above the bustling freeway. Soon, the biomedical community would be excited by the promodulin story, but they would only have the positive side of it.

♋

In January, 2006, Wolfgang Schmidt and Yan Ishikawa published a paper in the journal *Science* that captured the imagination of psychiatric and drug researchers around the world, almost guaranteeing Schmidt a Nobel Prize. Sadly, no credit was given to the hardworking, young American Ph.D. who had made the discovery and paid for it with his life. The paper described a previously unknown protein that had been cloned from rat brain and its function elucidated. Promodulin was shown to regulate mood and to maintain normal psychic functioning in laboratory animals. A homologous protein cloned from human brain and shown to regulate neuronal plasticity (growth of neurons) in cultured, human brain tissue was also described. Some preliminary experiments strongly suggested that conventional psychotropic drugs might work by exerting weak effects on the protein, promodulin. It was not claimed, but obvious to readers of the *Science* article, that if drugs could be devised with more powerful and specific effects on promodulin, then a revolution in the treatment of mood and psychiatric disorders might follow—along with billions in profits for the lucky drug company that solved the puzzle.

However, the playing field was not level; Apex pharmaceutical's investment in death had given that company a leg-up. It had already developed a molecular screen for promodulin-related drugs. They had to only sort through thousands of small molecules until they found their magic bullet. Others could not possibly catch up; besides who could possibly compete with the resources of Apex?

Large pharmaceutical or biotechnology companies eager to take advantage of such a rich discovery normally enter into negotiations with the innovator university and its inventors for rights to use a newly discovered protein as a tool for drug discovery. Such negotiations tend to be laborious and highly competitive—consuming months of time and millions of dollars.

Perhaps, because of the inconceivably high stakes involved, several companies, abandoning intellectual property concerns, went after the exciting protein on their own. Though it was never discussed publicly, only one other company was successful in its efforts. Genplex, a much smaller player than Apex, not only cloned the protein and successfully developed drug screens, but also had the extreme good fortune of an early screening hit or discovery, thus putting Genplex on the same footing with Apex.

What was announced in public in the loudest Wall Street terms was that Apex Pharmaceuticals, the largest drug company in the world, and Genplex, a much smaller, but successful, player, both had powerful new drugs that acted through the recently described promodulin system and held great promise for the treatment of psychiatric disorders. Chemical structures of the new drugs and how the molecules were discovered remained a closely guarded secret. The competition correctly guessed the new drugs to be small molecules of some complexity, but that was of little help to their scientists. The competition soon gave up.

Wall Street anticipated new products with sales in the billions, and Apex and Genplex stocks went through the roof. Internal pressure to successfully develop their respective drugs soon reached the boiling point. Apex's falling earnings needed bolstering, and Genplex's patent on their blockbuster recombinant protein for the treatment of blood disorders was about to expire, putting 50 percent of their future earnings at risk. Neither company returned the frantic telephone calls from an international law firm in Munich. There would be time to deal with litigators later; should the need arise.

The stage was set: Genplex and Apex, like David and Goliath, were firmly locked in a battle to the death. Winner take all.

3

Genplex Pharmaceuticals Research Headquarters, Madison, Connecticut

August, 2008

Jerrod Wesley, Genplex's young Vice President for Research and Development, strained his eyes as he tried to count the distant sails floating in the haze over Long Island Sound. It was past 6:00 p.m. and he should be out there with his sailing friends in the regatta. The one with the bright red spinnaker might even be his own boat, *Sea Sprint,* sailed by his crew of drinking buddies. Where was the bastard, anyhow? He shook his head; the empty company helipad shimmered in the late afternoon heat. Sometimes the glass office on the fifth floor penthouse just didn't make up for the personal sacrifices. Jerrod looked to the east. It was too far to Groton to be able to see the monstrous enemy that called itself Apex Pharmaceuticals, but he could almost sense them plotting their next move to screw him. Jerrod shuddered; this was not paranoia on his part; he was a pawn in a chess game of enormous proportions.

He turned at a rap on his heavy, glass door. It was Wanda Lassiter, his long-suffering administrative assistant. She was very efficient, alarmingly attractive, and a recent divorcee. Jerrod nodded and she stuck her head in the door and said, "Dr. Vettori's helicopter is still on the ground in New York with engine trouble; he just left in a limo. He said to meet him at eight-thirty sharp at Il Tosco and no guests, please." The young Vice President bit his lip as he considered inviting Wanda for a drink before dinner but he discarded the dangerous thought when he spotted the small Asian male in an ill-fitting white lab coat waving a yellow pad; as usual, he was in an animated state of excitement.

Wanda smiled and said with a wink, "It looks like Dr. Chen needs to see you immediately, Sir."

Jerrod mumbled, "What's new?" but said aloud, "Let him in Wanda and you go home. It's been a long day." Wesley knew that most chemists were happy to work in the shadows of the higher profile biologists, but not Chen; the young chemist would do anything to be recognized. He had survived on peanut butter while a graduate student at Cal Tech and he intended to make the sacrifice pay off. Although possessed by unbridled enthusiasm, Chen was usually worth listening to.

Wanda waved her patented bye-bye, and Chen bounced into the office, sprawling on Jerrod's leather couch without being invited. Jerrod chuckled and said, "Hello, Dr. Chen; what do you have that is so pressing at this late hour?"

"New chemistry work! High yield of drug!"

"Chen, are you referring to the new process that Professor Abraham proposed to us last week?"

Chen nodded. "Axilon now cheap; we beat Apex competition. Kill their lousy drug, Medulin. Get new process patent."

Wesley considered that it was about time Abraham suggested something useful. He had tolerated the alcoholic, egomaniac consultant from Yale only because he had to. Rhinner Albright, the CEO of Genplex, was a Yale Law graduate and thought everyone at the overstuffed place walked on water. Whatever, this was last minute good news, and if true, would help him survive another difficult evening with his demanding Italian boss. At some level, Jerrod loved the old man, but Dr. Vettori instilled fear in many hearts, including his own. Alonsio Vettori was Genplex's President of Science and Technology, meaning that he was in charge of research and development—Wesley's operation—the molecular biology research center in Oxford, England, and manufacturing. He was housed in the New York office with Albright and the business brass. The significance of the New York location had more to do with good restaurants than with a strategic business location, and that was fine with Jerrod. He laughed to himself; it could be a lot worse; he could be working for the tyrants at Apex. If half the stories he had heard about Apex's management were true, it would indeed be a frightening place to work.

There, the science was run by business and management and nothing the company said or published was believable. At least at Genplex *he* ran the science, if not his own life. Even though some of Jerrod's employees pretended to resent his absolute demand for scientific honesty, most understood it was really for the best. That did not prevent the occasional argument over authorship of scientific papers or inventorship on patents, but these matters were easily sorted out by bringing the disagreeing parties together and having an open discussion. Honesty, unlike dishonesty, is contagious in professional settings with transparency.

⚴

Wesley slowly stirred his Jack Daniels on the rocks. His boss was already thirty minutes late, but such powers demanded total dedication and Wesley would wait. How had he gotten himself into such a situation? Was it money, ambition, greed, or all the above? It certainly wasn't marital stability. The not-so-long-suffering Susan had recently packed her bags for a job on Wall Street, at least until he found a life outside of Genplex. Fortunately, their smart, pretty daughter, Courtney, was tucked away at Choate, a prestigious boarding school, just up the road in Wallingford. If there was a divorce, at least she would not be trampled by it. The walls of ivy grew thick there and shed more than rain.

However personally distressing, the situation was just as well for now, he grumbled to himself. His small company was at war with a monster, and he was the general on the battlefield. The last general in Jerrod's family had been Nathan Bedford Forrest, a great strategist who never really yielded to the Yankees. He could only pray that a little of that resilience remained in his genes; he was going to need it.

His cell phone jangled, and the homely woman on the next bar stool gave him an annoyed look. The hard luck creature had been eyeing him and probably thought it was a woman more attractive than she on the phone, but no such luck, it was his boss.

There were no apologizes, nothing. "Dr. Wesley, I will be there in five minutes; please have our table ready." The tall, gaunt man finally arrived and the pretty cocktail waitress, who ingratiated herself to him by speaking Italian, took his drink order, a Manhattan with double sweet vermouth. Wesley resisted gagging and ordered his third Jack-rocks. Angelina giggled at Jerrod's obvious reaction to Alonsio's repulsive drink order and sauntered off to the bar.

Vettori took a couple of sips from the sweet cocktail, and then looked Wesley in the eye. The old devil wore horn-rimmed spectacles with thick lenses like the bottom of a Coke bottle. They made his eyes look huge, like those of a goliath grouper eyeing its prey. "Jerrod, it has been too long since we have spoken. My phone never stops ringing—Mr. Albright, the board, Wall Street analysts, and every little prick in the world who thinks he has some interest in Axilon. They all call, yet you, with all the answers, do not. I must tell you, this is totally unacceptable." Every word was emphasized with waving hands, Italian sign language."

"Sir, with all due respect, such things move slowly, and I have been swamped dealing wih the FDA's questions about our Phase I protocol that we submitted with the IND—Investigational New Drug Application." Thinking that he better move on to the good news and save his ass, Wesley said, "Alonsio, I do have some good news; I just learned today that we have finally solved the synthesis problem. Dr. Chen told me that Abraham's suggestion worked, and we can now make Axilon in high purity for a thousand dollars per kilo, maybe less. Naturally, Chemical Development will have to qualify the new process, but that shouldn't be a problem."

The old man eyed him suspiciously and said, "Are you certain that Chen knows what he is talking about? Might he stretch the truth a bit to please his boss?"

Don't argue, Jerrod thought. "Sometimes he does, yes, but I saw the preliminary data and it looks good. Better quality, too; we avoid some troublesome impurities with the new process."

Vettori was always looking for an angle. In this case it was a way—any way—to speed up the process and beat Apex to Phase I safety trials in humans. He moved his fingers like he was unscrewing the lid of a jar as he spoke. "So, when I relate this new result to Mr. Albright, he is going to ask me how much this moves up the time and events schedule for the first dose in healthy, human volunteers. The shareholders are all over him; even one week might be worth two dollars a share."

Wesley looked out across the bustling restaurant; a lady at the next table was eating the most delicious-looking veal dish he had ever seen, and his stomach growled loudly. He found courage in his embarrassment and spoke the truth. "Alonsio, *please*, a few fleeting points in the share price are irrelevant; the only thing that matters is doing the required work by the book, and by that, I mean both the regulatory and the scientific books. No shortcuts!"

Vettori sensed that he had pushed his most important player to the limit, and it was time to back off. The last bit of juice would be extracted from him before this was over, though. To extract the juice and crack the nuts was his job. "Of course, you are correct, Dr. Wesley, the right way is the only way, but you do understand it means everything to beat Apex to the market?"

"I understand." Yeah, he understood the importance of winning, but he also understood the amazing resources of the mightiest drug company in the world. Did Alonsio understand that Genplex was still a relatively small company and that its competitor was a monster?

"Good, let's order." Vettori waved his hands impatiently at the poor waiter who had been orbiting, needing to move the table.

The remainder of the meal was as relaxed and pleasant as it could be with the old man—happy chit-chat about Jerrod's daughter and concern for the quality of Jerrod's meal for which he had waited so long. Actually, it was the best veal Milanese that Jerrod had ever tasted and the expensive Borolo was perfect. Alonsio drank little and had only a small arugula, radicchio, and endive salad. In between beatings, life could be good.

℘

Jerrod pulled the big, black BMW 750-LI into the drive of his Madison home and set there for a moment before he keyed the garage remote control. It was a beautiful colonial set well back on a wooded lot and only a short walk to the quaint, little downtown business area and Long Island Sound. He looked at his Rolex and saw that it was almost one in the morning. The tired scientist activated the garage door opener and watched it rattle up. As he eased the car into the garage, he spoke out loud, "Beautiful home, wonderful town; too bad no one is ever here to enjoy the damned place ... that I paid two and one-half fucking million dollars for, by the way."

Jerrod dropped his rumpled clothes onto the floor, made a nightcap, and headed for the shower. He had no more than adjusted the steaming spray when his cell phone jangled. He started to ignore it, but then considered it might be Alonsio. The intense executive had an annoying habit of reviewing conversations in his mind and calling to inform you of your mistakes that he let slip the first time through the issue.

"Hello?"

"Hello, *Romeo*, and just where have you been all evening? Was she pretty?"

Susan! "*Jerrod*, not Romeo, and no, the six-foot-five, bald sociopath that I had dinner with wasn't very pretty."

Susan laughed. "Alonsio ... a romantic evening, for certain. Bet the two hundred dollar bottle of wine was good, though."

Wesley sighed, "And just what is it that you want this time of night, Susan? Are you drunk?"

"Yes, a little, I guess. I had several glasses of champagne; in celebration, you know."

She was playing games. Wesley took a sip of his own drink and decided to humor her for the moment. "Celebrating what, your new job?" Susan should have just reported to Blendon and Grimes, a medium sized investment bank specializing in pharmaceutical and biotechnology companies. Armed with an undergraduate degree in biology from Ole Miss and a newly acquired MBA from Yale, she had recently accepted a position as a biotechnology financial analyst. Wesley's accurate, but wisely unspoken, opinion was that she had no clue about any of it. He had married the best looking girl he could catch at Ole Miss, and though she was smart enough, she wasn't even on the same page with the Wall Street wizards. The most important position she had held prior to this was president of Chi Omega at Ole Miss. She had been one of the coeds the late Southern writer, Willie Morris, would have called a *gold chip*.

"Jerrod?"

"Nothing; go ahead."

"Well, I have a *really* new job—way better than the Blendon and Grimes thing with that little dip-shit investment bank." She paused for a moment, but her husband remained cautious, fully suspecting one of her traps. "OK, it's with the Sirius Financial Investment Bank, the biggest boy of them all, so there."

Sirius? The *brightest fucking star in the universe!* Jerrod's head churned and his heart pounded; how on earth had Susan pulled this one off? He put his most obvious concern aside for the moment and asked, "And how did you get out of the employment contract with Blendon and Grimes before you even reported for work?" Jerrod had been the witness to her signing the damned thing. It seemed iron clad, inviolable.

"I didn't, Sweetie; Sirius cut them in on the Amgen private offering—*no problemo*, as your boss would say."

Jerrod thought, maybe not for you, but a *huge* fucking problem for me. "So, Susan, with all due respect, why do you think the most successful investment bank in the world would burn millions of dollars to hire little ole you? Really, now."

"Jerrod, the answer to that question lies in why you are there alone in Connecticut, jerking off, and I am luxuriating in the best suite the Palace has to offer. You have never understood me, much less appreciated me. *Sirius does.*"

"Susan, I really don't want to get into all that tired, old shit again, so let's just stick to Sirius and their motives; shall we? Let me just suggest that they are not known for their sensitivity, so they most likely had motivations beyond making you feel good. Normally, they eat small children for breakfast and spit out the bones. Could it just possibly be, just possibly, that they hired you because, number one—they are Apex Pharmaceutical's primary banker, and number two—you are married to Apex's biggest problem's Vice President for Research and Development? Just what might your dumb husband reveal in the troughs of ecstasy during one of your weekend conjugal visits?"

"Fuck you, Jerrod! You keep that shit up and there won't be any more of what you so crudely define as *conjugal visits*."

Jerrod considered how the powers that be at Sirius would do almost anything to gain a leg up in the Axilon vs Medulin competition. Sirius and their investors owned many shares of Apex, and the company had a monopoly on their investment banking business. They had everything to win or *lose*. Susan was just another way to hedge their bet.

It's late; drop it for now. "Susan, will you be coming home on Friday evening?"

"I, I just don't know."

"Fine; Courtney and two of her girlfriends from Choate will be here for the weekend. I plan to take them sailing and then cook lobsters on the grill. I'm sure Courtney would appreciate her mother's presence, so come if you can; it's your shot to call."

Jerrod was steaming when he hung up the telephone; his nervy, bitch of a wife had become a monster. It was as if the MBA program at Yale had infected her with unbridled narcissism. He knew she was in over her head and was being used against him, but Susan didn't and didn't want to hear about it. He stared into the glass for a long minute and then downed the remaining amber liquid in one gulp. He felt better after the shower and slept like the dead.

4

Scared Man

Jerrod looked up from his work as Wanda strode into his office. Her big, baby blue eyes sparkled in the sunlight reflected off the distant water. The pretty girl's form-fitting sweater and short skirt left little to the imagination. Her coy smile signaled that he had been caught again—nailed—admiring her wares and that she didn't mind one little bit.

"Jerrod, do you know a guy from Apex named Dr. Wally; first name is Alton; I think?"

Jerrod thought for a moment. Wally? Apex? Then he put it together; he had never met the man but recalled that he was head of toxicology for Apex. He had been at that company for a long time and was highly respected in his field. In fact, he had written the definitive *Handbook of Nerve Cell Toxicology.* "I know who he is; why?"

"Well, he's at the back security gate, and he demands to see you, Jerrod."

"*Demands*? I guess you had better show him in then." Jerrod replied with a chuckle.

Wanda said, "Will do." As she was walking away, she turned her head and said with a laugh, "You give yourself away when you blush."

Presently, Wanda showed Wally into Jerrod's office. The toxicologist was overweight and somewhat disheveled in appearance. There were signs of his breakfast over-easy eggs on his out-of-date tie, and Jerrod could have identified him as a scientist from one hundred yards. Beyond that, the man looked tired, worried, and his left eye twitched uncontrollably. Here was a man with a lot on his mind.

Though uncomfortable with the situation, Jerrod smiled warmly and shook the man's limp hand which felt cold, clammy. "Good to meet you, Dr. Wally; I've heard lots of good things about you and your work. What brings you to Genplex?"

Wally clawed at the annoying twitch and responded, "Likewise, good to meet you, and thank you for your time. The, ah, reason I'm here is that I'm looking for a—a job—a position in your toxicology department."

Wesley was happy with his own senior toxicologist but knew this was not just a casual inquiry. Something was about to unfold, and he was going to listen. "Dr. Wally—Alton, I am confused. Why on earth would you be looking for a job; you are part of the superstructure at Apex and one of the most respected toxicologists in the country?" Wesley knew enough about Wally's pristine reputation to suspect that he had hit some sort of brick wall with management, and this turned out to be true.

"I, I'm under fire. To be blunt, the management of the company doesn't like my toxicology group's findings on Medulin." Wally opened his briefcase with trembling hands and pulled out a thick report and held it before Jerrod's face.

He obviously didn't mean disrespect or to share the report, but it was the upset, unthinking man's stage prop and a necessary accoutrement to continue his story. More than that, Wesley sensed that it was a ticking time bomb and averted his eyes too late; his near photographic memory had captured the cover of the document. It bore the label: *Medulin—Rat Two-Year Toxicology Report.* Amazingly, it also displayed the chemical structure of Medulin, the significance of which the biologist seemed not to appreciate. But Jerrod did; he had a Ph.D. in organic chemistry and chemists never forget important chemical structures. He had just become privy to one of the most valuable and dangerous pieces of information in the world. To make matters worse, Medulin's structure bore a striking resemblance to that of Axilon, at least a patent attorney might argue so.

"Alton, you can continue, but please put that away; it is not meant for my eyes."

"Sorry, you are right, Sir; it is meant only for the company *and the FDA*. I guess I just wanted you to feel the weight of my burden. The report doesn't damn Medulin but there are certain unusual findings that question the safety of the drug and demand new studies be conducted to resolve the issue."

"And new studies take time," Wesley chimed in.

"Yeah, and new studies might also kill the damned drug, at least that's what they fear. Management is concerned to the point that they are demanding that I launder the report. The company has hired an outside toxicology consultant who says the reported observations are speculation on my part, not fact. The man is a well-known hired gun for the industry, part of the data for dollars crowd."

Wesley looked out the window at the water, now dark under

building clouds. There would likely be a blow tonight. "And you have refused to sign a doctored report?"

"That's correct. They have given me a week's leave to think about it and decide on my future. Obviously, they don't know I'm here, and I'd like to keep it that way."

Jerrod said, "I am sorry that you have to suffer through this, and I must say that I am amazed that a company of Apex's stature would take such risk. I can tell you; we don't do such things here."

The toxicologist smiled for the first time. "Despite the Medulin hype, the bastards do have their problems—earnings are below expectations and falling. The new CEO, Maxwell Hall, promised the shareholders the world, but he hasn't delivered, at least not yet. He is a desperate, unethical bastard, and it all flows down from him. Likely, people above me were threatened as well."

Wesley thought, *and we know who their number one shareholder is.* "OK, Alton, I'd like to help, but I have to consider how. I have a perfectly competent head of toxicology, and I suspect there should be a fire wall between you and Axilon, given the relationship to Medulin and the possible legal ramifications. Maybe we could establish an experimental toxicology group, and put you in the arena where you do your best work—cutting edge investigations, something like that. But I need some time to think about it and look at my budget. May I call you at home in few days? Today is Thursday, so why don't I call you at home on Monday morning at 9:00 a.m.?"

"Yes, that would be fine, and I like your proposal. I'll await your call."

"And, Alton, please don't ever bring any more Apex documents into this building."

Alton grinned sheepishly and said, "I will not—promise."

Jerrod watched the defeated man shuffle out the door, marveling at how callously a big company could destroy the best of people who have contributed so much. Apex would interview people until they found a yes-man who wouldn't know a dead rat from a light bulb.

Jerrod had reasonable assurances from Alonsio that he would be allowed a weekend in peace with his daughter. Likely, Alonsio agreed to this because Jerrod had not yet found the courage to discuss Susan's new position at Sirius with him. It was Friday evening, and he was relaxing with the *Wall Street Journal*, waiting for his daughter and her friends to arrive. He was praying for a nice weekend weatherwise for the girls; heck, Susan had even condescendingly agreed to return to Madison for the Saturday evening cookout. He was thinking that a gin and tonic might be nice when the door chimes sounded. Jerrod thought it might be the girls but it was UPS with a delivery. He tore open the outer cardboard box and found a letter attached to a heavy, sealed envelope stamped confidential.

Strangely enough, the package was from Alton Wally, and Jerrod became more disturbed as he read the words. The short letter begged secrecy and requested that Jerrod place the package in a *secure place*, where it would remain until Dr. Wally either requested its return or until it was clear that *something untoward has happened to him.* That would include his unexpected disappearance. It concluded, "Should worst come to worst, please examine the contents of the package and see that it falls into the proper hands, preferably those of the FDA." For reasons that weren't clear, he listed his brother, James, as next of kin and provided his telephone number. *Next of kin?*

The gin and tonic now seemed mandatory and he walked over to his elaborate, glass bar and poured a double shot of Bombay into a tall glass. Jerrod added a little tonic, squeeze of key lime, and plenty of ice, and the cold concoction was ready to go. A few sips calmed his nerves and he was able to consider the situation in more analytical terms. Likely, it was the Medulin rat report, the unaltered version, intact with all the ugly findings—*rat poison!* Wally's fear had advanced to paranoia and he had badly over-reacted, hadn't he? Monday morning he would be apologetic and embarrassed and hopefully request the damned thing back. In the meanwhile it would rest securely in Wesley's heavy home safe. If he could only rip the chemical structure of Medulin from his mind and throw it into the safe with the report!

The doorbell rang again, and this time, thankfully, it was three giggling girls with enough baggage for a month's stay. Jerrod was delighted and hugged them all at once. Free of the rigors of Choate, these girls were ready to play.

Jerrod proudly escorted the girls to a nearby seafood restaurant which was popular with the tourists and locals alike. The starving girls dove into fried scrod and clams with corn on the cob, and a good time was had by all. Jerrod grinned; he could tell that his guests were ready for a break from the Choate cafeteria. The happy group played silly card games well into the night, and though Jerrod feared a late evening discussion with Courtney about her mother's new life in New York, thankfully, it never happened. Still, Jerrod was unable to sleep that night; he simply couldn't get Alton Wally and the mysterious package off his mind. First Susan's new job and now this ... it was as though Apex's toxins were seeping under his door from all directions.

Despite pressing concerns, Jerrod and the girls were up early for sailing and enjoyed a stiff westerly breeze which pushed the *Sea*

Sprint along at a breathtaking pace. He watched his daughter sail the fast J-Boat with pride. He and the other two girls served as crew until it was time for the tricky maneuvering back into the yacht club.

When they returned home, they found Susan poring over Sirius financial documents. Sadly, the preoccupied woman seemed to take little joy from Courtney and her cute friends. The woman's mind was elsewhere, and Jerrod now realized how far Susan had moved on to what she perceived as a better life. Thankfully, she became part of the festivities when the caterer arrived with the wonderful steamed lobsters and all the trimmings. She laughed and raised her glass and seemed the old Susan, but Jerrod wasn't fooled for a second. He knew that the Susan part of his life was over. She hurriedly departed for the city on Sunday morning as Jerrod and the girls prepared for another fine day on the water. They might even sail across the Sound to Long Island for lunch if the breeze held.

Wesley glanced at his Rolex; he had to call Alton in ten minutes. What next, he wondered? At least it had been a marvelous weekend with perfect sailing weather; the breeze had held without turning into a gale. His cook-out with the help of a local caterer had been a success, and even Susan had mostly behaved, though it had definitely not been a conjugal visit. Courtney was a mature, intelligent young lady and made life fun for whomever was around her. If she had inherited anything other than good looks from her mother, it lay dormant. Jerrod found Wally's home telephone number in his address book and keyed in the number. The telephone at the other end rang and continued to ring; there was no answering machine—nothing. He grew more concerned throughout the day as his repeated calls went unanswered. Wanda's check with directory assistance revealed that he did indeed have the correct number.

There didn't seem a logical next move for Jerrod, but he remembered entering Alton's brother's telephone number in his address book. James Wally answered on the first ring. Unlike his brother, James Wally spoke in an uneducated, inarticulate manner, but he seemed honest and sincere. Jerrod said only that he and Alton had a business relationship and that Alton had missed an important telephonic meeting. Jerrod not only needed to get in touch but also was concerned about Alton's welfare. No mention was made of the edgy circumstances or the strange package in his possession.

James had been having a similar experience and said that he was on his way out to the old family farm on Roast Meat Hill Road where Alton lived with his menagerie of Portuguese water dogs and miniature horses. It would not be like Alton to abandon his animals for any period, much less miss an important meeting. The man was compulsive, if nothing else; perhaps his telephone was malfunctioning. Jerrod didn't think so, but he said that he would appreciate a report when James sorted it out. Jerrod felt a sinking feeling deep within the pit of his stomach as he hung up the telephone. What in hell had happened to Alton Wally, and what hurricane had the poor man sucked him into? Jerrod shivered; he knew deep within his bones that he might never speak to the talented toxicologist again.

Later that evening, Jerrod was paying bills when the telephone rang; it was James Wally, an extremely upset James Wally. "My brother, Alton, is dead," he sobbed. "Before I go on, I'd like to know the nature of your relationship with my brother."

Keep it simple, stupid, Jerrod thought. "I'm head of research for Genplex here in Madison, and I was calling Alton to offer him a job—he was highly respected in his field, and I needed his services. What on earth happened?"

James coughed several time to regain his composure. "I drove out to the farm, and when I pulled up in the drive, his pack of Portuguese water dogs came out jumpin' around and barking their heads off. Now, my brother loves his dogs and don't never let 'um run free like that, so I knowed something was bad wrong. Then, they all raced off to the lake, looking back at me and a barkin' and whimperin' for me to follow. At first, I ignored them dogs and went up to the house; it was unlocked and nobody was home. I got this scared feelin', see, and went down to the lake where them dogs was at. His naked body was floatin' face-down in the water and his dogs was a swimmin' all around him, trying to help him like Portuguese water dogs is supposed to do. But it was way too late. My brother had done drowned."

The bereaved brother broke down for a moment, but then regained control and continued, "I called the cops and they finally came out there. The coroner's preliminary report said that it was an accidental drowning."

Jerrod felt like he might throw up. "What about the *naked* part? Isn't that rather odd?"

"No, no, not in Alton's case. He, he was kindly a nut that way, you see, and he swam that way—naked, I mean, most every day, year-round with them water dogs. Despite his appearance, he was an extremely strong swimmer, so I just don't understand none of this. Too bad them dogs can't talk, theys witness to ... somethin'. Somethin' really ugly."

Jerrod thought that maybe he did understand, but he kept it to himself, expressing his condolences and offering to help in any way.

He also asked James to let him know if the police came up with anything new, since he had reservations about the official cause of James'
brother's death. The two men said their good-byes, and Jerrod wondered if he would ever hear from James again. The funeral would be
on Wednesday, but there was no way in hell he was going to be seen
there. Jesus!

"Damn," Wesley exclaimed aloud, "What should I do, now?" He
imagined he could feel the heat radiating from the package in his
safe; it might as well contain nuclear weapon-grade plutonium. General Forrest and his boys would have dropped this bomb, but could he
muster the courage to do so? Maybe later.

5

Apex Pharmaceuticals Headquarters, Groton, Connecticut

Maxwell Hall was a tiny man with a big ego and a bad disposition. He had been ridiculed as a kid and abused by every bully in his school. He was smart though, very smart, and had found solace in his Wharton MBA, which he used like a ladder to reach the top of the American business executive world. The little man didn't really like women but had married three of them as necessary trappings for his business success. None of the three wives had given birth to children and that was fine with Maxwell. The third one he had kept because she was both well-positioned in East Coast society and would be far too expensive to dispose of in divorce court, though he often strangled the woman in his dreams.

Melinda Pierce Hall was a product of Manhattan society, and the elegant woman stood a full six inches taller than her husband. She spent far more time in her Park Avenue penthouse than she did in their Groton waterfront mansion which she loathed. Melinda occupied her time with important charity events and had little time for Connecticut Yankees and local riff-raff. That was fine with Maxwell who would rather tend to business than deal with the bitch. His few sexual needs were fulfilled while on his extensive overseas trips. Melinda could be relied upon to show up at the company Christmas party, and that was about it.

Maxwell had recently become the President and CEO of Apex Pharmaceuticals, the largest diversified pharmaceutical company in the world, after falling earnings and an embarrassing balance sheet compelled the board of directors to remove Murray Schwartz from that position. Murray remained on as Chairman but had little real power beyond presiding over expensive board dinners and serving as a yes-man for Hall.

Maxwell, never Max, ran his fingers through his preacher-style, bouffant hair-do and blew cigar smoke across his massive desk in the general direction of Murray Schwartz. The impressive office was furnished with British Empire era designer furniture and provided a panoramic view of Long Island Sound and the sinister looking nuclear submarines that often lurked there. Maxwell found delight in the thought that old Schwartz probably missed his former, opulent workplace. Too fucking bad; if he hadn't been such a weak, sniveling failure he might still be here, Maxwell thought. Now, he would be forced to participate as a rubber stamp in real decision making. Maxwell let the old fool ramble on; it was entertaining, really.

"I, I don't like it one bit; in fact I can't be a party to such a thing. How can we ... murder one of our own employees just to achieve some dubious leg-up on the competition? Besides, the last time I checked, murder was against the law."

Hall took another puff of his big Cuban Coronas Especiales and licked his mustache. "Gee, Murray, you killed a lot of people with all those big drugs you marketed during *your time*. Shit, all drugs are poisons; aren't they, but that's the business we're in. So, why does killing one of our own uncooperative, little piss-ants bother you so much?"

"Yes, it's true; most drugs have their nasty side effects, but they help a lot more people than they hurt."

"Do tell. Well, if we had let Alton Wally take his imaginary toxicology findings to the FDA, then there would be one hell of a lot of sick people deprived of the wonder drug benefits of Medulin. Shit, Murray, there are forty million Americans with anxiety disorders, more with depression, and God knows how many schizophrenics. More importantly, we would have been deprived of the billions in sales the analysts at Sirius predict. And we, Sir, would be unemployed."

The old man frowned and made a show of fanning away the acrid cigar smoke with his hand. "I don't like words like *had let*. What have you done, Maxwell?"

Hall poured two fingers of Glenlivet Single Malt into a glass and handed it to Schwartz. "You had better drink this, Murray."

Schwartz tossed the amber liquid down with trembling fingers and then looked his nemesis in the eye. "OK, let's have it."

Hall grinned expansively and exhaled a thick cloud of cigar smoke. "It's done. Man swims alone in his lake every day, he takes a calculated risk. Two days ago Alton Wally got unlucky. Maybe he had a cramp; maybe he didn't, but he drowned, naked and alone with his dogs."

Schwartz looked around the office—might these walls have eyes and ears? "You cruel bastard; I know you think you are one clever son of a bitch, but maybe, just maybe, someone will figure out that this was no accident. Then what? What if we are implicated in this, this ... awful crime?" His bald head was spinning, and he couldn't find the words, *felony homicide*, that he was searching for.

"Not to worry, Murray; it was a professional job and can't be traced to us, no matter what. The money came from a source in Indonesia. The less you know about it, the better. So relax."

"Accepting that as true for the moment, what about poor Dr. Wally's toxicology report? What about the raw laboratory notebooks and the necropsy slides and so on?"

"All copies of the report have been accounted for and destroyed. Original laboratory findings have all been replaced with clean materials. One of our senior toxicologists is now a very rich man. Bastard Wally was over-reacting, anyhow. We're not exactly talking about thalidomide here."

Schwartz wondered just what the hell we were talking about, here. In the 1950s and 60s, thalidomide had caused the birth of over ten-thousand tragically deformed babies when pregnant mothers in Europe had used the presumably harmless drug as a tranquilizer or as a treatment for morning sickness. The children were born with small, seal-like flippers rather than arms and legs; this previously rare condition was known as phocomelia. Frances Kelsey, an astute official at the FDA, had figured it out, and despite tremendous pressure, prevented thalidomide marketing in the United States by two large pharmaceutical companies—Grunenthal and Richardson Merrell.

"What prevents some alert FDA auditor from figuring this out, Maxwell?"

An evil grin crossed Hall's face, and he assumed a condescending tone. "My good man, the term, *alert FDA auditor,* is an oxymoron."

Murray thought about Frances Kelsey and looked out the window, wondering how such sinister things could happen in such a beautiful place. His daydream was interrupted by a gruff voice, "Now, we need to talk about Genplex and Axilon."

Schwartz pretended to listen with interest while Hall completed his own biased comparison of Medulin and Axilon. "So, even though Medulin is clearly the better drug, you never know what is going to happen in this business. We have to continue to promote Medulin in every, and I do mean *every* way we can. Worst possible scenario is we lose the drug despite our best efforts; then what? *Then what* is that we have to be prepared to pounce on Axilon, to steal Genplex, whatever works for us"

Maxwell Hall almost felt a pang of pity as the broken, old man limped out of his former office. He chided himself for the moment of weakness and selected a good brandy from his collection and poured two fingers. Nothing was going to stop Maxwell Hall, nothing; he ruminated. He polished off the brandy and reclined in his plush, leather chair and was soon dozing, dreaming of a distant time when *he* was the target of bullies and the object of practical jokes. *Little Max* the bastards had called him, and where were they now? Just for laughs, he had even hired a detective to run down a few of the most annoying of them and he had been gratified by the former cop's findings. They were menial workers, all inconsequential people. The one he had hated the most, Big Dave Brassfield, was locked up in a Federal Correctional Institution in South Carolina, a real hellhole even for a prison. Dave had been their top football player and leading ladies man, or so he imagined. He was also one cruel son of a bitch and tormented defenseless Little Max in front of his equally stupid buddies or any silly girl that would watch and giggle. Big Dave loved to pull Little Max's pants down and show the girls his tiny penis—tee hee! TEE HEE!

But today he was grateful for all that Big Dave had taught him that helped him rise to the top. Dave had taught him all about the need to get even, to take unfair advantage of the weak, and to work at the sub-rosa level. They can't get you if they don't know who did it; can they? Maxwell laughed; he had peed on Big Dave's homework, put sand in the gas tank of his expensive convertible just before the big football parade, and replaced his football uniform with one half the oaf's size minutes before kick-off at the state championship game. The Golden Wave had lost 34 to 18 to a lesser team, and the local paper blamed it all on Brassfield the next morning. Seems the fool had never found a uniform large enough to fit, and he had never made it on the field. His popularity waned considerably after that.

Maxwell never did follow up on his plan to kill the bastard, but it had been a good plan, and planning is never wasted; consider the unfortunate Wally drowning, for instance. Originally, Big Dave Brassfield had been the focus of that plan. It was a matter of economy of thought, really.

6

August, 2010

Jerrod was tired, and he had not been reassured by some things he had learned at the ACNP Meeting, a large clinical pharmacology meeting. Nothing new or all that profound had been learned about the reality of Medulin, but several of their Axilon clinical investigators, who were also likely performing clinical studies with Medulin, had hinted that the two drugs were running neck and neck and, in fact, competing for the same patients. There was also the rumor though, that Apex was recruiting patients at an alarming rate, seemingly attempting to drain the finite patient pool of quality patients. Both companies had chosen to initiate Phase II trials in generalized anxiety disorder, major depression, and schizophrenia with other targets in the works. The presumption would be that the Phase I safety trials in healthy human volunteers for Medulin, like Axilon, had been clean, but what was Apex's hurry? Caution usually boded well for a new drug. Why kill an invaluable asset with impatience? Jerrod considered that it was just another example of the business interests running the science—an increasingly risky scenario.

Larry Reynolds, MD, Director of Clinical Research for Genplex, and Jerrod had been called back a day early by Alonsio, and Jerrod was looking forward to a good night's sleep after several restless evenings in a bad hotel in New Orleans. The passage of time since Katrina had not improved the Crescent City. Alonsio's need to be informed about every little thing led Jerrod to wonder if the old tyrant wasn't a candidate for Axilon. At least he found the thought amusing as he turned onto the I-95 exit toward Madison and home. Make that his dark and lonely home.

Despite all, Jerrod was still married to Susan but had seen her less and less often over the past two years, partly because Courtney had graduated from Choate and moved on to Duke University. When he had seen his absentee wife, he was subjected to her incessant grill-ing about Axilon. Is it safe? What are the side effects? Does it have any useful therapeutic effects? Susan was parroting the questions that Sirius demanded she ask, but she wasn't smart enough for coy trickery that might pry out some valuable nugget at a weak moment. He gloated in the fact that she was being well-paid for nothing and wondered how much longer her relationship with the financial conglomerate could last. When, not if, that ill-based relationship failed, what then? he ruminated.

He thought about the toxicology report that had killed a good man and might destroy an empire. It had been so easy to procrastinate. Indecision about exactly what to do with it, along with fear for his family, certainly had helped. Jerrod shook his head; where had two years gone? At least knowing the structure of Apex's drug was no longer an issue. This information had been disclosed with the publication of the patent applications for both drugs. By now, half the chemists in the industry were diligently trying to rip off the structures of Axilon and Medulin with their me-too versions. One of them might actually become the winner; nothing fair about this business, he thought grimly.

Presently, Jerrod turned into the dark, tree lined lane that led to his rambling colonial home. He was at first surprised and then disturbed when he saw light shimmering through the trees. He had left no inside lights turned on; someone either was, or had been, in his home. Jerrod switched off the lights of the BMW and left it parked in the middle of the narrow drive. He silently eased his way along, sticking to the darker shadows, avoiding light from the house whenever possible. Once he froze after the serenade of summer insects abruptly ended after he stepped on a twig that broke with a loud snap. Finally, they resumed their raspy songs, and Jerrod advanced to the front door, with key in hand. He held his breath as he entered the house. Although he saw no one, there was music playing softly in the background. The door to the kitchen stood open and he could see a coffee cup on the counter. He jumped as a clatter came from the direction of his great room. The safe! The fucking report! Jerrod kicked himself for not carrying a gun, given his circumstances. His eyes fell on a cut glass vase, one of Susan's favorites; it had a heft to it and was decorated with an attractive design with razor-sharp edges. Jerrod said a little prayer and bolted toward the great room, but his ankle caught on an antique table leg, and a heavy, metal lamp crashed to the floor.

Shit! All surprise had been lost, and his ankle was in pain, but he managed to limp forward into the great room, still brandishing the vase. The safe, which had been professionally drilled, stood open and its contents, including his stash of emergency cash, were missing. The safe cracker's tools were still scattered about the floor, but no masked figure pointed a gun at him. Jerrod's attention was diverted by the sound of one of the garage doors rattling up. He tried to run for the garage but his ankle wouldn't support his weight. A powerful engine roared to life, and tires squealed. The scared scientist opened the door to the garage just in time to see a black Jaguar convertible with lights off vanish down the dark drive at an alarming rate of speed. A noxious cloud of burned rubber hung in the air.

Jerrod powerlessly limped down the lane after the fleeing vehicle, and then, just as he remembered his abandoned BMW, there was a tremendous crash, the sound of metal shearing and glass shattering. He thought the driver had crashed into his BMW! But no, as Jerrod came upon the horrible scene he could see that the driver had swerved to miss the BMW and collided with a substantial copper beech tree. Even in the dark Wesley could see that no one could have possibly survived such a crash. A bloody figure slumped over the steering wheel. Susan! It finally occurred to him that it could be Susan, caught up in her desperation for substantial information about Axilon. Jerrod was relieved that it was not Susan; the BMW's high beams revealed the body to be that of a man. His features were almost unrecognizable, but it was a man and definitely not Susan. Apparently, the airbags had failed to inflate, and the driver never had a chance. A blood-splattered satchel sat undamaged on the seat beside the driver. Jerrod went back to his car and retrieved his driving gloves. He slid them on and removed the satchel and found it to contain the entire contents of his safe. He found the envelope containing the toxicology report and Wally's letter and put them in his trunk under the carpet covering the spare tire. He closed the satchel, which still contained ten thousand dollars, personal financial documents, and some Genplex confidential information and placed it back on the seat next to the driver. He then removed his cell phone from his jacket pocket and called 911.

As he sat on the hood of his car, waiting on the police, he considered that it was silly for him to have thought the victim was Susan; though she didn't know the combination to his safe, she surely didn't know how to crack one. But Susan, or Susan plus Sirius, could have been in on it. Then there was Apex to consider, or maybe it was just the random robbery of an expensive home in Madison. The first two seemed more likely, and that scared the hell out of him. Jerrod couldn't get around the thought that Susan might be somehow involved; who else knew that he was supposed to be out of town? The sirens were close now and he had to regain his wits.

Two Madison police cars arrived on the scene, and two officers remained to investigate the crash scene while two others accompanied Wesley back to the house. Both Officers Rollins and Smith were overweight, lazy union types who had little interest in what they saw or who had robbed some rich jerk. Jerrod thought they were officious pricks, but he had no option other than to accompany them down to the station to make his statement. He was reminded of the security system during their questioning, and yes, he knew he set it before he left. Once again, he thought of Susan; only she and Courtney knew the code.

When the cops were through with Wesley they informed him they would be back in touch and likely would have a positive identification of the deceased suspect. He thought, yeah, only because the FBI would do the work. Jerrod remembered reading some really damning articles about the Madison cops in the local paper, but he still found their lackadaisical attitude unbelievable. His good night's sleep was rapidly going south. On the drive home, the only traffic he met was a police wrecker towing the remains of the impounded Jaguar.

When he entered the house, the phone was ringing. Who? It was almost midnight, and none of his guesses about the late night caller's identity were anywhere close.

"Hello, Dr. Wesley, James Wally, here; you know, poor, dead Alton's brother."

"Ah, yes, James; what brings you to call this late at night?"

"Oh, I'm sorry to awaken you, Sir."

"Unfortunately, you didn't."

"Thought you might wanna know, Alton's house is burnin' to the ground as we speak. Fire trucks is here, but it's way too late, and Fire Chief Dennis says a lot of accelerant had to have been used. I'm on my cell phone just standin' here watching the flames eat our old family farm house up. A lifetime of memories is gone," he sobbed.

Be cautious, Jerrod thought. "I'm awfully sorry, James, but why are you calling me? What can I possibly do to help?"

"Cause them bastards that killed Alton did this too. I jist listed the place with Jefferson Realty last week, and maybe that alerted them to, to … somethin' or other, I don't know what, though. Maybe they ransacked the place looking for whatever they killed Alton over and burned it to cover up their tracks. Or maybe they was concerned about what a new owner might discover hidden in the house."

Jerrod thought that sounded about right. "James, my house was broken into tonight as well. I interrupted a burglary in progress, and the perpetrator was killed in an automobile accident while trying to escape. Don't know if there is any relationship between these events, but it seems pretty odd to me. Cops are trying to identify the dead intruder as we speak."

The two men said their good-byes and agreed to stay in touch. These seemingly disparate crimes were likely connected in some way. Why would Apex suddenly be looking for that toxicology report again after two years? And why would they believe that he might have it if they were? "Or maybe they didn't; it was Susan and Sirius that burgled his home," he said aloud. "Maybe the dead guy can be tied to Sirius."

Jerrod found sleep elusive for what remained of the night. He had those horrible dreams that sometime permeate the half-awake mind. Killers lurked in the bushes outside his home and they were always some ghastly form of Susan. Several times he sat up fully awake, and she stood there, pointing her weapon at him, until the phantom faded to a lamp or ticking clock beside the bed. Finally, he gave up on restful sleep and rose from his bed to escape the lucid dreams. No matter, he had to catch an early Metro North train to New York.

❧

Vettori was so angry that his fingers shook as he held the *Wall Street Journal* page out for Jerrod to see. "Mr. Albright is jumping up and down," he said. The old man stabbed an article on the cover page with a long, bony finger. The headlines screamed: *Genplex Losing Race to Industry Leader, Apex*. The article described the new approach to the cure of major mental illnesses and how the right drug based on promodulin would likely be successful. They projected Medulin would be it!

Jerrod's heart beat increased when he read the next paragraph. *Susan Wesley, a new healthcare analyst at Sirius Financial Investment Bank said in a recent interview, that while both Axilon and Medulin looked promising, Apex is enrolling thousands of patients in Medulin trials and already making note of certain important therapeutic advantages. Genplex, on the other hand, is plodding in their effort and remains silent. Clearly they either have problems or simply can't compete with the industry leader.*

Following that, there was a lot of financial information about markets for psychotropic drugs, problems with available drug products, and physicians' pressing needs for new drugs to treat mental illness.

Jerrod finished reading the piece and looked up at Alonsio and shrugged.

"So," Vettori asked, "Who is this Susan Wesley woman that seemingly knows more than we do? Perhaps we should hire her."

Wesley thought that Vettori obviously knew who the analyst was and this was just another of his not so subtle traps. Shit, why didn't I tell him before now? "My wife, I'm afraid."

Alonsio's eyes became very large behind his thick glasses, and he spoke slowly, making little strangling motions with his bony hands. "And, Dr. Wesley, why did you not tell me about this? This is a major conflict of interest and I can't wait to discuss the damned mess with Mr. Albright and the lawyers."

"Perhaps I should have, but my wife and I are basically separated, and I seldom see her unless Courtney is home. She lives here in New York and does as she likes; the truth is, I have no control over what she does or doesn't do. I will say that when she left she said she was going to work for Blendon and Grimes, but that never happened. I believe that Sirius hired her because they thought they could get to Axilon through me. They overestimated Susan, and perhaps this article is an act of desperation on her part. Neither Sirius nor Apex can be trusted, in my opinion. If you haven't heard, my house in Madison was broken into last night; the perpetrator had drilled my safe and removed its contents. He was killed in an automobile accident while trying to escape. I don't know who he is, make that *was*, or what he was looking for but the police are working on it."

The old man sighed deeply and banged his pencil on his desk top, breaking it into several pieces. "I believe what you are telling me, Dr. Wesley, but you are like a slimy thing that lives under a rock at the bottom of the sea for not telling me earlier; now I am at a *disadvantage.* But let's forget your wife for a moment—how could you have possibly let Apex get so far ahead of us? That article makes it sound like we have thrown in the towel." His arms waved as if he was doing so.

Jerrod reddened and raised his voice. "I can assure you, Sir, we have not *thrown in the towel.* We have proceeded cautiously according to the clinical study plan that you approved based on the budget that you also approved. As you have reminded me many times, *the budget is the budget,* and that's what we are working with. We have been very cautious in our picking of clinical investigators; there are many traps in psychotropic drug clinical studies. We have already met more than one scurrilous investigator in our interviews. Screw up, and we might end up before Congress. It has happened."

"Calm down, Jerrod, you have answered my question well enough, and I believe that you are doing a good and methodical job of what we agreed upon. However, assuming the article has some truth to it, how can they possibly be enrolling patients as though they are in the middle of a Phase III clinical program, supported by a large body of Phase I and Phase II safety and efficacy evidence? The FDA is still the FDA, is it not?"

Jerrod wondered about that. Had the bastards somehow gotten

to the FDA? Perhaps that would not be much of a leap for murderers. On the other hand, the FDA has a limited record of corruption. Jerrod did not like to ask for favors, but he knew it was time to call in some chits; he had to have answers, and quickly. "Sir, I don't know the answer to these questions, but I will do my best to find out."

Vettori slowly rose from his austere, Italian glass desk and walked to the windows that wrapped around his corner office. He waved his arms over the panoramic view of Manhattan and sighed. "This office could be yours, Jerrod, but we simply must be first to market this new class of drugs. I'm sure you know what I mean by this. We will discuss this again next week here in New York at the budget meeting, and Mr. Albright will be there. In the meantime, the Gulfstream V is at your disposal, and you already have a large travel and entertainment budget. Do something!"

7

Earlier that Year

Harvard University Medical School

Alan Werner stood well over six feet, though the gaunt man was stooped in posture. He had a certain charm, presence, though, and with a full head of reddish hair crowning a handsome face, women often gave him a second look. He was considered a good husband to his unattractive wife, Irena, and doted over his two children who attended Hebrew school. Werner had held the exalted position of Chairman, Department of Psychiatry, Harvard University Medical School for five years, and he was liked by most and respected by all. In addition to his duties as chairman, he also ran his own research program and maintained a small, but important, clinical practice. Most of his patients were politicians or celebrities, and he most certainly did not enter them into drug company studies. There were plenty of lesser physicians that did not mind soiling their hands for the money.

In fact, he viewed all drug company-types with a high level of disdain, especially the pompous asses like the one that sat before him. However, Maxwell Hall controlled a vast empire with a lot of money and Werner's expanding schizophrenia program required some of it. Werner was polite, even slightly fawning, as he, in his own mind, manipulated Hall. He had carefully explained his latest findings regarding disturbed sleep patterns of psychotics, though it was obvious the little shit had no idea what he was going on about. Now, it was time to talk money, *real* money—the kind of money that made the cogs and wheels turn.

Hall smiled broadly, "Congratulations on your successes, Dr. Werner. I think my unrestricted medical grants committee will see their way to enrich your program by one-million dollars to spend any way you choose, provided Harvard doesn't take too big of a bite. You know how I hate overhead."

Werner knew exactly what he meant by that; the parasites in the

Dean's office would suck you dry in a minute. "I can assure you of that, Mr. Hall; it will all go to the betterment of medicine. So, how shall we proceed?"

"My bean counters will be in touch shortly, Dr. Werner. You should have a check by the end of the month."

Mission accomplished; it was time to usher the slimy bastard out of his office. He had some *much sweeter* fish to fry. Werner took an obvious glance at his watch and said, "Thank you so much for coming, and I think I can speak for both myself and Harvard in saying that we sincerely appreciate your contribution."

Werner stood to dismiss his guest, but Maxwell Hall remained seated in his chair. Hall said, "Dr. Werner, Alan, there is another matter of importance I need to discuss with you. Have I *bought* myself another few minutes?"

Werner's tone of voice changed, dripping impatience. "Of course, you can have all the time you want. How might I help you?"

"I'd like for you to shed some light on a rumor that's circulating in the industry. Word on the street has it that you have been offered the job as Director, Center for Drug Evaluation and Research ,CDER, at the FDA. Is that true?"

The psychiatrist reddened slightly, and his hands trembled. How did this get out? He had mentioned it to no one. "Yes, but I don't know where you came by such *personal* information."

Hall grinned broadly; this time it was more evil than friendly. "Let's just say I have my sources. Are you going to take the job?" Hall, seemingly enjoying himself, pushed back in his chair with his hands behind his head.

Werner sensed trouble, and he got up and looked out his window at the vast place of learning that was Harvard Medical School. It calmed his nerves, and he said, "I haven't decided yet; I love Harvard and have a secure place here, so the probable answer is *no.*"

The professor's desk was a cluttered mess, typical of academic propeller heads. Hall brazenly leaned over and rearranged a few decorative items; they were little glass ducks; and he placed them in a row. "If you took the job, you would rule a vast empire and control all drug approvals in the United States. Lord knows the process could be improved; we both know that it is more bureaucratic than scientific and certainly not fair to the customer, the pharmaceutical industry, or to sick patients who need better therapy."

Why was this man here, trying to convince him to take a government job? It can only be for the wrong reasons. "You sound convincing, and so has the FDA Commissioner, who is trying to fill the vacant position, but again, the likely answer is *no!* Do I make myself clear enough?"

Hall laughed and leaned back and lit up one of his most aromatic Cuban cigars. He blew smoke in the angry psychiatrist's face as he selected a folder from his leather case. He examined it briefly, and then made a show of carefully placing it on Werner's desk, leaving it closed. "Dr. Werner, isn't it considered bad form for a psychiatrist, or any other doctor for that matter, to ah, have *sexual relations* with their patients? I am pretty certain that Harvard takes a dim view of such goings on. Humm?"

Werner was bright red now and stood and walked toward the door. He shouted, "Mr. Hall, I have no idea what you are talking about, and I think it is way past time for you to leave!"

Hall laughed again and opened the folder which contained several photographs. The one on top was a photograph of the professor with his family, all smiling radiantly, taken from a recent Harvard publication that featured articles on key faculty members. This produced little reaction other than a quizzical look. Hall said, "Now, I only show you that nice one to set the stage," and dumped the remaining dozen or so photographs on the desk. "Hope you like pornography; I know I do." Three perfect smoke rings added an explanation mark.

The frightened man grabbed the high quality color prints and looked at them one at a time. They clearly showed Harvard's Chairman of Psychiatry having sexual relations with not one, but two, very attractive, sophisticated-looking women. Werner's mouth worked but no sound emerged. A Jewish guppy, Hall thought.

"John's quite a good photographer, isn't he? I'll have to remember to give him a raise. My, you do have good tastes in which patients you sleep with, don't you? One, the wife of a U.S. Senator and the other a television news anchor lady—goodness! You obviously have talents with women that I wouldn't have suspected."

Werner's face twitched, and he began to shred the damning photos with trembling hands. "What the devil do you want, Hall?"

"Ah, simple enough; when I leave, you get on the phone and call the Commissioner at FDA. You accept the job and run CDER. Given your standing in the academic community, I'm certain that you will be able to keep your Harvard appointment, and you can probably negotiate with FDA that you keep your small practice—*have your cake and eat it too*, so to speak. Once you have moved into your new office in Bethesda, you take orders from me. And, oh yeah, I will more than make up for your lost income; you'll be on the bonus system, just like those big pharmaceutical execs you despise so much. And, by the way, don't worry about those prints you just ruined; there are lots more where they came from. You certainly have some novel ideas about sex. I actually took some notes for future reference."

8

Thirty-thousand Feet, Descending to John Wayne Airport

Irvine, California

The massive aircraft lurched and bumped as it dropped down through the turbulent air over the mountains. Jerrod opened his eyes and was treated to the smiling face of his pretty private stewardess; Becky was her name. She held a small tray out to him with the Jack Daniel's he had ordered hours ago back in White Plains, where the sleek G-V nested securely in a climate-controlled hangar.

She said, "Boy, you're an easy customer. I got almost as much sleep as you did. You still want this drink?"

Jerrod stretched and grinned, "Absolutely, with some fresh rocks, thank you. I had a really good sleep and am ready to go, even on California time."

The big jet, with its ninety-three-foot wingspan, lurched and turned with its powerful Rolls-Royce engines backing down, whining angrily. Becky winked and said, "Gotta buckle up, Honey," and was gone, leaving Jerrod alone with his thoughts.

He frowned and shook his head as he looked around the opulent corporate aircraft. Normally, riding as the single passenger in a thirty million dollar toy would have bothered him, but not tonight; he was seeking answers and didn't care how he got them. This extravagant piece of aluminum shit would be chump change if they could get Axilon approved and introduced to the hungry market.

Jerrod had arranged a dinner meeting in Newport Beach with one of Genplex's most trusted clinical investigators and his close personal friend, Charlie Cox. Jerrod and Charlie had done the world together,

45

attending scientific and medical meetings wherever they occurred. They had shared their lives in some of the best restaurants and worst dives the boondoggle circuit could offer up. The two men truly knew one another and trusted each other, implicitly. A black Lincoln Town Car was pulling up on the tarmac as the jet neared the general aviation facility. Becky joined Jerrod at the bottom of the ramp and waited for the pilots to off-load Jerrod's bag and some gifts he had bought for Charlie's family.

Becky said, "I hope you enjoyed your flight, Dr. Wesley."

"I did, indeed; it could not have been better."

She gave him a coy look and said, "Looks like you're working tonight, Hon."

He laughed and said, "Maybe next time."

Becky feigned a look of great disappointment. "I'll take that as a rain check and, by the way, I'm from here, Irvine, originally, so I know all the ropes."

Jerrod said, "I bet you do," laughed again and imagined the sights hidden beneath that tight, little stewardess uniform as he walked toward the car. He scolded himself for thinking that way—he was weakening under the heavy load of deprivation from his non-marriage. Hearing Charlie's latest war stories wasn't going to help, either, whether they were true or not. Some were.

"We're here, Sir, Roy's, best Pacific Rim food in the world." Jerrod's eyes blinked open as the big limousine easily moved out of the Newport Center Drive traffic and stopped in front of the expensive restaurant. He asked the driver to wait for him during dinner and moved through the crowd into the bar. As expected, Charlie sat near the end of the long, glass bar, holding court over several surgically-perfect Newport Beach beauties. As soon as he spotted his friend, Charlie dismissed the women with a wave and walked over and hugged his friend, not caring what anyone might think.

The two friends caught up over several drinks and ordered from the interesting Asian menu. Jerrod's order included a very expensive bottle of California Chardonnay that was not readily available in Connecticut. Charlie raised his eyebrow a bit, and Jerrod said, "Hey, Bud, you deserve it—only the best." After enjoying the outstanding seafood and draining most of a second bottle of the buttery wine, Jerrod asked, "Could we talk business for a moment?"

Charlie had gotten an early start and was a bit flushed. He replied, "I thought women were serious business," with a laugh. "Sure, anything—shoot!"

"I know you are involved in the Medulin clinical program. I fully understand that you can't disclose confidential information regarding the drug, especially your center's findings, but I am really confused about what Apex is up to. Word on the street is that they are enrolling thousands of patients over multiple centers as though they were in the midst of an ambitious Phase III program, which is impossible. You probably saw the *Wall Street Journal* article?" Charlie nodded and Jerrod continued, "Well, as you might guess, my ass is grass with Genplex management, and I have to understand what's happened to the playing field here. Right now, we are pushing Axilon ahead carefully and scientifically, enrolling limited numbers of patients in early Phase II studies seeking reasonable proof of efficacy, as mandated by FDA." Jerrod threw up his hands and shook his head in an unusual display, reminiscent of his Italian boss.

Charlie Cox looked his frustrated friend in the eye for a long moment. "Listen, I assumed you knew about this or I would have filled you in before now. Truth be known, there no longer is a level playing field at FDA. Do you know Alan Werner?"

Jerrod took a deep breath. "Yeah, Harvard guy; recently surprised a lot of people by taking the director position at CDER. I also remember some story about his ugly wife following you around at some European clinical meeting."

"I'll ignore your second comment even though it's true," Charlie replied with a grin. "Lots of people were surprised when he left Harvard, but now he's at FDA pulling drug approval strings. He's the root of your problem."

"I don't see how; director is a high-level, bureaucratic position, several levels above the therapeutic heads, in this case, David Kendall, who is the Director of Psychiatry Products. Kendall is pretty smart and would be tough to bully."

Cox rubbed his Miami Vice-type beard, enjoying the rasping sound. "You'd think, but things have changed with Werner's arrival. The Commissioner has given him free reign to run roughshod over the drugs bunch. What Werner has done is assigned himself a whole new level of scientific and regulatory power. He alone now selects *therapeutically advantageous* products for special treatment. If such drugs show promise in very small, early Phase II studies, then enrollment is immediately opened up, by Werner, for massive trials, hence theoretically speeding up the NDA submission for the miracle drug."

"And now, Medulin is such a *miracle drug*?"

"Yes," Cox responded.

Jerrod looked at his friend a long moment and said, "I sense corruption, or at least unfairness, in this sort of arbitrary *winner picking*."

"Unfairness, yes; corruption, I don't know; unbridled Harvard arrogance, for certain." The agitated clinical investigator drained the last of the Cake Bread Chardonnay into his glass and downed it in a gulp. "You know, I have a good relationship with David Kendall and work with him on several committees. I spoke to him about Axilon, and he said all he could do was treat your drug fairly but in the plodding, old way. He has no say about Werner's picks other than to monitor the results of ongoing trials. Yet, both he and I know that the two drugs are not markedly different in terms of their efficacy."

Jerrod scratched his head, "I know Kendall pretty well, too, and I can talk to him, but based on what you say, it's a waste of time."

"Yes, and it would take the CEO of your company, Albright, I think, to get in either Werner's or the Commissioner's office, and then he would fail."

"Charlie, I think I'm screwed, so we might as well go out and finish getting good and drunk. I've got a limo waiting, and the driver knows where the good bars in Newport Beach are."

Cox grinned his agreement. This was his thing.

$\mathcal{L}$

Wesley never made it to his company-owned suite that night and the tired limo driver literally poured him out of the plush vehicle and onto the plane with the help of ever-efficient Becky. It was 6:00 a.m.

She grinned at the sick scientist and said, "A little green behind the gills, I see. A bit of Miss Becky's special treatment, and we'll have you up and running in no time."

Jerrod groaned and nodded. He needed some special treatment all right; he had to call Vettori as soon as he sobered up. After a double bloody Mary, he slept throughout the long flight until Becky awakened him with a steaming cup of hot double espresso as the plane was landing. Soon, he was in his BMW speeding down the Merritt Parkway. His head was clear and traffic light, so he dialed Vettori on his cell phone and delivered the bad news. The old man remained unexpectedly calm on the phone, but Wesley knew he was boiling on the inside. The messenger could always be shot later, perhaps at the budget meeting on Thursday. Plenty of bullets would be available.

He had always thought of the Medulin toxicology report as being his ace in the hole, but now he wondered. Was the new head of CDER really a dictator that picked winners and losers with little regard to the supporting evidence? Charlie said he did not suspect corruption, but Jerrod did. So far everyone who had touched the drug had suffered the consequences, with either Apex and or Sirius pulling the strings. Perhaps it was time for Wesley to become the manipulator rather than the manipulated and squeeze some information out of his naïve wife. There would be a window of opportunity over the following weekend; both Susan and Courtney would be in town for one of Courtney's infrequent visits. The girl had hinted that she had a personal problem she needed to discuss with her parents—both parents. What now? Was she pregnant, getting married, or had she contacted some awful STD? Jerrod wondered. Girls today were at such risk, especially pretty ones. Whatever it was, he would not love her less for it.

A quick review of Jerrod's phone mail revealed a call from the Madison Police Department; The intruder who had died in his drive had been identified. Abramo, Fingers, Anesthasia had a long rap sheet in this country and abroad. He was an expensive, for-hire criminal who specialized in breaking and entering and was an expert at safe-cracking. He was thought to have retreated to his home in Sicily and had not been known to be in the U.S. until his death. Law enforcement had no leads on who might have been paying him, but based on his history; someone likely was. Someone big. They agreed to keep Jerrod informed and that was it. *Someone big*, he thought—right.

9

Genplex Budget Meeting

The headquarters of Genplex occupied the top three floors of the Banister Bank Building, favorably situated on Park Avenue in New York. Their fine conference room looked out over the best of Manhattan. The meeting room was long and narrow with an expensive, inlaid mahogany conference table that ran almost the length of the room. There was a large screen that occupied one wall and some sophisticated computer projection equipment suspended from the ceiling. This courtroom with its Genplex executive judges had been the scene of numerous executions, and Wesley figured he was next. His only allies in the room were Wanda Lassiter, his administrative assistant, Larry Reynolds, Genplex Medical Director, and Fred Wilson, Comptroller for the Madison site. Otherwise, there were other divisions of Genplex present, each fighting for their share of the total budget pie. Senior company executives looked on with distrust etched in their faces; they always thought they were being flimflammed for the sake of a bunch of science fair projects. One hostile environment.

Jerrod had been standing and defending his position for over two hours and was feeling the strain. He knew he had to somehow spend most of his budget on Axilon, the company's top priority, yet at the same time, keep research and lesser projects viable. Finally, he had no more juice to give—nothing left to say, so he concluded his budget request, thanked the group, and started to sit down, when Rhinner Albright called him back to the front and center.

"Dr., Wesley, I'd like to personally thank you for your excellent presentation and your effort to fairly distribute our precious dollars. I know how tough it has been."

Jerrod said, "Thank you, Sir," and nodded toward his team, recognizing their contributions.

Albright continued, "Now, just one more question. If, now if, mind you, we could come up with a lot more dollars to throw at Axilon, what could you do for us?"

The room filled with whispers and murmurs as Jerrod's competitors for budget dollars wondered whose ox was about to be gored. Vettori demanded, "One meeting, please!" and the room quieted. Jerrod's first thought was that his boss had not shared the new concerns regarding the FDA with Albright, or was he just running his trap line? Keep it simple, stupid, he chided himself.

The tired speaker took a drink of water and replied evenly while looking directly at his boss, "Unless we start new Phase II pilot studies in other psychiatric disease states, this budget will allow us to do everything the FDA will agree to over the next budget period." His medical director vigorously nodded his agreement from the sidelines.

Vettori stood to speak but was waved down by the CEO. "Alonsio, hold on, let's cut to the chase; you told me that Alan Werner at FDA has given the Apex drug some sort of special status that allows them to proceed more rapidly than we can, no matter our funding of Axilon. Is that correct?"

The old man stood and scowled at the audience. "Yes, Dr. Wesley reported that to me after a fact-finding trip to the West Coast. Apparently, this is an arbitrary decision by Werner, the first of many that he will make."

Now, Albright was standing too. He brushed imaginary crumbs from his expensive suit and looked Jerrod in the eye. "What are you going to do about this problem, Dr. Wesley?"

Jerrod felt his blue shirt dampen in the armpits; he should not have removed his jacket; he sure as hell shouldn't have worn a blue shirt to a budget meeting. Jerrod said, "With all due respect, Sir, there is little I can do. I have a good, working relationship with David Kendall, who runs the Division of Psychiatric Products, but my line of communications ends there. I should add that Kendall doesn't agree with this nonsense any more than we do. The only hope is that someone higher up in the company, like you, Sir, can get to the Commissioner, whom Werner and his organization, CDER, report to, and plead our case. Werner has built firewalls around himself."

Albright sighed and then managed a faint smile. "Thank you, Dr. Wesley, I appreciate your candidness. I will do what I can. Alonsio, please find a time on our calendars when you can accompany me to Washington."

Jerrod struggled to suppress a smile; for once he had reflected a bomb back from whence it came.

By the time the meeting was adjourned, it was early evening and Jerrod invited his team to dinner at Tuscany. Both Reynolds and Wilson declined, pleading previous arrangements. That left Jerrod and Wanda, who was delighted by the unexpected invitation, to meet at the big clock in the lobby of the Waldorf at 8:00 p.m.

Jerrod blinked at the approach of the beautiful, young woman. She wore a low-cut, azure sundress that matched her eyes and accommodated the late August heat. Gossamer curls of her fine auburn hair framed her face and evening makeup enhanced her beauty—a true goddess of summer, Jerrod thought.

A slight smile crossed her full lips when she saw Jerrod suck in his breath in awe of her. He had changed into more casual sporting attire and the two made a stunning couple. A shrewd operator, Jerrod had made dual reservations at Tuscany, an excellent, but loud and busy, Italian restaurant and Restaurant Daniel, a romantic and very expensive French restaurant. The decision to cancel Tuscany was easy when he learned that he and Wanda would be alone.

Daniel was packed with happy patrons—mostly older men who could afford the pricy place with women who could not. Jerrod and Wanda enjoyed the wonderful food and wine matched perfectly to the late summer season. The awful meeting and haunting issues were forgotten for the moment, and the world seemed to belong only to them. A place noted for the pollination of fleeting romances had once again done its part.

Reality returned the moment the couple stepped out onto the sidewalk. Heat, humidity, and honking horns dominated the scene. A faint odor of leaking sewage clung to the heavy air. He was suddenly sober, and the magical evening seemed over. But was it? Wanda clutched him by the arm and said, "I don't want it to end. A girlfriend recently introduced me to a smart club a short walk from here—Dance! Dance! Good drinks, fun bands, and a chic, upscale crowd. No Euro-trash."

Jerrod laughed at her girlish enthusiasm and said, "Lead the way, my dear."

It was still early for the Manhattan club scene, so they readily found a table, ordered drinks, and enjoyed watching the colorful patrons of all ages and sizes flow through the doors. Pretty soon they were caught up by the music and each other and spun effortlessly about the crowded dance floor. They matched the throbbing beat with their steps for a long time before they collapsed at their table and ordered one last round of drinks. Wanda smiled sweetly and reached across the little table for Jerrod's hand, but before she touched his fingers, she hesitated. Wanda's warm smile evaporated, and her hand came to her mouth in an expression of shock.

"Oh-my-God," she exclaimed.

"What?"

"Jerrod, whatever you do; don't turn around," she replied. "Your wife, Susan,is seated at a table behind you. She's with two older men I don't know."

Ignoring Wanda's plea, Jerrod stole a quick glance, pretending to drop his napkin and fetching it. He knew neither man personally, but he had heard Maxwell Hall speak at meetings. The other man, the one holding Susan's hand under the table, was none other than Anders Boreson, head of Health Care Investment Banking at Sirius. Susan had pointed out his picture in the Sirius Annual Report; he was a tall, skinny man with a mop of blond hair on a head that bobbed around like it was mounted on a steel spring. Jerrod's first thought was to confront them, be the obnoxious ass of a wronged husband, but he decided, no; he wasn't exactly all that innocent himself.

Jerrod placed sufficient money on the table to cover the bill and a generous tip and said, "You get up and walk out, and I'll follow."

As the couple made their way through the happy crowd, Jerrod chanced another glance at Susan and her friends. All three were laughing with champagne glasses held high. There was obviously something important to celebrate other than Susan's new boyfriend. Jerrod considered that at least he had some useful ammunition for Susan's weekend visit. Now he looked forward to it more than ever.

Wanda said good night at the door to her room in the Waldorf. She gave Jerrod a wistful look and a peck on the cheek, and that was it. He knew it was over with Susan, and he was ready to move on, but disappointed this was not the moment. There would be other opportunities, moments, he knew that, but damn it, he had seen Susan in action and he was more angry at her unbridled arrogance than her unfaithfulness.

It had been a long day and Jerrod was soon snoring blissfully when his room telephone rang at 2:00 a.m. At first disoriented, he finally found the phone; it was Wanda.

"Hello, Jerrod, sorry I woke you, but I can't sleep. Could you come down to my room? *Please.*"

Jerrod answered in the affirmative before he was fully awake. He threw on a promotional T-shirt and some faded jeans, brushed his teeth, and tossed down some left over, cold coffee. He felt the beginnings of an erection as he and Frank Sinatra counted the floors. Finally the big doors rumbled open on the twelfth floor, and Jerrod sprinted to room 1203. He suddenly wondered if he had the right room but knocked lightly. Chains rattled, and the door opened a crack.

"Jerrod?"

"Yes, Wanda, I believe you called and requested my presence," he laughed.

The door pushed open, and Jerrod stepped into the dimly lit room. He let out a low whistle; he had imagined that Wanda would be beautiful naked, but he had no idea—nothing could have prepared him for the full-bodied beauty that stood before him. Nothing. The passion lasted until daylight, when they finally fell into a deep sleep in one another's arms. A great void, left by an eternity of loveless nights, had been filled to overflowing for both lovers. Their souls had been renewed, visited by some god greater than hate, and their spirits soared. There would be plenty of time later for the inevitable questions and regret, for concern about what they had done to their working partnership at Genplex. Nothing would ever be the same. It never is.

10

A Daughter's Revelation

ate summer is a time to be prized along the Connecticut Shore. Long Island Sound has finally reached a hospitable seventy-two degrees, and the cold wind and gloom have been replaced by balmy temperatures and deep blue skies. The quaint, little beach towns swarm with summer people, spending their last days enjoying the beaches and seafood. The annual runs of bluefish and stripers are at their peak, and fishing boats and colorful sails dot the deep blue, ever-rushing water as the big tides rise and fall. Even the rich people of Madison, who pretend to hate their annual migrants and the money they bring, bask in the golden light of late summer.

Courtney had chosen the perfect weekend for a visit, though she would soon drag another dark cloud over a family that was already disintegrating. The Sound sparkled in the distance in the late afternoon sun's waning rays as Jerrod, Susan, and Courtney enjoyed a nice Chardonnay from a nearby vineyard while they relaxed on the stone patio of their Madison colonial. Cherishing the peaceful moment, they sipped their wine in a silence broken only by calling gulls in the distance. The smell of the sea and sweet autumn clematis blooming on a nearby fence permeated the air, and life's problems seemed a distant reality.

Courtney tried to force a smile, but the corners of her pretty mouth fell, and tears welled up in her big eyes. "At first I thought it was the place, you know. Duke is a very good school and there are some old Choate classmates there, but something was missing, I thought. Early in the semester, my grades were good, but then they fell off, and I had a hard time concentrating on my work. Finally, I lost my appetite and had difficulty getting out of bed in the morning. I felt so depressed, but there was no reason; I had friends, dates, everything you could possibly want. Jennie, my sweet roommate, became alarmed about my behavior and suggested I see Dr. Barrington, the school psychiatrist."

Susan started to interrupt, but Jerrod held up his hand. "Let her finish."

"OK, well, I did see the doctor, and he diagnosed me as having a major depressive episode, real depression, not some imaginary neurotic sort of thing. He prescribed Prozac, and I have been taking it for two weeks."

"And?" Susan demanded; her impatience near boiling over.

"I feel somewhat better, but I hate the side effects. Stuff makes me feel jazzed-up; you know, jittery—hard to describe."

Jerrod took a sip of wine and pursed his lips; he sensed where this was going next and didn't have long to wait.

Susan got up, hugged Courtney, and said, "Oh, Darling, you don't have to take that awful stuff; Mommy has a lot of influence with Apex Pharmaceuticals, and I feel certain we can get you into one of their protocols for Medulin, their miracle drug for depression and all sorts of problems."

"No!" Jerrod shouted, "No way in hell are we going to put my daughter on an experimental drug we know *nothing* about. In the first place, Prozac is a perfectly good drug, and it has been used safely in thousands of patients. Medulin may not even be safe." The unopened toxicology report loomed large in his mind. The narcissistic bitch was out of control.

Susan reddened, "I assure you; it *is safe*. Besides, you just heard Courtney say she has been taking Prozac for two weeks, and she does not feel a lot better."

Jerrod shook his head at her ignorance and blurted, "Susan, if you knew anything at all about this business, then you'd know it takes fluoxetine, Prozac, four to six weeks to achieve its maximal therapeutic effect. The side effects abate over time as well. We *are* going to give Dr. Barrington and Prozac a chance."

The angry woman stood and said, "We'll see."

"We'll see nothing," Jerrod retorted. "You can't enter Courtney into *any* experimental drug protocol without both our signatures. She's not twenty-one."

By now, Courtney had run for the comfort of her bedroom in tears and the altercation escalated after Susan said exactly the wrong thing.

"Yeah, we *will see*. I know Maxwell Hall personally, so there."

This time the lady spider was caught in her own web and for once would not be eating her mate. The smile that cracked Jerrod's angry face was a rare one for him—primal, nasty. "Yes, Susan, I know you do; why, I enjoyed watching you and Hall and your goofy-looking boyfriend living it up at Dance! Dance! the other evening. Was the champagne good, Honey?"

Susan's mouth fell open in surprise, but no words followed for once. She finally sputtered something unintelligible that might have been *spying bastard,* stormed out of the room, and was soon on her way back to the city. It was the second time in a week Jerrod had felt good, really good. He would speak to his lawyer soon. He made a mental note to call Dr. Barrington as well. He would offer his strong support and approval before his nutty, about-to-be ex-wife got to Courtney's psychiatrist. For now, he was taking his daughter sailing; his J-24, *Sea Sprint,* was rigged and waiting at the Madison Yacht Club.

☙

Jerrod knew that the altercation that had just occurred had not helped Courtney's condition one bit, and it was his responsibility as a father to make up for the added pain caused by it. The sun and exhilaration of slicing through the dark water with the wind in her face would help, but it was really his ability to convey his love for his daughter that mattered. He desperately needed to explain to Courtney what had happened between her parents, but he could not; it was beyond him. He pushed a tear away and searched for new resolve.

11

Naples Psychiatric Hospital, Naples, Florida

The Snake Strikes

Dr. Jonathan Smith had received an urgent page to examine a patient participating in the center's Medulin clinical study. Stacy Larkin had been in his major depression protocol for almost three months, no patient longer than she. Ramona Sanchez, Smith's study director was disturbed with Larkin's rapidly increasing Hamilton-Depression Rating Scale, Ham-D. Stacy had initially responded remarkably well to treatment, presumably Medulin and not placebo, in the well-controlled trial. But she had recently taken a turn for the worse. The forty-seven year old mother of three was not only suicidal but also exhibiting strange neurological side effects. To further complicate the woman's mental problems, there was possibly dementia.

Smith was shocked by the woman's unkempt appearance; she looked more like an untreated schizophrenic than the woman he had almost been ready to pronounce cured of depression a month ago. Her hands shook, and her lips rolled uncontrollably, much like the irreversible dyskinesia produced by long-term treatment with schizophrenia drugs. Her eyes were blank, and she seemed not to recognize her physician.

Dr. Smith tucked the stethoscope back into his white jacket; her vital signs were normal. Billy Larkin was a drywall hanger and seemed pretty confused himself, but he knew enough to be concerned and hovered by his wife's side. The psychiatrist asked the man, "When did you first notice a change in Stacy's condition?"

The concerned husband cleared his throat and struggled for words. "Started just after our last visit, doctor. First, the shakin'

58

showed up, and then, then the bad mood returned. Real bad. And God, her mouth started a-movin' all around-like. Yeah, and you increased the dose of that damned drug at her last visit, too. Remember?"

The psychiatrist was perplexed; he had never seen anything like this in his many years of practice. And he didn't know about the slight elevation in dose; the protocol required pushing the dose in even the best responders, which Stacy Larkin had been. Why would a twenty-five percent increase in dose make any difference? Maybe it was the long period of treatment; after all, she was in the three-month cohort of patients.

"Mr. Larkin, I'm afraid I must hospitalize your wife. The neurological symptoms worry me greatly. I'm going to call in Dr. Elizabeth Andrews, a neurologist here at the center, and have her evaluate Mrs. Larkin. Dr. Andrews will likely order some tests and get some answers rather quickly. I am immediately discontinuing Mrs. Larkin's medication and I have to notify the company. They will also break the blind and tell us for certain what medication she is taking. She will be included in the statistical analysis as an initial responder who was discontinued after three months treatment because of adverse events. Don't worry, Mr. Larkin, the sponsor will cover all costs related to your wife's hospitalization." The poor man nodded and fidgeted with his Budweiser hat; he understood not one word of it, but it scared him half to death. He didn't know what he would do without his Stacy. Crazy or not, she was way smarter than he was.

Just north of Naples in Bonita Springs, Dr. Smith's second tragedy of the day was brewing. Benny Jackson, like Stacy Larkin, had been on Medulin for over two months and had also responded well to treatment. However, on this day he had awakened with a severe headache that quickly evolved into a psychotic episode. The flashing lights and bells in his head soon became compelling voices that demanded he do extraordinary things. By noon, he was completely crazy and running around the house naked, shouting obscene things. The electric wiring of his house was causing burns on his arms and legs; he imagined. The container of Elmer's glue he ate for lunch did not improve the way he felt, and the voices demanded that he take a drive. This seemed a good idea, so he took Bonita Beach Road to I-75 and turned south towards Naples and the Everglades. His vintage Corvette was soon moving slowly down the busy interstate, weaving from lane to lane. This mightily displeased several truckers in big rigs, and they blew their powerful horns and made obscene gestures at Benny.

He could feel the power surging through his body and would have none of it. The Corvette screeched to a halt crosswise in the center lane, and the naked man stepped out of the car. Several fast moving vehicles with horns blaring narrowly missed him before he spotted his quarry. The heavily-laden Peterbilt eighteen-wheeler was bearing down on him at almost eighty miles-per-hour. Benny laughed hysterically and stepped directly in front of the speeding truck. He held out his hands, fully intending to stop the monster in its tracks and teach the operator some respect. The horrified driver slammed on the brakes, but it did little to retard the impact of tons of flying steel with soft, human flesh and brittle bones. Later, the driver would testify that the fool had literally exploded before his eyes. Although Benny's brains were scattered over several hundred feet of I-75, enough remained intact within a large piece of skull for possible study. It was frozen in the coroner's pathology lab and promptly forgotten.

While Benny Jackson's remains were being scraped off I-75, an intense neurological evaluation of Stacy Larkin was in progress. Every tool available to Beth Andrews was employed—CT, NMR, and PET—and the gestalt of all the findings was a clear picture of advanced brain pathology that defied logical explanation. A less astute observer might have diagnosed the patient's condition as Alzheimer's disease. Indeed, areas normally affected in Alzheimer's disease showed extensive pathology, but so did other areas normally associated with mood, psychotic behavior, and even normal ambulation. Tracks involving the major neurotransmitters, acetylcholine, serotonin, and dopamine were severely affected. Satisfied that she had learned all the complex data had to teach, Dr. Andrews picked up her desk phone and dialed Dr. Smith's extension.

Smith answered, but his normally strong, in-command tone was missing, and he sounded very upset. Finally, he regained control and explained to Beth what had happened on I-75 in Bonita Springs that morning.

"Jon, I'm afraid what I have to report is not going to improve your spirits. Your other patient, Stacy Larkin, has extensive, generalized brain pathology, unlike anything I've ever seen. Areas associated with mood, psychotic behavior, and even normal movement showed severe degeneration. The lesions are too widespread and non-specific to be any know neurological disease. I think this woman has been exposed to some potent neurotoxin. What drug did you say she was on?"

Neurotoxin? Smith wondered just how many patients were being administered this damned stuff, not only in his studies, but also the other trials around the country. Jesus!

"Jon?"

"Sorry, my mind was drifting all over the damned place. She has been on either placebo or Apex's so-called *miracle drug* Medulin for three months. Don't know if you are aware of this or not, but the new guy down at FDA, Alan Werner, has a program to fast track selected drugs based on limited safety and efficacy data. Medulin was the first. Any chance what you saw had nothing to do with the drug study? Environmental toxins?" the frustrated physician asked hopefully.

"Possible, I guess, but not likely."

"I'll know soon; I have to call the company, and they will break the blind."

Dr. Smith placed an urgent call to Regulatory Affairs at Apex and waited over the evening for a response, but all was not well at Naples Psychiatric Hospital.

At precisely midnight a bell rang in poor Stacy Larkin's head, and she sat bolt-upright in her hospital bed. Her husband was snoring peacefully in the chair beside her in the dimly lit room. The tremors in her muscles seemed better, and she managed to extricate herself from the covers and slipped to the floor without falling. The ringing bell in her head was replaced by Dr. Smith's voice.

It demanded, "Run! Run, Stacy, run or we're going to cut you up in little pieces and feed you to the spiders! Ruuuuuun!"

Stacy pushed open the door to her room and ran down the mostly deserted hall, clawing at her face and ears, screaming incoherently. She could *see* her doctor now, and he was not only yelling but chasing after her as well. He had taken on the appearance of a big, black, hairy spider with great fangs. Atlas Glass Company had sworn that no human force could break the large window at the end of the hall that provided a panoramic view of the beautiful Japanese garden, but it shattered like a light bulb when she collided with it. As Stacy Larkin fell the six floors, her trajectory took her well out into the koi pond, but it was shallow, and her neck was cleanly broken on impact. Now, there were two deaths in the Smith Medulin clinical study.

The rising sun found Maxwell Hall seated across his conference room table from three of his top clinical research scientists, all three medical doctors with advanced training in specialty areas. Steaming coffee and doughnuts sat untouched. The angry executive frowned at his bombastic Regulatory Affairs Director, Bob Shepard. He didn't get it and neither did his associates. Ken Joseph, Director of Biostatistics and Data Management and Russell Turner, Medical Director, were as silent as stones. Thankfully, his exasperating head of research, Yuan Li, was on vacation in China, as usual. He made a mental note to replace him as soon as possible. Apex simply did not have deaths in clinical trials and certainly not with Medulin. Both patients had major depression and had committed suicide on their own. Either the dose of the drug had been inadequate or there was a mistake in the randomization schedule, and they were on placebo. Hall favored the latter and he, personally, would deal with Jonathan Smith and the FDA.

Fed up with foot-dragging fools, Hall ordered the three to get out of the room and get busy and *correct* the randomization schedule to show that both deaths were suicides that occurred while the victims were on placebo. Depressed patients kill themselves all the time. Don't they?

Hall's first call would be to Jonathan Smith, and then he would call Alan Werner. Hall was so angry he dropped the receiver twice while dialing the number. "Doctor, we have broken the code, and both patients that died in the study were on placebo. They were obviously depressed patients with suicidal ideations and subsequently acted on them. The clinical report form should reflect that reality."

There was a long silence. Finally Smith said, "In the case of Stacy Larkin we collected a large body of evidence that she was suffering from extensive brain degeneration and dementia before her death."

Hall sneered, "Then, you Doctor, violated the protocol by entering a patient with Alzheimer's disease, or whatever her pre-existing problem was, into the trial in the first place. What were you thinking about? Obviously you believe she was on active drug, don't you?"

Smith was put off by the fast-thinking bastard, but he wasn't going to fold so easily. "I believe Mrs. Larkin developed the problem on the drug, and I'm sticking to my informed medical opinion."

"I'm not interested in your opinion, informed or otherwise, Doctor. Do you have a so-called *body of evidence* that she was not sick when she entered the study?"

"No, the diagnostic work was not done on her until she began to evidence neurological symptoms. But you should talk to Dr. Andrews; she's a true expert on such issues."

Hall interrupted the irritated doctor, "In other words I am correct, so let's move on to the guy who thought he was Superman, Benny Jackson. Do you have *any* proof that he was on active drug or that he did not commit suicide because of his depression?"

"No, but I have routine blood samples from both patients, and I plan to have them analyzed for presence of the study drug."

Hall laughed, "You do that, Doctor; you do that." Even high doses of Medulin produce miniscule blood levels of the active drug, and developing an assay has been a major issue in Medulin's development.

The difficult radio immune assay required can only be done by Apex's Metabolism and Pharmacokinetics Department. "What we have here is a clear case of two deaths in a clinical trial of an experimental drug. Both patients were on placebo, and there may have been protocol violations, even medical malpractice, in entering them. You may face FDA disqualification as a clinical investigator in this country."

The angry physician stammered, "I'm not through with you yet, Hall; I, I'll see you in jail!"

"No, Doctor, this discussion is over. By the way, what are Apex's outstanding payments due to you?"

Smith winced. "Over a million dollars, but you owe for all our clinical work, no matter what."

"Yes, almost two million to be exact, and if you ever want to see one penny of it, you will cooperate and continue on despite two placebo deaths. I will deal with the FDA and believe me, they will not be causing problems. You also forgot to mention the two deceased patients' packaged drug supplies—or was it intentional? Forget that nasty little idea; they are missing, and so is your not-quite-trustworthy study nurse, Ramona Sanchez. Now, get to work!"

12

Axilon Wavers

Despite pressure from all sides and his secret relationship with Wanda Lassiter, Jerrod felt reasonably good about life in general, including the progression of Axilon through early efficacy studies. Sometimes he wondered if it was just being in love that made things seem so bright. He had expected their affair to produce almost immediate problems, but Wanda was very circumspect, and her professional attitude remained intact. She only became his passionate lover late at night in the colonial at the end of the long, dark lane.

Jerrod had contacted a well-known divorce lawyer at a large family practice firm in Stamford, Connecticut, and she was taking a preliminary cut at an action plan for a scenario he might survive. He would hear her ideas in a week or two. The lawyer had been very clear about keeping his own relationships, if any, quiet. It thrilled him to think he might eventually be rid of his treasonous wife and all the baggage that came with her. Jerrod chuckled at the thought that Susan and bobble-head would make quite a pair. Wanda's voice on the intercom brought his revelry to an end. "Jerrod, please pick up line three; Larry Reynolds is holding, and he sounds excited."

"Hello, Larry; what's up?"

"I don't want to discuss this on the phone; may I come up?"

A few minutes later, Wanda let the red faced doctor into Wesley's office. Usually well-dressed, the man was disheveled and appeared to have not slept recently. He collapsed into the chair across the desk from Jerrod and sighed deeply.

Jerrod remained silent with his hands folded in his lap, letting his upset medical director collect his wits. Finally, Larry spoke, haltingly at first, "It's the Foster depression study; the one we thought the results were so exciting; well, our audit group just had a look at it and found some *irregularities*."

Jerrod's hatred for such words was reflected in his sharp tone. "Irregularities? What the hell do you mean by *irregularities*?"

"Maybe worse than that. Foster, he, he may have fudged the whole damned Axilon depression study."

Jerrod felt ill and pushed back in his leather chair, looking at the ceiling. He tried to find inspiration in several interesting water stains from a recent storm. The principal investigator of the study, Raymond Foster, was a respected clinical investigator in the industry. To complicate matters, he and Larry Reynolds were close personal friends, going all the way back to medical school at Penn. Had the friendship been taken advantage of in some way? Had Reynolds' group failed to monitor the critical study at all? Jerrod almost shouted, "How could he have rigged a study that your group carefully monitored? Who was the clinical research associate assigned to Foster?"

Reynolds replied, sounding like a hurt child, "I take full responsibility for whatever happened. The CRA for Study Number 312 was Jolese Monroe, the young girl we hired from Pfizer. She was obviously too green for the job, but I felt that Foster's work was so good that it would be excellent training for her in how things should be done. I was wrong—dead wrong."

"Dead is the right word," Jerrod quipped, "and that's what we're going to be if we can't salvage this thing. I can hardly wait to inform Dr. Vettori of this failure on our part."

Reynolds looked ready to faint—or throw up. "I, I'm sorry, Jerrod, there is nothing to salvage here. Foster's so-called patients weren't even real people, at least not *living* people. It was Jolese who finally caught on to the scam, and then she informed me. I had no choice other than to bring the auditors in. The patients all quietly reside in a Syracuse cemetery where Foster copied their names from tombstones. The too-perfect data looks like it was generated by a computer because it was."

"Have you confronted Foster with this? What does he have to say for himself?" Wesley queried.

"No, but what could he possibly say, under the circumstances?"

"Listen, Larry, you are the Medical Director for this company and this mess *is* your responsibility. You and the regulatory affairs group and the audit people will get on a plane tomorrow and fly to Syracuse and confront this, this goddamned criminal. Unless he has an excuse that I can't even imagine, the FDA is going to disqualify him, and he is going to jail for a long time. Beyond that, I want a status report for every Phase II Axilon study, and I want a preliminary audit of every damned one of them. We had better have our act together when we discuss this with New York management."

Reynolds, severely chastised, slunk out of the room feeling Jerrod's penetrating glare all the way. My God! Jerrod felt ill, but not too ill to question his own judgment in hiring the man. Reynolds was a knowledgeable academic physician for certain, but was he also a weak fool who didn't understand how many crooks there were in this business? Out of every ten clinical investigators conducting psychotropic drug trials in this country, three or four were incompetent, and one was an outright crook. Success was all about selecting the good ones, and even then you had to watch them like a hawk.

A few minutes later Wanda walked into Jerrod's office with a stack of financial documents for him to approve. She was shocked by his appearance; his color was bad, and his face had big problems written all over it. She was deathly afraid it had to do with their relationship. "Jerrod, what's wrong; is it about us?"

"No, no, Wanda, I know what you are thinking, nothing to do with us. It has to do with Dr. Reynolds and the Foster study. He let it slip through the cracks, and the whole thing is apparently bogus; damned patients don't even exist."

"Axilon?"

"Well, this doesn't have much to do with the drug other than to say that a study that we thought was highly positive no longer exists. Foster will be disqualified by the FDA and likely face some serious criminal charges. I did a little research, and in 1989 an investigator supposedly conducting clinical trials on drugs for arthritis faked eighteen trials for nine companies. Federal Judge sentenced him to four years, fined him two-million dollars, and demanded restitution to the wronged companies. The fool also lost his license to practice medicine."

Wanda asked, "Dr. Reynolds and Dr. Foster are long time friend; aren't they?"

"Yeah, and that may be the basis of the whole damned mess. Foster may be in some sort of trouble, drugs, maybe, and saw an opportunity to take advantage of their relationship. Larry assigned a green CRA, Jolese, Jolese somebody, to the case and she was fooled until it was too late."

"Hawkins, Jerrod, Jolese Monroe is her name. Honey, what ever are you going to do?"

"Do? Well, for starters I have dispatched Reynolds and a team to confront Foster. He may not know we know, and we are going to give him an opportunity to explain, although there are no believable explanations that can save him. No way!"

Wanda's voice cracked, and she pushed away a tear. "Jerrod," she asked, "will Dr. Vettori blame you for this, possibly fire you?"

Jerrod rose from his desk and looked out over the Sound, ochre-pink in the fading light. Screaming gulls circled over a bluefish feeding frenzy in the distance. Was he just another menhaden caught in a bluefish feeding frenzy? "Maybe, and he may demand I fire Reynolds first, which I would cherish doing at the moment."

Wanda laughed, "But you won't, not unless you have to."

The astute lady had him there, and he laughed too. He felt better, and they made plans to enjoy a late evening. This mess could simmer until Reynolds returned with his assessment of the failed study and hopefully some recommendations. Alonsio would blow off later about not being immediately informed, but so what? He'd blow off no matter what.

Wanda reminded him that he was late for his monthly research meeting, and he hurried to the downstairs conference room where he found his preclinical staff patiently waiting for him. It was a healthy mix of senior Ph.D.s of many disciplines and selected members of their junior staff. He was met with a hail of *Hi Chief* and other friendly greetings. To these people *Chief* was a term of endearment. Jerrod's research team all respected him, and some actually adored him. He tried a smile, but he was near tears; it was these wonderful people that made it all worthwhile. Maybe he should have remained in the lab where he belonged. He took his seat, and the meeting began; it was very informal, and big pots of strong coffee and piles of pastries from a good Madison confectionary shop kept their engines stoked.

The subject of the day's meeting was newly prepared analogs of Axilon—an effort to identify improved back-ups to the company's most important drug in development. Chemistry had been busy, and many new versions of Axilon had been synthesized and evaluated in appropriate biological screens. Some compounds deviated significantly in structure from Axilon and others even ventured alarmingly close to Apex's competitor drug, Medulin. The structure-activity relationships of these new molecules would no doubt be informative. Which chemical modifications improved the biological activity of the basic Medulin molecule, and which detracted from it?

As the slides flashed by, Jerrod felt that significant progress was being made, and he commented on it several times. He knew that scientists thrived on praise, and he lavished it when appropriate. The meeting was nearing an end when a young cell biologist, Harold Philips, a Yale graduate, was presenting the effects of selected compounds on neurons in culture. Jerrod let out a whistle and rose from his chair; all of the analogs close to Medulin in chemical structure, including Medulin itself, showed significant toxic effects on human neurons. Unlike normal neurons, those exposed to concentrations of

Medulin and its close analogs were swollen with inclusion bodies and eventually died. The neurotoxicity was both dose and time dependent and fully reproducible. Transferring treated cells to clean media with no drug did not reverse the progression to death.

The group saw this more as a positive finding for Axilon, but for Jerrod the implications for Medulin eclipsed everything else. Now, he likely knew what was in that damned Apex toxicology report—what had been hidden from the astute eyes of the FDA. Axilon and Medulin shared molecular mechanisms of action in their therapeutic effects, but the similarities ended there. Something about Medulin's structure enabled it to be a poison on the same neurons on which it initially exerted beneficial effects. It was an important observation, but one made in a vacuum. How could Jerrod's people have known of Steve Lewis' frightening conclusions regarding possible pitfalls of manipulating the promodulin system? The critical data had burned with the young scientist in that horrible automobile crash in Munich?

He pondered what his moral responsibility in this matter was. Likely, he would notify Apex of Genplex's findings on Medulin, and they could, no would, hide this too, but he would consult with corporate counsel before proceeding. This new information gave him a little leg up after the awful Foster fiasco, but where would it lead? Nasty, little thoughts danced around in Wesley's head. Did Axilon also possess a modicum of this deadly biology that would only be seen once the drug had been marketed and millions of patients had taken it? Unfortunately, history teaches that only the market can answer such questions as it sometimes does in unfortunate terms. But it was not his job to speculate and certainly not to share such thoughts with management. He would ask Harold Philips to continue to challenge Axilon by pushing the studies to the limit. That was his moral obligation.

⅌

Wanda glanced at her glowing dash, and the clock said it was 10:45 p.m., a few minutes earlier than she normally arrived at Jerrod's home for the evening. As she made the first curve in the dark drive near the scene of the recent fatal accident, she caught a glimpse of a furtive figure darting across the drive into a dark stand of oaks. It could have been a kid, neighbor, anyone, but she was unsettled by the experience and phoned Jerrod and asked him to have the garage bay open and be standing there, on guard, when she arrived. A few minutes later, Susan's garage door rattled down behind her, and she was safely inside. Jerrod notified the Madison Police as he had been instructed, and they agreed to swing through the neighborhood.

Wanda was more disturbed by the experience than Jerrod was. He shrugged it off, not believing for one minute the intruder was the spawn of Fingers Anesthasia. "Do you think our blind is broken?" she asked, only half kidding.

He laughed at her silly reference to their affair and said, "Wanda, quite frankly, I love you so much I just don't care anymore. Besides, it will happen at some point no matter what. I'll be ecstatic when the world knows how much I love you. Remember that old song, *Shout-Shout*, sung by Ernie Maresca in the 60s? Well, that's the way it's going to be, Honey"

Wanda's frown was replaced by a smile. "Yeah, but you have to pay attention to your expensive lawyer. You, no, *we* have to survive this financially, you know."

The two settled down with whiskies on the patio and enjoyed the evening. Twinkling stars lit a dark sky, and it was cool with little humidity. The wonderful smell of the sea permeated the air, and fall was just a cold front's breath away. Wanda pointed at a bright streak in the heavens, a falling star, but said nothing. They both knew it belonged to them.

Wanda took a sip of her drink and said, "There's not much wrong with this picture."

"No, unless you can't afford it," Jerrod quipped, making light of her ruminations.

"In fact, I feel *needy* at the moment; let's go to bed."

The Kelsey Point breakwater horn moaned in the distance; a fog was moving in from Long Island, and the glittering stars would soon be extinguished. Wanda looked out into the darkness, shivered, and followed her boss into the palatial home with quickening steps. She still wondered who lurked out there.

Jerrod was tired the following morning and reviewed boring budget documents with little enthusiasm. He looked at his watch frequently and had decided an early lunch might help when Wanda informed him that his friend, Charlie Cox, was on the line. It would be awfully early in California for Cox to be up and around.

"Hi, Charlie; what's up?"

"Obviously I'm not in California. I'm on a road trip making presentations to client companies, and I picked up a little scuttlebutt at Lilly. Do you know Jonathan Smith?"

"Yeah, premier investigator. We tried to hire him to do some of our Axilon trials, but Apex had him locked up."

"Word is he had two deaths in one week in his Medulin depression trial. Both patients apparently committed suicide by violent means. Company swears both patients were on placebo."

"How violent, Charlie? How did they do it?"

"One crashed through a sixth floor window at the hospital, and the other tried to subdue an 18-wheeler with his bare hands on I-75 outside of Bonita Springs, Florida," Charlie explained.

Jerrod let out a low whistle. "Sounds a little violent for garden-variety suicide due to untreated major depression, doesn't it?"

Charlie chuckled. "Apparently they were both stark raving mad at the time, so if this is true, and I believe it is, then placebo dosing makes little sense." Anticipating the next question, Charlie said, "We have not seen any hints of such psychotic behavior in any of our Medulin or Axilon studies, but we are keeping a closer eye on the outpatients."

The two chatted about personal issues for a few minutes, and then Jerrod tossed out a lure on an unlikely fishing expedition. "Charlie, if you don't mind, one more question; do you, by any chance, know Raymond Foster?"

"Yeah, Ray is another one of the better thought of clinical investigators in this country; why?"

"I can't say until I have more proof, but we may have a big problem with the man and his work. Any scuttlebutt about Foster circulating on the street?"

"No, wait, I believe he was divorced recently, and his wife Sarah claimed he was mean and abusive and drugs were involved in some way."

"What kind of drugs, Charlie?"

"Maybe benzos, Xanax and Halcion. Hell, I don't remember; maybe I never knew. You ask too many questions sometimes, Jerrod."

"That I do, but fortunately you're often the man with the answers, Chuck."

They both had a good laugh and hung up, but the word *benzos*, benzodiazepines, resonated in Jerrod's mind. Maybe being too sloshy-headed to conduct legitimate studies plus a chronic need to feed his habit, his divorce, and his own, expensive lifestyle had led to Foster's demise. Perhaps his wife had caught up to his nasty, little secret first, but unfortunately she had not shared it with the FDA or their mutual friend Larry Reynolds.

He was ruminating over Reynolds' lapsed judgment when Wanda said Larry was holding on the other line. Jerrod thought his timing was ironic, and he had better have something useful to say.

"When we confronted Foster, he wasn't surprised and remained calm. He listened politely while our auditors ran through the whole thing, and then he asked everyone to leave except me, and that's when he broke down. He had known he was done for a long time but couldn't find the inner strength to give up the drugs; yes it was all about drugs. He was waiting, praying for this day, for someone to save him and his clients."

Jerrod cleared his throat, feeling a bit of the poor man's pain. "What was he on, benzos?"

"Yeah, Librium, Valium, Xanax, Halcion, almost any damned benzodiazepine he could get his hands on plus Vicodin and Percocet. I told him that we, by law, had to notify the FDA as soon as possible, and we would also file a written complaint to them within thirty days. He knows that he will be disqualified by the FDA and may go to jail. He agreed to notify other drug sponsors before the end of the working day. He apologized, if that's worth anything."

"Larry, it's not worth shit, and you know it's not. And what about our other studies?" Jerrod queried.

"The audit group and my CRAs have blitzed them all as well as one can without compromising the statistical power of the studies; they were of the new adaptive design which allows in-study assessments and refinement; you know. They look clean as a whistle, and the other three ongoing Phase II Axilon depression studies should cover the loss."

Jerrod expressed his relief and asked Larry if he had heard about the Medulin deaths. Larry said he had not but would keep his eyes and ears open for such information. Jerrod did not mention preclinical research's recent shocking observations on Medulin.

Feeling a bit relieved, Jerrod started to punch in Vettori's extension but changed his mind. Rather, he dialed his daughter's cell phone number and waited, but there was only her recorded voice directing him to leave a message. He asked her to call but knew she would not. Lately, she had been evasive, almost hostile, when asked about her condition and response to her medication. It was easy to suspect Susan was meddling again. Jerrod knew Courtney could not be talked into a trip home anytime soon. Maybe he would stop off in North Carolina on his next trip south. Why in the world would Courtney listen to her crazy mother? He never would understand that mother-daughter thing.

13

Nightmare in New Orleans

The old clock in Saint Louis Cathedral's middle spire chimed as it had since 1720, marking the hours, year after year. Melodic notes reverberated among the three steeples of the cathedral and throughout the historic neighborhood below. Some say the chimes are the cries of the old church that had quietly witnessed flags come and go, worlds change, and yet it had survived. Hurricane Katrina had only been a slap on the cheek. Bones of great people lay buried beneath the church, and some had rested quietly there almost as long as the landmark had ruled the site. On this night, though, some may have turned in their graves; their moldering disturbed by a sinister presence nearby. The last note of the third chime echoed throughout the French Quarter, and it seemed unusually quiet, bound up by darkness.

A man's head emerged briefly from a murky alleyway off Chartres Street. His dark eyes moved furtively, searching the night ... Discarded plastic cups and McDonald's boxes and wrappers rattled down the pavement in the light breeze. A few persistent revelers moved slowly along the filthy street, sipping their last drinks of the evening. The man, if you could call him that, grinned and pulled back further into the shadows of the alleyway. Three young girls were coming down the street, and they were very drunk. They had partied non-stop for three days and were in a state of near exhaustion, making them easy prey. Their escape from the workday world was over, and they were looking forward to a few hours sleep before they caught their flight back to Cleveland.

Marcel Boudreaux had been on the streets for four days since he had slipped away from the mental hospital. Long, disheveled hair cascaded over his wild eyes, and his face was unshaven. But for his filthy, blood stained pajamas, Marcel might have been mistaken for some dangerous animal that had escaped from the New Orleans zoo.

72

He was tall, gaunt with long wiry muscles, and at thirty-two years of age, quick and powerful.

Marcel had suffered from severe depression all his life; one of his many psychiatrists had called it schizoaffective disorder, a big word that meant he was not only plagued by depression but also by a disordered thought process. It was true that he had crazy ideas all his life, compelling ideations about girls and blood. His dreams flowed with blood, but he lived in a state of emotional paralysis; his depression was a lead anchor that kept his restless ship in the harbor. But that was before he was entered into the Medulin inpatient study. Right away, almost with the first dose, he had felt better, though his dreams and compulsions had increased. He tasted blood, craved blood, and finally tossed away the heavy anchor and was, for the first time in his adult life, a free man. His study nurse had been so cute, and it was a shame she had to be the first to die. It really wasn't his fault; the careless doctor should not have left the scalpel on the table. After all, he was as mad as Stephen King's *Cujo*.

Marcel whispered, "Never trust an idiot," and chuckled at his cleverness.

The disheveled murderer closed his eyes and breathed hard as he recalled how he had cut her throat and lapped her blood while he raped the horror-struck nurse. For that memorable moment, he took his instructions directly from Count Dracula, his long-time hero. Marcel looked forward to many more such adventures with his mentor, and another was close at hand.

He heard the girls laugh as they stumbled nearer. Saliva dripped from his mouth and oozed down his chin; he reached down and squeezed his erection. Oh, so big, he thought; he was ready. Although it seemed like ages, the unfortunate girls finally crossed the entrance to his dark, alleyway lair, and Boudreaux sprang like a cat. His ape-like arms enveloped the three as though they were one, a six-legged being, and he hurled them into the darkness. Their muffled screams were lost to the late night Dixieland band that still blared nearby. The foursome hit the filthy pavement hard and Boudreaux was pleased with the resounding crack of a skull. He knew she was down for the count. The rapist extricated himself from the tangle of arms and legs, and one of the other two girls, she was short and pudgy, stirred and moaned slightly but posed no risk of escape. The third girl was more athletic and less intoxicated than the other two and managed to stager to her feet. The light was poor, and Boudreaux's tackle fell short, but he managed to catch the horrified girl by an ankle and jerk her down; he was upon her like a cat. Medulin was about to claim three more victims.

℈

Dr. Abraham Snyder was the Director of the New Orleans Psychiatric Treatment Center. He also maintained his own practice and conducted clinical trials for pharmaceutical companies. Most drug trials in psychiatric medicine are conducted as outpatient studies, but generally the FDA wants to see some inpatient trials conducted in sicker patients. Such studies tend to be more expensive due to hospitalization costs and are typically more problematic. Snyder was a highly-regarded expert at the conduct of such trials and normally maintained tight control over both the inpatients and those who were responsible for their evaluation and treatment. Although most of Snyder's trials had their dropouts due to side effects or lack of therapeutic response, no patient had ever simply vanished in the middle of a clinical study, and certainly no patient had ever killed their study nurse on the way out the door. Not on his watch. Even so, just such an unusual event in a clinical study had become the focus of a criminal investigation and an intense manhunt by the New Orleans police.

Snyder was both embarrassed by what would be seen as his failure and concerned about possible litigation. The crazy bastard that killed the girl had never been married but did have living parents. The psychiatrist suffered from his own narcissistic personality and did not believe an important doctor like himself should have to put up with the two nosy cops that sat across from him in his office. One was a slick-looking Italian dude, and the other was an attractive female who somehow knew medical jargon. Mary Lou Campbell did not bother to mention that she had a Ph.D. degree in abnormal and criminal psychology, and that she and her partner, Frankie Panacea had extensive experience at solving cases involving insane killers. Snyder smirked at their thinly-veiled attempt at a good cop-bad cop act. How could he know she was always the smart interrogator and the greaser cracked heads? It was no act.

Mary Lou leaned forward over the physician's cluttered desk. "Dr. Snyder, what drug did you say Mr. Boudreaux was on?"

"I didn't say because I don't know. He was an inpatient in a double-blind, two-arm trial comparing the Apex drug, Medulin, with placebo. I'm blind to the drug."

Mary Lou considered telling the arrogant shit-head a thing or two, but said, "I would have thought you would have broken the blind by now, given this is a murder investigation, and you and this hospital may be implicated in some way."

Snyder reddened and replied, his tone patronizing, "Lieutenant, only the company can break the blind, and I have notified them of our little problem with Marcel Boudreaux. They will get back to me in due time."

"And you will believe whatever they say?" Frankie chimed in.

"Of course; they would be in violation of the law if they lied."

"We will require copies of all paperwork on Mr. Boudreaux, Doctor; in a case like this all physician-patient confidentiality rights are suspended, at least in New Orleans. Also, we will need to impound remaining drug supplies for that patient. You can speak to your lawyer about that, but you could really be helpful if you would summarize the results of this man's treatment leading up to the murder and his escape."

"I *will* speak to my lawyer about all of this, but as for Mr. Boudreaux, he has battled major depression all his life and was already hospitalized here when we started the study. His parents gave informed consent, and he seemed to respond rather quickly to whatever he was given. Unfortunately, as his depression improved, he began to show psychotic symptoms that may have been previously masked by his profound melancholia. However, there was no indication that he would become a homicidal maniac."

Mary Lou thought something smelled a bit fishy and pursued the psychosis angle. "Had this patient ever been diagnosed as having schizophrenia?"

"Umm, no, that would be a clear violation of the Apex protocol."

Mary Lou was making a note to investigate that idea further when her cell phone jangled. She left the doctor's office for a few moments, and when she returned, she said, "The bodies of three young women have just been found in an alleyway just off of Chartres Street. They had been raped, and their throats sliced open with a very sharp instrument, probably not in that order. Sound familiar? Doctor, I suggest you call your lawyer immediately!"

With the help of a secretary, the officers impounded all the relevant paperwork; patient history, recent case report forms, protocol, and remaining packaged drug supplies for Boudreaux and then were gone.

Mary Lou remained quiet for a moment as Frankie expertly merged with the heavy New Orleans traffic; then she said, "I'm not exactly certain what crime Snyder is guilty of, but he and that clinic are in for one hell of a civil mess. Those four victims—young girls— likely have parents and they can't be too pleased about Snyder, the hospital and their lack of security, or the company that made the drug, assuming he was not on placebo."

Frankie flashed a smile and replied, "I'm willing to bet Boudreaux wasn't on sugar pills when he committed those gory crimes. And, you're right about the law suits; judges just love arrogant bastards like that doctor."

Mary Lou said, "We'll see," as an urgent call came in over their police radio.

☙

Maxwell Hall paced the floor; he simply couldn't believe it. A confirmed Medulin patient had gone ape shit and was roaming the streets, murdering women, shit, innocent girls, in New Orleans. This time a cover-up was impossible; the damned cops had Boudreaux's drug supplies, and it would be easy enough to confirm he was in the drug-treated arm of the study. He picked up his steaming mug of coffee, but his hands were shaking too hard to drink it, and he hurled it at Russell Turner. Fortunately, most of the scalding liquid missed Apex's clinical director, but he stood up and backed away, scared, wondering what the crazy bastard might do next. Yuan Li, President of Research for Apex remained motionless, wishing he had stayed in China. The more time he spent around Americans, the less he liked them. They were all nuts in his opinion.

Hall narrowed his eyes and looked at Burns. "You will extricate us from this mess and somehow put some positive spin on it. I can only work so much magic with the FDA. Speak, Doctor!"

"We , we have one chance to rectify this as I see it. Last night I spoke to Don Black, my CRA on the project, and he had scrutinized Boudreaux's previous medical records. It turns out the patient has quite a history; one psychiatrist after the next has diagnosed him as having a major depressive episode, major depression, or melancholia. A Dr. Pierce McCafferty at Whitfield in Mississippi had made a note of probable schizoaffective disorder with depression being prominent. This strongly suggests a protocol violation, but because of the overwhelming support for the major depression diagnosis, it was either overlooked or ignored. I can imagine a scenario whereby the powerful antidepressant actions of Medulin freed him from his bonds and allowed him to act on whatever had been stewing in his tormented brain for years—maybe a lifetime. How this affects the study I cannot say."

"Well," Hall spat, "we're going on with the study although this mess definitely affects the situation. Dr. Snyder violated the protocol by entering a crazy person, so, who is surprised when he goes nuts? When the dust settles, we will have Susan Wesley put something out that whitewashes these Medulin study problems. The sooner this Boudreaux moron is captured, the better. What the hell are the New Orleans cops doing anyhow? And you, Burns, please jot down the contact information for this Dr. Cafferty at that Mississippi nut house."

"*McCafferty*," he corrected as he jotted down the psychiatrist's telephone number from his address book.

"OK, then, everybody out of here and get to work and no more problems! Got it?"

Hall poured another cup of black coffee and with no more obvious targets sipped on it for a few minutes before he dialed the number on the slip of paper. After several irritating transfers through an obviously antiquated switchboard, Dr. Pierce McCafferty was finally on the line. Surprisingly, the doctor had heard about Boudreaux on the television morning news and had figured out that the fugitive killer was none other than his former patient. He also understood the possible legal ramifications for the New Orleans hospital and Dr. Snyder and that he could become a key witness for the plaintiff, whoever that might be.

McCafferty had requested the conversation be off the record and Maxwell Hall dutifully responded by switching his voice recorder on. "Mr. Boudreaux was hospitalized in 1995 because he was a clear and present danger to himself and others. He was both suicidal and homicidal, hearing voices; very destructive voices telling him to kill, kill, kill. He was carrying on conversations with the voices inside his head, and his thought process was totally disordered. He was sedated and restrained; eventually, a high dose of chlorpromazine got his schizophrenia-like symptoms under control. His depression was stabilized with imipramine, and he was released to his parents. I never saw or heard from him again until now."

Hall laughed and said, "You use cheap drugs, Doctor."

"Err, yes we do, Mr. Hall; Whitfield is indeed a low budget operation."

"Doctor, maybe Apex could help you with your financial problems. How about a sizable grant to do an open study aimed at finding new applications for Medulin in your patients who don't respond to available drugs? I assume your silence means yes, so I'll have Russell Turner contact you in the morning. Our lawyer too, if that's OK?"

Hall grinned as he cradled the phone; he sure as hell knew how to ward off future problems. Money was the key. The only key.

14

Halloween, October 31, 2010

The Irma Jean Walters Nursing Residence was located two blocks from Tulane University Medical Center, situated on a dark, tree-lined street a short walk from the French Quarter. The four-story frame structure had been substantial when built as a boarding house almost one hundred years ago, but time and insatiable New Orleans termites had riddled the structure, which was set to be razed at the end of the current academic year. A number of the nurses-in-training had already moved into a nearby, gleaming, new glass and steel structure with a modern security system; but some sixty students still resided at *Irma Jean*, as they called the crumbling place. The nursing students often kidded about the spooky nature of the place and that Irma Jean Walters must have been a witch, a definite possibility in New Orleans. After all, the Crescent City had been the birthplace of several famous witches.

The spooky old building seemed a fun place to be on Halloween. Studies had been put aside for silly outfits and punch spiked with pilfered laboratory alcohol. It was a room to room party, and here you might find a girl dressed as a pirate, and there one dressed in body paint only. Voodoo priestesses were common. As the evening wore on, the alcohol took its toll, and one by one the nurses either passed out or fell asleep; some even found their own beds. There had never been any real security at the Irma Jean Walters Nursing Residence, and this night even the service entrance had been left unlocked.

Marcel Boudreaux giggled as he parted the dense foliage of oleanders that concealed his hiding place and watched the last of the nurses moving from room to room. Many were asleep in their silly costumes, and a few undressed before him. His powerful erection escaped from his filthy hospital pajamas, and he tried unsuccessfully to put it back. That distracted him from the real task at hand, and he went back to counting his toes; he was up to one hundred and still counting. Presently, the moon went behind a cloud and it became too dark to hunt for more toes. Boudreaux sighed and looked up just in time to see a young girl snake out of her costume, and then he remembered why he was here. He missed the nurses and what they did for him—missed how they came around and brought him food and drugs and bathed him. He knew they were here; he had seen them, watched them on his nightly peregrinations, seen them come and go in their clean, white uniforms. Marcel knew they needed him too; nurses needed patients, and he clearly was one. Besides, he couldn't stand living in the dumpster behind the meat market any longer, though the food was good. He didn't understand why the girls wore strange costumes, but he was sure they would dress like nurses for him. So many had over the years.

Marcel reached into his pocket and pulled out a scalpel. The blade gleamed in the filtered light from the residence as he turned the sharp instrument in his hand. He sliced his tongue just to test its sharpness, and his blood tasted good, so good. Satisfied that he was ready, he eased from his hiding place and ran from shadow to shadow to the service entrance at the rear of the old structure. Should he knock? He tried the latch, and the door swung open with a slight screech. It smelled musty inside, much like his dumpster, but he pushed ahead through the deserted kitchen and dining room. The next door easily swung open into the hallway of the first floor living quarters. Doors lined both sides of the hallway; some were open, some closed, some ajar. Oh, but the way it smelled—the heady aroma of women, perfume, and menstrual blood filled his nostrils. He realized that his erection, lost to toe-counting, had returned in spades. So many rooms! So many nurses! So little time! He slowly shuffled down the hall, chanting under his breath, "Eeny, meeny, miney, moe, catch a nurse by her TOE!" Marcel giggled as he wondered how many toes a nurse had. Soon, that question would no longer be a mystery.

The girl's piercing scream reverberated throughout the old residence.

Marcel turned to face a fearful Brittany Patterson. Brittany had been returning to her room after a shower when she spotted the ghoulish beast sneaking down her hallway. Her white bath towel lay crumpled on the floor, and the very drunk, naked girl brought her hands to her mouth, wobbled slightly, and then fainted. Marcel looked around and no threats emerged from doorways; either they were all passed out or thought Brittany's screams were part of the Halloween festivities. The crazy man grinned; this girl would make a very nice nurse for him indeed. He picked her up as though she were nothing and kissed her gently on the cheek; he had only to dress her in a clean, white nurse's uniform and she would be ready for duty. He marveled at her many toes and then pushed into a darkened doorway to his right—room 117. He latched the door behind him and then felt for the light switch. The room was not vacant; both single beds in the room were occupied, one by a New Orleans Voodoo queen and the other by a gaudily painted nudist. Boudreaux decided that the two looked liked patients back at Whitfield. They would not be competing for his nurse's time! Recalling that the door to the room next door stood open and was unoccupied, he deposited the two very drunk girls there and shut the door before returning to his responsibilities with his new nurse.

He found a crisp, white uniform for her in the closet and some undergarments in a chest. Sliding her panties over her plump legs got him going, and he removed them and had sex with her. He cursed himself for the quickness of the act and continued to dress the girl, who was slowly regaining consciousness. As Brittany's world came into focus, she did not understand her circumstances. She was dressed in an ill-fitting uniform; had she dozed on duty? Someone or something was pulling on her toes, but her legs dangled off the bed, and she could not see. What the hell? She sat up and her heart fell; the horror from the hallway was lying on the floor counting her toes. Eyes wide, Brittany sat up in bed but did not scream for she had no voice. Boudreaux grinned and held his finger to his lips and said, "Shush, you'll wake the other patients. You're my nurse now."

15

Matters that Matter

Maxwell Hall squinted as he looked at Alan Werner through the blue haze of his own cigar smoke. Somehow the fool thought he had found release from Hall's grip as the power of the important bureaucratic position enveloped him. Hall's mind wandered as the psychiatrist droned on in his academic monotone. He wondered how anyone could be such a pig—there were papers piled up on his desk and documents in the corners of the office stacked to the ceiling, likely unread, stone-walled. The cigar smoke could only improve the musty smell of the place; hell, the FDA stank in more ways than one, as far as he was concerned.

"Look, Mr. Hall, I'm certain we do understand one another, but you must agree that some point can be reached where I can't support you and Medulin any longer—when the body of evidence against the drug becomes so persuasive that even my voice no longer matters. Don't you see? Like a coach, I can call the plays, but I can't force the outcome of the game if the players fail."

"Look, Werner, I'm a busy man; what the fuck is so important as to bring me to Rockville? Spit it out Man!"

"The reports, these damned reports on Medulin—they don't come to me first, you know! They go in to David Kendall at the Division of Psychiatric Products. Then he informs me if it involves a priority drug. David's got red flags up all over where Medulin is concerned. He can't accept or doesn't care that the two suicides were on placebo and he's going bonkers over the poor nurse's murder and the missing psychopath. Where the hell is the guy?"

Hall answered in a very condescending tone. "Werner, I will leave the science and medicine to you, but goddamn it, Medulin is a safe drug. If Kendall doesn't believe the company regarding what the two patients were taking, then he should send in the FDA auditors. We are the first to admit that Boudreaux was on Medulin but the lunatic

81

was a clear and unfortunate protocol violation. His history is unambiguous in that regard and at least one qualified expert is willing to testify to that. You have no leg to stand on and if you find one, I'll cut the damned thing off at the knee—got that?" Hall threatened.

"Now, on a related matter, your brilliant David Kendall seems to be sucking up to Genplex. I know for a fact that there was at least one forged Axilon study, and it's a similar drug. Why aren't you giving them flack?"

"Look, Hall, I didn't give that drug any special priority to begin with. They have conducted Phase II in a careful and methodical manner with no significant adverse events. The bogus study was faked by a generally well thought of investigator, and they caught him and reported it to the division. The investigator, Raymond Foster, has been disqualified. He's toast and will face criminal charges."

"That's all very nice, but I want you to think about our little deal; what I'm paying you for and what you're doing for me so I keep my mouth shut about your *extracurricular activities*. I don't give a shit what you ever did at Harvard; I only care about your seeing to Medulin's progress and not helping Genplex."

The deflated psychiatrist collapsed back into his chair as Hall stormed out of his dismal office. But the psychiatrist was not one to stay down and ruminate about things; he glanced at his watch; he was meeting Glenda Snaps in ten minutes. One could certainly forget his worries traversing those high hills and deep valleys. She was a young medical reviewer at FDA, and he really did need a personal assistant. What a nice, new odalisque Glenda would make! Hey, with the newly-found money, the sky was the limit. Ultimately, crooks like Hall got caught, and the sooner he did the better. No one would ever suspect a brilliant, much-loved physician like himself of anything unseemly or dishonest.

Wesley thumbed through the draft report for the Ardsley generalized anxiety disorder study. He grinned; it looked pretty flawless. He considered calling his friend David Kendall at FDA and giving him a heads up, but then he realized what a big mistake that would be. Kendall would carefully review the final report when it was complete and polished. He realized that he was tired and not thinking clearly; the long nights with Wanda followed by endless days of pressurized work on Axilon had worn him out. The low light of late autumn lent the Sound a golden glow, and a few fishermen moved about, seeking a trophy striper as the big fish migrated south to the Hudson River. It was a nice moment to reflect, and obviously he needed to do so; he understood that he was a procrastinator. He always had such a long list of things to do that difficult or unpleasant matters, particularly family matters, were often pushed to the bottom and left undone. Jerrod sighed and scratched a couple of words on his yellow pad, underlining them both repeatedly. One was *Courtney* and the other was *lawyer—divorce filing.*

He instructed Wanda that he was not to be disturbed. He would call Barbara Barnes at Barnes, Waddle, and Stein in Stamford after he talked to his daughter. He had not attempted to call Courtney in some time. She had not returned his calls, and he had just let it slip. This time would not be different, but for the first time Jerrod left an angry message in the answering machine, urging her to call her father ASAP.

Jerrod was frustrated by his daughter and believed that Susan must somehow be behind whatever the problem might be. He had not spoken to his wife since her last trip home when he confronted her with her tryst in the New York nightclub. Now, he was angry enough to call her but thought it unwise to mention the divorce filing.

Jerrod, "What do you want?"

"I want you to drop your sword for a moment and discuss a common issue—our daughter, Courtney."

"Jerrod, I ... OK."

"I cannot get Courtney to answer the phone and she will not return my calls. I'd like to know what is going on here."

"Based on your angry tone of voice I think you are accusing me of something, Jerrod, and I won't stand for it. Do you always have to be such a bastard?"

"Sorry," he said. "It's just that I am very worried about Courtney, given her illness."

"I speak to Courtney at least once a week, and I can assure you that she is fine. Dr. Barrington is taking wonderful care of her."

Jerrod thought that Susan was just a bit too quick and smug with her answer. And since when did she like Barrington's approach? "Thank you, Susan, I feel better," he lied. "Will you please ask her to call her father and fill me in on her life? After all, I do love her and pay her bills."

"She will call you, Jerrod; I promise."

Jerrod made a mental note to get down to Duke whether Courtney called or not. One of his friends, Buster Paxton, was a Duke graduate and usually had some extra football tickets. A little father-daughter bonding might be in order.

Much to Jerrod's surprise, his cell phone rang a few minutes later, and it was Courtney. She said that she was much better and had once again become consumed with academic activities, parties, and boys. "No, Dad, it isn't necessary to come down; I have finals coming up, and I know you don't like college football. I love you, and I'll stay in touch from now on—promise—bye."

Courtney folded her cell phone and placed it on the dresser. She opened a drawer and pulled out a sizable box that contained medical supplies and removed a blister pack containing white capsules. It bore the label: *Medulin Capsules, 100 mg, A Product of Apex Pharmaceutical Research.* The girl popped out two of the small capsules and swallowed them without water.

Courtney smiled broadly and said out loud, to herself, to no one, "Thanks to Mom and her friends at Apex, I feel like I can conquer the world." She shook her head remembering that her father would have preferred she take that Prozac shit forever. Like hell she would; soon, she would receive an almost unlimited supply of Medulin from her mother.

Courtney's closet overflowed with new clothes of bright, even psychedelic, colors. She selected a very short, bright red skirt and held it up to her naked body, admiring herself in the mirror. She smiled approvingly, but this time it was not the pretty smile of a young girl; it was the smile of the devil about to welcome some new and unfortunate soul to the flames of hell.

16

New York

Jerrod felt a lot better about Courtney's welfare and removed her from his immediate list of worries. He smiled and remembered the good times they had while she was a child growing up in Connecticut. He chuckled as he remembered Courtney's first boyfriend, a pimple-faced, little geek, if there ever was one. But then, as she began to mature, she developed both a personal and physical beauty that attracted many boys. She had her choice of them and generally chose well. She sang and played the piano and was the best of ballet dancers, but oddly she was not a great athlete. Jerrod laughed as he recalled his daughter's feeble attempts to make the Choate varsity field hockey team. She had been graceful and flowing without being quick. Still, Jerrod had loved those family trips for athletic events held at New England's best prep schools, Exeter, Groton, Kent, Hotchkiss, places he had never even heard of as a pubic high school student in rural Mississippi. Courtney had no real point of reference to appreciate all that she had been given. She did not associate with the old pictures of a young and very naked Jerrod Wesley in the midst of his grandmother's chickens in Plantersville, Mississippi. He had been remiss in never taking Courtney to his home state of Mississippi. In fact, he had not been *home* in many years and the very thought of the steamy Magnolia State clawed at his heart. Perhaps next summer he would find the time.

The Wesleys had been a close-knit family for a long time and Susan had been very much a part of it. Perhaps she had even come to live her life through Courtney, and when Courtney grew up and became her own woman, Susan began flailing about, unsuccessfully searching for a new definition of her old self. Not finding it, she had resented Jerrod's success and his comfort with it. Only, he didn't feel too comfortable at the moment as the driver merged the stretch limousine into the mass of Midtown Manhattan traffic. The genteel life

85

of the past was lost to honking horns and blaring sirens. He would meet with Alonsio Vettori and Rhinner Albright in thirty minutes. As usual, he was being pressed for an update on Axilon. He felt like a freshly-picked orange headed for the Donald Duck Orange Juice factory. The bastards would squeeze the last drop.

Albright looked thinner and older, and new lines etched his worried face. Undoubtedly the board was putting undue pressure on the haggard executive regarding Axilon and the company balance sheet. From the scowl on Vettori's face, he was sharing in the pain, and Jerrod knew he was about to experience some of it himself. Thank God, New York was one hundred miles away from his office, and these floggings were relatively infrequent. The lash marks never quite healed before the next meeting, however.

The three sat in Albright's cozy, private conference room armed with steaming coffee and doughnuts. Vettori turned to Albright and said, "Here he is; it's your meeting, Rhinner."

Albright nodded and took a sip of hot coffee, gathering his thoughts. "Jerrod, thanks for coming in; there are several issues we need to discuss. First, there is the issue of the unfortunate depression study, conducted in Syracuse by Dr., Dr. ... Fredrick."

"Foster," Jerrod corrected.

"Yes, that scalawag, Foster. Now, I want you to tell me exactly how this happened; as you know we have had a rash of adverse publicity about the study, some have even questioned our honesty. The anti-pharmaceutical company factions have had a field day with this."

Jerrod looked the angry CEO in the eye and said, "I make no excuses and take full responsibility for the mess."

Vettori stood up and said, "Very admirable of you, Jerrod; you have learned well from me and now that that is out of the way, how did your clinical group ever let such a thing happen?"

"It was a little like most automobile accidents; it was caused by a series of mistakes and bad judgments, some on our part. First of all Raymond Foster was a well-respected clinical investigator, and I do mean *was*. Second, he was an old classmate and friend of our clinical director, Larry Reynolds, who trusted the bastard explicitly. And because of these factors, Larry assigned a very green CRA to the task of monitoring the trial. This was intentional; Larry thought that Foster was so thorough and exacting that the girl could learn from him. Right. It was all made up—patients, completed case report forms, data, all of it. She, the CRA, finally figured it out and informed Larry. We confronted Foster and reported the violation to the FDA immediately."

"It was your clinical director's lack of oversight; he should be fired immediately!" Albright asserted.

"Sir, with all due respect, Larry is a very knowledgeable clinical scientist who has learned his lesson. He almost had a nervous breakdown over this."

Vettori nodded, "I tend to agree; he is a hard-working, conscientious man and deserves another chance. Besides, he knows the clinical aspects of the drug better than anyone."

Jerrod felt relief at Larry's reprieve. He said, "Thank you, Sir. We have made preliminary audits of all of the other Axilon studies just to be certain, and they are fine. The other depression studies should carry the day, so there has been no real time lost—just money. Most of the data is in-house and Biostatistics and Data Management is gearing up for all the work that will go into the end of Phase II submission and meeting with the FDA."

The CEO looked right at Alonsio and observed the old man's face closely as he asked Jerrod, "Are you telling me that we will be able to start our Phase III program in anxiety, depression, and schizophrenia on time?"

Vettori nodded like he knew what he was talking about, but Jerrod answered, "You never know until you have the stats in hand and confirm that the study has jumped through all the FDA's arbitrary hoops, but there is a high probability that the anxiety and depression studies will be fine. I have less confidence in schizophrenia, and I can't say why, other than it is a more difficult field of study." That was partially true but Jerrod also wondered about the emerging data involving psychotic patients on Medulin.

Albright seemed satisfied, even relieved, by the progress report on Axilon. The discussion turned to Medulin, but there was little to say other than there were possible adverse reactions associated with use of the drug. Perhaps more could be learned if the AWOL psychopath could be captured, but that was far beyond Jerrod's jurisdiction. The discussion had gone his way, and Jerrod felt confident, perhaps overconfident, and pushed the limits of his position.

Jerrod said, "Dr. Vettori, it would be very useful if you could enlighten me on the outcome of your attempt to meet with the FDA. Did anything get agreed upon?"

Alonsio looked at the floor and said, "Mr. Albright and I spoke to the Commissioner with little success."

The CEO reddened and cut Alonsio off. "Bastards stonewalled us is what they did. Said that what the Director of CDER did with someone else's drug was none of our damned business. He didn't make me feel much better by assuring us that Axilon is being handled in the *most professional manner*, either. In other words Werner is off-limits, period."

Vettori raised his eyes from the floor and looked at Jerrod through his thick glasses. "A man like Werner with all that power and no one to challenge his decisions is doomed to failure in his arrogance. In the meantime we will very carefully answer every question the FDA throws at us; will we not, Dr. Wesley?"

Jerrod agreed and the meeting was over. He shook hands with his superiors and left the conference room only to be confronted by a secretary in the outer office.

"Dr. Wesley, your driver called to say that he is hopelessly backed up on I-95 and won't be waiting to take you back to Connecticut. Want me to arrange a London Towne Car?"

Jerrod grinned and answered, "No thanks, Betsy, I think I'll just have an early dinner in the city and board a train. I don't think I had better forget what the real world is like, everything considered." Betsy laughed and escorted Jerrod to the door. Once on the street, he called Wanda and asked her to pick him up in New Haven later that evening. Then he walked the few blocks to his favorite steak place, Smith & Wollensky. The green and white three-story, free standing restaurant nestled among glass and steel skyscrapers had been a popular destination for hungry businessmen for many years. He glanced at his watch; it was 5:30 p.m., too early for dinner but about right for a happy hour drink. As usual, the place was already filling with the Wall Street crowd, spinning lies about their trades and the millions they had made that day. Guys in dark business suits hustled attractive women wearing stylishly short skirts and blue blazers. Jerrod loved to people watch and this was the spot, as long as Susan went elsewhere; he snagged a strategically located table in a quiet corner and ordered a double Jack.

A heavy set guy held court at the end of the long bar and Jerrod immediately thought of his friend Charlie Cox, still hard at work at his office in California. The man was tall, overweight and about fifty; Jerrod guessed. He moved around with the help of a cane but did so with a practiced grace. He seemed familiar as people across a room in Manhattan often do, but Jerrod couldn't place the man, likely a salesman or trader for a brokerage house. One of the pretty women looked equally familiar; she was short, animated, with black hair, flashing eyes, and a quick laugh that carried over the din. He could tell that she and the heavy guy were colleagues because *Big John*, as Jerrod nicknamed him, was obviously hitting on the other women.

There was a commotion when a nerdy-looking guy, likely a scientific advisor of some sort, joined them, but then the crowd closed in, and the show was over. The thought of Susan thrashing about in this piranha infested environment caused Jerrod to chuckle in his drink. His wife had little opportunity to acquire street smarts and could drown in a single martini with one olive.

Soon, the place was so crowded that there was standing room only, and Jerrod decided on a quick trip to the plush men's room and then dinner. Remarkably, his neighbor at the next urinal was none other than Big John, who grinned at him and muttered something about *the target rich environment outside.* Jerrod laughed and nodded but did not make his acquaintance, fearing where the evening might lead. After bumping into a scruffily dressed guy with a stuffy nose and a logo on his shirt that claimed he was a small game hunter, meaning pest exterminator in NYC, Jerrod escaped to the hallway. The City was a laugh a minute.

Jerrod's dinner upstairs was served by an older, highly polished waiter in a white coat, and the meal was excellent. He relished the restaurant's famous split-pea soup and followed that with a rare Porterhouse steak, hash browns, and asparagus. The merlot was way overpriced but resonated perfectly with the steak. Unlike the bar scene, the restaurant was filled almost entirely with visiting businessmen, alone, in pairs, and groups. Several were Japanese road warriors as was the well-dressed gentleman seated directly across from him. Jerrod marveled as he watched the tiny man consume a very large lobster and then a gigantic portion of prime rib, one of the largest in the city. Two bottles of wine and several drinks no doubt aided the digestion.

It was a brisk fall evening, and the short walk to Grand Central Station felt good. He caught the last Metro North train with a bar car but opted for a relatively empty coach near the front of the train where he could nap. The evening had been a nice change, and he soon fell asleep, wondering who the almost familiar couple in the bar at Smith & Wollensky had been.

17

Irma Jean Walters Nursing Residence

Driving rain did its best to extinguish the powerful police spotlights that deprived the decaying, old building of the storm's darkness. The surrounding French Quarter seemed deserted, its denizens in hiding, waiting, wondering. Powerful gusts from a late tropical depression ripped at swaying trees whose shadows danced like crazed witches on the wet pavement. The NOPD arrived in force after an excited call from campus security who had wisely evacuated the Irma Jean Walters Nursing Residence. Only one door remained locked, and the lunatic inside held a nurse's life in his pathetic hands.

Mary Lou Campbell and Frankie Panacea, both NOPD lieutenants, waited in the unmarked Crown Victoria idling in front of the dormitory. Rain drummed on the roof, and wipers served little or no purpose. They waited for their cue in silence as they had many times before.

Frankie finally laughed and said, "Nice night for ghoul hunting. Do you really believe Boudreaux is hiding in there, Mary Lou?"

"Highly likely and we're probably lucky he didn't kill them all, based on what I was told about the party that was going on when he slipped in. Apparently, the girls all got soused on stolen lab alcohol. "

Frankie made a disgusted face and strained to see through the sheets of rain. "Yeah, guess they were pretty drunk, and he may have killed one of them, Brittany Patterson, already. Security said they heard only his voice inside the room. He's probably armed and certainly dangerous, insane, actually, so if talking fails, we both know where this is going to end up."

The police radio crackled; it was their commander. "Mary Lou, Frankie, we're all in place, so go ahead in, and do whatever you can. We've got a SWAT team waiting for our signal to go if you fail to talk him out, so good luck to you and Frankie and that young woman in there."

Mary Lou said, "Let's go," and they splashed their way to the dormitory and paused once inside the entryway. Both wore the same bullet-proof garb as the SWAT team but carried their standard police revolvers. Their mission was one of mercy, not firepower. They found room 117 easily and stood outside the door, listening for voices from inside the room. Mary Lou knew that all her education and training that had finally led to a doctotate in criminal and abnormal psychology was about to be challenged.

Frankie raised his revolver to pound on the door, but Mary Lou grabbed his arm and shook her head. She rapped on the door gently and called, "Mr. Boudreaux, are you in there?"

There was a long silence before a man's voice answered, "Yes, but go away, I'm sick—a patient—and my nurse is taking care of me."

Frankie and Mary Lou looked at one another; maybe the girl was still alive. "Mr. Boudreaux, I am Dr. Mary Lou Campbell, and I am here to help you."

"Help me? Help me? Do you have any more of those pills that made me feel good, Doctor? I don't feel so good no more; it's like my brain's gone *all mushy*, and I can't count my toes no more."

Mary Lou felt the first hint of optimism. "How is Nurse Patterson, Mr. Boudreaux? Would you please send her out so we can discuss your treatment, Sir?"

Boudreaux answered with a hysterical, lunatic laugh followed by several audible grunts. Then he said, "She's real busy right now. Maybe later."

Frankie raised his gun and whispered, "Let's go, damn it."

Mary Lou shook her head, "Patience!"

She then called out to the murderer again, "Mr. Boudreaux, we have any drug you might need at the hospital and lots of nurses; they have a nice clean bed and some good, hot food waiting for you."

Only a pitiful whimpering sound could be heard over the driving rain outside. The two cops listened for a long time before Boudreaux spoke. "Please, get 'um out of my brain! Them worms is eatin' my brain! I can't stand it no more; I have to ... *git 'um out!*" The insane man's bloodcurdling scream was followed by a loud thump. Either a sack of potatoes or a body had hit the floor, the latter seeming more likely.

Mary Lou called for back-up as Frankie's strong shoulder hit the door. It was so old and termite riddled that it offered little resistance, and Frankie literally fell through it as it splintered. Mary Lou rushed past Frankie while he recovered his balance. Her weapon was raised, but there was no need for that. Death had not removed the lunatic's beastly grin. A deeply buried scalpel projected from an empty eye socket, and the missing eye watched the proceedings from the floor nearby. It had no doubt witnessed Boudreaux's desperate, fatal attempt to excise the demon from his tortured brain. He would never know that his particular demon had a name, not Satan, not Lucifer, not Beelzebub, just Medulin.

Another of the drug's victims lay bound on the bed; Brittany Patterson was naked and tied up in such a way as to make sexual contact convenient. She was alive, but barely, and made gurgling noises beneath the gag improvised from a strip of Boudreaux's filthy pajamas. Her carefully pressed uniform hung beside the bed. Tears streamed down Mary Lou's face as she gently removed the gag and loosened the tight ropes that bound the nurse. She had been abused in just about every manner a human being could be, and maybe some day she would tell her story. It would probably take a very long time for that, however. Mary Lou covered her with a sheet and called for medical assistance. The SWAT team that waited outside the door would not be required and did not need to gawk at the naked victim.

Pelting rain continued as the Crown Victoria eased away from the crime scene. Mary Lou said, "Frankie, I don't know the whole story, but it has something to do with an experimental drug that either made Marcel Boudreaux crazy or crazier than he already was. Remember how evasive that psychiatrist, Snyder, was about the whole affair? I feel that we did all we could have possibly done under the circumstances, but this smells like litigation to me. I suspect that we haven't heard the last of it; Jesus, Frankie, someone needs to pay and pay big for what happened to that poor, little nurse. God knows how many times that pathetic creature raped her. Let's not forget the nurse murdered at the psychiatric center or the three girls brutalized in the alley, either. They were innocent creatures who died awful deaths."

Frankie felt sick but managed a broad smile, showing his amazingly white teeth. "Yeah, but we saved Brittany Patterson, and that counts for something."

Mary Lou gave him the look; she didn't necessarily believe that. She would have done anything to save them all.

℀

Maxwell Hall had just walked into his office; it was well before 9:00 a.m. and his secretary was already telling him he had an urgent telephone call. He pushed the button for extension number two, and an excited voice spoke loudly.

"It's over!"

"What's over, and who is this," Hall demanded.

"Sorry, this is Dr. Snyder, Abraham Snyder. Marcel Boudreaux, the Medulin patient that killed the nurse, is dead."

"Dead? How so?"

"If you can believe NOPD, and I do; it was death by his own hand. When the cops tried to apprehend him, he killed himself. Not exactly a suicide, mind you."

"Go on," Hall urged.

"He cut out an eye and tried to exorcise the demons in his brain with the same scalpel he used to murder the nurse during his escape," Snyder explained in an emotionless monotone.

Hall was breathing hard now. "Did he hurt anyone else?"

"He held a nurse captive and pretty well brutalized her, but she'll live. Can't imagine she's too happy about all this though. Her name is Brittany Patterson, and the vulture lawyers will be calling her soon, I would imagine. Don't forget; he probably murdered those three girls in that alley as well."

Hall said, "Leave Miss Patterson and the legalities to me, Doctor. You complete the Medulin trial with no more problems; you hear."

18

A Creature of the Night

Like many college towns, Durham, North Carolina had a number of bars that stayed open until the early morning. They featured loud music and cheap beer, catering to students attending the local colleges of which Duke was the academic and drinking frontrunner. The Durham cops had long since given up on checking the fake identification cards carried by most underage students. Generally, order was maintained, but the authorities were hands-offish toward rich kids from powerful East Coast families. They'd learned this the hard way; the bastards had too many lawyers.

Two o'clock in the morning was no longer a late hour for Courtney Wesley, and like other nights recently, she had outlasted her two girlfriends who had wisely gone home around midnight. Really, nothing much good happens in Durham watering holes after midnight, and most wise students keep that in mind. The Purple Ace was still bustling with young people—students too drunk to be wise, local trash pretending to be students, and criminals pretending to be local trash, and looking for a purse to snatch or a pocket to pick. The bar smelled of stale beer, perspiration, and perfume. The band was as smashed as the clientele, and their loud rock music reverberated throughout the dark bar. The dance floor was packed, and it was clear that no one had a particular partner or cared. Flashing, colored strobe lights over the dance floor froze bodies in contorted positions as over one hundred individual engines stoked with cocaine and alcohol sought release through their gyrations.

Courtney smiled as she entered the Purple Ace; she knew she would quickly attract attention with her heavy make-up, see-through blouse, and short skirt. She felt the powerful bass notes throb through her body in concert with the urgings brought on by the dominant effects of Medulin. Although Courtney only knew that she felt good, powerful, even, she could not know that this night the Medulin cir-

94

culating in her body was crossing the thin line between its useful therapeutic effects and the drug's ability to produce a toxic psychosis shortly before it destroyed the brain. She fingered the folded straight-razor in her tiny purse; the cold steel felt good, ravenously hungry.

Until this night, the voices had been just whispers, but tonight she could finally hear them urging her, urging her ... to what? Courtney skillfully elbowed her way to the crowded bar. She could feel hungry eyes devouring her body, and oh, how her energy surged; electricity flowed through her veins; could they see the sparks? A black boy she was certain had never seen the inside of a college made a great show of yielding his bar stool to her. *Super Fly* was out trying to nail him-self a white co-ed, she decided. Courtney accepted with a coy smile and then tossed down the shot of Absolute that Jamal had offered her.

Courtney had little experience with blacks. There had been a few on free rides at Choate, carefully selected and generally harmless. There were more at Duke, and quite frankly, she couldn't stand their ways and avoided them like the plague. That was her prerogative, but tonight the voices told her to do something about the problem and *Too Cool* Jamal was at the wrong place at the wrong time. They both had several more shots, and Jamal was losing his inhibitions. He was bobbing and weaving and everything was funny to him. The foolish boy assumed she was also drunk as a skunk, but little did he know about Medulin; Courtney was as sober as her Baptist preacher on Sunday morning and about as crazy.

Much to Jamal's surprise, she agreed to go out to the boy's car with him for a *ride*. The rusting Lincoln with oversized, polished wheels sat in the far corner of the dark parking lot. It went as pre-dicted, but Jamal moved so quickly she almost became the victim. In one motion, the strong boy, who had played high school football before being expelled in the eleventh grade for masturbating in class, slammed Courtney against the passenger-side door and proceeded to unbuckle his pants. The rape was on, but Jamal hesitated at the girl's high, thin laugh. Courtney's uppercut was delivered with strength be-yond her own, and the boy's neck snapped back. He was out cold and with the load of alcohol on board would sleep for a very long time. She finished removing the heavy boy's pants with difficulty and ex-amined his impressive equipment, shuddering that the damned thing had been intended for her. How many girls had he raped right here on this very spot on nights like this? Courtney wondered.

The straight razor flicked open and glittered red as blood in the bar's flashing neon light. It was easy, and only took three carefully di-rected slashes of the sharp instrument to castrate Jamal Washington.

Super Fly had been gentled and would likely not be happy when he awakened with his balls in his mouth. Probably, he would be loath to share his story with his fellow miscreants, but so much the better if he did. Duke girls were safer now—at least for a while.

Courtney could not have predicted that Jamal would show up early the next morning at the local emergency room with his testicles in a zip lock bag, begging that they be reattached. Unfortunately it was too late. When questioned by the police, he told the truth, he had been too drunk at the time to know who did it.

19

December's Cold

I t is said that there are only two seasons in Connecticut: winter and road work season. Though this is meant as a joke, it is not to the many commuters who live in that state. Winter had arrived right on schedule, and wind-driven sleet and snow peppered Jerrod's windows. Despite his Southern roots, Jerrod enjoyed the spectacle of a good New England winter, though he knew that it was difficult for the many employees who could not afford to live in the immediate, highly affluent area. Yet, most were dedicated and slogged their way through the icy mess to their offices and labs.

He smiled as he watched Wanda in action through the glass wall. She had her telephone receiver pressed to one ear, and someone else was on the speakerphone. She was as skilled at negotiating and problem solving as she was at love making, and that covered a lot of territory. Wanda had placed herself in the middle of some altercation and would undoubtedly solve the problem, leaving him free for more important issues. Unfortunately, he had plenty of those at the moment; the statistical package for the end of Phase II Axilon submission was nearing completion, and a meeting with David Kendall and the Division of Psychiatric Products at the FDA was scheduled after Christmas. Jerrod looked forward to the meeting; both the anxiety and depression submissions strongly supported moving forward into Phase III. As he had feared the schizophrenia results did not look solid, and in some cases Axilon had actually exacerbated the disease.

New Phase II programs would be immediately implemented in panic disorder, with or without agoraphobia, and bipolar disorder. In his own mind, Jerrod had written off schizophrenia as a potential indication, along with any other disorder involving psychotic behavior. Axilon was a virtual gold mine without schizophrenia, and Albright and Vettori were just going to have to accept that. Jerrod dreaded the inevitable rehearsals for the FDA meeting. Alonsio would preside no

97

matter what; the old man would torture the data and Jerrod along with it. His boss would also demand to know a lot more about Medulin than Jerrod knew. Charlie Cox had said the word on the street was that, although there had been no more deaths related to Medulin treatment, dropouts due to psychotic behavior were excessively high after long term treatment. That said, Apex was charging ahead as though there was no tomorrow. Jerrod frowned; the Medulin toxicology report weighed heavily on his mind again. Time had passed; maybe he should destroy the damned thing.

Although Apex cast an ugly shadow over Genplex and Axilon, Jerrod felt good about the company's progress with the drug. Apex with its hellbent for leather Medulin program might even find eternal flames, leaving Genplex as the clear winner. The Apex program was being driven by business sorts who had no clue about science and medicine. Now, if he could just keep Alonsio and Rhinner at bay, he might get it done.

Whether he liked it or not, it was time to deal with Susan and face their impending divorce. Barbara Barnes had filed on his behalf, and the negotiations would probably begin in January. A settlement would clearly be desirable for everyone concerned but might not happen. Susan's salary and bonus on Wall Street were greater than Jerrod's, earnings, but she did not feel secure with it. However, Barbara's negotiating skills were legendary among divorce lawyers, and she had almost ninety days to negotiate a settlement before the hearing. There was nothing else he could do for now other than meet Barbara's demands for personal and financial information relevant to the filing. He would eventually be a free man and start a new life with Wanda Lassiter.

The one nagging issue that haunted Jerrod's days and kept him awake at night was his daughter, Courtney. Once again, she had disappeared from his life; she did not return his calls or answer his e-mails. His only proof that she was still alive and at Duke were the monthly bills that seemed to be growing by leaps and bounds. Discussing it with Susan was not an option; Barbara demanded that they only spoke through her, and the lawyer clearly knew what she was doing. Surely, he should just trust Courtney, and she would grow out of whatever real or imaginary problem clouded their relationship. Jerrod, in his state of paranoia, could only guess that Susan had told Courtney some implausible lie about him.

Courtney ambled slowly across the big green that separated the depressing Gothic buildings. She heard Seth call to her but kept her face down, pretending not to hear the handsome boy's hail, and hurried up the steps of her classroom building. Although they had been close to a relationship, she had dropped Seth Simpson without warning and refused to return his e-mails and calls. She ignored him and entered the classroom building, but by then the athlete was upon her and grabbed her by the shoulder and spun her around. He stood there, breathing hard. Seth was over six feet tall and wore his Duke football letter jacket with pride. A shock of sandy brown hair fell over his right eye, and he pushed it away in a gesture of frustration and anger. He had never been so unfairly rejected by a girl, and his hurt pride demanded an explanation.

"Let me go!" she cried.

"Like hell, I will! Why haven't you returned my calls? How can we be in love one day and then no word, nothing ... this?"

"Seth, it isn't you; it's me; I'm sick, and I did not want you to see me this way. Now, let me go, damn it. I'm late for class. I'll call, I promise."

Seth held on to Courtney and looked her in the eyes. He felt ill, nauseated; her eyes were bloodshot and her face ashen, shrunken; her formerly beautiful teeth were greenish, and her breath fetid; she had aged years in the month since he had seen her. Cancer? He slowly released his grip on her arm and stood there, stunned, as she ran crying into the dark hallway. He looked at his hands, held open before him, hoping he hadn't caught whatever horror had consumed his beautiful Courtney.

Heads turned as Courtney dropped her books with a clatter while climbing into the silly child's desk. She finally gained her composure and looked up at the teacher. Dr. von Hautig, all three hundred pounds of her, was standing behind her desk, tapping a pencil impatiently. She was paid to teach Anthropology 202, and that did not include suffering fools. She said, "OK," and cleared her throat and began the lesson on the evolution of early man. Courtney was very tired from the previous evening's hunting, and the fat woman's monotonous voice soon lulled her to sleep. She was dreaming of dark, squirming things when von Hautig's big fist slammed down on her desk.

"Wake up!"

Courtney's exhausted brain returned to life, and she jerked awake. "Whaa ... I'm so sorry."

"No one sleeps in my class! Gather your things and get out! Now!"

The fat woman's nylon panty hose made a swishing sound as she waddled after Courtney, insuring the humiliated girl's rapid exit from the classroom. Several students laughed at the spectacle, but the ones who saw Courtney's face did not. Her eyes glowed blood red, and her lips were stretched back, exposing filthy teeth in a frightening grin-snarl. She foamed at the mouth as though she had rabies. Later, when questioned by the police, the student witnesses would not reach agreement as to what they had observed other than to say that Courtney did not look remotely human when she fled the classroom.

℘

Although Durham normally enjoys mild winter weather, precipitation had moved up the coast and collided with a cold front from the northwest. A thin coating of ice lent a sparkling, fairyland beauty to the drab campus. Wind-blown sleet clattered against darkened windowpanes. It was 2:00 a.m. and a very good night for sleeping and dreaming of holidays and Christmas. There was the promise of home and beautifully wrapped gifts, and ugliness was surely put away for the season.

Dr. Lydia von Hautig lived in a small, comfortable cottage suitable for an assistant professor without a family. It was situated on the edge of the deep forest that surrounds Duke University and was quiet and private, ideal for serious study. The second rap on the door woke the woman, and she raised her naked bulk from the bed and looked at the glowing tableside clock. Who would be calling at this hour and in this weather? She switched on a light and found her tattered housecoat. Covering her ample body as best she could, Lydia made her way down the hall to the entryway. She threw the switch to the porch light, but it was burned out. A peek through an adjacent window revealed the form of a young woman with a backpack, a lone, dark silhouette surrounded by glittering, white ice.

Lydia's first reaction was fear; she seldom had unannounced visitors appear at her door and certainly not in the middle of the night and in this horrid weather. However, the woman was blessed with a scientist's deep curiosity and a modicum of empathy, despite her tyrannical ways in the classroom. She opened the front door a crack, keeping the safety chain in place.

"Who is there?"

For a moment there was only an icy blast of howling wind, but then a girl's voice. "Courtney, Courtney Wesley."

Lydia hadn't known who to expect but certainly not the likes of Courtney Wesley. "What in the world do you want this time of night, young lady?"

"I couldn't sleep; I've come to apologize for my behavior and I've brought you ... a little *something* as a peace offering. May I come in; I'm freezing."

"Uhh, yes, certainly, come on in out of that awful weather," Lydia answered as she unlatched the safety chain with a metallic clatter.

Lydia nodded at a series of pegs beside the door and the shivering girl hung up her dripping wet coat and backpack. Courtney concealed her hatred of the bitch with a faint smile. She stood before the older woman in a form-fitting sweater and ski pants that displayed her fine figure to some advantage. For the moment, her face was almost normal, even pretty. Lydia von Hautig was a lesbian with a well-known appetite for young girls, and Courtney was about to play her like a violin. Courtney's mind raged with blood lust and a pressing need to humiliate, punish the obnoxious teacher as she had been humiliated and punished in front of her friends and classmates.

"Dr. von Hautig ... Lydia," she whispered, "I've come to show you just how sorry I am for disrupting your classroom ,and I've brought you a very special gift."

"Oh, honey, you shouldn't have; it's OK. It really is."

Courtney was breathing hard now. "Oh, Lydia, I know what you *really* like, and I've brought just that to you—me and my young body." The woman was dumbfounded at her good luck and said nothing as Courtney pulled the tie to her bathrobe. Lydia let it fall to the floor, and Courtney began massaging Lydia's massive, pendulous breasts. She sucked in her breath as Courtney kissed her hard on the lips and then touched her private parts.

Lydia threw her head back and moaned, but her expression of sexual ecstasy was cut short, and her eyes bulged from her head as the straight razor sliced upward and onward through layers of skin and fat until its mission was ended by hard bone of her rib cage. Lydia's failed scream came out as "Uck! Uck!"

Courtney laughed and said, "And oink, oink to you, too, pig," as the dying woman collapsed to the floor, her insides spilling from the massive wound.

Courtney wiped the bloody blade on von Hautig's discarded bathrobe, donned her wet coat, and was off into the raging storm. Snow had replaced the freezing rain, and her tracks would soon be covered. Courtney had no clue as to her destination, but she knew that the raging engine from hell that burned inside of her did know, and her feet moved ahead, deliberately, one at a time.

20

A Father's Worst Fears

Wanda had taken the day off for Christmas shopping, and Jerrod was alone in his office, shuffling papers and ruminating about how he had gone wrong with Courtney, when the telephone rang. It was Dr. Amanda Griffith, Dean of Students at Duke; he vaguely remembered meeting her at a parent's orientation during Courtney's first week at the school. Jerrod was immediately consumed by a feeling of panic; he knew this could not be good. The Dean of Students doesn't call you without good reason.

"Dr. Wesley, I am afraid I have bad news for you."

Jerrod swallowed the metallic taste in his mouth. "Yes, go on," he replied, pulse racing.

"It seems your daughter has gone missing. Her roommate has not seen her in several days, and she has not attended her classes. Do you happen to know her whereabouts, Dr. Wesley?"

Jerrod was breathing hard; he *had known* that something—some damned thing—was wrong all along. His daughter was just not right in the head.

"No, Dean Griffith, I do not. I have found it impossible to communicate with her recently, but perhaps her mother knows something I don't."

"I'm afraid not; I spoke to Mrs. Wesley yesterday, and the last time they spoke was a week ago." Griffith cleared her throat and began again with difficulty. "Dr. Wesley, I, I have to inform you that there is more to this ... students disappear all the time—drunk, shacked-up, drop out without warning—but in this case it may not be the usual childish nonsense."

Jerrod was impatient and interrupted the struggling woman, "Damn it; please be direct with me!"

"Sorry, but this is very difficult. The last time your daughter was seen was in Anthropology 202 class three days ago. She was involved in an *altercation* with the teacher, Dr. Lydia von Hautig. Courtney was late to class and then dozed off. Apparently Dr. von Hautig exploded and threw her out; Lydia was not known for her tolerance."

"Courtney was taking drugs for her depression under Dr. Barrington's care. Say, just what do you mean by *was not known?*"

"I'm afraid Dr. von Hautig has been brutally murdered. Her body was found in her home by the campus police when she didn't show up for her morning class. She had been eviscerated with a sharp instrument. The forensics lab believes she died the night following the classroom altercation with Courtney. I'm not necessarily saying that ... your daughter was involved in any way."

"Just what are you saying then, Dean Griffith?"

"Only that the police consider her as a person of interest in their investigation. We, the administration and the campus and local police, have interviewed a number of students and faculty who interacted with Courtney, and they all said the same thing. She was ill, not herself at all, and looked awful. She had suddenly dropped her boyfriend without explanation, was staying out to all hours, and her grades were slipping."

"Jesus!" Jerrod searched for words, "What does Dr. Barrington have to say about all this?"

"She hasn't seen Barrington in months."

Very loud warning bells went off in Jerrod's mind; he had finally connected the dots, and they drew an ugly picture of lies and deceit on Susan's part. She had gotten supplies of Medulin from her friends at Apex and given them to Courtney just as she had threatened. Courtney had been much better for a time but then went straight downhill as the toxic drug poisoned her previously agile, young brain. What crimes had Courtney committed in her psychotic state? Was it too late for her? Was she even alive, and if so, was she remotely human?

"Dr. Wesley?"

"My apology, Dean Griffith; I'm in a state of shock."

"I'm sorry, real sorry; I'll let you go, but we'll be in touch. In the meanwhile, if you learn anything useful, please share it with us. In a sense we're all in this mess together."

Jerrod agreed, hung up the telephone, spoke to a secretary, and then left the building, heading directly to the law offices of Barnes, Waddle, and Stein in Stamford. It would probably take him at least an hour to get there on I-95 South with its congested traffic and numerous 18-wheelers. The heavy traffic would move only at a creep from Bridgeport to Stamford.

♃

Jerrod could not have known or imagined that Courtney also traveled on I-95, heading north. She was far to the south, passing through Roanoke Rapids, near the Virginia border. Perhaps Courtney didn't look her best but she had looked good enough for Clem Hawkins to slam on his brakes and pick her up as she thumbed a ride on an I-95 entrance ramp. Clem had just returned from a tour of duty in Iraq and was still shell-shocked from an improvised explosive device that exploded under his vehicle. His two friends in the HUMV had died instantly, but Clem was somewhat more fortunate and survived the ordeal with a horribly burned face. What Clem didn't know was that Courtney had passed up several other offers from nice families in fancy vehicles. Clem and his inconspicuous, rusted-out green Chevy pickup truck were just what she had been looking for.

ℒ

Barnes, Waddle, and Stein occupied the top two floors of an impressive glass and steel tower in Stamford, Connecticut, just off I-95. Barbara Barnes' spacious office overlooked several other modern buildings, and there was a glint of Long Island Sound in the distance as the fickle winter sun played hide and seek with scudding clouds. Barbara was a tall, impressive lady who was almost always dressed in an immaculate, black suit of the latest design. Today, however, she was dressed in tennis garb, having come directly from her downtown athletic club to meet Jerrod. He had called her on her cell phone, so she had a good idea of the magnitude of the emergency.

"OK, Jerrod, let's have it—all of it. Today the meter is not running, and you have all the time you like." Barbara put down her coffee cup and picked up a pen and began scratching on a yellow pad as Jerrod waded in, edging toward deep water.

"First, let me thank you for seeing me on such short notice; obviously I have interfered with your tennis game."

Barbara nodded patiently and smiled a little, and Jerrod continued. "I think I have to start at the beginning, and this may take a while, but I will get there." Jerrod began with the toxicology report, which he carried in his case, Wally's death, their findings on Medulin, Susan's relationship with Apex, and the whole story leading up to Courtney's depression and their argument over Courtney's not taking the experimental drug. Finally, Jerrod struggled through Courtney's disappearance that coincided with the death of her instructor.

Barbara let out a low whistle. "My God, Jerrod, so many issues! I'm so sorry about Courtney. You actually believe that she has been taking this drug, Medulin, and it may have induced a sort of psychosis that has led her to do things she ordinarily wouldn't do, don't you?"

Jerrod nodded his agreement, and she continued. "I think we have to compartmentalize these issues; finding your daughter is obviously the highest priority, but may not be easy. We have some excellent private investigators that work for us, but let's put that issue aside for the moment and come back to it later. For many reasons, it is an absolute priority to confirm that the poor girl is held in the grip of this horrible drug and that she did not take it voluntarily. Like it or not, we have to talk to your wife, since only she and Courtney know the answer to that critical question. I have a pretty good relationship with her lawyer, Carroll Anne Johnson, and I am going to work through her. Carroll Anne has to listen to me, and Susan may not."

Barbara asked her secretary to make the call, and she continued while they waited. "Jerrod, I think I understand why you have remained silent about Dr. Wally's report, or what you believe to be a toxicology report that damns the drug, Medulin. The problem is, you may have knowingly withheld vital evidence relevant to a murder, and that's a felony."

Jerrod sighed and responded in a tired voice, "I feared for the lives of my family and for myself. I still, to this day, don't know for certain what's in that damned envelope."

Barbara smiled. "You mean the one that was almost stolen and cost an intruder his life?"

"Yeah, that one, the one I have right here in my case." Jerrod unlocked the black, leather case and removed a large envelope that contained the letter and the still-sealed, confidential package. It seemed heavy, hot in his hands, and he perspired profusely.

The discussion was interrupted when Barbara's secretary buzzed to indicate that someone was holding; it was Carroll Anne Johnson. Barbara started to explain the situation regarding Johnson's client, when Carroll Anne said, "Barbara, stop; you don't have to go through all that. Susan called me when Courtney went missing, and I can confirm that she was taking the Apex experimental drug, Medulin. That is all that I can say at this time. I believe you understand?"

Barbara nodded her head vigorously so that Jerrod immediately knew the truth. Then she spent a few more minutes ironing out several pressing details regarding the divorce filing with Carroll Anne, Susan's lawyer.

When Barbara turned around to face her client, he was ripping open the thick envelope. It's contents might send a number of people to jail, including Jerrod Wesley. He would punish himself for the rest of his life for finding endless reasons for putting off what he knew should be done. Might he have saved Courtney from all of this? Tears streamed down his face when he pulled out the same toxicology report that Alton Wally had brought into his office months ago. Jerrod read the summary in silence; certain phrases and sentences jumped off the page ... "delayed neurotoxicity and cell death in regions of the brain associated with normal cognition and behavior ... lesions in the critical regions rich in acetylcholine serotonin and dopamine-secreting neurons." Furthermore, the summary stated that all rats treated with higher doses and/or for longer periods of time showed catastrophic changes in brain architecture and associated chemistry. There was more than sufficient data to support the conclusions, and it was consistent with their own findings with Medulin in human cell culture. Jerrod was now certain that Apex had not shared that data with the FDA either.

Barbara said softly, "It must be bad."

"Yeah, and I was wrong to sit on it for so long. So, now we must do the right thing; how should we proceed?"

The smart lawyer made a pyramid with her long fingers and rested her chin on it. "This law firm will take care of it on your behalf. There are two issues—the FDA and the police. Preventing more Medulin deaths should be our priority. That and finding your poor daughter."

After a long discussion, it was decided that the report would be delivered to Averill Hampton, Commissioner, FDA, along with a letter explaining the circumstances. An urgent e-mail would be sent to Hampton's office as soon as possible to alert him to the issue. As a second priority, a copy of the letter and the cover of the report would be delivered to the Madison Police Department. Barbara explained that Jerrod might be off the hook because the coroner had ruled Wally's drowning as accidental. He need never mention that Alton Wally had flashed the report in Jerrod's office prior to the frightened toxicologist's untimely death.

Jerrod was happy with the plan but could not imagine the possible ramifications; would there be a war between the FDA and Apex or just another cover-up. What would the lazy Madison Police do now?

The discussion then turned to Courtney, and Barbara proposed that the *only* possible approach was to put a good private investigator on the missing girl's trail. Like most big law firms, Barnes, Waddle, and Stein kept several on retainer. It was agreed that Jerrod would meet with Sam Lugar before the work day was over. Sam was a former CIA operative and had a record of success at tracking down lost people who didn't want to be found.

21

On the Road Again

The old truck bumped the curb and jarred to a halt beside the Garden State Parkway rest stop. Clem Hawkins pushed the driver's side door open and stumbled into the parking lot amidst a cascade of empty Budweiser cans. The keys were in the ignition, and the truck idled roughly, fumes from the faulty exhaust system seeping up through the rusty floorboard. Courtney coughed and reached for the ignition switch to turn the truck off, but her eye caught something on the seat; it was Clem's billfold. He had forgotten it in his drunken haste to pee.

She smiled and thumbed through the bills, finding that it contained several hundred dollars, likely his military rousting out pay. She almost put it back but then remembered how the repulsive bastard with his horribly burned face and fetid breath had pawed at her and slobbered on her the prior evening. Clem owed her; didn't he? Besides, he was already a lucky man—she had seriously considered slitting his throat when he put his filthy hands on her. Courtney slid over behind the wheel, struggled briefly with the column-mounted manual transmission, and finally merged with the flow of traffic after narrowly being missed by a speeding 18-wheeler. The girl's thought process was disordered, but she realized that even though Clem was likely guilty of *something*, he would call the cops as soon as he sobered up enough to realize that his truck and money had been stolen. It would be all too easy to apprehend her at a toll plaza if she stayed on the parkway, so she took the first exit without regard to where it might lead her. She figured there was a New Jersey road map in the glove compartment, and she would find her way; the voices left her no other choice.

※

Jerrod winced at the man's powerful grip as he shook hands with the big private investigator. Sam Lugar stood well over six feet tall and had the square face and bulging muscles of a Hollywood actor—more of a Clint Eastwood than a John Wayne—but he was real, a no-nonsense, CIA-trained operative. Barnes, Waddle, and Stein used Lugar to locate big-time delinquent dads who often luxuriated with their money and younger women on distant tropical isles. Normally they left a trail of breadcrumbs a foot deep and a mile wide and were easy enough to find. That would not be true in Courtney's case; she was psychotic, unpredictable, and extremely dangerous.

Sam suggested he start his search with her dormitory room at Duke University. She had left most of her clothes and possessions there and possibly some clue as to what she had in mind or where she might be hiding, or more likely traveling. The private investigator was not discouraged by the fact that the local cops had already searched her room and found nothing of interest. There was likely someone around who knew something of use.

"Jerrod, I also feel it is very helpful that an APB was put out on Courtney in regard to the murder investigation. Her picture is posted and recorded in police computer systems all over the country. She will get stopped for some minor traffic offense and be recognized. That is the best-case scenario. The worst is that I have to track her to hell and back, but one way or the other, we'll find her."

Wesley agreed to call Dean Griffith, fill her in on the situation, and request her cooperation. Lugar would begin his search in Durham the following day. He would drive all night, which was no big deal for him. It was after 7:00 p.m. when Jerrod bade Lugar good luck and left the law offices. It was dark and the wind was howling, so Jerrod was glad his car was in the lower level parking garage. He skillfully negotiated the big BMW through the Stamford traffic and up the I-95 entrance ramp. He groaned; the northbound lanes were a sea of slowly moving taillights and honking horns. As usual, the southbound lanes were wide open and traffic was flowing. Making the best of the situation, he called Dean Griffith and settled his business with her—the university would cooperate fully—they, too, had a lot to lose in this mess.

Jerrod was missing Wanda, and he called her cell phone; she was still at the office. Wanda sensed his frustration and agreed to meet him at an out of the way Westport restaurant they sometimes frequented in search of a nice, but private, meal. The Broken Spar was on the water at the end of a narrow lane. It was a charming, little seafood restaurant, frequented mostly by wealthy locals. Jerrod had suffered a long day and needed something pleasant to anticipate. Given the traffic situation, she might even beat him there and have his Jack on ice waiting.

Remarkably, they crunched into the oyster shell parking lot at the same time. The hour was late, and only the cars of a few die-hard drinkers and the staff remained in the lot. Their fear that they were too late for dinner was quickly dismissed by a friendly hostess named Shirley who said they would serve diners for another hour, at least. In fact, they were offered free oyster shooters for their late patronage. Jerrod took his in one gulp, the prescribed manner, but Wanda sipped and then chewed and chewed. Jerrod laughed until it hurt—the look on her face! God, he loved her so.

Finally relaxed, Jerrod shared his trying day with her. Events had been set into motion that would gain unstoppable momentum over the next twenty-four hours. The happy couple took their time with drinks, wine, and a nice striped bass with lobster cream sauce. I-95 would have died its usual slow death by dinner's end, and they would enjoy a quick ride back to Madison.

The roar of heavily laden jets on full power lifting off the runway was deafening, but Courtney had slept for two hours despite the noise and fumes. Now, it was time to come to life and make her next move. The old truck was parked in a dark corner of the Newark International Airport long-term parking lot for Terminal B, and she was about to play out a scam she had seen on television. The lot was mostly full as early holiday travelers escaped the East Coast for the Christmas season in warmer climes. Rain that had moved in while Courtney slept was becoming an icy mix. Travelers with heavy bags found slick going as they made their way toward the distant terminal. Courtney watched several individuals and families unload their luggage before she spotted what she was looking for. An elderly woman in a heavy coat had struggled to get her bulky bag out of the trunk of a silver Lexus and would walk right by the old truck. Courtney watched her like a hawk as she struggled by, leaning into the howling wind, blinded by the stinging sleet. She pulled her bag on rollers with her right hand, and her purse strap was looped over her left shoulder. Her keys dangled absently from her left hand; she had yet to find a secure place for them. Courtney opened the truck door; its loud squeak obscured by a Boeing 767 blasting through the skies overhead. The truck's cab light had burned out long ago.

The cunning girl timed it perfectly, stepping from the shadows and colliding with the unsuspecting woman. Courtney cried out in feigned surprise but steadied the old woman, preventing her from falling. Courtney apologized profusely for not having seen her in the sleet and darkness. More angry than hurt, the woman would have nothing of it and hurried off toward the passenger terminal grumbling about *today's rude youth*, all the way.

Courtney shouted, "I'm sorry," into the wind as she fondled the keys to the Lexus. The unfortunate victim would only think of her keys in a week or two when she returned home. In the meanwhile, Courtney would have the use of a fine car that was not sought by the police. That would buy her the time she needed. Courtney loaded her pack into the Lexus and drove toward the closest toll gate where a bored attendant bought her story that an emergency had prevented her from taking her scheduled flight. She took the exit for New York City, only 16 miles away, and merged with a sea of headlights.

22

The Truth

Averill Hampton, Commissioner FDA, was a slight man with a bushy head of gray hair and a similar mustache; he wore thick glasses with large, plastic frames from another time. He was the consummate bureaucrat and had risen through the ranks, successfully obstructing one government office after the next. He had an extremely high opinion of his ability and an elevated sense of *self*, despite the fact that he had been unable to deal with the practice of medicine in an earlier life. He had not liked blood or the whiny patients that bled; in fact, he still didn't like people, period, unless they could do him some good. Notwithstanding his failure as a practicing physician, Dr. Averill Thomas Hampton's diplomas from Princeton and Emory School of Medicine were prominently displayed on the walls of his large, but worn office.

The package from Barnes, Waddle, and Stein had arrived as yesterday's e-mail promised. There was a cover letter from the law firm informing him of important information relevant to Apex's drug Medulin. Two attached documents provided further support. He had read every word of the package twice and did not care for the obvious take-home message, so he read Barbara Barnes' letter for the third time. He sighed; there was no other interpretation of the lawyer's claims. The attached toxicology report clearly demonstrated that Medulin was toxic to the rat nervous system, so the one submitted to the FDA was fabricated, or was it the other way around? There was also some fairly believable evidence that Alton Wally, Apex's head of toxicology, had been murdered as part of the cover up, and now the cops were involved.

And who the hell was this Jerrod Wesley, and why did Wally go to him? The letter was extremely vague as to why this Genplex research executive sat on this hot potato for so long. Hampton looked at his hands as if they were contaminated; he wasn't much of a turd fondler, and this baby was about to be passed along to CDER where it belonged. One thing Averill Hampton could do was delegate.

He called his assistant, Juanita Cassandra, into his office and requested she send a form letter to Barnes, Waddle, and Stein, informing them that the information had been received and would be reviewed by *qualified experts* at FDA. He took pleasure knowing that this nothing response would irritate the lawyers to no end. He asked Juanita to make copies of the Medulin package and then to call Alan Werner and request his presence ASAP.

By the time Werner arrived, Hampton was almost gleeful. Although he had gone to great lengths to hire Alan Werner, he had quickly learned to dislike the know-it-all Harvard prick. A broad grin crossed Hampton's face at the thought of Werner's *therapeutically advantageous* drug sinking in quicksand, and Werner being sucked down with it. The last damned thing he was going to do was approve some unneeded drug that had not undergone adequate testing.

"You asked to see me, Averill? What's up?"

Hampton pretended to be reading the disquieting documents, then picked them up and waved them in Werner's face. He said with furrowed brow, "Some pretty troubling information relevant to the development of Medulin has been sent to my attention by a Connecticut law firm. These are your copies, and getting to the bottom of this is obviously your responsibility, so study them carefully, and let me know what your action plan is. Oh, and please take a minute, and read the lawyer's cover letter right now, and tell me what your knee-jerk reaction is. Coffee?"

Werner frowned and quickly scanned the document. "Yes, and make it black."

Hampton sat back in his chair and enjoyed himself as he watched the psychiatrist read the letter. Werner's mouth opened and closed, making little Os; the man looked just like a skinny goldfish, out of water, sucking air. The Commissioner smirked as he considered that he was about to find out just how fast on his feet Alan was ... or wasn't.

Werner completed the letter and placed it back on his boss' desk. He said, "Well," as though he had solved the problem.

"Well, what?"

"An obvious fabrication. The legitimate report with all the required supporting data is filed with the Division of Psychiatry Products."

Not that simple, Hampton thought. "OK, and what about the death of the toxicologist who supposedly wrote *both* reports? Sounds a bit fishy to me."

Werner took on his preachy tone; he was back in control. "Not if you think about it; the *accidental* death of Apex's toxicologist obviously inspired this ... this fraudulent attempt to discredit Medulin."

Hampton sighed and said, "According to the letter, Genplex's research head Wesley received the documents prior to Alton Wally's death. As you can clearly see, the date on Wally's letter corroborates this. I'm certain that express mail records will be consistent with that."

"Maybe so, maybe not—most anything can be altered or fabricated. And what about this Wesley guy? Why did he sit on this so long? I think he and Genplex are in this up to their eyeballs. Cheap industrial espionage, if you ask me."

Hampton reddened. "Look, some important information has been sent to the FDA in a very professional and legal manner. We have no choice but to look into it and reconcile the two very different toxicology reports. I am going to start by having Juanita copy David Kendall on this information. After you both have had an opportunity to digest the material, you will meet with David and then direct the Division of Psychiatry Products' reviewing toxicologist to audit the toxicology study and compare the two reports. I want to know about any discrepancies immediately!"

Hampton watched the angry man hurry out of the room; his answers had been too quick and glib. Did the bastard already know something about this, or did he just sense that his ass was on the line? Kendall already had red flags up all over where Medulin was concerned; this was really going to be interesting.

Maxwell Hall lit up a Cuban cigar as soon as security called to inform him that his unnamed visitor had arrived. If the bastard was going to ruin his Saturday off, he was going to pay for it. And why all the cloak and dagger secrecy? It was snowing heavily, and Hall could only imagine how tough the drive up from Washington must have been. He considered that this could not be good news and cursed under his breath. He did not need any new problems at the moment.

The two men shook hands, and Werner gladly accepted a cup of black coffee even though it was tepid. There was only small talk while Werner warmed up and relaxed from the treacherous drive. It didn't take Hall long to tire of such pleasantries, and he blurted, "OK, let's have it—what the hell is going on?"

Werner explained the situation exactly as it had unfolded and handed copies of Barbara Barnes' letter, Alton Wally's letter, and the toxicology report to Hall. "Maxwell, I can't make this go away. The Commissioner neither likes nor trusts me and he has also fully engaged David Kendall and the Division of Psychiatry Products. They are going to audit your damned toxicology study and try to reconcile the two reports. What the hell have you done?"

Hall blew a cloud of acrid smoke in Werner's direction. "Alton Wally was a fool; no one agreed with his findings; why, the bastard was making some things up and exaggerating others. It could have been the end of Medulin, but it turned out to be the end of Wally instead."

"My God, you not only fabricated the report but also killed one of your own employees?"

Hall took another deep drag off his cigar and blew perfect smoke rings toward the ceiling. "We did what we had to do, and as for Wally, the police case is closed; he drowned swimming in his own lake alone and naked. Very risky thing to do in my opinion. And as to the report submitted to the FDA by Apex, I assure you that everything will be found to be in order."

"Don't underestimate the FDA," Werner countered, "they have good toxicology auditors, and David Kendall hates Medulin almost as much as he hates me and my fast-track program. I think this is a huge problem that the rat neurological findings are consistent with the clinical adverse reactions we have seen in Medulin studies. I am warning you, Maxwell, Kendall is coming after you."

Hall angrily mashed the cigar stub in an ashtray. "Alan, you seem to have forgotten who you really work for; maybe I should remind you of a few things."

"No, no need," the excited psychiatrist blurted. "Quite the contrary—I came here to warn you so you could be prepared for this ... this damned thing. Let's not forget that Jerrod Wesley down the road at Genplex is somehow right in the middle of this mess."

"Alan, this is no surprise; we knew that Wally had made contact with Wesley, and we were afraid that information, some damned thing, may have been passed on. We even sent a high powered operative in to search his house and crack his safe, but unfortunately Anesthasia was killed trying to escape when Wesley came home early. Fortunately, he couldn't be traced to us. It was too dangerous to make a second attempt with Wesley alerted, so we took a chance."

"Big chance, in my opinion; maybe you underestimated Jerrod Wesley?"

Hall squinted and gave Werner a nasty look. "Maybe, but we have new worries with him now. There is a lot of inbreeding going on here, but to make a long story short, Wesley's estranged wife covers Apex for Sirius Financial Investment Bank and through Apex, meaning me, she obtained Medulin supplies for her daughter at Duke who was suffering from severe depression. The girl improved for a while, but then went off her rocker, killed a teacher, and disappeared. She has not been found. The good news is that there is no way to prove that Medulin had anything to do with the killing."

Werner was dumbfounded; was there no level of bad news that Maxwell Hall couldn't brush off as though it were nothing? Sooner or later something would stick and then what? "Maxwell, that is definitely not good news; if that crazy girl keeps on killing innocent people, it will be blamed on Medulin—on all of us. Maybe it's time to ... uhh."

"Cut bait?" Hall provided. "No, I don't think so. And as for Courtney Wesley, the police are looking for her, Wesley must be looking for her, and *we* are definitely looking for her. She'll turn up and soon— just another loose thread to pull."

"Now, I have to go; I am making an important speech on drug company ethics at a PMA meeting down the way at Pfizer. You know what you need to do at the FDA, so fucking go do it!" Hall searched for another cigar while he watched the Harvard psychiatrist slink out of his plush office. What a wimp! Hall scratched a note on his pad to speak to Bernie Bothwell, the newly rich toxicologist who had *fixed* the Medulin report—and what a job he had done!

23

'Tis the Season

The late afternoon sun played tag with scudding clouds that brushed the western horizon. A few errant rays of sunlight cast a cold, pink glow as the last snow flakes from the winter storm fell into the frigid water of Long Island Sound. Jerrod's big colonial was almost buried under a blanket of snow, but Wanda rested comfortably with a hot rum toddy in front of the big stone fireplace. She was relieved when she heard the rattle of the garage door; Jerrod had finally returned from a long Saturday afternoon of Christmas shopping. Thank God, Manuel had plowed the long drive. Jerrod shouted a greeting and told Wanda to enjoy the roaring fire while he unloaded the BMW. She assumed he had gifts for her and complied, smiling, considering how fortunate she was to have Jerrod. When Jerrod made trip after trip back to the cold garage, she grew curious and met him at the door.

"Jerrod?"

"Yeah, I guess I got a bit carried away. I bought a lot of gifts for ... Courtney. She ..." He struggled to finish the sentence but broke down entirely, dropping an armload of Christmas presents on the floor.

Wanda ran to him and held him close. What greater horror could a father endure than *this*? "Oh, Jerrod, she'll be found; so many people are looking for her; you must have faith."

Jerrod did have faith, and he had a great inner strength that his Southern Baptist parents had instilled in him, but this had already gone too far to have much hope. "Yes, Wanda, she will be found, but even if she's alive, then what? What has she done? What will they do to her?"

"No, Jerrod, it's not what has she done; rather, it's what have your wife and her so-called friends done *to Courtney* with that poison they encouraged her to take? I just don't understand how any mother could take such a foolish risk. I know you feel responsible, but you are not; *you informed Susan of the risks and told her not to do it!* Now, come in here and sit down in front of this fire; I am going to make you the best damned drink you ever had. We will get through this together."

Presently, she served Jerrod a warm rum drink that was a bit stronger than her own. He sipped the drink and seemed to find solace in the flames, though there were no easy answers, no cure for the damage done by the drug. *Cure,* he thought; that's it! There is no cure, but we have all the tools required to find a cure ... or a treatment, something, to help heal the damage done by Medulin. He resolved to spend the remainder of the weekend on the Internet looking for a place to start, contacting experts in the field, and praying for ideas. Jerrod knew most of the nerve cell recovery experts personally; they were a pretty small clique. The same tools being applied to brain and spinal cord injury might apply here. Something had to work.

There was a scraping sound and then a scream as a stray cat flushed from her hiding place in the darkness of the alleyway. The figure of a girl moved furtively to the edge of the shadows but shrank back at the laughter of last minute holiday shoppers. She shivered; the frozen, gray slop that New York City called snow was freezing her feet. Courtney put the cold from her mind, easing forward until she had a good view of Estrada, her mother's Central Park West luxury residence tower across the street. She didn't have to count up to the twenty-third floor—she knew exactly which one it was. Her mommy and *that man* were up there—on the warm and secure side of the window decorated with a fancy Christmas wreath. Even her muddled brain understood that something had gone sour with her drug treatment. Daddy had known better. Just the same, she would be wishing Mommy and her friend a merry Christmas, but not quite yet.

Courtney's dormitory room was still cordoned off by yellow police tape when the two men arrived. Her roommate had been assigned new quarters and the room held as containing possible evidence, though none had been found. The campus cop turned the key and pushed the door open for the big private investigator.

When the light came on, the cop let out a low whistle; the room had been ransacked and was not as it had been left after the last visit by law enforcement agents. Courtney's clothes were strewn about the room, drawers pulled open and their contents scattered on the floor.

The cop exclaimed, "Jesus Christ, Sam, someone's been here—someone who was not invited, much less escorted!"

Sam Lugar had seen most everything in his long career and wasn't remotely surprised that the *enemy*, as he saw them, were also looking for the girl. After all she might be able to damn the largest pharmaceutical company in the world.

Lugar said, "Well, Officer Jones, I'll just sort through this mess as best as I can, but the police record should indicate that there has been illegal tampering with evidence here." Lugar found little of interest but did take note of a road map of New York and New Jersey on which New York City had been circled many times in red ink. Susan Wesley lived in midtown Manhattan; was there some connection?

Lugar thanked Officer Jones and walked the block to the parking structure and his Mercedes. His cell phone rang, and it was his assistant, Lindsey Fortune. She explained that she had just received a report that a woman matching Courtney Wesley's description had stolen an old pickup truck and some money from a wounded Iraq veteran named Clem Hawkins. Though the unfortunate victim was a little shell-shocked, his description was quite detailed, and it was almost definitely the missing girl. He also identified her from a recent photograph.

"Not only that," she continued, "the stolen truck was found an hour ago by the police in the Terminal B parking lot at Newark International Airport. Maybe she skipped the country. She left the parking ticket in the truck, and we have the time she entered the lot. I checked with the airlines, and no one of her name was listed on any passenger list on flights leaving that night, but that doesn't mean anything. So … oh, yeah, the cops have prints and will look for a match with those lifted from her personal items."

Sam said, "Good work, lady. I don't think she took a flight out—probably too loony to purchase a ticket and board a flight without attracting attention. I think she either stole a vehicle or begged a ride out of there. A rental car seems highly unlikely. I think I might even know where she was headed. By the way, we've got company in this investigation. Someone else is looking for Courtney Wesley, and we need to get to her first. OK, do you have reports from the Port Authority of automobiles being stolen from that parking lot that evening?"

Lindsey responded, "No, Sam, but the problem is that the car would not have been reported missing if the owner hasn't returned. Besides, women don't usually steal cars; do they?"

Sam answered her sexist question with a laugh and asked her to run down Susan Wesley's address in Manhattan for him. Snow or not, he was heading back up north. He would update Jerrod along the way; at least he could say the girl was likely alive.

It would be a slow trip to Manhattan, Sam thought, as he pulled his Mercedes out into the winter weather. He decided to make the best of it and work along the way. Jerrod answered his cell phone after one ring.

"Jerrod, she's alive."

"Sam? Thank God! Where are you, man?" Jerrod responded in a relieved voice.

"I'm just leaving the Duke campus. I didn't find much to go on in Courtney's dorm room other than a hint that she was headed for New York when she left. Unfortunately, an unauthorized person or persons had ransacked the room before I got there. Hate to say, but it looks like someone else is also looking for her, Jerrod."

There was resolve in Jerrod's tone. "*Competition*—I'm not surprised; you also said she is alive—how do you know that?"

Sam went through his assistant's telephone call in some detail and explained that the Newark International Airport waypoint strengthened his belief that Courtney was headed to New York. "If so, she would be there by now; the airport is only sixteen miles from the city. My guess is that she is looking for her mother."

Sam was fishing, looking for Jerrod's knee-jerk reaction, Jerrod thought. "It could be—they were a team and had me fooled." Suddenly it occurred to him that Courtney's visit to New York might not be about warm and fuzzy. "God, no, she's figured out that Susan and her allies have poisoned her, maybe destroyed her. She's going to New York to seek ... *restitution*."

Sam responded in a quiet tone, "Yeah, that's my guess, and she's in a homicidal mode and unable to distinguish right from wrong. I know it's painful for you to hear this, but she's killed once over a minor college classroom altercation and robbed a guy. This would be an easy next step. The issue is: do we concentrate on warning your wife or finding Courtney?"

Jerrod thought for a moment and said, "My priority is obviously finding my daughter, but I think we have a moral and perhaps legal obligation to inform Susan of Courtney's probable whereabouts. She'll have to form her own conclusions as we have done. I'll call Barbara Barnes as soon as we hang up. We'll discuss the issue, but my guess is she'll want to call Susan's lawyer, Carroll Anne Johnson on the record. If I know Susan, she'll make the wrong interpretation. You can't protect fools from themselves." Jerrod immediately regretted having blurted out the damning statement, even though it was the truth.

24

The Audit

Bernie Bothwell looked up in surprise; he had instructed his secretary to admit no visitors. He had copious amounts of new data to review and little time before reports were due. He blinked; there, standing in his doorway was none other than the President and CEO of Apex, Maxwell Hall. Generally a business executive would hesitate to walk through the smelly toxicology laboratories and animal rooms to reach his office. Who knew what they might step in?

Hall laughed at the expression on Bothwell's face. "Thought the stink and rat shit would keep the riff-raff out, did you? Not this time. I needed a walk and had to talk to you in private and this is really private. How's the extra money treating you? Probably got a new car in the garage by now?"

Bernie frowned—be careful. "No new car but my wife and children have benefited immensely from the added income." It was a little, white lie; he had recently ordered a custom, candy red BMW M-3 convertible. "The new house has a lot more room for the kids and Kate has her own sewing room."

Hall thought that he didn't really give a shit if Kate was growing a penis for Christmas, and that was enough for pleasantries. "Listen, Dr. Bothwell, we have a code red situation brewing. Alan Werner just paid me a surprise visit, and it seems that a Connecticut law firm has sent the damned original Medulin toxicology report to Averill Hampton, the FDA Commissioner. He in turn involved Werner and David Kendall, who hates us already. The Commissioner has demanded audits to reconcile the two reports. Not only that, but I just got a call from Regulatory Affairs, and the reviewing toxicologist and two FDA Field Investigators will be here next week to audit the damned study. Ordinarily we don't get such a warning, or so I'm told."

Bothwell was ashen and looked ready to throw up. "How the hell?" he managed.

"Bernie, bloody Jerrod Wesley had the report all along. We were right on when we broke into his home and tried to find it, but too bad we failed. Here is a copy of the whole package as received from the lawyer. Alton Wally mailed it to Wesley before his, ah ... unfortunate demise. It is not clear why Wesley sat on it for so long."

Bothwell thumbed through the information; yes, it was indeed the original report. He remembered every word of it and had destroyed every copy—except one. "This is it! What the hell did Werner say to the Commissioner?"

Hall frowned and replied, "Told him he thought it was a fake, and that Wesley and Genplex were behind it. That they were trying to discredit Medulin and Apex for the sake of Axilon, which Werner didn't assign any special status."

"I see. Well, he apparently didn't buy Werner's explanation, if we're going to have auditors here next week. So, we had better be prepared for them when they arrive."

The reality of the situation is that not a great deal of the revised report was altered, just the section that deals with neurological aspects. All the rest is virginal and quite legitimate. Original supporting data for the neurological section, notebooks, tissue slides, everything has been replaced by clean material obtained from untreated rats. Naturally the summary and conclusions have been modified to fit the new shoe."

Hall gave the alarmed toxicologist a penetrating look. "You could not have done this alone. Others must be involved."

"Yes, Raj Peretranian and Shirley Blake assisted in the work. It was done late at night, and there were no witnesses."

Hall wasn't reassured. "And what about the people who did the original work for Alton Wally? I assume they are still here?"

"Yes, they are, but they are low-level technicians and have no clue about any of it," Bothwell insisted.

"The FDA will likely interview whoever they can get their hands on, so see that the Indian and the woman, Blake, are on vacation out of the country for ... fucking forever as far as I'm concerned. That will leave you as the manager and the know-nothing technicians for the FDA to torture. That work?"

Bothwell faked a smile and managed, "Yes, Sir." But he worried about the one thing that had not been mentioned, the omnipresent rumor mill. Who had said what to whom in that critical period just before Alton Wally was found floating in his own lake? Would the FDA conduct random interviews and threaten dangerous information out of people? They would have plenty of time to snoop around; they would be here for days, even weeks. They would track every notebook entry all the way to summary data in final reports. Nothing was a given. Perhaps this would not be the standard, general compliance audit; maybe they would put a 100 percent effort into reconciling the differences between the two reports. He wondered if his small *squirrel fund* would get him to South America if this shit went wrong. Maybe he should not have been so quick to blow the bonus Hall had given him.

Hall pulled out a Cuban cigar and stuck it in his mouth without lighting it. "I'm not interested in discussing this with the Justice Department, Bernie; you better understand that."

The scared toxicologist nodded that he understood and smiled, but as soon as Hall was out of sight, he ran to the men's room and threw up breakfast.

♌

Wanda Lassiter rapped lightly on Jerrod's office door and then stuck her head inside. "Heads up! Security just admitted an FDA toxicologist, Dr. Roger Paisley, and he's on his way up to see you."

Jerrod frowned; surprise visits from the FDA regarding audits were not unusual, but he had never heard of Roger Paisley. Another FDA official had originally been assigned to Axilon. Jerrod shrugged his shoulders and said, "Show him in when he arrives."

The overweight bureaucrat was red faced and puffing when Wanda introduced him. The elevator was being serviced, and Paisley had to take the stairs. Jerrod smiled and welcomed the man warmly, apologizing for the inconvenience.

Paisley explained that he reported to David Kendall and was the reviewing toxicologist for Medulin. "So, you probably already understand why I am here?"

Jerrod nodded politely and said, "My time is yours."

Paisley mopped his brow with a handkerchief about as dirty as his over-easy egg-stained tie. "This Medulin toxicology report that you and your lawyers mailed to the FDA—I want to go through every detail regarding how it came into your possession, starting with your first conversation with Alton Wally. I also want to understand the timing of your decision to involve the FDA. OK if I tape this for future reference?"

"Certainly, and I'll try to be as accurate as I can." Wesley went through the whole story leaving out few details. He described how he had not expected Wally's first visit, how Wally was under threat to bury the negative findings, the mysterious circumstances of Wally's death, how Jerrod had received the package and procrastinated. Finally, the break-in and death of the suspect. He did not mention that

Wally produced the report on his first visit. Somehow that seemed too personally damning.

"Dr. Wesley, I genuinely appreciate how candid you have been, but why did you finally send us the report?"

"Well, I should have sent it when we generated some really ugly data regarding the toxicity of Medulin on human neurons grown in culture, but I didn't. We sent that information to Apex with the expectation that they would inform you. I guess they didn't?"

"No."

"I'm not surprised. You will have a copy of that report before you leave Genplex. After that discovery we heard the rumors of clinical side effects and deaths of Medulin patients. Still, I did nothing until my daughter, Courtney, was given Medulin without my knowledge. She, she was a good student at Duke but then *lost her mind* and did some awful things after receiving the drug. A lot of people are looking for her. That was the final straw. But, please remember, I did not know for certain that sealed package actually contained the damned report until I opened it in my lawyer's office with Barbara Barnes as a witness. We immediately mailed it to the FDA."

"Dr. Wesley, I am sincerely sorry about your daughter, but it is my job to ask who gave your daughter the drug? Was she in a protocol?"

"No, I'm sorry to say my wife, Susan, gave it to her. She is a security analyst for a firm that covers Apex and she is quite close to the company and its top management. Too damned close it turns out."

Paisley shook his head. "All sounds terribly illegal to me. You say the cops are looking for your daughter?"

"Yes, along with my private investigator and perhaps others."

The man was truly moved by what he had heard but didn't know what else to say about the horrible situation with Wesley's daughter. Instead, he concluded with business. "The FDA has informed Apex that we are going to audit the suspect rat toxicology study next week. That is not our normal procedure, but apparently that's what we did. Two Field Investigators under my direction are going to settle in and go through every dose record and necropsy slide, particularly information related to differences between the reports and neurological findings. What do you predict that we are going to find?"

Jerrod looked out at the Sound. For once the sun was shining. "I'm afraid you will find nothing, not one bloody thing. Based on all that I have seen, Apex is capable of almost anything."

Paisley finally laughed. "Don't underestimate the FDA, Dr. Wesley; sometimes too clean is just as bad as dirty."

As Jerrod showed the toxicologist out, he thought of the fabri-

cated Axilon clinical trial and how all the ducks had lined up in perfect order before they were shot from the sky and found to be rubber
ducks. Wanda provided Paisley with a copy of the cell biology findings on Medulin and the letter that had been sent to Apex, and then
the official was gone. Jerrod thought that despite the man's unkempt
appearance, Paisley was first class and just might solve this vexing
puzzle.

25

Merry Christmas

December 25, 2010 rolled around right on schedule despite the dark clouds that swirled around Jerrod Wesley. Genplex was closed for the holiday period, and Wanda and he would spend a few precious days together before she caught the train to see her mother in Philadelphia. Another blanket of snow had fallen, and it continued with no end in sight. Christmas music tinkled in the background, at times lost to the howl of the wind and hiss of the blowing ice crystals. Oak and hickory logs popped and snapped, burning brightly in the big fireplace, warming the two lovers on the couch who were lost in the glow, lost in each other. Champagne glasses clinked and they laughed and kissed. The couple had exchanged gifts earlier, and no one had mentioned Courtney's colorful presents piled high under the Christmas tree. Would they ever be unwrapped?

Presently, it was time to retire to tender love-making, though both yearned for the day that marriage would end a serious affair carried on in dark corners during stolen moments. It was particularly painful that they could not attend the many holiday parties as a couple. Jerrod had undressed and climbed into bed, and Wanda was still in the bath suite when the telephone rang. It was Sam Lugar.

"Jerrod? Hi; how are you? Listen, I'm in position on Central Park West and it's snowing like hell right now. I checked into a cheap hotel nearby a few days ago and I have been quietly patrolling the area around the Estrada ever since. Fancy digs by the way."

Jerrod grunted. "Hard place to be alone at Christmas; any luck, Sam?"

"Well, first of all, I don't think I'm alone; two guys seem to be following me. So far they've held back, but I keep seeing the same two thugs wherever I go. The good news is I think I have seen Courtney a couple of times, standing outside the Estrada, looking up. Then she just melts into the Christmas mob—gone, poof. With any luck at all, I'll have her soon."

"Thank God," Jerrod exclaimed. "Have you seen Susan? Hopefully she's in hiding."

"Hiding? She's sure as hell not in hiding—comes and goes with her funny-looking boyfriend at all hours. She ..."

The thunderous explosion could only have been from a gunshot. When the ringing in Jerrod's ears subsided, there was only the sound of honking horns and screaming sirens.

"Sam! Sam!" but there was no answer. Sam's luck had finally run out, and his life had been ended by a well-placed .357 magnum slug behind his left ear. His cell phone was still clutched in his right hand, mindlessly relaying postmortem events. Repulsed Christmas revelers darted around the growing pool of red without offer of help. The cops would surely come.

Courtney had witnessed the killing from her dark alleyway hiding place. She sensed that the two big men who had murdered her stalker were also looking for her and plotted to kill her as well. She had to move and quickly—her mommy and the man had just returned. They were all dressed up like they had been to a Christmas party. She thought her mommy looked really pretty, but the fancy clothes didn't do much for the odd looking man.

Within minutes, the police and ambulances arrived at the crime scene, attracting a large crowd of gawkers as they cordoned off the area with yellow crime tape and snapped photographs of the dead man for evidence. Courtney chose her moment and hurried for the gaudy entry of the Estrada. Though she wore ragged jeans and a dirty sweatshirt, she was well-covered by a heavy Diane von Furstenberg winter coat that she had stolen. The thick fur lining of the hood obscured her twisted face, and she looked like any other rich New Yorker caught in a blizzard.

⅋

"Wanda! Wanda!" Jerrod screamed.

Wanda emerged from the shower dripping wet, holding a towel before her. "Jerrod, what on earth is the matter?"

"It's Sam, Sam Lugar. I think he was killed while I was speaking to him on the telephone. He was outside Susan's apartment in New York."

"Killed ... are you certain; who in the hell could have done it?"

"I don't know, but he said two men were following him. He also said that he had spotted Courtney in the area and was close to apprehending her. God, I can't think—what to do!"

"Jerrod, start by calming down. Then get on the telephone and call your lawyer. Despite the holiday, she'll know exactly what to do."

Wesley looked out the window; there was only snow and more snow. Deep drifts were forming and visibility approached zero. The foghorn complained in the distance.

"Forget it! There is absolutely no way for you to get to New York tonight."

Jerrod nodded and picked up his cell phone and dialed Barbara Barnes' home number. Her husband, Robert, answered in a rather harsh tone but apologized for his rudeness once he understood there was an emergency. After a short delay Barbara came on the line.

"Jerrod?"

"Oh, God, Barbara, I think Sam's been killed. I was speaking with him on the telephone. He was outside Susan's high rise, and there was a gun shot and then nothing but New York City street noise. He said that he had spotted Courtney a few times in that area, and two men, thugs he called them, had been following him. Other than to call you, I didn't know what to do."

"My God, Sam dead; I just can't believe it. Whatever has happened, you did the right thing by calling me. I'm going to contact the Central Park precinct which has jurisdiction over Central Park West. Probably start with the detective squad; maybe even reach the crime scene. I'm going to give them your name and number, inform them of the two possible suspects, and let them know that your daughter, a mentally ill fugitive, is in the immediate area. As for Susan, I feel we have to do something, so, once again, I am going to notify her lawyer. She can do as she pleases, but it is Christmas, you know."

Jerrod considered that Susan might even know about the murder, given her allegiances, but said, "OK, do it."

♎

Courtney's hands shook as she removed the electronic card key from her pocket. Her mother had given it to her some months ago when she came for a visit. Had the entry code been changed? As she reached for the card reader slot, there was a loud buzz and the glass door swung open before her. A grinning black gentleman in a doorman's uniform welcomed her in from the cold. Before he could engage her in conversation, a group of loud visitors at the door demanded his attention. There was an elevator waiting with its door open in the B bank that accessed the twenty-third floor. The door closed with a rumble, and she was up and away before the old man had finished signing in the group of visiting merrymakers headed to a wealthy investment banker's Christmas party in the penthouse.

The elevator ride to her mother's floor seemed to take an eternity, and the grating music didn't help, yet it was just a matter of minutes. She stood motionless for a time, fingering the straight razor in her coat pocket. It felt cold and hungry to her touch. She knew that it was still flecked with the blood of her previous victims, but soon there would be more, so much more. She turned left and silently crossed the hundred feet of plush carpet, pausing for a moment to run her fingers over a massive piece of expensive furniture that served no purpose. She started to knock but remembered the card key. There was a low buzz, and Courtney pushed the heavy door partway open. Mommy was listening to Christmas music, but no one was in the living room to the right or the office to the left. Courtney was breathing hard; revenge was hers for the taking, and the time was *now*. Her coat and gloves fell to her feet, and a flick of the wrist revealed the razor's gleaming blade. The master bedroom was at the end of a dimly lit hallway and Courtney was there in a flash. The bedroom door was ajar, and the girl chanced a peek.

He, the man who was pretending to be her daddy, was there, asleep in a reclining chair. A half-empty glass of amber liquid rested on the small table beside him, and its strong whiskey aroma drifted across the room and repulsed her. His ostrich-like neck stretched awkwardly over the back of the chair, and his head with its mop of red hair bobbed with his loud snores. Her mommy's voice rose above the sounds of the shower as she sang along with the Christmas music playing on their expensive Bang and Olufsen sound system. Bing Crosby was dreaming of a white Christmas—how appropriate.

The slash was delivered with a power beyond that of any normal, young woman, and the investment banking genius' throat was cut from from ear to ear. Anders Boreson died with a quiet gurgle.

Satisfied that the bad man who was not her daddy was dead, Courtney turned her attention to her mother. The room was full of steam, and the distorted figure of the woman who had destroyed Courtney's life moved easily to the music behind the shower's frosted glass. The girl removed her clothes and entered the shower with the straight razor concealed behind her back.

"Hello, Mommy!"

Susan's eyes grew large and she brought her hands to her mouth, but her scream was silent. "C ... Courtney?"

"Mommy, why did you and that bad man hurt me so?"

"We ... tried ... to ... help ..."

Her foolish words were cut short by the flash of the straight razor waved before her eyes by a trembling hand.

"Anders!" she screamed, "Anders!"

"Mommy, I'm sorry; he's dead. I just killed him, and now I have to kill you too."

Susan's foolish move for the shower door was blocked by a slash of cold steel. Her scream reverberated throughout the apartment, but it, like her life, was cut short. Sparkling droplets of condensation on the shower door disappeared in a deluge of crimson, smeared by flailing hands, and then all was quiet except for the hiss of the shower and Bing Crosby's gentle voice. Courtney had dispatched her mother with the technique perfected on Anders Boreson—a single powerful cut to the neck, severing everything that mattered. Still clutching the blade, Courtney dragged her mother's lifeless body from the shower and tossed her into Boreson's lap like she was nothing.

She whispered, "I know that you would rather be with him for Christmas than with Daddy and me."

The bloody girl returned to the shower and enjoyed her first good scrub in weeks. She dried carefully with a big, fluffy bath towel that smelled nice and then turned to her mother's closet. It was crammed with overpriced garments that meant nothing to the demented girl. She finally selected some designer jeans and a nice sweater and tried them on after removing the price tags. They fit perfectly as did a new pair of hiking boots. A search of the residence, billfolds, and purses provided several thousand dollars in travel money. She slipped her heavy coat back on and was half-way out the door when the telephone rang.

Curious, or merely from habit, she picked the up the receiver and said, "Hello," in a voice muffled by her gloved hand.

"Susan? God, I'm so glad I got you. I have to warn you ..."

Courtney grinned, showing green teeth, and made good her escape.

26

Lay the Dead to Rest

Jerrod stared at the worn, old pine floor as the choir and congregation sang the last refrains of *Safe in the Arms of Jesus*. Somehow it brought his tragic daughter to mind more than his murdered, estranged wife. Susan was beyond rescue and would soon be laid to rest and have to answer to God for what she had done. Indeed, Courtney was the fallen angel who he prayed was *safe in someone's arms*. Though she sat far back in the old chapel, Jerrod could feel Wanda's love and support flowing through his wracked soul. However, it was Barbara Barnes that sat by him and touched his hand. Thank God for a good lawyer who had become a fast friend and always seemed to know what to do.

Just a few days before, it had been Jerrod who provided the comfort to Barbara when her long-time associate, Sam Lugar, was buried. Although a careless moment had placed the tough man in his grave, there he would find his own peace. Sam had been a man who had placed honor and virtue above all else. He had come so close to rescuing Courtney from herself. So very close.

And now what? Although he was convinced that Courtney had killed Susan and her lover, the NYPD was not. It was logical for them to believe that the three murders that took place at virtually the same time at the same place were somehow linked. To further convince them, several witnesses had come forward and given rough descriptions of the men who had killed Sam on that busy street. The old, black doorman at the Estrada was half-blind and didn't remember admitting two tough-looking thugs, much less an ordinary-looking girl. He simply wasn't a reliable witness. The security camera revealed nothing of interest, either.

Maybe the cops would catch the two murderers; maybe not. He had to talk to Barbara about who else they might put on the case, if anyone would take it knowing the risk.

The snow transitioned to rain, and the brief thaw turned the dirty snow to mush. The trip to the cemetery was heart-rending. No matter what she had done, Susan had been a loyal wife at one time, and he *had* loved her. Jerrod had loved her with all his heart, and she had given him his beautiful Courtney. The finality of it all washed over him like an angry, gray sea as the late afternoon rain and gloom slid toward darkness. Thankfully, the graveside service would be brief. Jerrod closed his eyes and tried to remember the good things; it was William Faulkner who said, "The past is never dead, it isn't even past." Indeed, he had met Susan in the shadow of Rowan Oak, the home place of that famous author. The past came to him through bitter tears, and it seemed like yesterday.

He had been an out-of-place nerd at a big Chi Omega sorority party at Ole Miss when he met the beautiful girl in the heart of her universe. Susan Carter was president of the prestigious sorority and surrounded by her football player date, fawning frat-cats, and jealous sorority sisters. Susan had come from Greenville in the heart of the Mississippi Delta and was the only child of rich parents who had also graduated from Ole Miss. Her father, *Buster* Carter, owned a towboat line that pushed hundreds of heavily-laden barges up and down the Mississippi River. Her mother, Cathleen Carter, had also been a Chi Omega, so Susan was a legacy on fast track to run the sorority and had become the chapter's seventy-fifth president. Despite his own cute date, Jerrod had fallen for Susan, almost at first sight. The only reason that he had been at the party in the first place was that his date, Mandy Leigh Pennebaker, had invited him in return for his help on an organic chemistry exam. She had made her B in the course and presumably that would be good enough to get her into medical school and fulfill her life's dream.

The evening ended in a friend's apartment in downtown Oxford where Mandy had too much to drink, not much in her case, and became aggressively amorous; she called it grateful. But Jerrod simply couldn't get Susan out of his mind and resisted the tipsy girl's best efforts. He called Susan for a date the next day, and much to his surprise she accepted. The rest is history—a history that had unraveled to this horrible end: an empty spool and then a broken line. Jerrod shook his head; it all brought a quote from Willie Morris' *My Dog Skip* to mind: *it's not the game, it's skip. He's gone for good.*

Jerrod shook his head and returned to the present; it was raining harder now, and his umbrella served little purpose. Someone, something, spoke to him, and he jerked around, but it was only the voice of the howling wind. He stood back from Susan's immediate family and said his last good-byes in his own way. Finally, it was all over, time to retreat and escape to Wanda's waiting arms. There, he would find solace and perhaps some answers.

27

Mid-January, 2011

FDA Commissioner Averill Hampton studied the faces of the professional bureaucrats seated around his conference room table. Although he wore his poker face well, he laughed inside. Expressions ranged from glee to fear to outright horror. Most notably, Alan Werner had developed a satisfying twitch along the right side of his tense face. There was almost no reason to hold this meeting to discuss the fate of Medulin; he could *read* the votes right now.

Hampton finally smiled, revealing his own position. "Gentlemen, we are assembled here today to discuss the fate of Apex Pharmaceuticals' new drug, Medulin. Despite this drug having been assigned special status by CDER, it has experienced a rocky road in its development; patients in company protocols have died, some violently. Now, we are even faced with possible fraud and worse. There are many issues, but the first thing we are going to discuss this morning is likely irregularities in an important toxicology study submitted to the FDA in support of the drug's safety." Hampton looked around the room to make certain that everyone was listening.

"To preface this discussion, Gentlemen, the problem came to light when a Stamford, Connecticut law firm representing Jerrod Wesley, head of research at Genplex, delivered a copy of a report that differed substantially from the one officially submitted to the FDA by Apex. You all know that story by now and how it all came about. The first order of business is to determine which report represents the true toxicological profile of Medulin. To that end, Dr. Kendall, David, what do you have?"

The Director, Division of Psychiatric Products, stood and made his own survey of faces before he said, "Sir, at your request, I recently sent a group inside Apex to audit the *official* Medulin report and compare it to the newly discovered version. I would like to thank Roger Paisley and his team of field auditors for getting this done in record time. Roger, would you summarize your findings for the group?"

Paisley struggled to drag his considerable bulk from the uncomfortable, government-issue chair and walked to the front of the room. By the time he spoke he was sweating profusely. "Ah, Gentlemen, I wish this was more cut-and-dried, but it isn't. The two reports are identical except for the neurological aspects. The notebooks, necropsy data, tissue slides, and so on all support the version submitted to the FDA. There was no evidence of central nervous system damage seen in any of the data we examined. However, when we really tortured the data, we thought it was just too clean. The usual random abnormalities we see in almost all toxicology studies were missing. There were also some questionable cases of connectivity between the various levels of data. The data in the newly discovered report looks much more believable, but there is no notebook or necropsy data to back it up. In my opinion, what we have here is a carefully orchestrated case of fraud that *I cannot prove.*"

Alan Werner practically exploded from his chair. This was better than he dreamed, and it was time for a little grandstanding. "You *believe* that the report was fabricated, but you have no proof? That's not worth the powder it would take to blow the thing to hell! You have nothing, and we can't rule based on *nothing.*"

Paisley was breathing hard and mopped the sweat from his brow. "I agree; that alone is not enough to make a decision on the drug; however, when one considers the *gestalt* of the thing, the picture becomes clearer. For instance, I have had an opportunity to review some interesting human cell biology data generated at Genplex that clearly shows that Medulin is toxic to human neurons in culture."

Werner shouted, "Genplex! My God, they are simply trying to damage their competition. Who would believe this?"

Paisley answered in a calm voice. "I, for one, do. This data was generated in a Genplex study comparing analogs of Axilon and Medulin some time ago. It was provided to Apex with the assumption that they would review it and then forward it along to the FDA, but they did not."

Werner was nearly boiling over, but his impending tirade was prevented by Averill Hampton. "Gentlemen! Gentlemen! Let's be calm here. Alan, we all appreciate your strong feelings about the value of this drug, but it is our job to protect the public, and if we err, to err on the side of safety. Now, it is my understanding that there is a building body of clinical adverse event data that is consistent with neurological problems. David, what is your thinking at this point?"

"Well, my thinking is that this drug worries me a lot. For one thing, there seems to be a trail of bodies wherever Medulin goes. First the Apex toxicologist, Alton Wally, then the two violent suicides in the Jonathan Smith study. Not to mention Abraham Snyder's patient—Boudreaux, I think—who killed Smith's nurse, raped and murdered three innocent bystanders in an alley, and finally kidnapped and raped a young nursing student, before he committed suicide."

Kendall glanced at his boss before continuing, "And this crazy business with Jerrod Wesley's daughter is most bizarre of all. She was illegally given Medulin by her now deceased mother who had some relationship with Apex. The poor girl lost her mind, but not entirely; seemingly she was functional enough to get even. The Wesley girl's mother and her mother's boyfriend were murdered in their upscale New York City residence. By the way, that was the same evening that a private investigator looking for the Wesley daughter was also killed outside the place. Oh, yeah, and Courtney Wesley knocked off one of her teachers before she left the Duke campus. That particular Medulin casualty is still on the loose. More subtle, but never-the-less important, are the growing number of psychiatric adverse events leading to drop-outs across the many Medulin trials."

"And," Werner interjected, "let's not forget that Medulin is probably the most effective drug for the treatment of psychiatric disorders we have ever seen. Your view seems to overlook that fact, Dr. Kendall! Those admittedly horrible *anecdotal* observations you mentioned likely have nothing to do with Medulin. Let's look at them in more detail. Apex reports that there were randomization errors in the Jonathan Smith study, and the two patients that committed suicide never received Medulin. They were on placebo. They ..."

"*Apex reports*! That is pure bull shit, and it will be revealed when the study is completed, and we audit the damned thing," David Kendall shouted.

Werner looked at Kendall as though he were pond scum and continued, "And as for the Cajun, Mr. Boudreaux, he was schizophrenic with homicidal ideations before Snyder ever enrolled him—a clear protocol violation."

Hampton held up his hand and asked, "How can we be so certain about that, Alan?"

"Mr. Boudreaux has a long history of psychiatric disorders; before he was entered into the Snyder protocol, Dr. Pierce McCafferty at Whitfield in Mississippi had made a diagnosis of schizoaffective disorder with depression being prominent. I have spoken to this man and have no reason to doubt him."

Kendall shook his head and said, "Snyder is a perfectionist; hard to believe he made such a mistake."

"All this makes me nervous," Hampton asserted, "but, this mess with the Wesley girl is nothing short of a disaster. How in the hell did her mother get her hands on a closely controlled experimental drug?"

Kendall, fearing another whitewash by Werner, blurted, "Susan Wesley had connections with Apex through Sirius Financial Investment Bank. She is—was—an analyst for them and covered Apex in some sort of a cozy relationship. However the woman got her hands on the drug, it was quite illegal; mind you."

"Yeah, and it makes me nervous that Jerrod Wesley is right in the middle of all this," Werner said, trying to divert a conversation that was rapidly going wrong. "Besides, we have absolutely no proof that the girl ever took one Medulin tablet."

Hampton stared daggers at the arrogant psychiatrist, registering his displeasure with the man's obstinate personality. He sighed and moved on. "Now, David, what were you saying about the dropout rates?"

Kendall nodded. "Not so much about the rates as the causes; almost all dropouts are from central nervous system side effects, and most of those are psychiatric in nature."

Hampton called a brief recess for a cooling down period and then brought them back for final considerations. He looked each of the participants in the eye before he spoke. "I am tempted to put Medulin on clinical hold until all of these issues are fully fleshed-out and resolved. I agree with Dr. Werner that Medulin has breakthrough therapeutic potential. However, I also side with the rest of you in believing that the drug potentially has dangerous side effects. It is very difficult for me to believe that all these horrendous observations are just random noise." He paused and looked up at the stained ceiling as if seeking divine inspiration.

"I would also submit to you that Apex Pharmaceuticals is likely guilty of wrongdoing on several counts, maybe outright fraud with regard to the toxicology report and handling of clinical trials. However, I am not yet ready to turn this mess over to the Justice Department, but I am close. What say you?"

After a long and heated debate with Alan Werner leading the charge for Medulin, a compromise was reached. The FDA would audit all ongoing Medulin trials with priority given to the clinical studies where glaring problems had occurred. Apex would repeat the rat two-year toxicology study with an independent contractor and FDA oversight. Since this was a long-term project, Apex would be required to immediately sponsor a study of the effects of Medulin on human neurons in cell culture, similar to the Genplex work. This would be done at an established academic laboratory with FDA oversight. A letter would be drafted to the company delineating these requirements in no uncertain terms. It would be signed by the Commissioner, Alan Werner, and David Kendall.

It was an unhappy decision that pleased no one, but before the work day was done, the letter had been drafted, signed, and sent by registered, express mail to Maxwell Hall at Apex. Hampton considered that it was a real loss whenever an important, new drug got into trouble, but fortunately, this time a seemingly safe drug from the same therapeutic class would be discussed at the FDA tomorrow.

28

A Rough Road, Driven with Care

The discovery and development of a safe and effective new drug that offers therapeutic advantages over existing treatments is a daunting, low probability undertaking that involves hundreds of scientists and physicians and places many millions of dollars at risk. *There are no shortcuts* to success, though there are endless pressures on those involved to take chances and speed up the process. A good Indianapolis 500 race car driver understands the fine line between winning and hitting the wall and doesn't cross it. Jerrod Wesley knew he was such a person, if a bit of a procrastinator, and he could live with his scientific and strategic decisions regarding Axilon. He shook his head as he considered the competitive program with Medulin at Apex. In his mind they were a bunch of dishonest fools and had not only hurt themselves but injured and killed others in their refusal to stop and reevaluate. There was a growing list of Medulin casualties, and his daughter Courtney was among the walking wounded.

Jerrod found a smile as the long meeting wound down; it could not have gone better from his point of view. A great deal of time had been put into the preparation of the Axilon end of Phase II meeting with the FDA. His scientific, clinical, and statistical people had been challenged by their FDA equivalents, guided by David Kendall at every turn. They had met, even exceeded, the challenge and had been forced to concede little. Unlike most drug company advocates, Jerrod had identified the therapeutic and safety problems upfront, even burying the schizophrenia application in his opening statement. Beyond that, the splendid data obtained from the depression and anxiety disorder trials had spoken for itself. He felt that David Kendall had been more than helpful at times; it was obvious that Kendall wanted to see this important drug move into massive Phase III trials and defeat Medulin. If his nemesis, Alan Werner, went down with it, so much the better. Jerrod smiled; seemingly things at FDA had changed for the better.

Jerrod's main problem had been ignoring his irritating boss who sat beside him. Often Alonsio didn't understand the proceedings and his twitches and near convulsions had been distracting. The old man had, thankfully, kept his mouth shut and now could share the heartfelt joy of victory with the others.

As they filed out of the crowded room, Alonsio said, "Jerrod, congratulations; you have done a fine job with this project, and we are all grateful. I know that you have accomplished this at a very difficult time in your personal life, and we are all the more grateful for your sacrifices. I will call Mr. Albright with the good news as soon as we get out of here. He will say that it is time to involve the business people and prepare the world for Axilon."

Jerrod nodded, quickly wiping away a tear, and made his way through the mob toward his people. They, too, had done a splendid job and deserved his praise and a good lunch. Somehow, the term *business people* resonated. Free trips to Japan with the hard-drinking, Genplex marketing types wasn't exactly his cup of tea; however, it was one of the trappings of success in the industry. But where was Courtney? How could he become a world traveler when he didn't know where his daughter was or what she was dealing with?

℥

The chill of the season permeated Maxwell Hall's office with the receipt of the FDA's letter detailing concerns and requirements for Medulin. Although Hall had received a heads-up telephone call from Alan Werner, Werner had downplayed the seriousness of the situation. The letter in Hall's hands was so damning, so hot, that it almost burned his hands. For once he was at a loss for words and could only shake his head as the Apex Chairman of the Board read his copy aloud. After a while, Schwartz finished reading the document. "Jesus! They don't trust us one little bit, Maxwell; they want studies repeated by outside laboratories under their oversight, and they actually want to audit all of our clinical trials before they are complete."

"I know, but that's what they say."

"And that bastard, Werner, where was he when they were deciding all this?"

Hall sighed. "He was sitting right there, fighting for Medulin, but the FDA Commissioner has taken control of the issue, and Alan is a lone voice in the wilderness. However, he may be the only reason the Justice Department isn't involved—yet."

The old man was ashen. "Are we going to jail, Maxwell?"

"I can't speak for you, Murray, but I, for one, do not intend to be incarcerated for even one minute. Let's not overreact; they haven't killed the drug, and the studies go on. Russell Turner and his clinical staff have made some meaningful adjustments in dosage and therefore we should see fewer side effect problems. I intend to push this thing as far as it will go."

"Well, you can't erase what's already happened out there; can you? And I have to tell you, Maxwell, that Wesley girl worries me a lot. All the trouble she's caused and whatever she has yet to do is going to be blamed on Medulin—on us. What have those two goons accomplished since you sent them out there to, to *exterminate* her other than to kill a harmless private investigator?"

"The *harmless*, as you call him, PI was close to catching up to her, which would have been a disaster for us. He was working for Wesley and his damned lawyer. Unfortunately, our agents have lost her. After the last murders they tracked her to Florida, to Miami, actually, and she melted into the streets. They'll find her though; Sergei Mogilevish and Vadik Nikolsky are real pros. Bastards are the best the Russian Mafia has to offer, and they know how to kill people and make bodies evaporate."

Schwartz gave the evil executive a hard look; he made murder sound like a work of art. "Not reassuring," the old man quipped. "Not reassuring at all. Every cop in the country is looking for her, and likely her father has someone new on the case. You have us way out on a limb, Maxwell, and you're just sawing away like it's no big deal. Don't you know when to cut bait and move on to more fertile water with fewer sharks?"

Hall made a great ceremony out of lighting up a cigar and blew several perfect, blue smoke rings at the ceiling. He sneered at the old fool as he replied, "I thought you knew me better than that, Murray. I think you're getting too old for this business. Maybe you should retire to some old folks home in South Florida."

Murray Schwartz had long ago made the decision to ride out his final days with the company in grace, no matter what Maxwell Hall said or did, but he snapped at Hall's Machiavellian display. Schwartz's face reddened and he spat back, "Maxwell, I know you have a low opinion of me, but I must say you are a *little person* in more ways than one. Unlike you, I can see the big picture and know when it's time to ride a new horse. Medulin is dead; fucking face it, and it's time to move on with something better before you destroy the company and us along with it. We'll all end up in a Federal Correctional Institution at this rate."

Maxwell grinned and said, "Gee, Murray, I didn't know you had that much piss and vinegar left in you. I'm interested in your line of thinking; exactly what new pony do you propose we saddle up and ride?"

"Genplex's Axilon just got approval to move into Phase III with the full support of the FDA. David Kendall loves the damned thing. Let's face it, Hall; Genplex just gained the upper hand." Schwartz sat back and relaxed; he had finally expressed his opinion about something and had a little girl's *so there* etched on his face.

"Surely, you don't think they're going to sell their pipeline front-runner to us under any circumstances?"

Once again, Hall wasn't even thinking inside the box, much less outside of it, and Murray replied impatiently, "No, I don't think so, but we could *buy the damned company*. We certainly have the cash, don't we?"

Hall chewed on the option for a moment and said, "Yes, I suppose we could. I had considered that possibility earlier but thought the stock price was too high. It's trading at one hundred dollars, give or take, and the price is mostly based on Axilon hype and ballyhoo. They have some earnings and patent issues. Their board would never let them sell the company. It would have to be a hostile takeover, and those don't work. Moreover, there's a lot of institutional ownership, and the only way we could get controlling interest is to send the stock into a nosedive, drive the shorts into it, and spread some rumors. That shouldn't be hard; our friends at Sirius could help with this. As a start, their new biotech analyst—when they find one—needs to initiate coverage of their stock, GPX, and see that it begins to tank. We could do a so called *creeping tender* offer and buy it all the way down and get a good average price."

"That may work, but one way or the other, we'll kill the bastards and get what we want," Murray concluded.

29

Key West

ourtney nervously fingered her straight razor as she turned off
Duval Street and entered the dark doorway of Roberto's Tattoo
and Piercing Parlor. This would be the last stage of her grand
transformation. Though she did not trust the strange people that
worked in the place, they were artists in their own right, Rembrandts
with tattoo needles and drug issues. Her face and body were already
adorned with tattoos and black makeup; the final piercing would
be completed before the afternoon was over. The art work and fa-
cial jewelry would complement her spiked, orange-red hair, and she
would no longer be readily identifiable as Courtney Wesley. Seemingly safe in Key West, Courtney 's condition had somewhat stabilized,
and Courtney had snagged a bartender job in a Key West dive that
catered to a weird assortment of wanna-be pirates, Goths, and heavily tattooed lesbians. Bat Cave was not visited by normal college students or executive-types, and the fearful cops came only when called.
Courtney had fallen in love with the curious patrons who shared her
new fascination with the macabre.

After an hour of painful piercing procedures, she selected her
jewelry, paid the large bill, and walked out a new girl. The addition
of a nasallang, lip ring, several eyebrow studs, multiple earrings, and
tongue stud completed the look. She would add the large crucifix,
black Victorian dress, and black, painted nails when she returned
home, a small apartment near Bat Cave shared with three other girls
of similar persuasion. Courtney did not share their proclivity for
drugs, knowing that she carried the heavy footprint of a really bad one
on her brain every day. All four girls were sought by desperate families and the police. Key West was a place where the fugitives would
not be noticed; nevertheless, they mostly avoided the busy streets by
day. Courtney had shed all forms of identification and had dumped

the last car that she had stolen. Any automobile, stolen or not, made it easy to track down people.

Courtney had stopped by the apartment to finish preparing for her next shift and entered the Bat Cave dressed in full regalia for the first time. It took her senses a moment to adjust to the darkness and noise. The bar was packed, and two bands played death rock and gothic rock simultaneously. The music stopped, and the menagerie of patrons whistled and clapped. Finally, Courtney got it; they were applauding her transformation into a true Goth—one of them. She, Courtney Wesley, was now a part of a dark, inner world, and *they* could never find her and punish her for what she had done or might do. From this point forward she would be known only by her Goth name, Samara. In a sense, she had been awarded her bat wings. Samara was ready to soar with the best of them.

Samara had mixed drinks for the late night shift for a full month and had gotten to know more of the regulars each evening. Most were harmless enough people enjoying a place where they could be different, but a few probably were dangerous. Remarkably, there was little trouble at Bat Cave; like a bumblebee on its favorite flower, even the craziest patron felt it a place for calm. Samara winked at the toothless pirate grinning at her and poured two shots of Old Crow over an ice cube without being asked. The routine and the regulars were established in her mind. She knew something about each of them, especially what they drank. Samara glanced at her watch and saw that it was nearing the end of her shift—there was no official closing time—when she spotted two men entering the bar who were not regulars and did not seem to belong. They were both large, powerful men who could be former wrestlers or professional football players going to fat. Yet, they seemed to be familiar in some other context. In her mind, Samara replaced their gaudy tourist clothes with business suits and immediately knew who they were. They were the men who had killed her pursuer on that bloody street in New York. How had they tracked her here? Key West was a good bet, and they were checking all the bars? Likely.

The two sauntered up to the bar and sat on stools directly in front of Samara's station. Both men looked through her when they ordered their drinks, vodka straight up. They sipped their drinks quietly while they surveyed the scene.

The fatter of the two said, "Wrong place," and turned to the girl. "Sam-ara," he read from her nametag, "have you ever seen this girl in here?" Both men spoke with a heavy Russian accent—Russian Mafia.

Samara took the picture and pretended to examine it carefully. She smiled and popped her gum. "Nope, don't get no regular co-ed types in here. Just look around you, man." Sweat trickled down her back; was the bastard going to recognize her? She fingered the razor in her pocket—she would kill at least one of them if he did.

The man downed his drink, turned to his partner, and said, "Let's go." As soon as they were gone, Samara ran after them, holding back in the darkness as she followed the red glow of two cigarettes bobbing across the sandy parking lot. A light came on, doors slammed and the dirty Mercedes headed for the single exit; it would come right by her.

She strained her eyes but managed to read the dirty New York license plate and jotted the number down on her waitress' pad. All she had to do was call the cops, and they would have the two wanted murderers. Samara considered the possibilities as she made her way back to her station. Calling the local cops might generate subtle clues leading to her. She couldn't kill them if she didn't know how to find them, so what to do? Then Samara remembered her father's lawyer; the papers had reported that the murdered investigator had been working for her, hadn't they. She still had Barbara Barnes card someplace; her father had given it to her just before she departed her old life for good. Once back inside, she borrowed a recently stolen cell phone with an East Coast number from a friend. Although her watch registered a very late hour—3:00 a.m., she dialed Barbara's home telephone number.

Three rings and a sleepy, "Hello, this is Barbara Barnes."

"Listen carefully and write this down," Samara hissed, like a snake. "The men who killed your investigator in New York, and I'm giving them to you free of charge. They are both Russians."

"Gi ... giv ... Go ahead."

Samara gave a very detailed description of both men along with a good description of the Mercedes and its New York license plate number. She said, "Good luck!" and hung up without waiting for a reply.

Barbara looked at the buzzing receiver; she was angry that sleepy cobwebs had prevented her from being her usual perceptive self. The caller had obviously been a woman and hissed like a snake, an intentional inflection. She jotted down the caller id number but knew that was a dead end likely not worth following up on. All she could do was wait until morning and call Randy Hull, the NYPD detective in charge of the case. She sensed the information was valid and might lead the police to Sam's killers and to the puppet master who was pulling their strings. Barbara shook her head; who had made this unexpected call and why?

Though the tiny island had been home to Samara for several weeks, she was witnessing her first Key West sunrise. Normally, that magical moment found the girl tucked in her bed, lost in a deep and exhausted sleep. The emotional experience of being inches from those who would kill her and having survived the moment had been a nerve-wracking experience as had the phone call to Barbara Barnes, although to a lesser extent. The emotional stress had stimulated her injured brain to an excited state—a do-loop of uncontrollable, racing thoughts and emotional electricity. The rising of the sun, a ball of red fire floating on a pink and blue horizon, somehow calmed, yet sad-dened, the girl. The sand was cool and damp as it filtered between her fingers, and small shells collected in her hand. Waves washed closer with the incoming tide, but she did not rise to avoid them. She had slammed all the important doors of her life, and there was nothing for her but sadness and loneliness and the sea could have her.

"Hello, strange creature; what's your name?"

Samara turned and looked up into the pale blue eyes of a hand-some, young man. He was tall with an unruly shock of blond hair and a spattering of freckles about his nose. He wore red athletic shorts and expensive running shoes—an early morning jogger. The gorgeous boy reminded her of Seth Simpson, her almost forgotten Duke football player boyfriend, and she managed a smile as he squatted beside her.

"Samara," she finally managed, "Samara."

"Are you OK?" he asked.

"Y ... yes," she lied.

"I'm Josh Ledbetter—make that Dr. Josh Ledbetter. I recently completed my medical training and have arrived in Key West to min-ister to God's lost children who hide here. You look like my first pa-tient; may I give you a ride someplace?"

Samara hesitated to interact with anyone outside the tight-knit Goth community, but this boy-like young man had a strange appeal she could not resist. It was as though he radiated a warm glow that soothed, encompassed. Besides, she was so tired that her legs were like rubber, and she might not make it the few blocks to her apart-ment.

Josh helped the wet, sandy girl the short distance to his PT Cruiser convertible and followed her directions. He explained as they drove that he was a medical missionary for the Southern Baptist Conven-tion, sent to Key West to help those poor souls who lived outside the system and were often beyond help. Samara told him a completely made-up story about her life, though she knew he knew she was fib-bing. Maybe someday she would tell him the truth.

Presently, they arrived at her dilapidated apartment complex, and Josh smiled and said, "Samara, if you become ill, or ever need help, here is my business card." Samara reached for the card, but Josh held on to it for a long second. "I suspect there is a pretty girl behind all that paint and heavy metal. How can I contact you?"

Samara blushed and almost turned and ran, but how could she dis this beautiful guy who had come to help and seemingly passed no judgment? "I have no phone, but I work at the ... Bat Cave. You can find me there any night after ten, along with a lot of other sick, lost souls."

Josh sped away with a laugh, and Samara stood there for a long time as the little convertible disappeared in the distance. She touched her nasallang, and for the first time wondered what she had become.

30

Some Flowers Bloom in May

Wanda laughed and squeezed Jerrod's hand. The happy woman's baby blue eyes sparkled in the early May sunshine. Though the Connecticut shoreline is seldom blessed with anything that sells as real springtime in May, an eddy of warm air had escaped from the south, providing a much appreciated, if fleeting, beautiful Sunday afternoon. Early spring flowers bloomed in profusion in the gardens of fine homes, adding to the optimistic feel of the season. Even the ubiquitous gulls complained less. It was a perfect day for a walk along the Madison waterfront, and Wanda and Jerrod joined many others in celebrating the end of winter's cold wind and gray skies. A few of the braver ones even wore shorts.

Wanda wiggled her ring finger at Jerrod, pretending to show off her engagement ring; it was an inconspicuous platinum band, thin, with no stone. It was not meant to be noticed but to bind the couple in their loving relationship until the day came when she could wear the big diamond that rested impatiently in Jerrod's safe. Then, their future marriage could be announced to the world. A few busy eyes at Genplex had registered the ring, but so far no one had chosen to comment, even though the cat was mostly out of the bag by this time. Most employees grieved for Jerrod and what he had been through—was still going through. They also secretly applauded Jerrod's relationship with Wanda and wished them the best.

The upstairs porch of the Madison Beach Hotel was a perfect destination for lunch after their long walk along the shore. The simple, but delicious, food complimented the splendid view of sand, birds, rocks, and water. A little girl chased crabs in a cold tidal pool, and Wanda watched Jerrod push a tear away. She understood; the pretty child could have been Courtney a few years ago.

Wanda touched his shoulder. "I'm sorry, Jerrod, so sorry."

146

He nodded, unable to speak, and wiped his eyes. Regaining composure, Jerrod said, "I've heard from Barbara."

"Yes?"

"She, she has somehow found another private investigator to take the case. Said she had a tough time after Sam's murder and none of their regulars would even consider such a dangerous assignment. Fortunately, one of them had a hungry associate who would take the work. The new PI is a fairly young black guy, former homicide detective from Atlanta, just getting started in the business. Apparently, the man has seen it all and isn't afraid of the devil."

"I guess there is plenty of devil to deal with in Atlanta. What's his name, Jerrod?"

"Jason Rand. Barbara says he may catch the Russians who killed Sam Lugar before the cops do; he has their descriptions and their license plate number. Naturally, that came from a stolen car, and who knows if they are still using it."

"Jerrod, who do you think made that call to Barbara and gave her that information about the killers?"

"I know what you're hinting at, but I don't think so. More likely someone close to them wants the bastards out of the picture. Sometimes I just want to get in my car and start driving, looking for Courtney, but that's just plain dumb. Unless she calls me or there is some substantial, new clue to her whereabouts, I am just going to have to trust in Rand and the police. And God."

Wanda saw that it was time to change the subject and asked, "How's Alonsio treating you these days?"

Jerrod grinned. "OK, I guess. He seems happy that our Axilon Phase II program was successful and that we now have a good chunk of Phase III up and running with carefully chosen investigators. On the other hand, he tells me that Mr. Albright is very unhappy about Wall Street and some funny business with the stock. Rhinner suspects that someone at Sirius is manipulating our shares. The share price takes these sudden, little dips for no reason, and then a big block of stock gets traded. Right now, it's just noise—nothing definitive. It's scary because our fundamentals aren't so hot, and Axilon's potential represents a good chunk of the GPX share price. Someone does a hatchet job on Axilon and GPX goes down the tube—at least until we prove them wrong."

"And more shares get traded in the meanwhile?"

"I think you get the picture, Wanda; what Mr. Albright really fears is that someone might try to hijack the company under these shaky circumstances."

♀

A short distance up the shoreline, in Groton, Maxwell Hall didn't give a damn about the nice weather as he paced about his office, wondering where his guests were. Sunday or not, they needed to be on time when they had an appointment with Maxwell Hall. He poured a small glass of cognac to calm his nerves, and just as he lit a Cuban cigar, security arrived with the two new Sirius employees.

The man spoke first as he shook hands with the Apex CEO, "Good to meet you, Mr. Hall. Sorry for our lateness; we got lost in that Pfizer rabbit warren. I'd like for you to meet our new biotech analyst, Lois Ackerman. I'm sure you've heard of her."

Davis Collingsworth had recently joined Sirius as Head of Health Care Investment Banking, replacing Anders Boreson after his untimely death. Collingsworth was English, an Oxford graduate, and had worked in London as an international investment banker with the Bank of England. His deportment was nothing like that of his predecessor; Collingsworth had a handsome, rugged look from his rugby days and exuded both mental and physical toughness. He had the richly affected speech of an educated Brit and used it to good advantage, particularly when dealing with what he saw as unsophisticated Americans.

Collingsworth introduced Lois with glowing accolades, as though she had discovered DNA while walking on water. However, Maxwell Hall knew all about Lois Ackerman—the analyst was a biotech hack from way back. She had the reputation as a hired gun that didn't let the facts get in the way of a big payout. Her expression was cold and calculating, almost reptilian. Lois Ackerman took no prisoners. Maxwell Hall had been instrumental in hiring the woman before Collingsworth came on the scene. No man would knowingly volunteer to have Lois Ackerman report to him, and frankly, Hall didn't care what Collingsworth did with her after the Genplex acquisition was a done deal.

Hall said, "I think we all know why we're here, so let's not waste time. Apex wants to buy Genplex in order to acquire Axilon. Your top management has agreed to bank the deal, which will be a creeping tender offer, meaning that we don't have to jump through the usual hoops related to Williams Act Provisions. We'll take care of feeding the shorts. As the price falls, your traders will buy every share of Genplex possible. This will continue until we have a controlling interest. The main problem is that Genplex management has played Axilon close to their chest and there has been no real Wall Street coverage of the drug. Apparently the public assumes the best, given the share price. OK, Davis, this is where you come in; let's hear it."

"Yes, I've had considerable experience in these matters myself—at the international level of course. If you'll just look at this simple prospectus I've prepared, based on the Genplex 10-K, you'll see the total number of shares, those owned by Genplex, and those outstanding and theoretically available. We should have little problem acquiring the needed number of shares, but time is not only money; it's everything. The share price needs to begin a steady fall. Now, our traders can help some by throwing lots of low balls; OK, Lois, you pick it up from here."

"Sirius will immediately initiate coverage of Genplex. I will get out an announcement and initial report based on public information this week. It won't say much other than plant some seeds of suspicion about this alleged miracle drug. No problem. First, I need to do some smoke and mirrors due diligence. I'll arrange a formal visit to the company—meet the CFO and the head of R&D. A thorough report will follow that key meeting. It will put some warts on Axilon—guaranteed. However, we simply must nail down my compensation before we proceed."

The discussion went on for another half-hour, and Hall concluded by saying, "Thank you for your time; I realize today is Sunday and you had plenty of other things to do. However, I can't emphasize the importance of this effort enough, and I needn't remind you that you both will have very large bonuses riding on the outcome. I'll put down the terms tomorrow, and you won't be disappointed. I'm not recommending anything illegal; just get the bloody thing done."

As soon as they were safely out of sight Maxwell grimaced and thought that those two arrogant asses would cast a nasty spell on just about anything they came in contact with, and Axilon was a wonderful place to start.

31

Clouds over Naples

Dark clouds boiled overhead as Dr. Jonathan Smith pulled his gold Jaguar convertible into his private parking place behind Naples Psychiatric Hospital. The tic-tic of the hot engine said something about how the powerful car had been driven. The muggy weather precisely reflected his mood. He didn't even notice the elegant landscaping and beautiful tropical flowers that provided privacy for the physicians passing through the entrance set aside for them. God, how he wished he had never heard of that damned drug, Medulin. In the end it had been the money that had broken his weak back; the thought of losing nearly two million dollars had been more than he could deal with, and he figured his new, trophy wife, Rhonda, would have left him. It had been several months since the FDA had paid him a visit. The auditors had looked in every nook and cranny but said very little while they were there. He had said even less—he was convinced that both Stacy Larkin and Benny Jackson had been on active drug when they died, and he wanted to scream foul play. He had remained quiet, however, hoping these FDA sleuths could follow the faint footprints to the truth and then throw Maxwell Hall in the slammer where he belonged. Smith thought he had detected at least a glimmer of excitement from them over the missing drug supplies and the study nurse who had disappeared into thin air. What had Hall done to her? Made her rich or killed her? The woman's family had heard no word and were frantically searching for her.

Smith removed his blue blazer and settled down behind his cluttered desk. The doctor groaned; his schedule indicated an unusually long list of patients for that morning. Most would be hypochondriacs, but some would have legitimate psychiatric conditions found in DSM-IV, the diagnostic bible for mental disorders. He wondered if he would find himself in the manual soon.

Smith examined several patients and remarkably most qualified for drug treatment and would be under his care for the foreseeable future. He was enjoying a well-earned coffee break when his assistant, Beverly, stuck her head in the door.

"How's it going today, Doctor?"

"Just fine, Bev."

"Well, Doctor, we've a tardy patient at the moment. Roberto Juarez is a Medulin outpatient in your depression protocol. He should have been here an hour ago for his routine rating and physical examination. Juarez had been reporting some difficulties, and we had planned to schedule an appointment with you to sort it out."

Given his morning ruminations, this was the last thing the psychiatrist wanted to hear and fearing the worst, reacted strongly. "Damn! Immediately seize his study meds and lock them in my personal safe. They can go back to the supply room when and if we find Juarez safe and sound."

"OK, but, Sir, don't you ..."

"No! After what happed to Larkin and Jackson, absolutely not! Send Julie in here right now!"

Presently, Julie Powell, Ramona Sanchez's replacement, stuck her head in the door with a quizzical look on her face. "Sir?"

"Where the hell is Juarez?"

"I wish I knew; we've repeatedly called his home number and his cell phone but no answer."

"Julie, now think; doesn't he have a large family? Shouldn't someone answer?"

"Doctor, I just don't know; our standard procedure when we have real concerns about a patient is to call the police and have them check the residence."

℞

Officers Terry McGuff and Monica Ray Watson were in the vicinity of 3456 Las Palmas Avenue when they got the seemingly routine call to check on a missing psychiatric outpatient. This is about as close to action as it gets in gentrified Naples, Florida, and they pulled up in front of the modest, but neat, home of Roberto Juarez and his extended family. Monica saw them first—rusty red footprints led from the front door to the street and ended abruptly at the curb.

"Look, Terry, that's blood. Call for back-up?"

"No, this may be some sort of medical emergency; let's check it out first. Probably nothing; this is Naples, you know?"

"Right as usual," she laughed. "Let's go."

The front door was ajar; both officers sensed real trouble and drew their revolvers. McGuff jabbed the door with his weapon, and it freely swung open with a slight squeak. The house was dark and very cool; an antiquated air conditioner hammered and hummed in the background. Several large, black crows cawed their objections from a nearby cabbage palm tree; otherwise it was quiet—too damned quiet.

Monica said, "It smells a lot like blood in here," and hit a light switch. "Oh, my God; there's blood everywhere. Terry, call for back-up and medical assistance. Right now!"

Although there was no one, dead or alive, in what of the house they could see from the entry, blood was indeed everywhere. There were puddles on the floor through which bodies had been dragged toward the back of the house. The walls of the kitchen and living room were covered with spatters, and several bloody handprints raked down the walls, recording the story of someone's last grasp at life.

The air conditioner cycled off with a clatter, and a hoarse breathing-gurgling could be heard from somewhere in the back of the house. Terry followed the ghastly sound with his police revolver drawn, leading the way, with his partner covering closely from behind. Both officers ducked low and charged the dark bedroom. The light was dim, but the dark lumps were immediately recognizable as bodies. Terry found a light switch, and Monica made a quick search of the other two bedrooms. The four children, two boys and two girls, had been neatly arranged in order of size on one bed. Their throats had been cleanly cut, and there was no sign of life. An older couple lay still on the other bed. The woman's throat was cleanly cut. The old man had been stabbed multiple times; maybe he had tried to resist his assailant. A naked woman about forty-five lay on the floor; she alone had multiple gunshot wounds but was still alive—barely. She was unconscious, but breathing and the awful gurgling sound originated from a gaping wound in her chest. It oozed frothy, red foam.

There was little they could do for the poor woman other than provide a pillow for her head and try to stem the flow of blood by applying pressure. Both officers were relieved to hear the sirens of approaching emergency vehicles, though they knew the shooting victim could not survive her terrible wounds.

℘

"Dr. Smith, sorry to interrupt, but you'd better take this call, Sir. In private."

Smith frowned at his assistant and apologized to the patient. Then he took the call in an empty examining room next door. "Yes?" he spat, fully anticipating trouble.

"Oh, sorry to bother you, Dr. Smith, this is Officer Monica Ray Watson, and this call is extremely urgent. We visited the Juarez resi-

dence as requested and found his family ... well, to be blunt, slaugh-
tered. Four children and an older couple, likely grandparents, are
dead, and a woman, the wife we think, is near death—dying. She was
shot, and the others butchered with a knife of some sort. Bloody footprints disappeared at the curb, so our best bet is that Roberto Juarez
killed his family and then fled the crime scene in his car that was
parked on the street. Every cop in Southwest Florida is searching for
him, but, Sir, you and your employees may be in danger. A police
officer is on the way to your office as we speak, but this is a critical
situation, and I would advise you to evacuate your patients and employees—right now!"

Smith paused for a moment, breathing hard, and said, "It will be
done. Everyone who can leave will leave—that excludes physicians,
nurses, and in-patients. We will lock the doors but welcome your pro-
tection."

He cradled the receiver and looked at the ceiling, mumbling
aloud, "I knew it. I just fucking knew it."

But Jonathan Smith personally had little cause to worry about
Roberto Juarez, who had other fish to fry. The crazed man's old
Ford Explorer rattled its way through the crowds of rich residents
and visitors and their expensive automobiles lining Fifth Avenue in
downtown Naples. He had always despised the real Americanos who
looked down on him and his family despite his good education and
modicum of success. His penniless father had brought his family
from the state of Oaxaca in Southern Mexico to realize the American dream. He had cooked in cheap Mexican restaurants while his
wife had cleaned gringo toilets to pay for their children's education.
He had not understood that the so-called American dream was reserved for white Anglo-Saxons. Spics and other such trash need not
apply. Though his father never once complained, the heavy weight
of bigotry had made Roberto sick, and then the drug had made him
crazy—homicidal. Roberto had killed his family to save them from
more disgrace, and now he would show the evil bastards who he was.
Roberto swerved to miss a big Mercedes driven by an almost blind
geezer and then noticed a group of expensively dressed, older women
emerging from a popular bistro.

He muttered, "Painted cadavers, fucking painted cadavers," and
then found his way to the Naples Pier without further incident.

Roberto lucked into an empty parking place in the small lot near
the pier's entrance and surveyed the lovely scene; as he had predicted, it was busy with sightseers and fishermen enjoying the warm day.
The sun had just broken through the clouds, and other people would
join them soon. The Naples pier is a wooden structure that extends

far out into the Gulf of Mexico. There are bait and gift shops situated near the half-way point and a covered structure at its end. The pier's designers had never considered what a wonderful place it would be for an ambush, but Roberto had. For the past several days he had thought of little else. Automatic weapons fire had filled his dreams; mutilated bodies of gringos had bloodied the sea. Sharks had churned among the bodies; that was the part he liked best.

After half an hour, Roberto decided the pier was as busy as it ever would be and stepped out of the car with an AK-47 assault rifle cradled in his arms and a bag brimming with loaded ammunition clips over his shoulder. The weapon would deliver six hundred rounds of 7.62 mm bullets per minute. A group of pretty young girls dressed in brief bikinis and eager for the beach below passed close by but were so engrossed in animated conversation that they paid no attention to the blood covered, heavily armed murderer.

He considered killing the rich, white bitches for what they were but walked on passing the ornate sign that designated the popular park, and then stepped up onto the structure. An obese salesman and his wife from Cleveland did take notice of the bloody killer, and the woman started screaming, more like screeching, at the top of her lungs—a big mistake. Roberto opened fire, and the two were riddled with bullets in seconds. There were yells and screams and a general stampede for the far end of the pier. Roberto laughed and walked forward, firing the automatic weapon in random bursts. Dozens of fishermen and sightseers fell, bleeding, dying. Some leaped and others fell to their deaths on the beach, but many more jumped into the water; some surviving the long fall. The crazed shooter reached the two shops and shot everyone cowering inside and then moved on. Several confused, brown pelicans flopped among the dead, and Roberto shot them just for fun, not knowing or caring that they were harmless, blind beggars. The survivors were crowding beneath the gazebo-like structure at the pier's terminus; many were either crushed or pushed over the side. Juarez inserted a fresh clip and emptied it into them. Finally there was no one left to shoot; he had shown them, hurt them, killed them, drowned them—all of the bigoted bastards. They would never look down on him again. Never! He grinned broadly and inserted his last clip into the hot weapon. Pleased with his success, he stuck the barrel in his mouth and pulled the trigger. A final ak-ak-ak-ak, and it was quiet until sirens screamed in the distance.

Jonathan Smith and Officer Terry McGuff were quietly discussing the death of the Juarez family when the urgent call came in on McGuff's police radio relating the massacre at the Naples pier and the fact that the probable perpetrator, Roberto Juarez, was dead by his own hand. The total body count at the site of the mass murder was conservatively estimated to be in the dozens, but it would be days before an accurate figure could be determined because of the number of victims that had either fallen or jumped into the Gulf of Mexico. The officer's presence was requested as soon as possible at the crime scene. Smith thanked him for his assistance and volunteered to help with the injured if he could. It was only after the shocked doctor was alone in his office that the full impact of the situation settled upon his shoulders. This horrible mess was not exactly his fault, but it could have been avoided if he had done the right thing when the moment presented itself. He had not; he had allowed himself to be bullied by Maxwell Hall and, as a result, dozens of innocent people were dead and dying.

Smith sighed and looked at his telephone; the only question was who to call first, Maxwell Hall or the FDA. He chose the former and punched in his private number with trembling fingers.

The telephone rang several times, and his secretary answered, further angering the doctor. Smith demanded that he immediately speak to Hall, and there was a long wait and then a familiar voice. "Hall, here, what the hell is so important as to pull me out of our executive meeting?"

"It's over. Medulin is dead. Roberto Juarez, a patient I am convinced was on active drug, has killed his family, and then shot dozens of innocent fishermen and vacationers on the Naples Pier before taking his own life. The awful carnage is all over the national news."

Hall exploded. "Now, you just wait one minute, Doctor. You have no idea what that patient was on."

"Bull shit! I was just plain stupid to listen to you before, and there is no chance this time, Maxwell. I have Juarez's packaged drug supplies secured, and within the next hour they will be shipped to the FDA as *evidence*. I am then proceeding directly to the university with a sample tablet, and my friends in forensic chemistry there will have a positive identification of the drug before tomorrow. Now, likely you have ruined me, and I will be disqualified as an investigator by the FDA and maybe even lose my license to practice medicine, but you and your company are going down with me. I shall feel responsible for the deaths of those poor people as long as I live. Do you feel no shame, you heartless bastard?"

"Jonathan, wait ..."

But Smith was already dialing David Kendall's number at the Division of Psychiatric Products and Hall was left to fluster. In light of the emergency, Kendall's assistant at the FDA soon located the busy man, and his familiar voice came on the line. Kendall was barely able to contain his rage, but listened patiently, while the upset psychiatrist explained what had happened, as best he understood it.

Smith continued, "I am convinced that Juarez was on Medulin, and I am on my way to express mail his drug supplies to you. I am also taking one tablet to a local university chemistry laboratory for a quick identification by mass spectrometry. When these things are done, I am going to the Naples Pier and volunteer my time to help in any way I can or to help the families of those poor people I helped to kill."

Kendall took Smith's cell phone number and agreed to confirm the receipt of the damning drug supplies and to stay in constant touch as the story unfolded. When he finally looked up from the yellow pad he was scratching on, his assistant, Janet, was standing there looking at him with a questioning face.

He said, "Looks like we have a disaster brewing. Please set up a meeting with the Commissioner in his office immediately. Alan Werner must also be there, no matter what. The subject is Medulin, and this is a top priority—lives are at stake."

32

A Healing Hand

Both bands quit playing and the rowdy Bat Cave patrons became quiet and turned to gawk when a tall, young man dressed in a blue blazer and neatly-pressed Bill's Khakis walked into the dungeon-like bar. Two painted ghouls rose and started for the intruder but were stopped in their tracks by Samara's eager greeting, "Josh, Josh, over here!"

Even more heads turned to see who was laying claim to such a clean-cut, suspicious looking outsider. Samara smiled broadly and motioned for Josh to come to the bar. She announced in a loud voice, "Everyone, listen up; this is Josh Ledbetter; he's a medical doctor and a friend of mine. He is here to help people like us, and he has already helped me. Now, go back to your own business."

Josh made his way through the mob of weird and wonderful people and seated himself on a bar stool in front of Samara. He said with a big grin, "You didn't tell me you worked in a real bat cave."

Samara giggled like a little girl. "About as close as you can get, I guess, and Josh, they are mostly harmless, despite appearances. By the way, none of these creatures can hang upside down from the ceiling. You slumming tonight?"

Josh laughed a comfortable, happy laugh. "As I told you before, I am in Key West to do the Lord's work, wherever I can find it. I would appreciate a cup of coffee; it's way past my usual bedtime, so make it black, please."

Samara poured Josh a hot cup of Bat Cave's strongest coffee, and he smiled his appreciation, making Samara's heart flutter. Was his mere presence healing her? She watched him sip the steaming brew and said, "How can I help you do God's work?"

"The people in this bar, your friends, are all here because they are hiding from someone or some thing—the law, their parents, spouses, work, discipline; who knows what?"

Samara nodded agreement and Josh continued, "Many are hiding from themselves, but the one thing they share in common is that they are all lost souls, hovering just outside the protective umbrella of the system. I am not here to make any judgment of them at all. I am only here to help. That is my mission."

"How so?"

"As I said to you on the beach, I am a board certified physician and am trained to treat sick people. As I look around this room, I would guess that any number of your friends need medical attention but are afraid or have no resources to seek it. I suspect that hepatitis, tuberculosis, drug addiction, AIDS and other STDs are prevalent here. I have a small office in an inconspicuous place and will see anyone who feels they need medical treatment, life counseling, or even financial aid to return to productive life—or to their loved ones. There are no gimmicks; the Southern Baptist Convention pays. Do you think I could make such an announcement to this group? I have my appointment book."

Samara was not prepared for this. "Err, ah—I'll have to ask the boss." Altar was hovering nearby, keeping an alert eye on the well-dressed stranger that might be a cop of some sort. "Boss, would it be OK, if Dr. Ledbetter made an announcement? He is a missionary offering free medical treatment to our people."

"You know this guy, Samara?" Altar asked. She nodded, and the owner said to go ahead and use the microphone.

Samara's heart skipped a beat as Josh stepped up on the stage and took the microphone from the disbelieving lead singer who thought Josh might be a narc. "Hi, folks! I know I'm strange-looking, but I promise I'm not a cop. Truth is I'm a doctor and a missionary, here in Key West to do God's work and help people any way I can."

Josh felt the crowd relax, and he knew he had their attention. He continued with his pitch, explained what he could do for them, and noted that his out-of-the-way small office was within walking distance of the Bat Cave. "I'll be over at the bar for another hour, and I have my appointment book right here. I will find time for you, no matter what, so please come on over and sign up. If you are uncomfortable with that, I'll leave a stack of business cards with my contact information with my friend, Samara. If there's sufficient need, I'll drop by once a week, but no more speeches. I promise."

No one came to Josh for an uneasy few minutes, but then a brave soul came forward and then another and another until his book was filled with appointments for the following week. He finished his coffee, bade Samara good night with a wink, and was off into what was left of the night.

Samara stared after the young doctor as though in a trance but returned to her real world that was the Bat Cave in response to a gentle nudge on the shoulder. It was Altar; he grinned and said, "I think you've got it bad for that pretty boy, Samara. Be careful, he's not one of us."

She nodded and got back to her bar tending, but the place was thinning out, and there was little to do. Several regulars were sound asleep at their tables. Someone had turned the TV on, and an excited talking head caught her attention. The location was the Naples Pier, illuminated by powerful searchlights as divers continued to remove bullet-riddled bodies from the water. Mary Hopkins, an investigative reporter for the local ABC affiliate, repeated the story from the beginning for new watchers and concluded by saying, "It is believed that an experimental drug called Medulin may have interacted with an unstable personality and played a role in the killings. The FDA and the Justice Department are making a full investigation of the circumstances of these heinous crimes. If you or anyone you know has ever taken this drug, Medulin, as a part of a clinical study for a drug company or for any other reason, please notify your physician immediately."

Samara couldn't watch any more of it and changed the channel. It was the first time that she had fully appreciated that others had had their minds distorted by this horrible drug and like her had done awful things. She thought maybe it was time to turn herself in, but no, she wasn't ready yet. Maybe Josh could help her; his mind was as clear as a bell, and his heart was golden. But how would her new friend and confidant view her when he learned that she had not only taken the lives of others but even murdered her own mother? Josh had been sincere when he said he would help without judging others, but he likely didn't have serial killers in mind when he said that. Did even the love of the Lord have its limits? Samara had a lot to consider but fully understood that Josh might be her last chance, one she knew she would take ... when the time was right.

33

Bad News Travels Fast

Although there had been no reason for the FDA to notify Genplex of the Medulin difficulties, the breaking story of Roberto Juarez and his mass murders had been all over the national news. Jerrod had received a heads-up from his friend, Charlie Cox, who, like other Medulin investigators, had been ordered by the FDA to cease Medulin clinical trials and quarantine every patient who had received at least one dose of the drug. The public safety was at stake. Predictably, the press was outraged by another arrogant, big pharmaceutical company that valued earnings over human life. The entire industry was tarred by Maxwell Hall's brush. The United States Senate might have to investigate the drug companies again, and congressional hearings were almost a certainty. Unfair as it might seem, several astute reporters had mentioned Genplex's Axilon as belonging to the same class of drugs and being worthy of suspicion.

Jerrod had plenty of time to think as his Metro North train rattled and lurched to Manhattan. One moment he felt elated that Medulin would no longer be hurting innocent, sick people and the victims of their lunacy. The next he would be positively ill over what the repercussions were doing to Axilon, to Genplex, and to the industry. When the long ride was finally over, Jerrod was grateful to exit the stuffy car. He usually ignored the mob of busy travelers when he stepped off the train into Grand Central Station, but today he looked at them differently and saw individual faces, the rich and happy, the frightened, the poor and desperate, and the sick. He knew that so many of them were mentally ill and could benefit from a wonderful, new drug like Axilon; yet he also knew that the novel drug could be killed in a second by an overzealous politician or an unscrupulous reporter seeking their moment of glory. But, at the end of the day, he was just the research guy; it was up to top management, Alonsio Vettori and Rhinner Albright, to decide how best to respond. That's what they got paid the big bucks for.

Jerrod walked into Albright's big office right on time to find Rhinner sitting at his desk angrily reading a Sirius document while Vettori paced the floor with a copy of the same document. Jerrod shook hands with his bosses, and they took their seats in Albright's private conference room. A large pot of strong coffee was provided, and Jerrod sensed the gravity of the meeting.

Once seated, Jerrod found a copy of Lois Ackerman's first report on Genplex and Axilon before him. Alonsio's eyes appeared even larger than usual when he spoke. "Dr. Wesley, have you seen this Sirius report?"

"No, I haven't; please let me breeze through it." Jerrod found it pretty generic and saw that its main purpose was for Lois Ackerman to announce coverage of Genplex. The only thing he saw that was highly objectionable was the way she questioned the safety and efficacy of Axilon, based on no real information. If nothing else, it was a red flag for her future intentions.

Albright said, "Jerrod, do you know this woman?" Jerrod shook his head as a negative response, and Albright continued, "She is a known hired gun in the financial community who has worked for a number of firms. She is despised on the street but is in demand to come in and trash companies that need trashing for an investment bank's own business reasons—in this case Genplex. She reports to a new guy there—some Brit named Collingsworth—I don't know the man, but I think he just came over from a bank in the United Kingdom To make matters more complicated, Sirius has contacted our investor relations people and requested a meeting so that an in-depth report can be issued on Genplex and Axilon. This all comes at the time of the Medulin fiasco and unbelievable negative press on the industry, especially Apex. Our shares are already down fifteen points; what do you have to say about all this, Dr. Wesley?"

Jerrod rubbed his chin thinking that Sirius was sending Susan's ghost after him. Will this nightmare never end?

"Dr. Wesley?" Albright repeated.

"Sorry, Sir, I was thinking. I can mostly speak about the research, and we are where we are. The Phase II program in schizophrenia failed, and we said so and cancelled all work on that indication. The FDA was highly impressed with our Phase II data in depression and anxiety disorders, and that is being drafted for publication, along with the negative data in psychotic patients. Phase III trials with Axilon are under way, and we have seen no big problems. If you want me to present this data to Lois ... Ackerman, then I will, but I believe that is your decision, Sir."

Albright responded, "You are correct about that, and the decision has been made. Next week this ... Ackerman woman will meet with our corporate and financial people and then with you and whomever you chose to assist you."

Jerrod thought for a moment and then replied, "I would be most happy to do so, but wouldn't it be a good idea to have a friendly analyst at the meeting as well—someone that you can at least rely on to be objective and set the balance?"

Albright smiled and said, "At times, Dr. Wesley, you actually can be brilliant."

Traffic was snarled and the big limousine crept along at an annoying pace. He should have returned as he came—by train. Jerrod wanted to be home with Wanda, but it would be another two hours. He decided to make the best of it and reconnoiter Lois Ackerman with some old friends and colleagues around the industry. He guessed that if anyone had locked horns with her it would be his former classmate at Ole Miss, Poppy Gruber who had been in investor relations at Pfizer for a long time. Jerrod found Poppy's number in his cell phone's memory and soon had the recognizable voice at the other end. Poppy had made so much hay with his Mississippi accent *up North* that he had cultivated it rather than hidden it over his many years in Connecticut. Jerrod was just as happy that he had lost his accent somewhere along the way but knew that it miraculously returned as soon as he crossed the Mason Dixon Line.

"Yeah, I know that Ackerman bitch. She has lied about and butchered so many of our newer products that she has been banned from the Pfizer premises forever. You say you have to go up against her next week?"

"I'm afraid so. We aren't Pfizer and it is a sensitive time for us right now. I guess you've seen reports of the latest Medulin disaster on TV? Axilon is being tarred by the same brush for no good reason, so we certainly have to be transparent right now, certainly not appear to be hiding anything."

"Yeah, somebody should shoot that Hall bastard at Apex; he's gonna be the end of our industry yet. Listen, old buddy, I recommend that you present the hard data on Axilon with no speculation; don't give her one smidgen of wiggle-room. Don't speculate about markets or any of the usual hogwash we give out. Just the cold, hard facts, you know."

Jerrod replied, "I tend to agree with what you are saying, and my management has consented to have a friendly analyst attend the same meeting. Don't know who that will be, but I'm going to assume *friendly*. Ackerman will be less inclined to lie if there is a differing opinion released to the public. Also, my part in this will be presented in Connecticut. The thought being, she'll be in less of a feeding frenzy out of home waters."

Poppy laughed, "Sounds like a plan to me, but I wouldn't count on nothin' with that witch. And for God's sake, don't let your bosses trap you into dinner with Lois Ackerman."

"Been there, Poppy?"

"Hell, yes."

Jerrod laughed and suggested that they meet for drinks in the near future. Somehow the vision of Lois Ackerman eating Poppy for dinner stuck.

Jonathan Smith managed a twisted grin when Maxwell Hall answered the telephone. The psychiatrist was angry, sweating profusely, and seriously considering murder as an option. Hall had trashed Smith's successful career, and the arrogant bastard could care less.

"Max, I thought I should bring you up to date on Medulin—share the misery, if you will. The tablet I selected from the Juarez supplies was indeed Medulin, not placebo, and the FDA has corroborated the results on the remainder. There is no argument that you can make about this, absolutely none, *nada*. The FDA has stopped all studies, as you already know, and the unfortunate patients who received active drug have been quarantined until further notice. Naturally, you will be responsible for all costs associated with this. Your miracle drug is dead, Hall, fucking dead!"

Maxwell Hall was already in a truly bad mood; just moments before he had received a call from Alan Werner stating that he was being quietly removed from his position at the FDA and would be returning to academia at some shit university in New Jersey. Hall's plant at FDA had been fired! But he repressed his outward anger and answered calmly, "Dr. Smith, you should know by now that drug research is an expensive, dangerous, high-risk proposition. Drugs fail; some drugs kill; that's just the business we're in. Now, I have moved on from Medulin. I have greater battles to fight, and I suggest you do the same. Do-you-understand-me?"

The audacity of the man! "You bastard, I may or may not be ruined, but you are going down. I will do my best to see that the Justice Department locks up your arrogant ass and throws the key away. You are going to burn in hell for all those people you murdered. Do-you-understand-*me*?

But Maxwell had already hung up and was dialing a number from memory.

A deep voice answered in Russian. "Speak English, Sergei."

"Ah, Mr. Hall ... and what does the big man want?"

"I want to make an addition to your assigned list of targets, but first, what of the girl?"

"We believe the girl is hiding in South Florida someplace but has likely changed her identity and looks and melted into the masses. That would be the usual way of things. No?"

"Possibly, people like her often hide in either Key West or San Francisco. Where are you and Vadik, Sergei?"

"Just leaving Key West."

Hall said, "Excellent. I want you two to put the Wesley girl on hold for now; I have two easier targets for you, and I will pay the same as for the girl but for each one of them. The first one is in Naples and the second in the DC area. Both are to be killed as soon as possible. In the case of the Naples physician, Jonathan Smith, it has to appear as death by accident. Automobile, I don't care, but no bombs or bullets. OK? Now, the death of Alan Werner in Washington will be a bit trickier—it will be death by suicide, and his body must be found with a note that I will provide to you. The suicide note will be typed, but you must see that it is signed by his hand. I believed you are skilled in such matters?"

Sergei agreed, and Hall gave him the necessary information required to find, identify, and kill both men. The unsigned suicide note would be sent to their next hotel by express mail. Hall indicated that the fee for Courtney Wesley would be doubled if the Smith and Werner murders were handled professionally. He didn't need her dead so much anymore, but Maxwell Hall hated loose ends.

34

Lois Ackerman

Jerrod grinned when he walked into the conference room; two of the biotech analysts had arrived early, and he recognized their faces though he did not know their names or affiliations. They were the two colleagues he had observed in action at Smith & Wollensky that night that seemed an eternity ago. A flash of recognition crossed the face of the big man with a cane and they both laughed as they shook hands. His name was indeed John, as Jerrod had somehow guessed at the time, John Mosley. John introduced his colleague as Amy Cooper. They worked in the health care division of Coonts and Swale, Ltd., a small, but highly regarded, New York biotech boutique. Jerrod was immediately taken by the woman's flashing eyes and quick wit. Though he knew enough to be cautious around anyone from Wall Street, he felt oddly comfortable with these two characters.

Their animated conversation came to an end when Jerrod's two bosses walked in with Lois Ackerman and Davis Collingsworth leading and Leonard Bagley trailing behind. Leonard was Genplex's longtime CFO. He was slightly built and wore thick glasses, looking much like the financial nerd that he was. Financial *genius* might be a better term; he had been with Genplex from the beginning and was responsible for much of the company's success. Bagley had seemingly made money appear from thin air back when there was none. He had been a master of European private offerings.

Ackerman paused when she spotted the competition across the room. Her face etched with contempt, she snarled, "I was not aware that *these two* were going to be here. Maybe I should just leave. I believe I requested a *private* meeting."

Collingsworth, sensing disaster, laughed and said, "Come now, Lois, John and Amy won't bite you. The more brains the better."

Jerrod thought what a lying manipulator Collingsworth was but kept his mouth shut. However, he was unable to suppress a wry grin.

The exchange was clearly unsettling to Rhinner Albright, but he made the necessary introductions and opened the program. Albright took his seat next to Vettori as Bagley delved into the financials. His presentation was long and thorough but contained no information that could not be found in shareholders' documents. Amy Cooper took copious notes and asked several questions for clarification, but Lois Ackerman took no notes and said not one word. It was as though she had no interest. However, the taciturn financial analyst came to life with Bagley's presentation of key patents and issues; she seemed delighted with the near-term expiration of Genplex's patent on their blockbuster recombinant protein for the treatment of blood disorders which put 50 percent of their future earnings at risk. She dismissed the company's efforts to extend the patent with an exclusive process as pure claptrap.

John and Amy took exception to her biased opinion and cited several concrete examples where this approach had saved billions in potentially eroded earnings of major products for other companies. Clearly they viewed things in a different light.

Jerrod had been unsettled by the hostile interactions between the two sets of financial analysists but sucked it up before he stood to present Genplex's R&D efforts. He presented a succinct overview of their basic research program and then moved on to Axilon, first explaining the preclinical basis of the clinical programs in anxiety, depression, and schizophrenia. Toxicology data was summarized, including a comparison of Axilon and Medulin on human neurons in culture. There was little discussion of the preclinical data, but Jerrod sensed the axe was about to fall. He had agonized over how to deal with the failed schizophrenia clinical program and had decided to present it in a straightforward manner in some detail. Now, he wondered about that decision, but at least the order of his presentation placed it last—following the highly successful anxiety and depression programs.

Both John and Amy became quite animated over the results from the anxiety and depression clinical studies; both sets of studies showed lofty response rates and highly statistically significant lowering of rating scales that measured therapeutic responses. Unlike conventional drugs for anxiety and depression, Axilon showed a quick therapeutic response—in as little as a few days. Side effects were few, and there were no real adverse reactions in either diagnostic group.

Amy commented excitedly, "This is amazing; there is no reason that this drug can't capture a significant market share—the benzodiazepines and SSRIs can't compete, and at least forty million Americans have anxiety disorders alone."

Lois Ackerman silenced Amy with a hard look. "I don't think so; the Prozacs and Valiums of this world have been around for a long time and are considered safe and effective, if used properly. Generic equivalents are available for several and are inexpensive. Moreover, the newer versions like Cymbalta and Effexor aren't better. We know nothing about the long-term effects of Axilon. I'll reserve my judgment until I see the schizophrenia data. Those patients have a real need for a new drug—a safe one that works."

John Mosley took exception to Ackerman's pedestrian views. "Lois, that isn't a fair characterization of those two drugs. Cymbalta also has labeling for neuropathic pain, and Effexor has a dual label for depression and anxiety disorders, which I'd eventually expect to see with Axilon, which, by the way, is one hell of a superior drug."

Jerrod grinned his appreciation and sipped his coffee; he was not to be hurried by the pushy bitch. He explained that the current Phase III program was in generalized anxiety disorder, but additional Phase II studies were ongoing in other prevalent anxiety diseases—obsessive compulsive disorder, panic disorder, post-traumatic stress disorder, and social-anxiety disorder. These claims would significantly enhance the labeling of the drug over time. The Phase III depression program would focus on major depression but would seek a broader patient population, including chronic dysthymics, depressed patients that generally don't respond to drugs well.

Jerrod finally had to talk about the schizophrenia experience but sucked it up and explained the negative experience with as much aplomb as their successes. Few patients improved and some actually worsened, though the relationship to drug was not statistically significant. Adverse reactions were few, and Axilon did not produce side effects such as movement disorders like conventional antipsychotic drugs do. Overall, it was solid evidence for a safe but ineffective drug in schizophrenic patients. Jerrod concluded by suggesting that drugs that worked through promodulin might not be the best approach for schizophrenia. They had added to the body of clinical pharmacology.

Ackerman said, "What a shame; the drug has fallen on its face where we might actually need it. You could have gotten a premium price for a unique and effective schizophrenia treatment, but what can you charge against generic drugs for anxiety and depression?"

Amy came out of her chair, unable to suppress her boiling anger. "Lois, you absolutely know better than that! It is obvious to me that while this drug may not improve patients with schizophrenia, it is far more effective than anything out there, new or old, for anxiety and depression, and it seemingly produces few side effects or physical dependence—addiction. It will be awarded better pricing than the newer drugs out there, for certain."

"We," Ackerman snarled, "shall see when the Phase III program and the long-term studies are completed. I have great concerns about the long-term use of this drug that acts through a previously undefined system."

Jerrod cringed when he saw Alonsio's head bobbing up and down. The old man stood and spoke in his booming voice, "Of course we do not have all the answers yet, nor did we claim that we do. That's why the FDA requires Phase III studies. We have presented solid data suggesting that the drug is very safe and effective for the treatment of anxiety and depression—that is all. Jerrod will publish the schizophrenia data, and that will be the end of that discussion. Do I make myself clear?"

Fearing further negative debate might go the wrong direction, Albright concluded the session and thanked the participants. Thinking better of it, he did not distribute the glitzy, new Axilon PR items he carried in his briefcase. Lois Ackerman and Davis Collingsworth hurried out the door as if they were trying to escape the plague, but Amy Cooper and John Mosley remained to share in the coffee and light lunch the company had provided. Both Coonts and Swale analysts were highly complementary of the presentations and predicted a great future for the drug. However, Lois Ackerman had left a foreboding, dark cloud boiling over the occasion. Were storm windows in order?

Jerrod knew that two reports would be written following the meeting and that they would reflect two markedly different interpretations of the Axilon data. Would the market believe information distributed by Sirius, an influential monster, or Coonts and Swale, an upstart biotech boutique? He feared he knew the answer but did not voice it to his departing bosses.

35

Crime and Punishment

J errod had spent a sleepless night, tossing and turning in anger over Lois Ackerman's calculated behavior the day before. However, it was a beautiful July weekend morning and Jerrod and Wanda were enjoying coffee and *The Hartford Courant* on the patio, putting problems aside for the moment. Several varieties of hydrangeas were in full bloom and filled the air with their heady perfume. Thoughts of business difficulties were slipping away in the warm sunshine when Wanda said, "Wow!" and continued to read an article on the front page of the business section.

"What is it, Wanda?"

"Sounds like one of your best friends is in real trouble," Wanda quipped.

"Really? Give me that thing, girl!"

Wanda laughed and handed him the paper, not comprehending the full ramifications of the article.

Jerrod read aloud, "Apex Pharmaceuticals' CEO Faces Serious Charges. The U.S. Attorney's Office for Connecticut and the U.S. Justice Department announced yesterday that Mr. Maxwell Hall, President and CEO of the massive Groton-based pharmaceutical conglomerate, Apex Pharmaceuticals, was indicted on fraud and felony Food, Drug, and Cosmetic Act charges following an investigation by the FBI, FDA, and Justice Department. A spokesperson from the U.S. Attorney's office said that although it is unusual to name an individual in such charges, the massive fraud and cover-up involving clinical trials with a once promising new drug called Medulin were largely of Hall's doing. The CEO's actions may have both directly and indirectly led to the death of several innocent individuals, and the U.S. Attorney's Office could not rule out additional felony charges."

Hall was not available for comment, and the company said they would issue a statement following conclusion of an internal investigation.

Jerrod grinned and took a sip of coffee. "They finally got the bastard, but oddly enough, he has not been incarcerated. The rest of the article is Hall's history and a lot about the Medulin problems. Apparently several of the clinical investigators screamed loud and long. I wonder if this will have any affect on the jerks at Sirius?"

"I thought you might like that, Jerrod; your life could be a lot easier now."

"Don't count on it. If I know Maxwell Hall, he'll just take this in stride and fight it until the Justice Department runs out of lawyers. He has a hell of a lot more money than they do, and he's an unrepentant liar."

ℒ

Sergei and Vadik had tailed Jonathan Smith in his gold Jaguar convertible for several days. His peregrinations were somewhat predictable; he was chronically late for his appointments and often exceeded the conservative Naples speed limits, driving erratically and weaving in and out of the big Lincolns and BMWs driven by aging retirees. The Russians agreed that Smith was an automobile accident looking for a place to happen, but otherwise inaccessible. Thus, the opportunity.

Dr. Smith usually made his final rounds around 9:00 p.m., parking in the hospital's poorly lit lot. The expensive Jaguar had powerful brakes, but Sergei and Vadik were experts in such matters. A few nicks in the lines and some simple adjustments converted the automobile into a sleek, unstoppable instrument of death. Even the most competent investigator would not be able to discern such small changes in a heavily damaged car. The Jag's brakes would operate normally at low speeds and conservative braking but would fail the first time they were applied strongly at a high rate of speed—Smith's normal driving behavior.

At precisely 10:15 p.m. Smith emerged from the hospital. Not noticing the dark sedan following him, the physician made his turn south onto the Tamiami Trail. As expected, traffic was light, and the convertible smoothly accelerated beyond the speed limit. He didn't touch his brakes for the first yellow light, and then he increased his speed substantially. Jonathan Smith was doing over seventy miles per hour when he approached the Golden Gate Parkway intersection. He had fully intended to breeze through another yellow light, but the traffic signal flashed red before he reached the intersection, and a mass of cross-traffic moved ahead. He cursed under his breath and hit the brakes hard. There was a moment of normal brake resistance followed by a loud pop as he streaked into the intersection. The collision occurred just behind the driver's compartment of a fully loaded Budweiser truck. The Jaguar exploded in a ball of flame which threw the beer delivery truck into the path of several other vehicles. When it was over, a dozen cars and trucks had been ruined and several persons injured, but there was only one fatality. There was little left of Jonathan Smith or his precious, gold Jaguar convertible.

The psychiatrist's family, friends, and associates would mourn his death but not be surprised. Smith had a history of inattentive, reckless driving—always late and in a hurry. Under the growing cloud of his recent professional misfortunes, such an accident seemed almost predictable. Others, to the north, would rejoice that Jonathan Smith would never testify against Maxwell Hall in any court of law.

The Russians had been delayed by the previous red light, but it required little more of their time to determine that they had completed the first portion of their assignment successfully. They would make a quick phone call, and then they would drive all night into the following day to the Bethesda Marriott where they would receive additional information and instructions.

Despite quantities of Red Bull caffeine and thoughts of more easy money, Sergei and Vadik were exhausted after the long drive to the DC area. Even though they knew their quarry was moving to another city and wasting time on rest was risky, they checked into the Marriott and caught a few hours of deep sleep before tackling the job.

Sergei grunted when he saw the heavy, wrought iron gate blocking their passage into the condominium complex. He fumbled briefly in his pocket and extracted the magnetic card that had been part of Hall's waiting package. Sergei inserted the card, and after a brief buzz the gate swung open, and the dark Mercedes entered. It was 2:00 a.m. when the Russians eased into a guest parking place and turned the engine off. Security was not evident, and there were no late night residents walking barking dogs. While their approach had seemed brazen, so far there were no obvious problems. Both Russians wore dark suits and their hats were pulled down over their eyes to obscure their faces. They wore thin plastic gloves, and Vadik carried a small black bag containing essentials for their criminal activity. The Gardens was a large, luxury condominium complex typical of that populous area, but they had clear directions to Alan Werner's residence. Ideally situated, Werner's condominium was an end unit located on the top floor. The dark stairwell would provide an ideal route for their escape.

Informed that one card served both the main gate and Werner's personal entry, Sergei slipped the card into the reader. There was no buzz, but the lock clicked. Vadik turned the knob slowly and carefully opened the door until the anticipated safety chain caught. The Russian grinned and made short work of removing the chain with his homemade burglar tool. There was sufficient light that the Russians could see that the front of the condominium was filled with packed boxes and moving materials. Medical textbooks were scattered about the room. They had arrived none too early.

The only sound was loud snoring emanating from a back bedroom. Good luck; their quarry was lost in deep sleep. Sergei carried a .38 caliber police special fitted with a silencer. It was an untraceable weapon provided by Hall for this occasion. Both men crept forward, and Sergei peeped into the bedroom. Werner was not alone in the bed! A small, but curvaceous, blond slept peacefully beside the psychiatrist; she was naked as was he. They had no way to know that the attractive woman was the wife of an important US Senator, nor did they care who she was. Trained by the Russian Mafia to expertly take care of business at hand, expected, or otherwise, Sergei walked over to the bed and shot her between the eyes. There was a modest pop—the silencer had done its job—and Werner stirred but did not awaken.

Vadik grinned and whispered, "Murder-suicide."

When Werner did awaken, he found the silencer of Sergei's revolver stuck in his mouth. Vadik switched on the light, and Sergei ordered the frightened man to sit up. When Alan saw the growing pool of red beneath his partner's head, he panicked, making a foolish attempt to escape. The two big Russians grabbed the skinny man and sat him down on a nearby couch. Vadik placed the suicide note and a pen on the coffee table in front of him.

Sergei said in an even voice, "We are going to kill you, one way or another. You sign this note right now, and your death will be quick and painless, as it was for your partner. Or ... we will torture you to death in slow and excruciatingly painful increments—your choice."

Werner looked around the room and saw no avenue for escape. He looked at the dead woman on the bed, bit his lip, and said, "Let me read it first, and then I'll decide."

His lips moved silently as he read the typed note.

To whom it may concern:

My decision at the FDA to give the drug Medulin preferential treatment has lead to immeasurable death, pain, and suffering. My judgment was clouded by my initial enthusiasm for the drug, and because of my influential position, others were led to do improper things as well. I did not have the courage to end the program when I knew it was doomed and the drug was a killer. In short, I have failed at every level, and I can no longer live with what I have done and a simple apology would not be adequate.

    Alan Werner, M.D.

The scared man picked up the pen and scratched his signature across the bottom of the suicide note, fully expecting to talk the two dim-witted fools out of killing him. Unfortunately, Alan Werner was a doomed man, and his persuasive gift of gab was for naught. He looked up in time to see the flash but probably never heard the shot as the hollow point slug destroyed his brain. The two Russians left him slumped over where he died. Ideally, the note was blood-spattered but safe from the flow of blood from the massive wound. The murder weapon was placed securely in Werner's hand once they had made certain his prints were all over it. Otherwise, they left the condominium as they had found it. The safety chain was reattached with the clever tool, and the two killers made their way quietly down the dark stairwell. Another expert *suicide* had been carried out by the Russian Mafia. A quick phone call was made and then a great deal of money was wired to an anonymous Swiss bank account. They did not receive a bonus for killing Werner's lover, though they requested one, citing unexpected risk.

36

Absalom

Samara smiled as she looked out across the busy bar; she had come to know many of the patrons. They were living their desperate lives as best they could while hidden from ordinary folks who would harshly judge them. A few, like Courtney, become Samara, had been dislodged from privileged lives. Most had come from miserable, even violent beginnings, and suffered through failure in their quest for normalcy. Some were here because they had been born different and had to prove it. Either way, Samara knew better than to inquire into their life histories, yet she listened when they needed to talk. She felt good because she had helped so many of them. Samara had become a conduit for her sick and injured brothers and sisters into the warm and healing hands of Josh Ledbetter. She even worked at his busy clinic two mornings a week for no pay other than the satisfaction of helping someone else. Sure, she had fallen in love with the young doctor, but she was a realist.

Samara's smile faded, and her line of thought was lost when a tall, black man impeccably dressed in an expensive suit and red silk tie sauntered into the bar. She immediately made him as a cop of some kind. Jason Rand found a vacant spot at the bar and gathered his lanky frame onto the stool. He looked at Samara intently, and she put her thumbs to her ears and wiggled her fingers and said, "Boo!"

That broke his trance, and he grinned broadly, revealing perfect, white teeth and said, "Sorry; I was staring—rude."

She said, "OK, you're forgiven; name your poison."

"How about a Bombay and tonic?" Rand responded without thinking.

"Coming right up—lime OK?"

He nodded, and Samara mixed him a double without being asked.

The presumed cop reached into his jacket pocket and pulled out a photograph and handed it to Samara. "Have you ever seen this girl in here?"

Jesus—she knew who it would be a photograph of even before she looked. It was indeed of Courtney Wesley and very similar to the one carried by the Russian thugs. Samara pretended to examine it carefully and replied, "Nope, but she must be a popular gal; two big Russians were recently making the rounds looking for her."

Rand registered no outward surprise; he had heard this several times since arriving in Key West and knew that they were likely the men who had killed his careless predecessor. "Popular? Depends who you talk to. All I can say is that she has some serious problems and needs help. If you ever see her in here, would you please give me a call?" Rand handed Samara his card and stood up, leaving his drink untouched.

Noting his private investigator designation, she said, "Depends on who you are working for ..."

"OK, fair enough. I'm working for her father and his lawyer, and it's important that I find her before others do."

Rand threw down a bill which covered the drink plus a large tip and was gone. Obviously the Bat Cave and its denizens made him nervous. A black cloud edged over Samara; she was nervous too; it seemed the whole world was searching for her. This high level of scrutiny, brushes with certain death, had become too much for her fractured self. Samara's injured brain balked at ever-growing layers of stress and helplessness, and she fainted dead away.

When she awakened she was looking into Josh Ledbetter's pale blue eyes and his hand was on her cheek. She was on a cot in his examining room, and her head was still spinning. Josh explained that her highly concerned boss had brought her in after she had collapsed behind the bar.

"Water?" he offered.

"Yes, thank you." Samara tossed down the cool drink and felt better at once.

Josh looked at her and said, "I think you are under some kind of severe stress and also haven't been hydrating properly. You must drink more liquids, OK?"

Samara looked up into Josh's pale blue eyes and said, "Can we talk?"

He nodded his assent and she continued, "Josh, can I trust you? I mean *really* trust you—I need advice, help in the worst way."

"I already know you are not Samara. I am a physician and a minister; more importantly, I am your ... friend."

She caught his blush and hugged him around the neck as she sat up. The first rays of morning sunlight were painting the fronds of tall palms surrounding the little clinic when she was done with her story. She told him her entire tale, omitting no detail that she could remember. Courtney Wesley was crazy and had been a homicidal maniac. She had no control of her actions but fully recalled what she had done—killed her teacher, her mother, and her mother's lover; she had witnessed the murder of a pursuer. Her father, the Russian Mafia, and every cop in the country were looking for her. She understood the role of Medulin but could not free herself of responsibility. Nevertheless, she did not want to die, or go to prison, or be locked up with people as crazy as she.

Josh shared her pain, pushing a tear away. This terrible thing challenged every bit of his medical and religious training, but it was clear to him that she had once been a righteous ship whose rudder had been hijacked by the devil himself. Her mother had obtained the drug and insisted that Samara, Courtney, take it. But why, and who else was involved? How could Josh guess the complexity of the circumstances that had brought Courtney to him? How could he know that their relationship put him in serious danger?

"Courtney, you say that you are better, improving; what do you mean by that? Do you still have homicidal ideations directed toward those who have harmed you?"

"No, I do not, but my brain is still very sick and doesn't function properly. I cannot control my moods, and I become depressed easily. I can think more clearly and I am no longer a risk to anyone else—promise." Overcome with feelings of hopelessness, Courtney broke down and began sobbing uncontrollably.

Josh held her close and said, "The Lord and Josh Ledbetter will take care of you." Yet, he wondered how; she had not known what she was doing, yet there would be those who would blame her for her heinous crimes. Would she be treated as criminally insane and incarcerated in some institution full of crazies who were still dangerous? Down deep Josh wondered if Courtney was really free of her homicidal demons; he guessed he doubted it. All he could do was pray to his Lord and do his best.

"We have to start someplace, and I believe that road begins with your father and perhaps his lawyer. He needs to understand that you are safe and on the road to recovery and involved in your rehabilitation. I think it is premature for him to see you, and I have to carefully consider how to contact him without revealing your location. This Russian killer business worries me, and we have to decide how to best protect you."

♆

The plan had quickly evolved; Josh was already scheduled to go to New York to a convocation of Southern Baptist medical missionaries, and Connecticut wasn't much of a side trip. The following week, Josh departed for his New York missionary meeting and landed at La Guardia uneventfully. He was actively involved in the organization, and it was two days of hard work before he had a free day for personal business. It occurred to him that he should have called Courtney's father the moment he arrived in the city, but he had been overcome by pressing responsibilities. He considered simply showing up in Madison, but that seemed way too risky. He had to call now. Even so, he knew he was taking several chances; one was that Courtney's father would not be in town. Another was that he would be ambushed and arrested as an accomplice when he arrived. His finger shook as he pressed the keys of the New York City pay phone. The phone at the other end rang three times without an answer, and he was almost ready to hang up when Jerrod picked up the call.

"Hello."

"Dr. Wesley?"

"Yes, who is this?"

"Sir, you don't know me, and let's say my name is Josh. I'm a physician and a friend of Courtney's. I am on a pay phone in the city, and I don't want to say much, but I can say that she is alive and improving from her sickness but is still at risk. I would very much like to meet with you ... at a place of your choosing. I am asking nothing other than you meet with me and we develop a safe strategy to get Courtney back to you when and if that makes sense."

There was a pregnant pause as Wesley tried to wrap his arms around what he had just heard. His first reaction was doubt.

"Dr. Wesley?"

"Uh, how do I, ah, know you are on the up and up?"

"You don't, and I don't know how to convince you other than to say that if you won't meet with me, well then, the Lord and His humble servant will have to figure it out. That said, Courtney loves you and needs you, Dr, Wesley."

Jerrod paused for a minute and replied, "You have an honest voice and I think I believe you. Can you come here to my home?"

"That is risky for me, and I know you have employed the services of a private investigator, but if it makes you more comfortable, I will come to your home. But you have to promise me that you will not have me followed back to the city or take advantage of me in any way. I am only trying to protect Courtney. She and a lot of other unfortunate people rely upon my help."

"How is noon, tomorrow, my house?"

"I have directions ..."

Jerrod looked at the buzzing receiver in his hand. What sort of turn of events was this? Was it an ambush? More Russians? He really didn't think so; the man, Josh, sounded so honest, believable. At this point he could only trust his instincts.

The following day at 12:00 noon sharp Josh knocked on the door of Jerrod's big colonial. He had been careful and parked his rental car in a public lot behind a quaint bookstore in downtown Madison. The walk had been long but pleasant enough, and none of the strollers looked the least bit menacing.

Jerrod opened the door a crack and gave the handsome, young man a good look before he let him in. "Coffee?"

"Yes, black, please."

Jerrod returned in a few minutes with two cups of hot coffee, and there was an awkward moment of silence.

"Nice, private place," Josh ventured. He didn't add that he had grown up in a similar home in Austin, Texas. He could have done most anything after his privileged upbringing as the son of a wealthy Texas oil man, but he chose to serve the Lord and help the less fortunate. It was obvious to him that Courtney had not started out among the poor and suffering. Life had dealt the girl a bad hand, and now he must help her.

"Yes, it is, and I'm sorry to be so tongue tied; I just don't know what to say."

"Dr. Wesley, I know this is hard after all that has happened, so I'll do my best to explain what's going on. First of all, I am a physician and a minister; I work for my church as a missionary. My mission is to help people who are lost, outside the system, in any way I can, and the church pays for it. They are generous in that regard. Truth is, I am pretty new at this, and S ... Courtney was my first patient, though I have acquired many others with her help."

"Is she sick?" Jerrod asked in a concerned voice.

"No, not really, other than her mind, but you know all about that don't you?"

"Yes."

"OK, then; Courtney has changed her appearance and is working under an assumed name. She is not well but definitely better. She is aware that others have suffered a similar fate, and she saw the Naples Pier massacre on national television. Nevertheless, she still blames herself for what she has done, and that is an issue that will be difficult to resolve. In my opinion, that reflects a basic goodness in the girl that gives me hope. "

Jerrod shook his head. "Why would she share all this with you?"

"Only because I have helped her and a number of her friends, and she trusts me. She couldn't live alone with it any longer, and I was there for her. The main thing is to do what's best for Courtney at this difficult juncture."

Jerrod's red eyes filled, and he pushed a tear away. "What are the options?"

Josh's strong fingers formed a steeple beneath his chin, and he looked up as if for divine guidance. "We need the Lord's help here under any circumstances, but one option is to do nothing; let her live her new life as best she can as the devil slowly loosens his grip. Naturally, I will do everything I can. The downside of that plan is that some very bad people, Russian killers, are looking for her and once came close. You probably know who they are and what they have done in the past?"

Jerrod nodded, and Josh continued, "The other option is to bring her home and let her face whatever music there is to face. There is probably no way that Courtney could be convicted for killing those people, but she could be put away in a mental institution for a very long time. Life with the criminally insane would not be very pleasant, much less safe. I believe you have a lawyer, and you need to discuss this with her; the law is beyond my pay scale."

Jerrod laughed for the first time; he really liked this straightforward young doctor. Courtney had finally had a stroke of good luck after a long run of the other kind. "I understand, but what is your gut feeling?"

"My gut feeling, may the Lord guide me, is that she should remain where she is for the time being, until she gets a little better and is more able to face life with the unquestionable difficulties to come. Courtney claims that she is no longer a risk to others, but she may still be to herself. Then, there will be the issue of her appearance. It will take some effort and money to, uh, change her appearance so that she looks like she did, if she wants. I don't think any of the alterations are permanent."

Jerrod just nodded; his guesses about his daughter's transformation were close to reality but he kept his mouth shut.

Josh said, "I think for now you should work on a plan with your lawyer to eventually bring her home and to work with prosecutors to insure fair and reasonable treatment. She would be safe for now if we could just *get rid of the Russians.* What in God's name do they want with this sick girl, anyhow? I will contact you periodically and eventually Courtney will call, but for now, please do not look for us. That would be very risky, indeed."

Jerrod was happy that Courtney was in good hands but frustrated that he couldn't talk to his daughter, hold her. His mind struggled for some reasonable avenue to take. "Wait, Josh, I would like to send Courtney a letter. Could you give me a few minutes to scratch out something?" The brief, but loving, note was complete within a few minutes; it said:

> *Dear Courtney,*
>
> *I am so happy to find that you are alive, improving, and in good hands. I am indebted to this fine, young man, known only to me as Josh, and thankful for what he has done for you—us. Now, we can all join together and work on a plan to address the issues and ease you back into your normal life as soon as possible. I know you struggle with guilt for what you have done, but please listen to your daddy on this one. Baby, you just happened to take a dose of insanity. The killer was Medulin, and the criminals those who pushed it after they understood its liabilities. My heart is breaking for all the innocent victims of this unspeakable conspiracy.*
>
> *Please take care of yourself and come home soon. I will be here, and you will have a normal life again. I promise.*
>
> *I love you so much.*
>
> *Daddy*

Josh read the note and carefully folded it and placed it in his jacket pocket. He looked up at Jerrod and nodded his approval with a smile. Then he was gone. Jerrod sensed a palpable void in his absence.

37

The Senator

Maxwell Hall smiled as he dialed the Senior Senator from Connecticut's personal number. Senator Edward Whitney was also the Chairman of the Senate Judiciary Committee and uniformly despised by his many enemies.

"Senator Whitney's office; how may I help you?"

Private number, baloney, he thought. "This is Maxwell Hall; I'd like to speak to Senator Whitney, please. It's urgent."

There was some mumbling in the background and then a strong voice, "Hello, Maxwell, how in the world are you?"

"Fine, Ed; so, how's the campaign going?"

"OK, I think, but the Republicans are making threats about all sorts of things. Bastards have me under the microscope. By the way, your contribution really made a big difference. The country needs more patriots like you, Maxwell."

"Thank you, Ed. Say, I need to discuss something of importance with you; it involves me and one of your biggest tax payers, Apex Pharmaceuticals. You have probably read about our little problem?"

The Senator's voice took on a cautious note; he knew Maxwell Hall quite well. "Yes, go on."

"Well, the U.S. Attorney's Office for Connecticut and the U.S. Justice Department indicted me, not the company, *me*, on fraud and felony drug law violations. First of all, as you know, it is highly irregular to indict an individual in such a matter. It has been a witch hunt, a vendetta, against me from the beginning. They claimed massive fraud and cover-up involving Medulin clinical trials. Now, I'll be the first to admit there were problems, as there often are with experimental drugs, but cover-up on my part? Hell no! I am the CEO of the company, Ed; do you think I have the faintest clue about the technical details?"

"Calm down, Maxwell, I certainly wouldn't think so. I believe you are a Wharton MBA, like me."

"Yes, that's where we first met."

"So, you think you have been screwed unfairly by the legal arm of the Federal Government. What do you want me to do about it, Maxwell?"

"I want you to use your powers to reduce and redirect the charges so they make sense and fairly represent the circumstances. Our internal investigations of this have revealed some irregular actions on the part of our scientific and clinical staff. I will hand them to you and they can be named. Maybe they are sacrificial lambs but it is for the good of your single biggest taxpayer and campaign contributor."

"Maxwell, you must understand, this comes at a really bad time with the campaign and all. The damned Republicans are just looking for something like this to pounce on. I'd love to help, but ..."

Hall interrupted the man in an angry voice. "Senator, first of all, there aren't that many Republicans in the fucking People's Republic of Connecticut, and secondly, my good friend, you will help or there will be *no* further campaign contributions from me! At least not for you. You probably know that your Republican opponent is strongly pro-business, and I can tell you the man is looking better to Apex all the time."

"I will not be threatened, Max; I can't help you. End of story!"

Hall laughed and said in a very patronizing voice, "OK, OK, let me help you with your decision making, Senator. Of the two million dollars I handed you *under the table* for your campaign, how much of it did you use for your little love nest up at Kent? Great place to screw your secretary, Theresa, I believe—and all the others. Ed, by the way, I'm thumbing through some really good photos as we speak. Goodness, I can't imagine how my guy got some of these."

There was a long silence before the Senior Senator from Connecticut spoke, "OK, I wouldn't want Hanna and the children to see those damned things, now would I?"

"Or the Republicans," Maxwell submitted.

"No, certainly not them, either. I will get on this as a priority, and we will both avoid ruination."

The conversation ended and Maxwell lit up a Coronas Especiales Cigar and blew smoke rings at the ceiling. He grinned broadly; once again, Maxwell Hall had outsmarted his enemies—no, make that the United States of America. There was a knock on the door, and his secretary showed Murray Schwartz into his office.

"Sit down, Murray, and have a good cigar and celebrate with me."

Schwartz knew better than refuse and stuck the overpowering

Cuban cigar into his mouth but did not light it. He wondered what new crime he had just become party to. "OK, what in hell do we have to celebrate now?"

Hall laughed sarcastically. "Oh, ye of little faith; put simply, the Federal charges against us are no longer a concern?"

"How, so?" Schwartz asked, not hiding his amazement.

"I had a conversation with Ed Whitney, our ever helpful Senior Senator from Connecticut and Chairman of the Senate Judiciary Committee. Turns out he feels our pain over these unwarranted charges and will reduce them to lesser civil charges against the company. We, in turn, will give up a couple of sacrificial lambs. Whatever residual charges we are faced with, our lawyers will string it out until the government prosecutors run out of steam and settle for pennies. They will persist only as long as this mess remains newsworthy."

Schwartz fell back into his chair, fearing the worst and knowing he would not be disappointed. "Why would that arrogant bastard feel ... our ... pain?"

"Would you believe we are old classmates? No, not good enough? Try two million dollars in under the table campaign contributions and a lot of this sort of thing." He tossed Murray the stack of surveillance photographs taken at the Senator's *fishing* cabin alongside the bucolic Housatonic River near Kent, Connecticut.

Schwartz undid the rubber band and flipped through the candid shots and selected one to dwell on a little too long. Hall laughed a bar room laugh. "Not exactly his skinny wife; it's Theresa Polanski, his very well-endowed secretary, I believe. One of many, but definitely the pick of the crop."

"Damn, one fine woman; so you honestly believe this thing is going to happen, don't you?"

"Yes, but we have to fire a couple of people we identified as being responsible in our internal investigations. I have selected Russell Turner, Clinical Director, and Yuan Li, President of Research. I will adequately compensate both of them so they will keep their mouths shut, but Burns will be a real loss. Li is worthless and can go to hell for all I care. Anyhow, they are very high level people and should satisfy the sharks' thirst for blood. We won't hurt for long; the Genplex acquisition will snag some great human resources. You have been bird dogging the purchase of Genplex stock; how are we doing?"

"Let's start with the analysts' reports; I have them here. Lois Ackerman did her job for certain; just let me read her conclusion."

Schwartz thumbed through the thick Sirius report on Genplex until he came to the conclusion. He read, "The future of Genplex is to be found in Axilon's success. This pipeline leader is clearly needed because of patent expirations of existing products. Unfortunately, it is not the miracle drug for the treatment of schizophrenia we had all hoped for. Extensive Phase II clinical trials showed no useful therapeutic effects for Axilon in psychotic patients, and we are left with old, ineffective, dangerous drugs.

Phase II trials in depression and anxiety disorders were more promising, and Phase III programs are in progress, but we have real questions."

Schwartz nodded his head in excited agreement with the document and said, "Now listen to this. The Prozacs and Valiums of this world have been around for a long time and are considered safe and effective, if used properly. Generic equivalents are available and inexpensive. Notably, the newer, more expensive versions like Cymbalta and Effexor aren't better. We know nothing about the long-term effects of Axilon in any patient group. In that regard, the structural similarity of Axilon to Apex's tragic drug, Medulin, continues to worry us."

Hall grinned his pleasure. "That is basically what I understand she said at the meeting at Genplex. Good, the woman is under our control and earning her big bucks. What recommendations are made in the report?"

"This is the best part—*Reduce GPX Holdings Down to thirty-five dollars per share.* Right now it's trading at sixty-five. That's another way to say Sell! Sell! That's the good news, but naturally the bad news is the Coonts and Swale report. Amy Cooper and John Mosley disagreed with Lois at every turn; their recommendation is a Strong Buy. Almost like they didn't attend the same meeting."

"Yeah, but Sirius is the big player; who cares about Coonts and Swale for goodness sake?" Hall quipped. But he did care and considered the wisdom of getting rid of them for good. Right now the truth was dangerous.

"Apparently some investors do, but the Genplex share price is still spiraling down, and Apex is riding the bear. According to Shelby Flint, our CFO, we should have a controlling majority and takeover by the time the stock hits Lois' thirty-five dollar share price."

Hall took a last puff of his cigar and then said, "OK, let's review our punch list; I'll fire Turner and Li as early as tomorrow, and they will have the cash they need to disappear for a long time. What you probably don't know is that two important loose ends—more like loose cannons—have been *taken care of*. The papers will be full of it by tomorrow, but to keep it simple, Jonathan Smith died in a horrible automobile accident in Naples, and Alan Werner committed suicide and took a Senator's wife with him. Nasty! Nasty! Apparently Werner left a signed, suicide note taking credit for the Medulin disaster and those that were hurt by the drug. Kind of messy for the government but good for us!"

Murray Schwartz's mouth opened and closed but no words were uttered. Really, he couldn't think of a single question regarding this mess that he wanted to know the answer to.

38

Time to Reflect

Wanda had been to visit her ailing mother in Philadelphia again and knew nothing of Jerrod's meeting with Josh Ledbetter. Jerrod had not only wanted to spare Wanda added pain but had also become increasingly paranoid about his telephone line security. Courtney's life was at risk. Barbara Barnes had also been unavailable until today due to a complicated, high-asset divorce that made it to court. Jerrod had picked Wanda up at the Stamford train station and was pulling into Barnes, Waddle, and Stein's parking garage for a much needed meeting when he said, "A lot has happened while you were gone; I was afraid to mention anything on the phone, but Courtney has surfaced, sort of, anyway. I'll save the details for our meeting, but for now you have a heads-up before we speak to Barbara."

Wanda smiled sweetly and said, "OK, I'll reserve celebration until I've heard the story. Speaking of heads-up, did you see the paper this morning? This version is the *New York Times*; there are two articles on the first page of the business section regarding deaths of people you know—people involved in the Medulin fiasco." She read both of the short articles aloud while Jerrod searched for a parking place in the crowded garage.

Jerrod whistled; both Jonathan Smith and Alan Werner were dead. "Quite a coincidence, isn't it?"

Wanda frowned, "Not believable, really. Do you think Maxwell Hall had them both killed so they couldn't testify against him?"

Jerrod answered, "Maybe; he's capable of most anything." But in his heart he knew Maxwell Hall had done it—at least paid for the murders. Thoughts of the two elusive Russian Mafia killers tracking his daughter were overwhelming. These criminals had killed Sam Lugar and intended to take Courtney's life. What the hell was their new private investigator, Jason Rand, doing?

186

They waited for Barbara for a few minutes before she walked into the plush conference room, looking a bit disheveled for once. "Sorry ... it's been rough but I'm all ears now." The attractive lawyer seemed to come to life with the excellent dark blend coffee that her assistant poured, and she listened attentively to Jerrod's story.

Jerrod told of the young missionary's visit and spared no detail. Courtney had encountered a true Good Samaritan in Josh Ledbetter and had likely been given a reprieve on life as well. The two main threats at the moment were the police, who might take her down an irreversible legal path with devastating consequences, and the Russian killers, who, according to Josh, *had come close.* Jerrod related how they had agreed upon a plan to allow her improve both mentally and physically in her new life while a sympathetic approach with the legal system was sought. That would be Barbara's not inconsequential assignment.

Barbara considered the situation and savored her coffee for a moment. "I think I agree with the plans you made; however, I share your concern for Courtney with the Russian killers being the greater concern. If the information I received was accurate, and I believe that it was, I do not understand why the police have not apprehended them. I now am certain that call offering the tips on the Russians came from none other than Courtney, and she must have gotten their descriptions and the New York license plate number when they nearly caught her. However, they must not have recognized her at the time. Josh did say that she had changed her appearance; didn't he?"

Jerrod nodded and said, "Yeah, and what about our own man, Jason Rand? Josh never mentioned him and probably wouldn't if that bit of information would provide some clue as to their whereabouts. Maybe Rand is on a cold trail far behind the Russians; another issue, did you see the articles in the paper this morning reporting the accidental death of Jonathan Smith, the Naples Medulin investigator, and the suicide of Alan Werner, the FDA proponent of Medulin?"

"No, I've been too busy to read the newspaper." Wanda handed her the *New York Times* with the articles circled in red ink.

Jerrod gave Barbara a minute to digest the content of the stories and then said, "My hunch is that the two Russians killed them both and Maxwell Hall paid for it to block their testimony. Both murders, assuming they were, sound like professional crimes, and our Russian friends are likely trained to carry out such high quality work."

Barbara looked at Jerrod in shock and said, "That's a stretch but an avenue worth pursuing—we *know* these miscreants killed Sam. Maybe Rand has uncovered something."

"Barbara, can you contact him right now—on the speaker phone?"

She dialed the number, and he answered immediately. "Jason Rand speaking."

"Jason, Barbara here; how are you?" Pleasantries were exchanged, and then they got down to business. "Let's start with where you are?"

"Orlando."

"OK, I want you to listen very carefully to the following question; to the best of your knowledge, have you ever, in this investigation, crossed paths with the two Russian Mafia-types that killed Sam Lugar?"

"Yes, I believe so. Following a hunch, I made the rounds of essentially all the bars and dives in Key West with Courtney's picture. I didn't find Courtney, but I did learn that two Russians had recently made the same rounds with a similar photograph of the girl. They were very thorough, but I don't think they found her."

"Jason, Jerrod here; listen, you probably came very close to finding Courtney as well. You may have even talked to a disguised version of her. We are happy with that and that the Russians moved on, apparently to greater things. We have heard from Courtney through a third party and know that she is OK, at least for the moment. I don't know why the cops can't catch these two killers, but we want you to find them and expedite that. Snag a copy of today's *New York Times* and look at the articles about the accidental death of Jonathan Smith in Naples and the suicide of Alan Werner in Bethesda. We—I—believe that Smith and Werner were murdered by the same two clowns. They may be working for Maxwell Hall, the CEO of Apex Pharmaceuticals in Connecticut. Maybe you can connect these bloody dots in some useful manner."

"OK, I'll try to put something together and find the two killers. My hunch is that they avoid being caught, not by being slippery, but by proceeding about their business like everyday people. Likely don't hide in dark holes with the riff-raff. Cops mostly look in dark holes. Who knows what car they are using by now? I'm on it!"

Barbara switched the speaker phone off and looked up. "Now, I have to think about just what a *sympathetic approach* might be in Courtney's case. Though impaired, she has committed first degree murder in two states, North Carolina and New York. One state will have to take priority in the matter, perhaps New York, since that was a double homicide. It will have to be decided there by the courts or, hopefully, just a judge, and then she would be extradited to North Carolina for a similar process."

Barbara took a sip of coffee and then continued, "A judge would have to determine whether she was competent to stand trial or not, and that could be complicated here. She may be ready to stand trial at some time in the future, but she was obviously not sane when she committed the crimes. I am not a criminal lawyer and will obviously have to bring one in, but, oddly enough, I know the attorney generals of both states. I graduated from NYU Law School with Mitch Bryant, New York Attorney General, and Judy Rigby, North Carolina Attorney General, was a roommate at Yale. I know them both well enough to get one free pass through the door. That's all I can say for now."

Wanda had remained silent throughout the discussion, but her sympathy for Courtney revealed itself. "And what if none of that goes our way? Something unanticipated comes up. Isn't it possibly a lower risk situation for Courtney to remain in her new life, playing out whatever role she has devised for herself? Could she safely do this forever?"

Barbara turned to Jerrod and shook her head ever so slightly; this was way beyond the hundreds of law books that lined her office shelves.

Jerrod looked out the window for a moment as if seeking divine inspiration. "That is *the* question, isn't it? Problem is that I don't know what life she is living or how safe it is. I suspect, *not very*, based on the fact that the young man said he was on a mission for lost souls outside the system. My preference would be to clear her slate and let her start a new life of her choosing."

Wanda said, "There is still the issue of timing, isn't there?"

39

Weighty Matters

Increasingly, Jerrod dreaded his trips to New York, and this sultry, hot August day promised to be the worst. The weight of the humidity and stink of rotting garbage had made Jerrod's walk from Grand Central Station unpleasant at best. Manhattan's usually crowded streets were uncharacteristically empty; most people try to escape the city when it simmers in late summer's grasp, but for Jerrod it was a reverse commute to hell.

Even the expected blast of cold air was missing as the large, glass doors of the Banister Bank Building swung open. The sweating doorman informed Jerrod that the massive structure's air conditioning was operating under brown-out conditions because of the heat and overtaxed electrical grid. Jerrod was already sweating and knew it would not be better on the top floors occupied by Genplex.

Tina Alberti, Alonsio's vivacious secretary, was dressed in shorts and a T-shirt, providing Jerrod's first pleasant surprise of the day. She laughed when she caught him gawking and said, "At least we have suspended the dress code for the duration; it must be one hundred degrees up here."

"I can see that; now I know I'm in hell," Jerrod quipped without smiling.

Tina giggled her sympathy. "Go on in; Dr. Vettori is waiting for you. But tread lightly; the big man is in a really bad mood. The devil, maybe."

Jerrod nodded thanks for the gratuitous warning and proceeded into his boss' lair. Vettori was pacing the floor, sweating profusely. Despite the heat he wore dark, wool slacks and a long-sleeved, blue shirt with growing sweat stains under the arms. His out of date tie was knotted incorrectly and spotted with last night's tomato sauce.

The old man glanced up as Jerrod entered his office. He sighed and stopped pacing for the moment. "Ah, Dr. Wesley, thank you for pulling yourself away from the cool breezes of Long Island Sound. How is the sailing these days?"

It was not so much a friendly question as a deflection of his own frustration to a person capable of living a normal life. Jerrod ignored the unfair insult.

Alonsio slammed his fist against his desk and boomed, "It has all gone to hell! Everything! Where-have-you-been while the ship was sinking?"

Jerrod looked him right in the eyes and said, "Mostly making certain that Axilon saves the company. What would you have me do, Sir?"

"That is the right answer, and none of this is your fault, but you simply *must* do what you can to help save the company. Mr. Albright is in here every five minutes, jumping up and down. The board of directors has threatened him, and apparently Bill Long, the chairman, is going berserk."

Jerrod thought, thank God for Connecticut, but said, "OK, specifically what is the problem that has everyone so upset?"

"*The problem*! Just take your pick." Alonsio made picking motions with his long, skinny fingers. "Let me start with the share price. Do you know what the share price is at the moment?"

Jerrod had learned the hard way to keep up with the daily price of the company's stock. "Ah, closed at forty-two dollars and change yesterday."

"That was yesterday." Alonsio walked over to his computer and squinted at the flashing numbers on the screen. "How about thirty-nine dollars and change as you say, Dr. Wesley?"

"Pretty bad, so what's behind it other than the Sirius report?"

"The Sirius report is part of it but would appear to be a small part of a greater game. Our stock is being actively traded; Rhinner and our CFO believe it is being manipulated by the arbitragers. Someone is throwing low balls, driving it down and there is at least one big buyer accumulating stock on the way down. The excellent Coonts and Swale report has been ignored. Totally ignored."

Jerrod dismissed an ugly thought and asked, "And who do you think is accumulating GPX shares on the cheap?"

"Leonard Bagley, our illustrious CFO, believes that it is the Apex thieves who are stealing the stock. In fact, he *knows* they are; damn it."

Jerrod nodded his head, suspicions confirmed, and said, "So, you think they are trying to quietly acquire control of the company? But, why?"

"Why? Isn't it obvious; they want your drug, Axilon, to replace Medulin, which was a huge loss for them."

"I," Jerrod remarked, "thought they—meaning Maxwell Hall—were in big trouble with the law. How can they possibly pull a stunt like that off under such difficult legal circumstances?"

"Dr. Wesley, apparently they don't sell newspapers on that yacht of yours—look at this!"

Jerrod kicked himself for not catching up on the news on the train ride from Connecticut; he had needed a nap and that was that. The headlines on the business section of the *New York Times* screamed: *Federal Charges against Maxwell Hall, President and CEO of Apex Pharmaceuticals, related to the ill-fated drug, Medulin, dropped.* The article went on to say that after further investigation all charges against Mr. Hall had been dropped and lesser, civil charges had been levied against the company by the Justice Department. An unnamed company spokesman was quoted as saying that two key senior Apex employees, Russell Turner, Clinical Director, and Yuan Li President of Research, had been terminated due to irregularities in the ill-fated Medulin research program.

Jerrod thought, two more dead men are taking the fall for Maxwell Hall. Who in the hell had he bribed this time—the freaking President? He folded the paper in his hands and looked up. "The man appears to wear bullet-proof armor; he must have gotten to someone really big this time."

"Yes, but it would not be smart to pursue that line with him."

Jerrod nodded but thought that there was something rotten that very much mattered and did need investigating. Change the subject. "Alonsio, why aren't we buying back our own stock at this bargain price? Don't we have ample cash reserves?"

Alonsio replied, "Jerrod, that would be the right thing to do; give the bastards some competition, increase our ownership, and stabilize the price. But, unfortunately we can't. What we have at the moment is a large amount of money tied up as illiquid cash equivalents. That is why Rhinner is in trouble with the board; he went along with Leonard Bagley's idea to invest the money overseas in some high interest deal to try to make up for lost earnings. It appears to be a successful idea, but the money is simply not available for other purposes. The board says it was sheer stupidity to do such a thing."

Jerrod nodded—with the precipitously falling share price they couldn't even borrow against the European investment. "So, there is nothing to prevent Apex from taking over the company?"

Vettori seemed to be looking older by the moment. "Not really; Mr. Albright is putting together a road show with Coonts and Swale, but that will only delay the inevitable. Maybe they don't even care what the share price is."

"What about the SEC; is this legal?"

Vettori explained, "Our CFO says yes. This method of acquisition is called a creeping tender offer. It avoids all the usual SEC requirements for a takeover. Generally, with the help of arbitrage, one company quietly gains a controlling interest in another. That means at least fifty-one percent of the voting stock."

"And they are close?"

"Yes, we think so. And when, not if, it happens, they will vote their own board in, take control of the company, and fire whomever they like, maybe everyone. They only want our assets, mainly Axilon."

"OK, I think I understand, but just what do you want me to do about this?"

"I don't know, but *do something*! Your entire future is at risk here, so get out of here and get busy."

Jerrod was used to the old man's ranting and was not moved by it, but he did understand the serious nature of the situation. *Something* was expected of him. He assumed that the ploy to take over Genplex was one hundred percent Maxwell Hall's brain child. No one else in the company had the street smarts or the gall to pull off such a thing. Maybe if Hall went, the deal would fall apart, and GPX shares would return to their previous lofty level. So far, Hall had evaded the consequences of his appalling crimes. He tended not to leave loose ends, but those Medulin charges could not have simply vanished into thin air. Someone in high places was pulling heavy strings for Maxwell Hall. Despite the old man's warning, was that a fertile direction to take?

⅌

"FDA, Division of Psychiatry Products, this is Pearl in Dr. Kendall's office. How may I help you?"

"This is Dr. Wesley, and I need to speak to Dr. Kendall right away. The issue is personal and very important." Jerrod's heart pounded as he waited for the overworked bureaucrat; would Kendall even take the call?"

"Jerrod?"

"Oh, hi, David, I know you're busy, but I really need to talk to you."

"Medulin?"

"Yes. I believe you know that my daughter, Courtney, was given Medulin and allegedly committed several felony crimes. There are a lot of people searching for her, including her father, but she remains very well hidden. Others have died, and some have even killed on the drug. And what about your former associate, Alan Werner? Not to forget Jonathan Smith, the Medulin investigator in Naples. Suicide? Accidental death? I don't think so. I thought I saw the beginning of justice with the charges against Maxwell Hall."

"But, they simply evaporated into thin air, like ... *poof*," Kendall interjected. "And you are angry, and so are we, but my hands are tied; I am not the judiciary."

"Well, David, my hands are not tied, and if I can find a way to bring that bastard to justice, I will. Do you have any idea how or why the charges against Maxwell Hall were dropped?"

"Yeah, I do; the Senior Senator from the State of Connecticut, who also happens to be Chairman of the Senate Judiciary Committee, threw his considerable weight around on Hall's behalf."

"Ed Whitney?"

"None other."

"Wow, any idea what the connection between the two might be?"

"No, other than to state the obvious—Apex is one hell of a big Connecticut taxpayer."

"Likely more than that going on here, and I'm going to find out just what the hell it is." Kendall wished him good luck, and they said their good byes.

Jerrod keyed Jason Rand's cell phone number from memory. The investigator answered after three rings.

"Hello, Jerrod; what's up?"

"Well, I am looking for some help. Listen, I know that you work for both Barbara and me, but I want this discussion to remain between the two of us. The reason is that what I want to do could put Barbara and her firm at risk, and I don't want to do that."

Jason hesitated for a moment and said, "Sounds heavy, but OK, shoot ..."

"Here it is: an influential Connecticut U.S. Senator, Ed Whitney, has pulled some strings, freeing Maxwell Hall from the jaws of justice. I firmly believe that there is some relationship between Hall and Whitney, and knowing how Hall operates, he must have some real dirt on the Senator. In those circles dirt comes in two forms—money and/or sex, the latter being the more fertile ground. I suspect that Hall supports Whitney under the table but has also managed to dig up something on the Senator through his own investigations."

"Wow, but what does that have to do with me?"

"Jason, you are well connected; do you have any connections who are good at digging into such political problems and finding out the truth?"

He laughed, "You mean a private cop in the *political espionage* business? Yeah, I guess I do. The one I have in mind was very busy during the last presidential election and kept some big names out of it. Expensive, though."

Jerrod replied, "What isn't? So here's the deal; you keep my name quiet. The guy will be working for you and paid by you, and you will report his findings to me. I will provide the money, and there will be a big bonus in this for you if the effort is successful."

Jason laughed and said, "I'll see what I can do, and oh, just to keep it simple, let's refer to the person as *Dick Tracy*."

October's chill and promise of winter replaced September's warmth, and Jerrod busied himself with the ever more demanding Axilon Phase III program as large, long-term safety studies and the international registration program got underway. It was a huge undertaking for a small company with limited personnel and resources. The Wall Street wars were left to New York as Jerrod traveled the world, meeting new investigators and setting up clinical trials for Axilon. Jerrod often thought about Jason Rand and Dick Tracy, but the only reports from Rand came second hand from Barbara. Jerrod was beginning to wonder if Rand wasn't just another dishonest opportunist, taking the money and providing nothing in return.

Jerrod awakened and looked out the window of the JAL 747 as it touched down on the wet tarmac at New York's Kennedy Airport. Though it was morning, it was as dark as night and pouring down rain. He sighed as he thought of the traffic; with the snarls and accidents, it would take hours to reach nearby Connecticut. Even beyond the city, I-95 would be a parking lot. Lightning flashed and thunder rolled as the huge aircraft pulled up to its gate. First Class allowed a quick exit, and he was at the head of the pack, running for ground transportation, despite legs of rubber after 13 hours in the air. Jerrod surveyed the small army of waiting limousine drivers waving signs marked with customer names. There, Wesley, but it was not held by a uniformed driver; it was Wanda. He was overcome with appreciation that she would fight this weather to pick him up at the airport from hell, but there she was, smiling, looking beautiful as always.

Wanda said, "Looks like JAL got it done," and they hugged and kissed. She pulled his carry-on bag as they headed for short-term parking. "Jerrod, since it's Friday and your working day is lost to this weather, I took the liberty of making a hotel reservation at the Waldorf. It seems to me that after your short turn-around time for the Tokyo meeting some R and R is advisable."

Jerrod was dressing, and Wanda was still in the shower when his cell phone jangled. He feared it was Alonsio, but, no, it was an unexpected Jason Rand. "What's up?" Jerrod asked with more than a little apprehension.

"First of all, I am sorry to take so long to get back to you. Dick Tracy has been out of the country, and I just now ran him down and met with him in person."

"OK, let's hear it." Jerrod pressed impatiently.

"Well, it's not good news, I'm afraid. Dick Tracy says that Ed Whitney is a dangerous untouchable. He doesn't hesitate to use his powerful position on the Senate Judiciary Committee as a weapon to destroy his enemies. He takes money under the table, but he's not the only one. Only a fool would stand up against him publicly."

Jerrod considered that Alonsio had known this all the time, based on his warning. "And Dick Tracy knows what he is talking about—is nobody's fool?"

"No, far from it."

"So, where does this leave us?"

"Back to plan A, I'm afraid. With regard to that, I have a lead on the Russians—they are Sergei Mogilevich and Vadik Nikolsky, former operatives of the Russian Mafia, who went out on their own. They stay alive by kicking back some of their fees to the big boys. The killers take contracts all over the world, but Maxwell Hall's money is keeping them in this country for the time being. Probably the FBI knows who they are but can't find them. A Russian contact of mine tells me they are in New York and that they frequent those God awful Russian clubs, so I am about to take up a new hobby. Wish me luck!"

Wanda was still drying off when she walked into the room. "Who?"

"Jason—good news and bad news." The news didn't take long to discuss, but the two lovers were very late for dinner.

40

Annual Fantasy Festival

Josh smiled at the pretty girl walking beside him. Samara was making a rather miraculous transformation back to Courtney. The ugly metal that had deformed her soft face was gone, and the tattoos were being removed one by one by a dermatologist with a gentle touch with a laser. Courtney's quick laugh had returned, and she had ample opportunity to use it as they made their way through the hilarious mob of revelers on Duval Street. October brings more than cooler weather to Key West, and the Annual Fantasy Festival was in full swing. Although many of the party people were naked, some wore ridiculous costumes. The Hemingway look-alikes, Jimmy Buffet Parrot Heads, pirates, motorcycle mammas, Bahamian street performers, sailors, fishermen, normal Key West denizens, and noted artists and writers had all become scantily clad Fantasy Festival revelers. Fat Midwesterners, accountants from New York, and schoolteachers from Peoria joined in, losing their crushing inhibitions for that one brief week.

Samara squeezed Josh's hand. She was so glad that he was not a prude. Though a physician and a man of God, he seemed to have escaped the chains of judgment that bind most people. Josh sought to help, not to judge, and she cherished him for that rare virtue. He would never be her lover, but he would always be her friend, mentor, guru. A couple of overweight women, clad only in silly, pink feathers, stumbled over a passed-out drunk on the sidewalk and ended up in a heap on top of him. Josh laughed and helped them up; they almost swooned at the sight of his handsome face. "Maybe time for a cup of strong coffee," he offered and looked for a policeman to rescue the old wino before he was trampled.

For sometime, they continued on their mission as chaperones at the craziest party in the world and actually managed to help a few people who were in real trouble. Samara liked the feeling of helping others. Life as a snooty, privileged prep school student and then as an expensive college coed had allowed so little time for charity. She knew that in spite of all she had suffered, done, she was becoming Courtney Wesley again, perhaps someone better. Could she find her new life here in Key West, helping Josh care for those in need? Samara knew it was not as simple as just remaining here and paying her own version of penance for her sins. She was improving, nearing the point where she could go home and with the help of all those who loved her, face the music. Then, and only then, would she be free to return to Josh and Key West for what remained of forever. Josh pretended not to see the tear that Samara quickly wiped away.

But what Samara could not know was there were damaged areas in the far recesses of her brain that would never heal. Though Courtney's brain had adapted as best it could, rerouting circuits that watched over normal people, modulated their emotional response to the vagaries of life, controlled their anger, and the overpowering need for revenge; her brain would never function properly again. Vital circuits in Courtney's brain, those that separate modern man from caveman, had been irreversibly damaged and quietly festered awaiting some unexpected insult which would cause them to explode.

℘

The efficient secretary showed Barbara into the large, cluttered office. It was obviously a place of hard work for a lowly public servant and not an executive showplace. Mitch Bryant looked up from the ominous pile of documents and his frown rapidly melted.

"Hello, Barb, you come to lend me a hand?" He nodded at the pile of documents with a grin.

"Always, it would be just like the old days when I tutored you through contract law at NYU."

Mitch laughed and replied, "I never was much for fine print work. That's why I went into criminal law and why I work in New York. We have the market for crooks cornered in this city."

"Well, not quite; there are plenty to go around. I'm here to discuss what we briefly spoke of on the phone, the difficult case of Courtney Wesley. You know that I am representing her father?"

"Yes, and I am intrigued, especially since no one has been able to apprehend the girl, and she committed two murders in this city on my watch. She must be pretty slippery."

Barbara nodded her agreement, "And one prior to that in North Carolina. As far as we know, that's all, though quite enough. I hope you have had time to review the brief I sent you?"

Bryant replied, "Yes, I read every word of it and was fairly familiar with the cases from news media reports. This drug, Me ..."

"Medulin," she supplied.

"Right, Medulin dosing has led to some very toxic effects on the brain, and hence behavior, of several innocent patients in clinical studies sponsored by Apex Pharmaceuticals. There were federal charges filed against the company's CEO, were there not?"

Barbara responded, "Yes, and they were unexpectedly reduced for reasons beyond me; suspicious reasons, I might add."

Bryant left her dangerous suggestion alone. "I see, but it remains a fact that several patients committed some pretty ghastly crimes on the drug, that horror in Naples was the worst."

"Yes, and I know your time is limited, so let's get to the real point of my visit, Courtney Wesley. She is the only surviving victim of the drug who actually committed a crime; though others were injured, and there will likely be litigation. We want to work out something with you that will allow fair treatment of Courtney in the courts of the state of New York."

"First, I have to ask you about her whereabouts. Do you know where she is?"

"No, we do not; a third party caretaker contacted my client, her father, Jerrod Wesley, and met with him. Jerrod believes the stranger is totally honest; the man is a physician and minister committed to helping unfortunates. However, we don't know who he is, much less where he is. His first name is Josh; he has contacted us routinely and provided updates as promised. According to Josh, Courtney is doing much better but is not well. We all want to agree on a plan to bring her in and treat her fairly and humanely. Can you help us?"

"Barbara, all I can promise is that I will do my best. I will make it clear that I don't want her prosecuted, but we have laws in this state that we have to abide by. In cases of insanity, for whatever reason, a judge has to rule. He is deciding whether or not she is sane enough to stand trial, and that stands apart from a jury's verdict of innocent by reason of insanity. Expert witnesses, psychiatrists, may be required, but I am concerned that she may now be well enough to stand trial even though there is little probability of conviction. When do you think you can surrender her to this office?"

"Reasonably soon, I hope, but that is out of my control. Pending the outcome in New York, she will have to be extradited to North Carolina. I am on my way to meet with Judy Rigby as soon as I leave here."

"Well, please give Judy my regards; she was your roommate at Yale, was she not?"

"That's correct, and I just pray to God she'll be as helpful as you have been."

"She will be, I'm certain, and just let me know when Courtney wants to turn herself in. By the way, whatever transpires in New York, there will be the overriding issue of public safety. Does this woman pose a risk to public safety if she is released under any circumstances?"

Barbara considered that as a really tough question that likely weighed mightily on Josh's mind. Courtney seemed to be at a critical juncture and it could go either way ...

41

Buzzards Circling

For once Murray Schwartz felt he had it over Maxwell Hall. He had gotten his hands on a copy of what is called a *confidential blurb* in the investment banking business from a contact at Coonts and Swale before it had been issued to selected investors. It was obviously a counterattack by Genplex; a cleverly worded investor alert document written by the Amy Cooper-John Mosley duo. The piece championed Axilon, reiterating its blockbuster potential. It also speculated, in not so subtle fashion, about a sub-rosa takeover, fingering Apex Pharmaceuticals as the likely suitor. Cooper's and Mosley's strong buy recommendation carried a six-month target price of seventy-five dollars, a significant increase over its current low level. A pressing need for Apex to replace Medulin with a new drug of blockbuster potential was mentioned in the disclaimers as a likely driving force.

Murray squinted at Maxwell Hall through the haze of cigar smoke that enveloped the CEO as he carefully read the document. Finally, he laid it on his desk and asked, "And when will this hit the street, Murray?"

"In a day or so; I can't be certain."

Hall took another puff of his big Cuban cigar and grinned. "That may give us the time we need. I'm calling Davis Collingsworth at Sirius right now. No more screwing around looking for bargains; I'm going to direct him to have Sirius go for the final block of stock that we need to close the deal at the market price. We may indeed push it to seventy-five dollars, but so be it. Hell, Murray, we don't need all that much more. I probably should get an exact figure from Herb Ziegler, our anal, overpriced CFO, and then make the call."

"I wouldn't," Murray replied. "Make a conservative guess and call Collingsworth right now. Ziegler will want to ruminate over the thing for a week and generate a hundred charts and graphs and waste valuable time. Just tell him what you did, and let him figure out whether that is enough or not ASAP. As chairman, I reiterate that I have the board of directors' approval for Apex to make this acquisition."

Hall nodded and punched in a number on his secure line, and Collingsworth answered almost immediately. "Hello, Mr. Hall, what can I do for you?"

"One hell of a lot, Davis." Maxwell Hall went through the situation as he understood it and wasn't surprised when Collingsworth knew exactly how many shares were needed for Apex to obtain a fifty-one percent controlling interest in Genplex and agreed to a ten percent overage to thwart any last minute funny business by Genplex or unknown investors.

Collingsworth said, "Mr. Hall, be sure that you file the necessary SEC documents once this is done; you have ten days to file the forms reporting beneficial ownership. There will be hell to pay if you do not, and it might even queer the entire deal."

Hall acknowledged the requirement and concluded by saying, "You and, unfortunately, Lois Ackerman are about to be rich, so get this done and quickly. Oh, and as far as I'm concerned, you can give that bitch a pink slip along with her big check."

Collingsworth laughed and hung up. He didn't waste any time; in minutes he was out on the trading floor capturing the attention of the biotechnology/pharmaceuticals trading group. "Genplex shares! Buy the final block at the market and do it now."

Shouts and applause could be heard as the traders got down to some serious work—there were four hours left until the market closed, and the traders imagined their slice of the pie. Computers hummed for the remainder of the trading day, and when the market closed, it was done. Apex Pharmaceuticals, largest such company in the world, had just eaten another little guy for breakfast. Apex now owned a controlling interest in Genplex and would soon take control of Axilon, a probable multi-billion dollar blockbuster drug. Davis Collingsworth would inform Maxwell Hall and then a long-planned series of events would be initiated. An announcement of the acquisition would go out over the wire, a detailed report, written by Lois Ackerman, hyping the event would be issued, and the required SEC-related documentation would be completed in a timely manner by Herb Ziegler.

※

"Hello, this is Rhinner Albright."

"Rhinner, this is Maxwell Hall; how are you, my man?"

Albright cringed at the sound of Hall's voice and its sickening, gleeful tone. He sensed he was dead meat but had to play the level-headed executive role. "I'm fine; what leads you to call me so late in the work day, Maxwell?"

"Well, our Chairman, Murray Schwartz, is here with me and we are calling you to inform you that we have successfully completed a legal creeping tender offer for your company, and Apex now owns a controlling interest in Genplex. Is your chairman, Leonard Bagley, around?"

"No, he's at his Los Angeles office. I could get him on the line, I suppose."

"No, no, not necessary; we'll call Bagley separately after we are done here."

"Do you have any questions, Rhinner?"

Albright looked off into space for a long moment until he found the words, "You bet your sweet ass, I do. What's your motive; why on earth would you choose to do such a hostile thing that affects so many people?"

Hall laughed. "Seriously, Rhinner, you know the answer to that question; we wanted Axilon, and you were stupid and left yourself in a vulnerable position in the market. It was like shooting fish in a barrel. You didn't buy back shares, even when they became cheap, and it was obvious what was happening. You should go back to business school and take corporate finance 101."

Albright reddened; he knew the board should not have allowed their ambitious CFO to invest their cash in illiquid instruments; now he could only kick himself. "OK, no need to get cute. Assuming what you are telling me is true, what are your intentions? I'm going to have to meet with our board ASAP and eventually with our employees and tell them ... *something*."

Hall grinned through a cloud of cigar smoke. Too bad he couldn't blow it into the incompetent shit's frightened face. "Fair enough; we do not plan to operate Genplex as a partially-owned subsidiary; I am sorry to say. We plan to merge it into Apex, and naturally the remaining shares will be swapped out for Apex shares pending board approval. Beyond Axilon, we will keep whatever assets we want and sell the rest. As far as people go, we plan to let them all go unless they are found to be critical, say, for Axilon development. You and the other top executives, including Vettori and that troublesome Jerrod Wesley, will be given high value packages. At the end of the day, you'll have nothing to bitch about."

Schwartz cringed. The bastard was actually enjoying himself, torturing the poor SOB that had just been informed that his dream was over; it was time to wake up and face unemployment. The dejected executive could only hope Hall was being honest about the severance package. His hand trembled as he dialed his lawyer's number.

Jerrod and Wanda turned down the colonial's long drive after enjoying a brisk, evening walk around Madison. Even as winter approached, Madison was still a lovely town; mums held on to a few orange and yellow blooms amid pumpkins, gourds, witches riding brooms, and all manner of fall decorations. Long Island Sound prolonged the waning warmth of summer for shoreline towns for a few precious weeks; just as it swept spring out to sea for what seemed forever. Jerrod and Wanda understood such things and loved New England and took every advantage of it together. Their engagement had been made public, and Wanda now wore her large diamond engagement ring with pride, though her original stealth ring would remain among her fondest possessions. The wedding would be planned as soon as Courtney returned home, and that now seemed a near-term thing. Life was nearing a sweet moment.

The couple laughed and ran the last yards to their front door as the first few big drops of rain spattered the pavement and the wind picked up, whistling through the trees, filling the air with a cascade of colorful leaves. Winter was nearing and soon a fire would be blazing in the big fireplace in the evenings, its glowing warmth to be enjoyed with a good red wine. Jerrod heard his cell phone ringing as soon as he burst through the front door. It was on the counter where he had unintentionally left it. Probably Alonsio—damn.

He caught his breath and answered the annoying device. It was indeed Alonsio, and he was not a happy man. "Jerrod, I can never find you when I need you. Where have you been? Surely not sailing in this cold?"

"Sorry, Sir. We were out walking, and I forget my cell phone; your tone concerns me; what's going on?"

Alonsio sounded like a dying man, far away in a tunnel. "It's over, all over. Watch the financial news this evening, then you'll see. Jerrod, Maxwell Hall has acquired a controlling interest in Genplex. The company will be absorbed, disappear, and we, all of us, will be terminated. We just concluded an emergency, telephonic board meeting, so the board of directors have been informed and have proposed no meaningful response; not that there is one. Only a few employees deemed critical for Axilon and other key projects will be retained. Apex will sell the products they don't want. I, I ...the main thing is you have to meet with your people in the morning and tell them what has happened and to start looking for jobs. Some will have heard and be angry, scared. Be honest, but be kind; tell them that we will help them as long as we can. Key executives will receive a package; I don't know about the others. This will take a couple of months to sort out. Sit down and write your speech tonight; it may very well be your last one to your people." There was a sob, and the defeated man hung up. Jerrod knew Alonsio was too old to start over and too ornery to retire. The old man was finally done and would likely never get over how the game had ended. A lost fumble on the one yard line going in.

Jerrod looked at the silly, little cell phone. How could such a tiny thing bring such heavy news? He was stunned but didn't fully understand the why of it. Had he been in denial? He switched on CNBC and called Wanda. Her high spirits soon fell as soon as she heard the news, but she rallied and supported Jerrod as best she could under the devastating circumstances. Dinner was a leftover pizza and a bottle of Jack Daniel's before the television. Much of the financial news focused on the takeover, and the more Jerrod heard about the genius of Maxwell Hall in acquiring Genplex and Axilon, the angrier he became. He was livid with the management of his own company for letting the takeover occur; he was angry with the investment firm that had engineered the deal, but he slowly focused and redirected his hostility to the right place—Maxwell Hall.

"Wanda, I have to tell you that someday, one way or another, that … criminal, Maxwell Hall, is going to get his due. Just listen to those talking heads; they think he's wonderful."

"Jerrod, easy; Wall Street loves takeovers and layoffs for balance sheet reasons, and it's not their fault. You have to get a grip and face reality; what are we going to do?"

"Do? I eventually want another research management position; perhaps I'll try my hand at a start-up biotechnology company. I'm pretty certain that Coonts and Swale can raise the capital for me. I have a good friend, Robert Honeywell, who started up a company specializing in infectious disease drugs, and he has done fabulously well. A lot depends on the package I get from Apex. Knowing Maxwell Hall, it will be very generous with lots of strings attached so I go away and keep my mouth shut. That, I will do up to a point, and I believe you know what that point is. You, my dear, will come with me and we will do it together—at least I hope so. This whole thing could be a blessing in an ugly disguise. While I am devising a business plan and talking to the many necessary people about a start-up, I will have a lot more time to help Courtney, and I feel, hope, she will return home soon."

Wanda smiled and said, "Jerrod, let's go to bed."

Jerrod shook his head; at the moment he would be a poor lover.

"Sorry, I can't. I am going to have one more drink, calm down, and then write my damned speech for tomorrow."

The following day was one of the more difficult ones of Jerrod's life. The word of the Apex acquisition had spread rapidly, and most employees overflowing the Genplex auditorium already knew almost as much about it as he did. There was not a dry eye in the place when Jerrod waded into his prepared speech. Rhinner Albright and Alonsio Vettori sat on the front row in uncomfortable proximity to an Apex Human Resources representative who was there to *answer any questions*. Several Genplex security guards lurked in the back of the auditorium, just in case someone lost it. Jerrod stumbled badly with the words and finally said, "Damn it," and wadded up the formal speech and stuck it in his pocket.

"How can a few empty words scribbled on a sheet of paper tell you how I feel about the takeover of our company by Apex Pharmaceuticals? And when I say *our company*, I mean just that. We have all given our best to make Genplex what it is today, and with the development of Axilon, the future seemed unlimited. Unfortunately, what we accomplished together in those few busy years made us an attractive target for astute players in the business. I personally want to thank every one of you for what you have contributed, for the long hours and sleepless nights, for your brilliant thoughts, and for making us what we have become. You can steal a company, or even a life, but you can't steal history and all the wonderful accomplishments that came before this dark day. You all know I am from Mississippi and love the writings of William Faulkner; he once said, *You must always know the past, for there is no real was, there is only is.*"

Jerrod pushed away a tear and described the conditions of the deal as well as he could and then introduced Albright and Vettori, who mumbled a few gratuitous comments before the Apex HR guy took center stage but avoided giving direct answers until he was shouted down. Most came away with the understanding that they had two months to find a job. Some loyal employees would hang in there until the last minute, hoping they would be chosen to stay on. Others would never return. None would ever forgive Maxwell Hall, and their names were added to the legions who despised the man.

42

A Brief Ray of Sunshine

I t was eight days before the takeover would be announced and a rare, quiet time in Key West. Fantasy Week was over and the throngs of tired, blistered, hung-over tourists had departed for the real world where naked princesses would resume their mundane lives as waitresses and law clerks in Peoria. It was a beautiful evening for a walk on the deserted beach, and gentle waves lapped the shore, reflecting the reds and yellows of the tropical sunset. The trade winds rustled the palm fronds high over head, pushing the heat of the day far out to sea.

The couple laughed and splashed in the receding surf as they made their way down the beach. Samara blushed as Josh took her hand. What was he thinking? He had always been sweet and caring, but that was his nature. Now, he was more than that—the way he looked at her. She reached up and gently brushed his unruly blond hair from his eyes, noting that his smattering of freckles had multiplied in the Florida sunshine. The tall young man bent down and kissed her. It was not a brotherly peck but a deep, long kiss filled with passion. Josh then held her by both hands at arms length, taking in her beautiful face, so recently free of ugly tattoos and primitive metallic trappings.

"Samara, no ... Courtney, in violation of everything I swore to myself before I came here, I am in love with you. I know this makes no sense given our respective circumstances, but I love you."

Courtney could not believe it, and her eyes filled with tears. "Oh, Josh, I have loved you from the moment I first set eyes on you. I love you with all my heart, but where can this go for you? I have so much to face before I am free to live my life as Courtney Wesley, much less ... Courtney Ledbetter."

"Yes, I know, and the time for you to go is nearing. We must make the best of what we have right now and then prepare for the long haul. I will stick by you through it all, and you know I am a man of my word."

Courtney answered with a smile; she knew who her man was.

The couple watched the brilliant red orb settle into the ocean, and then they were intimate for the first time on the deserted beach. For that wonderful evening they never left the comfort of each other's arms. They made love, napped, laughed together, and made love again until the rising sun and arrival of early morning shell collectors put an end to it. The ensuing week was a blur of happy work and quality time together, but they both knew that the time for Courtney to pack her bags and face the music was nearing. However, the winds of change that rattled the shutters of Courtney's tortured soul were as unpredictable as the trade winds that brushed Key West were predictable, and no one could have possibly imagined what would happen next. To say the least, her lover's fervent prayers were not rewarded.

ℒ

It was a slow night at Bat Cave, and an out-of-uniform customer in a dark suit had switched the TV to CNBC. Courtney had picked up the remote control to rectify the annoying situation when the name of her father's company flashed across the screen with a familiar picture of the Genplex's Madison Facility in the background. She froze in place as the two talking heads described the brilliance of Maxwell Hall's take-over of Genplex in excruciating detail. How could she know that her father and Wanda were watching the same news cast and experiencing the same gut wrenching emotions? Genplex would soon be no more, just another meal for the monster that was Apex. One Wall Street commentator gleefully announced that all of Genplex's senior executives would be fired, as would most employees, and then there was a short piece on the brilliant Jerrod Wesley and his wonder drug, Axilon. He, too, would soon be road kill. The arrogance of them!

Courtney stiffened; Maxwell Hall, the man who had poisoned her and killed people who got in his way, had now made her father *road kill*? This man who had done so much wrong had now ruined her father despite his endless hard work and dedication? Fired him? Hall had gotten away with so much and now this? Courtney's head pounded; the recesses of her injured brain overflowed with a hot lava anger and hostility. The few layers of inhibition that kept the animal within her at bay were woefully inadequate and simply ceased to function. Courtney's eyes narrowed to slits, and she drooled from the corners of her mouth. The angry girl walked out of Bat Cave without speaking one word to anyone and was never seen there again.

Two hours later, an unsuspecting Josh Ledbetter walked into Bat Cave and was surprised not to find Courtney at her station behind the bar. The other bartender was doing double duty and wasn't in a chatty mood but had said that a news program about a pharmaceutical company in Connecticut had set her off, and she left looking extremely upset. Fearing the worst, Josh had rushed to her apartment and banged on the door until a sleepy roommate materialized.

"Samara ain't here. She's split; just stormed in here and packed up most of her shit and was gone. Nothin' else, jist gone, man."

"Where," Josh probed, "did she go, Gathra?"

"Didn't say, and I didn't ask—way it is 'round here; people is always runnin' from something and don't leave no itinerary."

"OK, OK, I believe you; now, think, girl, what was she wearing?"

"A wearin'? Dirty jeans, tennis shoes, Duke sweat shirt, baseball hat—looked like a boy; if you can imagine that."

Josh couldn't, but the only way out of the Keys was U.S. 1, and she had to either be hitchhiking or driving a stolen a car. If she was hitchhiking, he might catch up to her before the night was done; if she had stolen a car, she could be well up the little chain of islands. Once she reached Miami she would simply melt into the vast city and disappear forever. The only hope was to call the police; they still had a good chance of catching her before she crossed the last bridge. Josh looked at his cell phone, shook his head, and then keyed Jerrod Wesley's home number.

Despite the late hour, Jerrod answered on the third ring. Josh explained the situation, taking as little time as possible. There was no discussion of what had set the girl off. There seemed little to do other than call the police, something they had avoided for so long. Given the pending charges against her, law enforcement would have no choice other than a full-fledged mobilization of local and state forces throughout the Keys. Jerrod at last knew where his daughter was, or had been.

Josh was well known and respected by the Key West police who were more than willing to listen when he walked into the station. He explained that Courtney was ill and probably not dangerous, though he wasn't sure about the latter claim. Within minutes, police cruisers were mobilized from Key West to Miami, and several road blocks were set up at key points along U.S. 1. Josh would remain at the station and provide whatever help was needed. Courtney would surely be apprehended.

⅊

The trade winds that had so recently ruffled her lover's hair pushed the little sailboat hard to the southwest. Steady tacking to the north would put her in the vicinity of Naples by the following evening. Her father had taught her well, and she handled the boat expertly with little fear of the rough water. There was no security at Pirate Joe's Marina and Used Boat Sales where she had stolen the thirty-foot boat. She simply selected a boat rigged much like her father's J-Boat, tossed her few things aboard, and sailed away. Courtney was fortunate; the owner had left the craft well stocked with supplies. She elected not to show lights, and the full moon provided all the visibility she required for navigation. The main concerns were avoiding the countless oyster bars and shoals, given the boat's considerable keel, and the Coast Guard. The latter was less of a concern because most stolen boats headed for Cuba. She would make her way across the hundred or so miles of open Gulf to Naples and then ditch the boat there. Once in Naples she would steal a car that would not be missed and drive to Connecticut. There, she would take care of Maxwell Hall once and for all. But where were those troublesome Russians? Would they be there, waiting for her? She'd kill them first if she had to.

43

Not Heaven

Two days after Courtney had set sail for Naples Jason Rand was pounding the streets of Greenwich Village in a driving, autumn rain. It was 2:00 a.m., and he was well into his punch list of New York Russian nightclubs in his search for Sergei Mogilevich and Vadik Nikolsky. The clubs he had visited so far had mostly been expensive, up-scale joints patronized by Euro-trash, tourists, and very few Russians. There was little chance that his quarry would visit such domesticated clubs that pretended to be something darker for the satisfaction of tourists.

Jason was tired, but He6eca seemed a lot more promising. At least it had a Russian name, that oddly enough meant *Heavens*, and was situated in a darker, more isolated section of the Village that made even him nervous. Sounds of Russian hard rock and thick cigarette smoke floated up the stairwell. Jason took a deep breath and proceeded down the stairs and stepped into another world. A tall, blond girl eyed him suspiciously and took his wet hat and topcoat. He noted that she had an artificial leg as she limped her way off to the cloakroom. He could feel his Walther P-99 snuggled against his chest under his suit jacket; it held twelve 9 mm rounds in the magazine, easily enough firepower to stop two big Russian thugs. The small, .25 caliber semi-automatic nestled against his leg provided back-up. He called it his voice of experience.

A trickle of sweat ran down Jason's back as he elbowed his way through the crowded dive to a single vacant seat at the bar. While Western restaurants and bars often smelled good, this place definitely did not. Stale cigarette smoke mingled with the odor of sweat and food offerings of dubious origins. Cheap perfume worn by the woman beside him did not help. The burly bartender muttered something to him in Russian, and he answered, *Vodka*. It was a good guess and a bottle of Stolichnaya and a shot glass appeared before him; the better stuff was apparently reserved for the Russians. He poured a shot of the clear liquid and knocked it down, hoping it would clear his burning eyes of the effects of the thick clouds of pungent, Russian cigarette smoke. He6eca was indeed a likely place; nearly all patrons were Russians and few smiled, though all talked loudly as older Russian men exchanged drinks and sometimes kisses and embraces with much younger, slender blond women. Rand guessed that the men were mostly mobsters and the women escapees from arranged marriages with Americans. Most of the women were pretty; some were beautiful. He felt uncomfortable, lit a rare cigarette, and did what he did best—waited and watched as blue clouds of acrid cigarette smoke and denizens of the strange world swirled around him.

Jason had been discretely observing the bar scene for over an hour. He had been hit on by several working girls but so far had not spotted his quarry. The tired detective was just about ready to give up and move on when they appeared. The two big men stood out, not because they were brutish and drunk, but because they leaned on two Asian women. Based on their scanty dress, they were likely hookers; expensive hookers paid for with Maxwell Hall's blood money. He knew the men were Mogilevish and Nikolsky but verified their identity with a glance at photographs provided by his contact. All he had to do was pick up his cell phone and call the police. Jason placed a large bill on the bar, not expecting change, and waited for the four revelers to find a table and settle in. But that was too obvious, predictable. Instead, they made their way to a knot of standing men and women drinking beside the bar very close to Jason. There was a loud exchange of greetings in Russian followed by much hugging and kissing. The smaller of the two instinctively scanned the crowd with his hard eyes, locking on Rand for a brief, but unsettling, moment. The larger of the two men reached inside his jacket, causing the jumpy detective to do the same. Rand relaxed; the Russian pulled out, not a weapon, but rather a large wad of bills. The money was eagerly accepted by a tall, lanky Russian man called Vlad. A livid scar across his face added to his menacing appearance. Jason figured Vlad and his friends were local Russian Mafia paid off for the privilege of operating on their private turf.

A few more words were spoken before Mogilevish, Nikolsky, and their lady friends bade their good-byes and hurried for the door. There was no opportunity to call the police, and Jason could only follow and hope for the best. A waiting car would end the opportunity. The group collected their rain gear and then climbed the steep stairs with difficulty. Jason decided to forget his hat and coat for the moment and followed the foursome up into the driving rain. Luckily, there was no waiting limousine and the party-goers splashed their way through the growing puddles to their next rendezvous. There were many other clubs in the area, and Rand could only guess they were hopping from one bar to the next, drinking and paying off whoever needed to be paid off.

A small, red neon sign flashed ahead; it read, *The Russian Bar* in English, but likely attracted the same crowd as He6eca. Rand ducked into a store front and waited, but again the group surprised him by turning into a dark alleyway just prior to the bar. Was there a side door, or had they sensed they were being followed? Jason was in a quandary; he knew these people were smart, and he remembered what had happened to Sam Lugar ... He pulled out his cell phone and keyed-in the NYPD contact number that Barbara Barnes had given him. A short conversation with a detective already involved in the search for the two Russians guaranteed a rapid response.

Rand did as he promised: maintained the cell phone connection and turned into the alley, presumably tailing the suspects. The stench of wet, rotting garbage was overpowering, but he took it in stride and moved down the narrow alleyway. He had taken no more than a few cautious steps into the darkness when there was a bright flash and the report of a high-powered weapon. The .357 magnum slug tore through the flesh and muscle of his left shoulder, and he hit the filthy, wet pavement hard. Rand knew he had made a serious mistake; the dim streetlight on the avenue behind him had made him a silhouetted target. It was not a life-threatening wound; he had dropped his cell phone and lost his line of communication. Walther P-99 ready, Rand fumbled briefly in the darkness for the tiny phone, but it was hopeless, and he soon gave it up.

They were still there; he could hear guarded voices whispering in the alleyway beyond him. Did the Russian thugs believe that they had killed him? Maybe. Had the women moved on to safety? Likely. Rand had no light, but there were twelve rounds in the Walther, and he had a spare clip in his pocket. He pulled off a single round from the prone position and then quickly fired two more times in the general direction of the brief image of two bulky figures revealed by the muzzle flash. His efforts were rewarded by a scream and a volley of shots fired in his direction. This weapon had a distinctively different report. He remained low and listened; it was quiet now, and the only sound was that of the rain which fell even harder. His next move wasn't obvious, but he heartened at the sounds of police sirens in the distance. In minutes, the alley was filled with blinding light as squad cars entered from both directions and slammed to a halt.

Relieved that it was likely over, Rand stood and dropped his pistol to his side, walking toward the bulky body of Sergei Mogilevish. The Russian lay motionless in a pool of blood, rapidly spreading in the flooded alley. Convinced his quarry was dead, Rand squinted into the blinding lights, dropped his weapon, and raised his hands. But where the hell was the other one? His question was answered by the rustle of cardboard boxes and clang of metal garbage cans as Vadik Nikolsky emerged from a pile of uncollected litter with his Uzi machine pistol raised. Raaaap! Raaaap! The weapon spewed its deadly rounds. Rand spun around and hit the pavement but did not avoid the impact of several 9 mm slugs. The detective's thoughts of imminent death were interrupted by three loud booms as a policeman dispatched Nikolsky with his sawed-off, 12-gauge shotgun.

It was over. The Russian killers were finally dead, and he, Jason Rand, could be counted among the living, at least for the moment. In addition to the flesh wound in his shoulder, he had suffered three wounds to his right leg; it was broken, he was bleeding profusely, and he needed help. The sirens of ambulances screamed in the distance, and heavily-armed cops were running all over. He tried to speak as the dark form of a detective in a hat and raincoat loomed over him, but the wounded PI fainted dead away in shock.

44

Sailor Take Warning

ourtney felt like a character in a fairy tale. She and her small vessel, *Silver Lining*, were one with the orange glow of the waning day. The sun began its descent behind the clear, unobstructed horizon, and for a fleeting moment she was treated to the illusive green flash, an often sought but seldom seen effect of optical acrobatics. She scanned the horizon, fully expecting to see a string of lights to her north as twilight passed into darkness, but there were none. Had she misjudged? Had strong currents wrestled her from the predictable arms of the trade winds?

The young woman smiled as the breeze freshened behind her back, pushing lingering doubts out to sea. She had ample food and water for several days, and if she stayed on this heading, she would eventually reach the coast of Southwest Florida; she had to—there were things that needed doing. Maxwell Hall, the man who had hurt so many people and made her dear father road kill, had to die. Perhaps a slow and painful death would be most fitting. Her sick mind processed multiple scenarios as she ruminated on the act.

Gathering clouds erased the twinkling stars, and soon bright flashes of lightning joined the rolling thunder that was the voice of a late tropical depression edging her way. It enveloped the *Silver Lining* slowly, seductively, until Courtney could only hold on as the wind and the fury of the churning sea had their way with the fragile craft. Eventually, exhaustion and the rhythmic pounding of the sea brought a restless sleep filled with lucid images of naked, fat Russians chasing her through the streets of Moscow. She screamed as the dream-Russians had their way with her and awoke with a start. It was morning, and she and what was left of the sailboat were hard aground on a broad, sandy expanse of deserted beach. The mast had snapped, and the sails were nowhere to be seen. The keel had been cleanly cut away from the hull by the sharp teeth of a distant oyster bar. The storm

215

grumbled far out to sea, and surf pounded angrily in the distance as the tide receded. The only living voices to be heard were the screams of gulls as they fought over the storm's bounty of dead creatures scattered about the deserted beach.

After pulling the plug to drain the boat, she removed her uncomfortable salt water-soaked clothes and arranged them to dry. The food and water stored in the watertight compartments were safe, and she enjoyed a simple meal of fruit and bread with bottled water. A quick search of her travel bag provided a dry bikini and a chart of the jigsaw puzzle waters off Southwest Florida. The lost girl frowned as she studied the chart; she figured she was north of Naples, but that was about all. This obviously wasn't Fort Myers Beach with its many businesses and high rise condominiums and hotels. It was probably one of the islands to the north—Sanibel, Captiva, Gasparilla—there were many of them and some were populated, while others were not. Then her eyes took notice of the Ten-thousand Islands to the south of Naples. What if she had landed there? Her remains would never be found. No, no, she was definitely north of Naples, but where?

"Please God, You delivered me here alive for a reason; now provide me with a car and a road to the mainland, and I will make Your world better," she prayed aloud.

After a while Courtney became bored with sitting and decided to climb the tall sand dunes that surrounded the broad beach to get a better perspective. Maybe she could see a boat or even a cottage when she reached the top. She was sweating and her legs were scratched from the masses of thorny vines that crept among the dunes. Courtney groaned; there were only a few hundred more feet of sand and then more water. Beyond the several mile expanse of water, what could be the mainland loomed hazily in the distance. Courtney was wrecked on a thin barrier island in the middle of nowhere. She walked down to the beach, an expanse of fine, white sand covered with pretty shells. The leeward water was calm and clear, unaffected by the storm. The tired girl sat on a little dune near the water and dozed for some time in the growing warmth of the morning. Presently, Courtney was awakened by a chugging sound. When she stood and shielded her eyes from the sun, she could see a boat in the distance. It was slowly approaching and holding hard to the beach. As it grew closer, she could see that it was a dilapidated, wooden affair with peeling, green paint. An ancient Johnson outboard motor emitted a cloud of greasy, black smoke. The single passenger, an old man, looked at home among piles of nets and rusting fishing paraphernalia.

Marion Garrard had not seen the girl; his eyes were focused on a dark blob that moved ahead of the boat like some large sea creature.

The old man fumbled about for a moment, and then a large cast net spiraled out of the boat and over the school of unsuspecting mullet. The lead weights hit the water with a circular splash and a hundred pounds or more of the little fish were captive. The old man struggled mightily to land his catch, but he simply didn't have the strength to pull it over the side and into the boat.

Courtney yelled, "Hello, let me help you," as she jogged down the beach toward the struggling fisherman.

The grizzled mullet fisherman jerked to an upright position and spotted the scantily clad girl splashing through the shallow water toward his boat. "Don't know who you are, but you damn near scart me to death. But yeah, I could use some help; come on aboard, young lady."

The large fish box was filled with mullet, and the fish were covered with ice in a matter of minutes. "Marion Garrard, here," he declared, as he extended a rough hand. "Who in the dickens are you, and what are you a doin' on this godforsaken sandbar?"

Be cautious, Courtney thought. "My name is Samara, just Samara, and my sailboat was wrecked on the beach on the other side in the storm last night after I was blown off course. Where in the world am I?"

"Whur? You ain't much of no whur, I reckon. Jist a big ol' sandbar kicked up by the last hurricane. That be Cayo Costa Island over there 'crost the big water. I live on the other side of that 'un in Matlacha."

"Mat ...."

"Mat-la-cha," he provided. "Ain't much—lil' ol' fishin' village on a spit of land on the road to the mainland. Them Yard Dog sangers made the place famous a while back. Fort Myers is right on up the road."

"And you sell your fish over there?"

"Yep," he nodded. "Sell some to the fish market, some for bait, and a few go in my gumbo pot. Make some right good gumbo, I reckon."

"Listen, Mr. Ga, Garrard; I need help. Would you please take me to the mainland, at least to someplace where I can catch a ride? I don't have any money," she lied, "but you can have my sailboat, at least what's left of it."

"I'd be most happy to take you to Fort Myers, and I don't need no money fer it, but I'd like to see that there boat, if you're jist gonna leave it here to rot."

Garrard anchored his skiff in the shallow, protected water and they crossed back over the island to the beached sailboat. The old man examined the boat while Courtney covered herself with a T-shirt and faded shorts, and then collected her few things.

He said, "Hull is mostly OK, and I can use this thing; pretty nice boat, really. I'll just leave a note that she belongs to me, and I'll tow her off the beach first good high tide."

Courtney laughed, "Good, glad you can use it, but I suggest we get the numbers off the hull and dispose of any papers inside right now."

It was Garrard's time to laugh. "Stole her; didn't cha?"

"I borrowed it, but it's in no condition to return; now is it?

Courtney enjoyed the cruise to Matlacha; the chugging skiff survived the angry water in Boca Grande Pass and then eased into the relative calm of Charlotte Harbor. An easy passage along the north side of Pine Island led to his fisherman's shack in Matlacha. Garrard never stopped talking; he knew much about the history of the area and its fish and fauna. He not only fished for mullet but also for whatever was illegal and commanded a high market price. He specialized in out-of-season pompano and grouper and was on a first-name basis with every conservation officer in Southwest Florida. Several got a nice bottle of whiskey every Christmas, and others took their cut in grouper fillets.

"You're welcome to stay the night or as long as you want. Don't have many pretty girls like you a comin' 'round here, I reckon."

Courtney smiled at the generous old man. His grin was like a New England fence missing several of its pickets. She realized that she could probably hide in Matlacha forever without being caught but said, "No thanks." Courtney was starving though and agreed to stay for a bowl of Marion's *world famous* gumbo soup, which he kept simmering in a big pot at low heat at all times. It was hot and nutritious, and she loved it. Two hours later she gave the fisherman a grateful hug in front of the Delta terminal at the Southwest Florida International Airport in Fort Myers, and Marion Garrard and his old Ford pickup truck clattered out of her life forever. Courtney stood there until he was out of sight and then walked across the street to the long-term parking facility. She was experienced at what to do next.

"A penny for your thoughts," Wanda quipped.

Jerrod looked at Wanda, realizing that he had been gazing into his drink, lost in fuzzy thought. Rumination was a trait he despised in people, but recently he had become prone to it. "I'm sorry, Wanda, it's just ... that ..."

Wanda hailed the waiter and ordered more drinks, allowing Jerrod to regain his composure. She reached across the little table and put her hand on his and said, "I know your losses at this point must seem uncountable, but I do not intend to let you fall among them.

Why don't we try to focus on the bright side—your company has been sold, but you are young, have money, and new ideas to pursue. Your phone never stops ringing; I know; I answer it," she said with a laugh. "You have a beautiful, sexy woman who loves you and will marry you. So, what's so bad?"

Jerrod sighed, "Thanks, Wanda, but what you say sounds better than my troubled mind's view of it. However, I guess I have to agree with you except for the Courtney part. Where in the world has she gone, and what is she up to? Things seemed to have been going so well for her. Why, Josh recently disclosed to me that they had developed a relationship and were in love. She was preparing to come home and face the music, when ..."

"When what?" Wanda asked, pushing him to spit out the hard bone he had been gnawing.

"I don't know; I just don't know. Damn! Truth is I'm afraid she's dead, taken her own life. Josh told me that the witnesses said it was a television news report about the Apex takeover that set her off. Maybe she felt somehow responsible ... I ..."

Wanda felt for him, wishing she could make his errant angel appear out of thin air, but she couldn't. "Jerrod, I don't know what leads you to believe that something bad has happened to her. There is no evidence of that at all."

"So, why didn't all those police with their roadblocks apprehend her, then?"

"Jerrod, there are a dozen ways she could have slipped through the net. She has certainly demonstrated her ability to avoid being caught so far. And remember, she did have a head start on the authorities."

"I know; I know, and I guess what we haven't considered is that there are other ways to leave the island, boats, planes, whatever."

Wanda replied, "There is no way she could have left by plane without being identified, but boat, maybe. You taught her to be an accomplished sailor, didn't you?"

Jerrod brightened, "That could just be it; she didn't own a boat but at this juncture she was fully capable of stealing one. That could be it. What we need to do is find out whether a small sailboat of the type she could manage alone was stolen in Key West around the time of Courtney's disappearance. I'm calling Josh Ledbetter right now."

Jerrod stepped outside the noisy restaurant into the brisk evening and dialed Josh's cell phone number. After several rings, Josh came on and listened patiently while Jerrod shared his idea. Josh was excited by the concept and agreed to meet with the local police right away and find out what vessels, if any, had been reported stolen in the immediate area. Jerrod and Wanda enjoyed their excellent seafood in silent anticipation before the return call came.

"Jerrod, there was only one boat stolen at about the time Courtney disappeared; it was a thirty-foot sailboat named *Silver Lining*. Older J- Boat owned by a retired couple and recently re-rigged. Could Courtney sail such a thing?"

"Absolutely, she grew up sailing a similar boat."

Josh was silent for a moment and then responded, "OK, they are already searching for the vessel, but not very actively, I suspect. I'll tell the police it is likely the key to finding Courtney, and they will alert police and Coast Guard contacts up and down the Florida Coast. It will likely be found, but she may be long gone. Oh, and another thing, there was a severe coastal storm that hit Southwest Florida about the time all this happened, so no telling where she washed up. It would have definitely been a trial for both the little sailboat and its captain. On the other hand, we don't know which coast she sailed along, but the west coast is the better bet."

45

The Trail Goes Cold

One week later, a U.S. Coast Guard helicopter spotted an old, green fishing skiff towing a damaged sailboat that once might have met the description of the *Silver Lining*. A small, fast patrol boat in the area was immediately dispatched and intercepted the old fisherman just inside Charlotte Harbor. Marion Garrard shut his laboring outboard down as soon as the siren sounded behind him. He had long ago learned not to try to evade the bastards.

Garrard squinted; shit, he didn't know 'um. "Sumpin I can help you boys with?" he asked as the patrol boat pulled up alongside the smaller craft.

"Likely so," one of the two officers replied. "We're looking for a stolen vessel, a 30-foot J-Boat that sails under the name *Silver Lining,* and that looks like what's left of her you have in tow, at least that's the name painted on her stern."

Garrard mumbled to himself, "Oh shit; how did we forget that?" but did not respond to the Coast Guard officer.

"Sir, could I see your registration for both vessels, please?"

The old man sorted through some papers in the boat's storage compartment and pulled out his commercial fishing boat registration. The officer made a fuss of examining the papers while his mate made a call. The man scratched some notes, handed the papers back, and said, "What about the other boat?"

"Don't have nothin'; jist found her a driftin' off Cayo Costa Island and thought I'd tow her in for salvage; you know."

"Why didn't you notify the Coast Guard, Sir?"

"Radio is busted."

The officer had no reason to doubt the old man since everything else on the boat appeared in disrepair. "OK, Mr. Garrard, I don't know anything about your salvage rights in this case, but I have to take the boat into my custody; it will be held as evidence in a murder investigation, at least for now."

The old man was genuinely shocked and searched for words. "Murder, you say?"

"Yes, murder. The person who likely stole this boat from a marina in Key West is a suspect in several murders. Her name is Courtney Wesley and she might call herself Samara. She is of college age. Have you seen such a girl, Mr. Garrard?"

"Nope, don't know no young girls and ain't seen none out here. Like I said, I jist found her a floatin' out there like she is right now. Girl might a drowned; thing looks all tore up from the big storm we had the other night." Garrard spit his chew of tobacco into the tossing water and grinned, showing a few brown teeth.

The officer looked at Garrard for a long moment and said, "Sir, do you still reside at the Matlacha address given on your boat registration?"

"Yep, and fer most of my life—my fishin' camp; you know."

"Well, you're free to go, but don't take any long trips; the police may want to talk to you."

Garrard waved as they departed with their captive in tow. He spit his remaining tobacco juice into the water and exclaimed, "Murder?"

※

Jerrod still spent many hours in his office in spite of the impending Apex takeover of operations. He handled his job in a professional and perfunctory manner but found time to invest in his future. He had just completed a conversation with Amy Cooper regarding the financing of a biotechnology start-up company dedicated to Alzheimer's disease when the news came.

"You say they found the missing boat, Josh?"

"Yes, off some islands near Fort Myers. The Coast Guard intercepted an old fisherman towing the *Silver Lining*, at least what's left of her."

"What's left of her?" Jerrod interrupted.

"Yes, the boat had been pretty well torn up by that tropical depression that came through. The mast and sail were gone as was the keel, but the hull was in good shape. Old man claimed he found it floating off Cayo Costa Island, and there was no sign of anyone, much less a young woman."

Jerrod chewed on the possibility of Courtney being lost overboard and discarded that unlikely notion. "Did the Coast Guard believe him?"

"Not one hundred percent. The local police questioned him as well and felt the same but didn't have any real evidence to hold Garrard on. His name is Marion Garrard, and he claims to be a mullet fisherman, but he's well known to the local authorities as an illegal market fisherman. That makes him a minor league crook, I guess, but a lot of the old timers resent the government's intrusion into their fishing rights."

"Josh, could you meet me in Fort Myers?"

"Sure," Josh responded, "anything that might help Courtney. Just let me know when and where."

"Our company plane is just sitting here on the ground doing nothing and I might as well use it one more time before it's all over. I'll land at the General Aviation Terminal at RSW at noon tomorrow; can you pick me up?"

"Yes, Jerrod, no problem."

"OK, get Garrard's coordinates, claims he lives in Matlacha, from the police and we'll pay him an unexpected visit tomorrow afternoon. I'm assuming he isn't dangerous."

Josh hesitated for a moment and then said, "OK, but the police may not want to tell me where to find the old man. If not, I'll figure it out myself; how many people could possibly live in Matlacha?"

Jerrod had little trouble gaining access to the idle corporate jet, and the quick trip from Connecticut to Fort Myers was uneventful. Josh was waiting as promised, and the drive from the airport to Matlacha was scenic and reasonably short. A few confusing dead-end lanes and back roads finally led to the old fisherman's camp. The ramshackle structure stood on stilts in a mangrove thicket at the edge of a small lagoon. An old pickup truck was parked in the drive, and there were several boats in various stages of disrepair tied up to the dock, but there was nothing that could be described as a reliable, commercial fishing boat in sight. The stench of rotting fish was strong. The old man was apparently out fishing.

They agreed to trespass and to wait for Garrard as long as it took and relaxed in two old folding lawn chairs on the dock. The two men passed several hours getting to know one another and catching up on their respective lives. Josh was exhausted and dozed off as the conversation waned, and Jerrod wasn't far behind when the arrival of a large bird caught his attention. The great blue heron lit on a piling very close by and examined the two strangers closely. Jerrod was familiar with the bird but had never seen one so up close and personal. The bird's formal dress reminded him of a Catholic priest ready to say mass, but its primeval eyes said otherwise. Was this some avian agent of the devil that plagued him? Further thought was interrupted by a loud squawk, accompanied by the expulsion of a voluminous string of bird shit, as the great bird flapped off.

Left only with the quiet setting and embracing sunshine, Jerrod soon joined Josh in sleep. Perhaps it was only minutes later when Jerrod snapped awake at the sound of a struggling outboard motor. He could see an old, green fishing skiff in the distance, surrounded by a cloud of black smoke. Jerrod nudged Josh to wakefulness and pointed out the arriving boat. As it slowly picked its way through the oyster bars that blocked the little inlet, Jerrod and Josh stood and waved, so as not to surprise the old man and maybe get shot. The boat approached the dock, and Garrard tossed Josh a line, and the skiff was secured.

"Didn't expect to see more cops so soon," he snorted.

Jerrod laughed and responded, "Sir, we're not cops," and extending his hand. "I'm the missing girl's father. My name is Jerrod Wesley, and this is Dr. Josh Ledbetter. He is a doctor and a man of God who had been a dear friend to my daughter, Courtney, before she disappeared from Key West."

The old man looked them over without saying anything for a long moment. "Reckon you know who I am, and I can save you a lot of time by sayin' I done told them damned cops everything I know."

Jerrod took a deep breath and said, "Sir, I mean no disrespect, and if you told the cops a little white lie, that's more than fine with me, but we need your help. My daughter, Courtney, maybe Samara to you, is very ill and is a danger to herself and others. She was under Dr. Ledbetter's care and was much improved but something went wrong and she, she ... snapped." The grieving father pushed away a tear, and his chin trembled.

Garrard was moved by what he was hearing but turned and pointed toward the water, looking to give Jerrod a moment to recover. "Looky there, old Joe's a comin' to dinner ..."

Josh, who had been quiet up until that moment, exclaimed, "My God, that's the biggest alligator I've ever seen and look at those teeth!"

The old man laughed a brittle, dry laugh and spat into the water. "Ain't no gator. That's salt water and Joe's a big ol' crocodile. I feed the lazy bastard fish heads every night, and he's just like a big ol' kitty cat; loves to have his head scratched. Ain't dangerous like a damned gator—never ate nobody." Sensing he had the moment, the old fisherman said, "Y'all hungry?" as he dumped a drywall bucket full of mullet heads and offal over the side. The big reptile tore into the repulsive mess like it was delicious.

Jerrod and Josh were more nauseated than hungry but knew they had to play along with the grizzled fisherman who obviously had his own sense of decorum. They changed their minds when he opened the door to the shack, and they were met with the delicious aroma of cooking seafood.

Garrard noted their reaction and said, "Smells good, don't it? Never stops simmerin'. I jist keep feedin' it crabs, shrimp, fish, and the occasional mullet; adds flavor to the gumbo pot; you know. He ladled out three large bowls of the steaming concoction and placed them on the dirty wooden table along with a pitcher of iced tea and three soiled glasses.

After the last shrimp was gone, Garrard admitted the truth, "She was here, all right, at least a girl who called herself Samara was here. I found her and her wrecked boat on a sandbar off Cayo Costa. Samara, Courtney, helped me net some fish, and I helped her. Right nice girl and purty, too. We came back here, and I fed her some of this here good gumbo, and then took her to the airport. She said I could have the boat in return, and I picked it up with the first good high tide even though I knowed it was stole all along."

Jerrod felt both relieved and exasperated. "Why didn't you tell the police this?"

Garrard scratched his beard and replied, "Cause she asked me not to and besides, I don't truck with no cops; you know."

"Did she say where she was going or how she was getting there?" Josh asked.

"Whur? No, all I know is that I let her out in front of the Delta terminal at that fancy, new airport."

Sensing that the old man had told them all he knew, they bade him farewell and returned to Josh's car. As they were pulling away, Jerrod said, "We can't incriminate the old man, but we have to tell the local cops that Courtney was last seen at the Delta terminal and let them investigate the situation. My bet is that she is way too smart to buy a commercial airline ticket and climb on a crowded jet. Probably, that was just a ruse for the old man's benefit, and she went directly to the parking structure and stole a car. We'll have to ask the cops to check on cars reported stolen from RSW. Could have stolen a car parked in the long-term lot that hasn't been reported yet, I suppose."

As they neared the General Aviation terminal at the airport, Jerrod's cell phone rang, and it was Barbara Barnes.

"The good news is that the two Russians, Sergei Mogilevish and Vadik Nikolsky, are dead, but the bad news is that Jason Rand got himself shot up in the process. He's in the hospital and will recover with a few scars to show for the experience. Rand killed Mogilevich but the cops got there a moment too late, and Nikolsky shot Jason before the police killed him with a shotgun. Pretty ugly, but at least Hall's hired killers are finally out of the equation. Any news about Courtney?"

46

A Chilling Time

Courtney's concerns had finally settled to rest on one rather daunting question: *Now that I am almost there, how do I kill Maxwell Hall?* She had only her straight razor that had been so effectively used before. But, this was different; she had no way to approach the high-flying executive, who undoubtedly was protected by electronic walls and armies of heavily armed soldiers. The thought occurred to her that she had almost no clothes suitable for such a mission and certainly no professional dress that might be needed to get near the bastard—inside his home or business.

Remembering a large mall in Cherry Hill, Courtney turned off the New Jersey Turnpike and easily found the sprawling shopping complex a short distance from the busy freeway. She managed to find a pleated, gray skirt, white blouse, blue blazer, and suitable shoes on sale at one of the major department stores and was headed back to the parking garage when a young woman with a familiar face walked out of Victoria's Secret. It was Shannon Morris, a friend from the Choate days. Their eyes met momentarily, but Shannon did not make the connection with the shoddily dressed girl. Grateful that she was not recognized, Courtney quickly disappeared into the mob of shoppers. Moments later she recognized another familiar face coming directly at her; it was Sandy Ahearn, a Duke acquaintance, who most certainly knew her grim story. This time she turned and ran; her sick mind in high gear. Every face was now familiar, distorted with hatred, and threatening. "Murderer, murderer, murderer," they yelled. Others came for her with guns drawn and knives flashing, and she ran and ran and ran until there were no more of them. Finally, she came upon her stolen 2005 Toyota Camry, sitting undisturbed in the dimly lit parking garage. The only sound was provided by water dripping from a higher level.

Her purchases secured in the trunk, Courtney fumbled to insert the key in the ignition with shaking hands. After what seemed an eternity, the little car sprang to life, and she sped back to the safety of the turnpike, pointing the car north toward Hartford. There she could hide among the politicians and miscreants that populated the city and not be bothered while she plotted her next murder.

Once in Connecticut the character of the landscape changed, and though it was mid-November, the forests along the way clung to remnants of fall; the little mountains along the Merritt Parkway and I-91 were awash in hues of red, yellow, and gold. The beauty of her home state calmed her troubled mind, and for those precious moments death and mayhem seemed far away. Able to think more clearly now, she realized that her mental health had never really improved; she had never been free of the shackles of Medulin that bound her mind. It had only been the loving care of Josh and the Lord's gentle touch that had held the devil at bay during those warm, wonderful Key West days. Now she was alone with the Devil, and they had important work to do. Lucifer's golden voice became more clear to her every day, and with his help she would play the hand she had been dealt to the last card.

Presently the skyline of Hartford, dominated by the capitol's golden dome, rose before her, and the shadow that clouded her soul darkened as she pulled into a shoddy motel on the outskirts of town. A cheerless, black woman took her money without ever really looking at her. The cheap room smelled of stale cigarette smoke, mildew, and recent sex, but it would have to do. The Elm Court was the sort of place that asked few questions, requiring only a small cash payment for the night, or for a few hours. What you did in that room was your business, and planning the murder of a big-shot was just fine with the management.

Surprisingly hot water was available. Courtney soaped every inch of her body and luxuriated in the healing spray until she realized she had not eaten all day. Fortunately there was a Mc Donald's of sorts next door, and her Spanish was good enough to order a Big Mac and fries to go from the surly, dark-skinned girl who refused to speak English. She snagged the last *Hartford Courant* from a battered display in front of the restaurant and returned to her room for the evening.

Courtney found the newspaper depressing; it mostly reported minority on minority murders and political corruption in Hartford. Seemingly all the schools were failing, and taxes must be raised again. Courtney frowned and turned to the help-wanted section of the paper. There weren't that many full-time jobs available, but as she scanned the few pages, a small add caught her eye. *Hall*—she couldn't possibly be this lucky—only in movies and novels—*Estate manager,*

Female with fluent English, college degree, and book keeping expe-
rience needed to manage staff of large shoreline estate. Beyond that
brief description of the job, it was suggested interested parties call M.
P. Hall and gave a New York telephone number.

Courtney remembered seeing the pay phone in the lobby and
made her way back through the littered parking lot, avoiding used
condoms and empty beer cans. Surprisingly the abused telephone
worked, and she dialed the number. She almost gagged on the smell
of urine as the telephone rang several times at the other end before a
most proper female voice came on the line.

"Melinda Pierce Hall speaking."

Courtney introduced herself as Samara Ledbetter and referenced
the advertisement for the estate manager position. She then told a
brief lie about her qualifications and experience, claimed she had
attended Kent School and The University of Connecticut, and then
worked in hotel management in Florida for four years. She was looking to return to New England for *personal reasons*.

Melinda Pierce looked at her cell phone—finally, someone with
an education and a brain that actually could speak English. "Young
lady, I am impressed with your qualifications, and you could be ideal
for this job. I don't know where you are calling from, but would it be
possible for you to meet me at the estate tomorrow afternoon, at say,
1:00 p.m.?"

"Yes, of course."

"OK, until then, the brief background is that this is Maxwell Hall's
home. Maxwell is a busy pharmaceutical executive (My God, the right
Hall!). I am Maxwell's wife and have to spend a great deal of time in
New York dealing with my own affairs. I need someone to run the
show to free up more of my time. I won't be around a lot, so this job
will require the manager to make everyday decisions on his or her
own." Melinda Pierce gave detailed directions to the estate in Groton
and bade her farewell.

"A gift from Heaven," Courtney whispered aloud. She noticed the
clerk at the front desk was now eyeing her closely, so she hung up the
receiver and scurried back to her room. Once she had every lock and
chain in place, she collapsed onto the dirty sheets and suffered a restless sleep. She was awakened several times by noises outside, voices,
tires squealing, sirens, and perhaps even gunshots, providing relief
from nightmares that were even more frightening. People chased her
screaming ugly accusations, people who became things.

Though Courtney had no idea what Melinda Pierce Hall looked
like, in her dreams she became an ugly shrew, a monstrous, fat rat
with long, yellow teeth and an appetite for human flesh. The horrible

woman was waiting for her, mouth open, salivating, when she opened the door to the Hall estate home that looked exactly like Dracula's castle in Transylvania that she had seen in the old movie. Courtney jarred awake for the last time that night. Sleep just wasn't worth it.

Finally an adventurous beam of sunlight found a small hole in a yellowed shade, and Courtney set up in the sweat soaked bed, feeling exhausted. She looked at her watch and groaned; it was 10:00 a.m. She had fallen back to sleep after all. Groton was a long way from Hartford; she also needed time to find the secluded estate. She felt filthy after a night on the unwashed sheets and took another quick shower and slipped into her new outfit. With a minimal amount of makeup she looked like any other attractive, young, professional woman seeking a job. The straight razor in her jacket pocket was not noticeable but readily retrievable when the need arose. She checked out of the motel and headed south toward her appointment. Traffic on I-91 was heavy, and she was relieved when she exited onto Route 9 toward Old Saybrook.

It was then that she realized that she was without a plan. Courtney assumed that Maxwell Hall would be at work, but how many gardeners, cooks, and housekeepers might there be on the premises? And when might her quarry return and how could she gain that bit of critical information? What if Hall was out of town? Would she have to somehow get herself hired? How, she had no substantiating papers with her, bogus or otherwise? Should she have given herself another day or so to fabricate a CV? She recalled the computers at the Old Saybrook library and glanced at her watch. If she skipped lunch there might be time to create something that was better than nothing. Ignoring the risk that she might be recognized in a library so close to home, she entered the modern facility and gained permission to use a computer. She was rusty, but her excellent word processing skills coupled with her newly-developed talent as an accomplished liar soon had her smiling as the words filled the two pages of the "Samara Ledbetter—Brief CV." It was more convincing than some real ones her classmates had shared with her at Duke. She only agonized over the hotel experience lie but finally decided on a couple of Key West hotels that she knew well enough.

After a few wrong turns, Courtney found herself on a long lane that crossed a pretty salt marsh. The lane led to a gate which allowed access to an island mostly covered by the meandering Hall estate. A bronze eagle with an infant in its talons soared above the heavy gate. A plaque below identified the estate as *Chateau des Aigles*. Courtney sniffed. Home of the Eagles was not an unexpected name for the abode of Maxwell Hall. Though of a privileged upbringing, she had never seen anything like this. How many people had paid the price so Maxwell Hall could live this obscene existence?

Courtney pushed the button beside the speaker and identified herself. There was no response, but the ornate gate swung slowly open, and Courtney passed under the eagle into a designated parking area for visitors. For anyone who loved the folksy, New England architecture common along the shoreline, the manse that rose before her would have been an out-of-place monstrosity. It was constructed of heavy stones and had turrets suitable for a castle. Perhaps it was a castle for its self-appointed royal master, Maxwell Hall, the Count Dracula in residence. What secrets did the somber place harbor in its dungeon? Courtney pushed the doorbell and in moments the massive wooden door swung open. She was expecting a butler or doorman but was surprised by the tall, blond woman who met her. She was in her late forties and was, or had been, beautiful. The slick, shiny skin of her face betrayed a long history of cosmetic procedures. Her clothing was casual but casual of the expensive, designer sort that one might see at a fox hunt or polo match.

"Hello, you must be Samara. I'm Melinda Pierce Hall and welcome to *Chateau des Aigles.*" Noting the look on Courtney's face, Melinda Pierce said, "Oh, I know; that's quite a pretentious name, considering it was known as *Sea Oats* when we acquired it some years ago. My husband's ego; you know."

Courtney knew all about Maxwell Hall's ego but smiled and nodded without comment.

"You are probably surprised that I answered the door; aren't you? Truth is, I let all the help go home at noon. Didn't want them snooping around while I was trying to hire their supervisor; you know. Come on in."

Courtney sensed another stroke of luck but probed for confirmation. "Gosh, you must feel all alone in this great home."

"Well, no, actually I enjoy being alone, even here."

Courtney considered that a *maybe* and didn't exclude the possibility of security hanging around but thought better than pursue it. She was escorted through a magnificent entryway and into a long hall. An opulent office to the immediate left could only belong to His Majesty. Melinda offered Courtney a seat in front of a massive, ornate desk and began to ask reasonable enough questions.

The interviewee replied, "Here, perhaps this will be of some help," and handed Melinda the bogus resume.

"Well, thank you, I almost never get useful paper out of anyone these days—so refreshing. Ummm ... let me see. Yes, the hotel experience in Key West—what responsibilities did you have?"

"Responsibilities? Quite a lot really. As an assistant manager, I filled in for whoever was absent and did whatever needed to be done. Spent a lot of time at the front desk, policed the maid staff, helped with accounting problems, and even tended bar on occasion. You need a drink, any drink, and I can make it."

"Really, I like that; you sound willing to tackle most anything?"

"Just about," Courtney replied with a warm smile.

"And how are you at dealing with grizzly bears?" she quipped.

"Ma'am?"

"By that I mean my husband, Maxwell. You'll be dealing with him a great deal more than me, and he's ... quite frankly a bastard at times. Most of the time, actually."

"I've probably seen worse in Key West," she lied. "Does this suggest that I would be here late most evenings and deal with your husband frequently?"

"Ah, yes, but I would think you would be accustomed to long days and late nights in the hotel business?"

"Yes, but since you have made such an issue of Mr. Hall, what time would he typically come home, say this evening?"

"Typical? There is no typical for Maxwell, but tonight he will be home by 8:00 p.m. because he is cooking dinner for me, at least if he knows what's good for him. And, I guess I didn't say, this job has free room and board as a benefit. You'll have your own suite on the upper level, and I'm certain you'll find it most comfortable and convenient. You are allowed to have visitors, and they will be impressed."

Courtney considered what a nightmare this job would be for the unfortunate soul dumb enough to take it. "That solves a big problem," she replied. "This neighborhood looks a bit pricy for me."

As a final step in the process, Courtney was given a tour of the massive home. She expressed awe and appreciation that she did not feel but took careful note of Hall's second floor trophy room. Apparently Hall loved to shoot helpless animals, and the walls were adorned with mounts of game animals from all over the world, many endangered species. In one corner of the room stood full body mounts of a doe and two tiny, spotted fawns. Beneath the great heads were expensive display gun cabinets with thick glass doors. Contained within these cabinets were literally hundreds of fine hunting rifles and shotguns; one of the most notable such collections in the world, her host had claimed. Most noteworthy to Courtney were the several full boxes of ammunition for each weapon on the shelves below. The locked doors would not prevent her from breaking the glass and taking what she needed. Now, she had choices if things got rough.

When the tour was over, Courtney said, "I just have one request. I am accustomed to hotels that are filled with people, and the vastness and emptiness of this place makes me a bit uncomfortable. So, would it be unreasonable if I asked to meet your security people?"

"No, not at all, but you'll have to come back tomorrow."

"Melinda, that won't be necessary; I didn't really come here seeking a job. Actually, I came here to *do* a job, namely to kill that bastard of a husband of yours ..."

The frightened woman brought her hands to her wide-open mouth and looked for an opening, an avenue of escape. But there was none. The flash of the straight razor blade paralyzed Melinda Pierce Hall, a helpless woman whose only defenses were money and lawyers.

"Please don't kill me; I'll do anything, pay anything, anything you want. You can have my husband and kill him if you like, but just don't hurt me. I can't stand pain. Please!" The distraught woman fell to her knees in tears.

Courtney and the Devil had become one again, and her face was contorted in a viscous sneer; saliva drooled from the corners of her mouth. She pressed the dull side of the blade hard against the fool's windpipe and asked, "Do you know who I am?"

Melinda did not look up to confirm that she didn't. "No! Please!"

"Look at me, you bitch. I am Courtney Wesley; does that ring a bell?"

Melinda looked up this time and took in the twisted face before her own. "Oh-my-God," she exclaimed as she finally understood. "You are the girl who was given the bad drug, Medulin, and killed those people. You hold my husband responsible, and you want to kill him, too. Oh-my-God."

"And let's not forget all those other people your husband murdered and the fact that he stole my father's company and made him *road kill*. The laugh of Wall Street!"

Melinda didn't know what the hell Courtney was talking about, but she said, "Maxwell has abused me in every way a man can abuse a woman. I hate him as much as you do and would love to see him dead and rotting in hell. But why kill me? I've done nothing to you or your family."

Courtney's killer instincts were raging within her now, and she needed to kill this scared rabbit, had to. She flipped the blade over, and it made a little cut into Melinda Pierce Hall's soft, white throat but did not slash. She pushed the whimpering woman to the floor in disgust.

Courtney tried to think. A large grandfather clock in the entry ticked off the executioner's minutes. Finally, she said, "I might not kill you if you cooperate."

The almost victim croaked a weak, "Thank you."

Razor in hand, Courtney moved her captive to the third floor bedroom, where she ordered her to strip. Then using her razor, Courtney cut cords from the lamps and bound Melinda securely, hands tied behind her and feet tied to the bed frame. The woman was gagged with a piece of sheet and placed on her side on the bed. The cords were tied so tight that the woman bled profusely, but she uttered no sound of complaint.

The crazed girl looked at her with disgust and said, "Looks like your boob job was about as effective as your face lift. There really is such a thing as more money than brains, and you're the poster child."

Evil smelling sweat was pouring from Courtney's body now, and she was almost overcome with the need to kill this woman who willingly shared her life with Maxwell Hall. But she resisted and said, "One tiny sound, and you are a dead woman."

She turned off the light and shut the door, proceeding back to Maxwell's office. As she entered the room, the telephone rang. Resisting the temptation to answer it, she let it ring until the answering machine came on.

"Hello, Dear, Maxwell here. You must be in the pool. Just calling you for a heads up; I will indeed be cooking dinner tonight for my sweetheart but will have a couple of unexpected guests along. Petrov and Anitov, my two new Russian bodyguards, will be with me. You won't like them; they are pigs, actually, but entertaining pigs. Better get that big package of T-bones out of the freezer to thaw. I have plenty of Russian vodka of all sorts, so we're set. Bastards run on raw meat and alcohol. I'll be home early—see you at 7:00 p.m." There was a click, and he was gone.

Courtney smiled a crooked smile; the hunt was on. But who were these two Russians, and what had happened to the last pair? Hopefully the police had killed them. But now the game had changed— she could have easily taken Maxwell with her straight razor, but that small blade would be woefully inadequate for the bodyguards. The extra firepower she needed to take the two Russians, who were likely bulky monsters trained in the martial arts, sat waiting in the trophy room on the second floor.

She bounded up the stairs and down the hall to Maxwell's so-called trophy room and took a quick visual inventory of the weapons. One case contained a collection of Uzis, which seemed especially appropriate for killing Russians. A heavy Civil War era musket taken from its mount above the fireplace served as a suitable club to shatter the heavy glass door. One of the machine pistols looked almost new, and she found a forty-round magazine that was full of 9 mm ammunition and jammed it into the lethal weapon. Uncertain about its operation, she pointed at the stuffed deer and pulled the trigger, but nothing happened. The safety was off; she switched it to the on position and pulled the trigger again. Still nothing. She finally figured out how to cock the machine pistol and chambered a round and tried again. There was a loud Raaaap! Raaaap! as bullets shredded the stuffed animals, but the powerful weapon almost flew out of her hand. Then, she knew she had to take careful aim and hold on tightly with both hands. Courtney had confidence she could do that; the main thing was to take out the two Russians without killing Maxwell Hall in the process. He needed to die a more protracted death.

Her eyes fell on another case that displayed a single, gold-plated, exquisitely engraved Beretta over and under shotgun. She rightly guessed that the thing cost a fortune and was Hall's favorite. Another swing of the musket and the beautiful shotgun belonged to her. She didn't know anything about hunting but selected a box of high-powered shells loaded with number two shot. The thought of killing Hall with his own favorite weapon had a certain appeal, and it probably wouldn't matter which shells she used up-close and personal.

Feeling she had all the firepower she needed, Courtney moved her weapons and ammunition back to Maxwell Hall's office where she planned to kill him. Then she remembered her car parked out front. That certainly wouldn't do! The dirty car fit nicely between two refuse bins behind the kitchen and would not be noticed. She opened the trunk and retrieved her small bag and backpack and returned to the house. There she changed her clothes and became more comfortable in a T-shirt, faded jeans, and worn sneakers. She was as ready as she would ever be, and now there was nothing to do but wait.

47

In a Lobster's Claws

Maxwell Hall stood beside the door of the big Apex auditorium, holding his unlit cigar in one hand and shaking hands with departing directors with the other. The meeting had gone as he predicted, and now he was being congratulated for his ingenious acquisition of Genplex and their wonder drug, Axilon. My, how they had clapped when he described how the competition had been crushed as with a powerful lobster's claws—appropriately the featured menu item for the dinner the night before. Maxwell loved theme meals, particularly when they celebrated a massacre. The last details had been tended to and forthwith Genplex shares would be swapped for outstanding Apex shares. Given the hostile nature of the takeover and issues regarding Medulin, the board members had insisted that Maxwell increase his security, but he was way ahead of them with that one. The two Russian killers lurked down the hallway at that very moment. The usual Apex security agents were curiously not to be seen.

Not far to the south of Groton, Jerrod Wesley sat in his Madison office studying the document that defined his next career. It was the comprehensive business plan for Plasma Therapeutics, a start-up biotechnology company that would focus on treatments for Alzheimer's disease and other debilitating neurodegenerative disorders. The thick document described new approaches to the complex diseases in exquisite detail. Paper commitments from several leading academic laboratories layered on additional, high-value, novel biology. An agreement had been signed with the health care division of Coonts and Swale, Ltd. to raise the necessary funds to start up the operation. Jerrod's waning responsibilities at Genplex had allowed him ample time to work on the plan. The investment firm believed in both Jerrod and his plan and thought the money would come quickly. For the past several weeks he had largely collected keys and files as tearful, former Genplex employees walked out the door to new lives. He sighed and looked out the window across the empty parking lot; it was pouring rain, and heavy fog hung over Long Island Sound. Usually, this shit waited until after Thanksgiving.

Despite his enthusiasm for the new company, Jerrod was in a funk. He hadn't realized how attached he was to his scientists until they were gone. Sure, some of the better ones would join him in the new company, but there would be no more than twenty—tops—to begin with. Much of the work would be done through academic contracts. And where the hell was his wayward daughter, Courtney, and what tomfoolery was she up to? Since she had quietly slipped away from Key West, Jerrod had searched high and low for an answer to that question. He knew that the key was there somewhere, hidden just below the surface of his mind. Maybe he should stop looking; perhaps there was some grand scheme that had to play out before the nightmare could finally be all over. His ruminations were interrupted by a soft knock; it was Wanda.

"How you doing, big boy?"

He laughed. "Fine now," and he meant it; the positive effect that wonderful woman had on his mood was greater than that of any drug, including Axilon.

"You just saved me—I was sinking in the mire when you knocked. The weather, the empty parking lot, Courtney ..."

"I know," she replied, "but this is almost over. Soon you'll be in the new lab surrounded by geeks and culture dishes again. You'll be so excited about your new company and its research that you'll forget about Maxwell Hall and what he did to you—to all of us."

Jerrod stared out over the water, and his eyes assumed its dark pessimism. He whispered, "I'll never forget or forgive Maxwell Hall."

It was at that moment the ugly realization of Courtney's intentions surfaced from its hiding place within the deep caverns of Jerrod's troubled mind. It was like the explosion of a flash-bulb—clear and obvious. Now, there was a new devil to wrestle with, but it was his own speculation, and no one would believe what he had no evidence for. He would live with his crushing revelation until it was over.

48

Sweet Revenge

Tic-tock, tic tock. The sound of the antique grandfather clock in the entry echoed louder with each count of passing time. Finally, Courtney could stand it no longer; her face twitched; then she screamed and fired a burst from the Uzi into the precious antique. The clock's decades-long count ended forever at 6:30 p.m., a very late and foolish time to be making unnecessary noise. But the place was as quiet as death; no one had heard the clatter of the machine pistol except her captive upstairs. What did Melinda think?

What did Courtney care?

Realizing that time was short, Courtney pushed away a tear and made her final preparations. Maxwell's study was just off the entry to the left. The curtains were partially drawn, and she could observe the trio as they approached without her being seen. She hid the shotgun behind a curtain, placed a comfortable chair before the window, and settled in; the cocked Uzi nestled lovingly in her lap. She had begun to nod when the slam of a heavy car door brought her to full wakefulness. It was Maxwell Hall and his two massive Russian bodyguards. Petrov held a bouquet of flowers, a thoughtful gift for the hostess, and Anitov carried a large bottle of clear liquor, likely vodka.

Courtney's features changed, and her lips drew back in an unearthly snarl. Her eyes became slits as she moved across the room and flattened herself beside the office door. There was the click of a key, and the massive door swung open. The two bodyguards preceded Hall into the foyer, as was their way, and he closed the door behind them. It was not an ideal scenario with Hall in the field of fire, but she had to shoot and shoot now; otherwise she was a dead woman. She checked her weapon; it was cocked, and the safety was off. Now!

She stepped out from the office doorway and said, "Hello, Max," as she unloaded the first burst into the Russian on her left. Raaap! Raaaap! A dozen 9 mm rounds tore through the big man, and he fell

237

to the floor spewing blood. Maxwell Hall dived to the floor and covered his head behind the fallen Russian, using Petrov's considerable bulk as a shield. The second Russian dropped his bottle of vodka and reached beneath his coat. Courtney put four bursts into the killer before his hand emerged, and Anitov fell face-forward in a growing lake of red.

Hall was crying now, begging for his worthless life, but Courtney ignored the fool and walked over and shot both Russians in the back of their heads for good measure. It was an unneeded precaution, but it somehow felt good to the blood-crazed girl. Besides, it scared the shit out of Maxwell Hall. She was trembling now and had the weapon leveled at Hall. It took all her inner strength—her remaining modicum of self restraint—to keep from pulling the trigger and ending it right then and there. But that would be too easy for him after all he had done; Maxwell Hall, like some evil moth, needed to twist and turn in the flame a bit, perhaps a lot.

"Stand up," she croaked.

Hall had regained his composure a bit and replied, "Who the hell are you, and what do you want?" as the blood covered executive struggled to his feet.

"Who? Look at me closely, Max; do I not look the same as I did when you dined with Mother and me? The night you brought us all those free Medulin tablets. Mother and I were so grateful, but that was before I killed her; wasn't it?"

The scared man's eyes widened as a glimmer of recognition flashed across his horrified face. *The fucking daughter!*

"You," he managed, "are ..."

"Crazy, crazy Courtney Wesley?" she offered. "Yes, that would be it; crazy as a shit house bug with no real hope of getting better. I've tried real hard to get well, and I've had some wonderful help, but it didn't work. There's only one thing that's going to make me feel better, and I think you know what that is."

Hall responded, "Do you know who I am? You hurt me, and they'll lock you up and throw the key away; maybe give you the gas or electrocute you, hurt you, torture you."

"Max, I don't know *who* you are, and I don't give a shit, but I do know *what* you are, and right now that's all that matters to me. You are a slimy, little, self-absorbed bastard who has no respect for the lives of others. You only care about money and your business, which for a long time was Medulin and is what brought you here to this end. Oh, and by the way, killing you won't make one bit of difference after all the blood I have already shed. The court may even show me mercy for the good deed I am about to do."

Hall had no response, and Courtney jammed the Uzi in his back and said, "March!" She directed him to his office and had him sit in the plush, leather chair behind his massive desk. "Be still, and don't move, or I'll shoot," she threatened. Soon he was firmly bound with a strong nylon rope she had located in the manse's shop. His hands were tied behind him and to the chair back, and his feet were tightly bound together and tied to the chair's pedestal.

Finally Hall remembered he had a wife and demanded, "What have you done to my wife?"

"Melinda Pierce is alive and well. She's upstairs, naked, and trussed up like a chicken. Naked, because I wanted to see what all the young men who are going to spend your money will have to look at. Not pretty, but they'll manage."

Maxwell had no reply to that disturbing thought.

"How much longer you live is up to you," Courtney explained. The girl walked to her backpack in the corner and retrieved a large bottle of capsules. It was labeled: *Medulin Capsules, 100 mg, #1000, A Product of Apex Pharmaceuticals Research.*

"I've been carrying these deadly things around since that awful night I killed my teacher, and I didn't know why. Now I do ..."

Courtney poured a small pile of the pills on the desk before Hall. She said, "Start taking the Medulin, Max; lap them up like the dog you are."

"No! I won't take those damned things."

Courtney smiled and replied, "OK, good enough." She walked over to the curtain and pulled out Maxwell's gold Beretta and cocked it. "I thought you might like to be killed by the most expensive shotgun in the world—so appropriate. Open your mouth."

℀

Jerrod Wesley's BMW slammed to a halt in front of the Groton Police Station. He left the big car double-parked with the engine running, and he and Wanda ran for the front door. He breathlessly explained who he was and the basic elements of his missing daughter's life of crime. Lieutenant Ramsey was familiar with the murders and amazed by what Jerrod had to say next.

"I have good reason to believe that my daughter is right here in Groton. She has likely come here to kill Maxwell Hall, President and CEO of Apex Pharmaceuticals; *the man who pushed the drug Medulin that hurt or killed so many people, including Courtney.* Maxwell Hall is not listed in the telephone directory, and I could not call him to warn ..."

"We know Mr. Hall very well; I'll call his number." The Hall tele-

phone rang several times with no answer until the answering machine
came on. "This is Lieutenant Ramsey at the Groton Police Department. We have a report that a wanted killer may be in this immediate
area with intent to harm you. Please alert your security, and take all
necessary precautions. We will immediately dispatch two patrol cars
to your estate."

"Sir, would it be possible for us to ride along? After all, Courtney
is my daughter, and you may need my help to safely bring her in if she
is indeed there."

Ramsey looked at Wesley. "You're serious about all of this; aren't
you? I'll dispatch two patrol cars to the Hall estate, and you two can
ride with me, if you agree to stay out of the way if it all goes wrong."

Jerrod said little as the cruiser raced through the streets of Groton
toward the shoreline, where the rich and powerful lived. He cringed
as he recalled how he had almost let this go; let the thing finally come
to its own conclusion, no matter what that conclusion might have
been. But something within him had balked at that hellish bit of dishonesty, despite the fact that the lie would have remained hidden in
his tormented mind forever. So, better late than never, Wanda and he
had rushed off into the night armed with the truth.

⚑

"No ... I ..." Hall bent over the desk and lapped the white capsules up with his dry tongue as best he could. When he finally choked,
Courtney provided him with a bowl of water.

Satisfied that he had recovered, she poured another pile of Medulin capsules, maybe one hundred this time, onto the desk. Courtney
leveled the twin over and under Beretta inches from his face and said,
"OK, go ahead."

The cycle was repeated several times until sirens could be heard
in the distance. Soon they grew louder suggesting that the emergency
vehicles, likely police, were crossing the salt marsh and heading for
the estate.

Hall spat a mouthful of capsules across the desk and said with a
smirk, "Too bad, Courtney, here come the cops; I'm saved, and you're
finally done. Maxwell Hall always wins in the end. Now fucking untie
me, bitch!"

Courtney was sweating now; she had not anticipated this and had
no contingency plan. "Max, *you have not won*; even if I don't shoot
you, which is unlikely, the dose of Medulin you just took will probably
kill you outright; that is, if you're lucky. Otherwise..."

Her attention was diverted from her captive as tires screeched
and doors slammed in front of the manse. There were three blue cars

with flashing lights parked in the drive. Two passengers remained in the rear seat of one of the cars, but she could not make out the two dark shapes. Her finger trembled on the trigger of the shotgun.

There was a loud rap on the door followed by, "Police, open up! Groton police!"

Courtney spun around and fired the two powerful shotgun shells directly into Maxwell Hall's grinning face, spattering everything he had ever known and every viscous plan he had ever schemed over his elegant office. The sick girl looked at the mess; there was no doubt, Maxwell Hall was finally dead, not that that fixed anything, but it certainly limited his future sins; she considered. Confident that the two loud reports of the Beretta had stopped the cops in their tracks; she sprayed two bursts from the Uzi out an office window well away from anyone outside. Now they would retreat to their cars and call for SWAT back-up, buying her some more time.

Melinda Pierce! Courtney thought of the woman and how frightened she must be by now and ran up the stairs to find her wide-eyed and bleeding profusely from her bindings. Courtney ripped the gag from the woman's mouth and looked at her tearfully. "Maxwell and his two Russian bodyguards are dead, and the police are outside. I think I delayed them a bit, but eventually they'll break down the door and discover what happened here. I'll untie you, and you can get dressed and let them in, if you like, but first, is there any way out of here other than that damned road?"

"First of all, thank you for killing the evil bastard; he can't hurt me anymore and now I'm about the richest woman on earth. Please don't untie me; let them find me like I am. I'll concoct some ridiculous story to throw them off for a while. Can you operate a powerboat?"

Courtney smiled and nodded.

"If you go down to the basement level, on the far left side you will find a door that leads to an underground passageway to our boat dock. It is a remnant of the original house that stood here long ago, and I don't know what it was used for, but we use it as an all-weather way to access our boats. The current conditions are awful, so you'd better take the Grady White. It's full of gas, and the keys are in it. There are heavy sweaters and rain gear aboard. On the way out, stop in the great room and remove that awful painting of Napoleon. There you will find a safe." Melinda gave Courtney the simple combination and told her to take the fat package of bills inside. The one hundred thousand dollars would take her a great distance from Connecticut and those who pursued her.

"You can consider that a tip for not killing me and a payment never to come back here again. Ever! Fair enough?"

Courtney nodded her agreement and hurried out of the room as the sound of more sirens carried on the thickening fog.

♄

There had been no more shots fired from the residence, and there had been no replies to the police's hails and loudly delivered threats and pleas. The heavily armed SWAT team had broken down the massive front door with a battering ram, rushed inside, and swarmed over the place. Lieutenant Ramsey and his men had followed closely, but there was no shooter, no resistance, nothing ... All that could be found was two dead Russians, the faceless remains of Maxwell Hall, and his tightly-bound, but very much alive, wife.

Melinda Pierce Hall told the lieutenant that she had expected two Russians and her husband for dinner but thought nothing of it when a third showed up. She believed them to be bodyguards and felt better for their presence until two of them grabbed her and took her upstairs and tied her up on the bed. She did not know where Hall and the third Russian were or what they were doing while this was going on. She had heard several bursts of automatic weapon fire and what sounded like two shotgun blasts, some more automatic weapon fire after the cops arrived, and then nothing until the officers freed her. She had no idea where the third Russian was or where he might be hiding. Maybe his name started with an *S*. Melinda Pierce reminded them that this was a vast compound, and there were many places to look. Dogs might help. No, there had never been a girl—*any girl*.

Ramsey was scratching his head when he returned to the cruiser. He sat in the dark and said nothing for a few minutes as the wind rocked the vehicle. The temperature was dropping, and fog was beginning to freeze on the windshield; it was indeed a depressing evening. Finally he spoke, describing the carnage he had seen at the crime scene and relating the story Mrs. Hall had told. "Only I don't believe a word of it; what we found at the crime scene and her story don't remotely resonate. Those two Russians had been killed the moment they entered the house, and there is no proof of a third one. So when she says there was no girl, I don't know whether to believe that either. She's lying about something—everything—and that just doesn't make any sense. Doesn't she want us to catch her husband's killer?"

"Maybe not," Jerrod provided. "Maxwell had a lot of enemies; perhaps she could be counted among them and is more than happy to see him dead. She is likely very rich now."

The frustrated cop looked at Jerrod blankly and said, "I didn't tell you quite everything. Would you mind walking back inside with me and looking at something? Lady, I'll have to ask you to stay in the car. It isn't pretty in there."

Wanda was grateful to be spared the horror of the crime scene, and the two men hurried back to the house. It was all Jerrod could do to concentrate on the scene before him; Maxwell Hall was still bound and hung forward in the plush office chair where he had died. What was left of his once arrogant face still dripped blood onto the desk, joining fragments of skull, skin, and brain tissue—gore from the shooting. Notably a number of white capsules were scattered over the desk top as well. A large bottle of the same capsules stood off to the side. He read the label without touching the bottle and looked up at the policeman.

"I suppose you brought me in here because you think I might know something about the drug?"

Ramsey nodded. "We often see illegal drugs at crime scenes, but that's not dope; is it?"

"If the label on the bottle is correct, then the drug is Medulin, an experimental drug developed by Apex Pharmaceuticals, which is responsible for endless death and misery. This is the drug that drove a number of unsuspecting patients crazy and led them to kill innocent and not-so-innocent people. Maxwell Hall was president and CEO of Apex and was up to his neck in the Medulin disaster and subsequent cover-up."

"And was this the drug that led to your daughter's problems?" Ramsey asked.

"I'm afraid so."

"Your daughter aside for the moment; what in the hell do you think was going on here with Hall and the drug on the desk?"

"I think someone was administering Hall a dose of his own medicine—literally trying to poison him with Medulin. Likely the murderer was someone who had been severely hurt by the drug and wanted to get even. We arrived, and they finished the job with two blasts from a shotgun, and then made their escape good."

The two men walked back into the foyer, and Lieutenant Ramsey put his hand on Jerrod's shoulder. "You called us because you believed that your daughter, Courtney, was on her way here. Do you believe that she could have done what you just witnessed?"

"Yes, I do, but I also believe that Melinda Pierce Hall played some role in this, if not the crime, then in Courtney's clean escape."

Ramsey sighed; he'd never seen anything like this. The lab people would arrive soon and likely the crime could be sorted out by lifting fingerprints from the murder weapons and abandoned automobile, but for now ... "Mr. Wesley, I know this has been very difficult for you, but would you be willing to return to the station with me and make a statement?"

Jerrod nodded, "Yes, whatever might help."

49

Sweet Surrender

The weather had improved, and the sun was struggling to break through the miasma when the couple finally pulled into Jerrod's lane. It had been a long twenty-four hours and a dangerous trip home to cap it off. The roads were covered with a thin sheet of black ice, compliments of freezing fog. Jerrod was beyond exhaustion and slept soundly on the back seat while Wanda negotiated the slick roads as best she could with the BMW. The icy limbs of almost barren oaks and sugar maples clattered overhead in the breeze, reflecting brilliant patterns of light as the sun pushed away the last of the fog. After a night of death and desperation, the new day offered promise.

"Jerrod, wake up; we're finally home—alive." She helped the tired man out of the car as the garage door rattled down.

"Thanks for driving, Honey; you saved me again. Let's go inside and have a nice breakfast with a mimosa or two, and then let's catch up on our sleep. I'm no good to anybody right now. He unlocked the door to the house, and they stepped inside and were immediately alerted that something was amiss. A television was on somewhere in the house, and the ABC Morning News was reporting the horrible murders in Groton. Jerrod looked at Wanda; he knew they did not leave a TV on. She shrugged, and they quietly made their way to the great room. The big flat screen television was on, and there was someone fast asleep on the couch in front of it. Courtney! After all this time, Courtney had finally come home.

The girl wore her old pajamas from high school; they were light blue, and the little birds and rabbits had almost faded away. She stirred and began to vigorously suck her thumb, a habit that had been difficult for her to break as a baby. Jerrod pushed a tear away and got down on his knees and ran his fingers through Courtney's fine hair. Her long eyelashes twitched and her big eyes opened slightly. "Da-Da?"

245

Eyes wide open now, she spotted Wanda standing behind Jerrod and began to cry. "You're not my Mommy! I want my real Mommy!"

"Courtney, listen to me, *I am your father*; tell Daddy what's wrong."

"Hungry! I want my bottle," the poor girl sobbed.

The daunting question as to how Courtney had gotten home so quickly was answered when a Grady White registered to Maxwell Hall was found hard aground on the Madison Town Beach that same morning. How the scared girl had navigated the heavy weather, islands, breakwaters, and rocks between Groton and Madison in the darkness remained a matter of speculation. Confronted with the facts, Melinda Pierce Hall had finally come clean and told the police the truth, at least as far as she understood it. Both her money and the expensive boat were returned, and no charges were pressed.

One thing that was all too clear was that Courtney had suffered her most severe mental breakdown since the first dose of Medulin. She had been treated in a secure setting at Yale New Haven Psychiatric Hospital, a seventy-three patient outpatient facility, for almost two weeks with little change. Jerrod and Wanda had been joined by Barbara Barnes for a consult with Dr. Leon Shively, a highly regarded Yale Psychiatrist and Dr. Betty Johnson, a neurologist specializing in brain injury and neurodegenerative disorders.

Shively explained, "There is absolutely no chance that Courtney is acting out. She has definitely reverted to a child-like state. Although the full truth may never be known, I think we all recognize that this poor girl has been through more horror in the past few months than we can imagine ... this in the face of an unknown degree of brain injury from that damned drug. I believe that what happened in Groton was the straw that broke the camel's back, if you'll excuse the non-medical cliché. From a behavioral point of view, I can't say for certain what her prognosis is. I would not recommend she be given any drug; perhaps she will make improvements or at least offer us some tips over time. Dr. Johnson ..."

"I have evaluated her neurological status using every tool we have here at Yale, and while I can definitely say there is neurological damage caused by Medulin consistent with what has been seen in other victims, I don't think there is enough injury to fully explain her psychotic withdrawal from reality. My belief is that she has been so severely traumatized that she has traveled back to a safe place, much like we see with soldiers shell-shocked or traumatized in combat; what we call combat stress reaction today. We have to remember that she was functional and improving in Key West, and she had to be extremely functional, if psychotic, to do what she did in Groton."

The physician took a sip of cold coffee and looked out the conference room window, buying time, seeking answers. Finding none she offered, "Dr. Shively and I have discussed this case extensively, and we believe that Courtney will require long-term care with frequent visits by familiar, loving faces to improve. For how long I just don't know."

Barbara Barnes pushed her chair back and said, "I don't want to make bad matters worse, but the medical problems are entangled with a lot of daunting legal issues. Courtney Wesley has allegedly murdered one person in North Carolina, two in New York, and now three in Connecticut. I am doing my best to deal with the legal systems in all three states and the FBI, but it will take your expert testimony and perhaps that of other experts to prevent her from coming to trial. A judge will decide. What we'd really like to see is the charges dropped due to the Medulin circumstances, but that will take some doing. Beyond the legalities I think we can conclude that a long and deadly nightmare is over, and Courtney will receive the care she needs."

50

Mending

Jerrod Wesley found a new place and a new peace. He was no longer afraid to answer the telephone, and he no longer grieved the loss of Genplex, though he carefully followed the latest developments reported for Axilon. He did not suffer from feelings of absentee ownership; rather he enjoyed a certain pride in what he had contributed. Though early in the game, his new company, Plasma Therapeutics, was doing well, and with Wanda's able help, he spent endless hours dealing with scientific issues, company business, and banking needs. Plasma Therapeutics was conveniently situated near Yale University and Yale New Haven Hospital, and he visited Courtney every day. Strangely enough she was the same little girl that she had been at age three or four, and Jerrod often brought her the cookies and stuffed bears she had loved then.

Despite the best of care and frequent visits by family and friends, Courtney remained the little girl she had become, seemingly free of awful memories that would otherwise haunt her and free of the lawyers and prosecutors that would torture her if they could. She even seemed happy at times, and Jerrod loved her for what she was. Sometimes in the dark of the night after a drink or two, he would admit to Wanda that he was thankful that the Lord had protected her from what she had done and might otherwise face. He knew that she had done part of it for him and loved her more for the risk she had taken. Although Jerrod was happy with the routine, he knew, but never mentioned, that Courtney could not occupy a precious bed in that busy psychiatric hospital forever. There would be decisions that had to be made.

In June Jerrod and Wanda were married in Las Vegas in a commercial wedding chapel. After everything that had happened and much gut wrenching discussion, they had decided that a large, celebratory, church wedding in Connecticut would be inappropriate. A quiet, understated reception for close friends and colleagues was held at their home in Madison a week later.

Early in July Josh Ledbetter spent a week with Jerrod and Wanda. He also spent time with Courtney, who did not recognize him, but she soon came to adore him. Josh spent late afternoons with friends at the Yale Divinity School, seeking advice from those experienced in foreign mission work. Josh had agreed to undertake a challenging medical and religious mission in Gambia, a small, but dangerous, country in Western Africa. In the evenings Jerrod taught Josh the fundamentals of sailing, and they enjoyed the local restaurants and New England seafood during his visit, but mostly Jerrod took pleasure in Josh's tales of Key West and Courtney's life there. Could it have worked for the long-haul? No one will ever know, but thanks to Josh, Courtney had found a modicum of happiness there.

After Josh had departed for Gambia, Courtney's demeanor changed; she was no longer cheered by Jerrod's visits; she had fallen into a severe depression. Perhaps there was no relationship to Josh's visit, but disturbing questions arose in Jerrod's mind. Questions he could not shake no matter how hard he tried ...

Over the next several weeks a gradual improvement was noted in Courtney's status. She smiled on occasion and could be cheered up when her mood was down. On the third of August, Jerrod was leaving Courtney's room after a promising visit when the girl surprised him by getting out of bed and hugging him. She said, "You are the most wonderful daddy in the whole world, and I love you."

Later Jerrod would recall her precious words and wonder if he'd actually heard a child's voice. All he could say was that it was somehow different, older. Maybe it doesn't even matter; those words would have to do; they were the last ones that Courtney Wesley would ever speak to her father.

Two days after Courtney's unexpected expression of her love for her father, Jerrod received an urgent phone call from Dotty Anderson, Courtney's duty nurse. "Mr. Wesley, your daughter, Courtney, has gone missing ..."

"*Missing*, what do you mean, missing?" Jerrod stammered. His mind was racing—this was so familiar, so *believable*.

"Uh, when I made the rounds with breakfast this morning, she wasn't in her room or anywhere else to be found. I'm afraid she's ... gone, slipped away during the night. I've left a call in to Dr. Shively; probably he can't help, but he will have to notify the police, given the girl's violent history. Is there any chance you have seen or heard from her, Sir?"

Jerrod ignored the gratuitous question. "Her things; what about her things."

"Strangely enough, Courtney took nothing."

Jerrod shook his head. "How in God's name could she just walk out of your hospital in her pajamas, unassisted without being seen? Don't you people have any security?"

Nurse Anderson took a deep breath and slowly responded, "Perhaps she didn't. Courtney wasn't a prisoner in this outpatient facility, and people come and go all the time."

"Didn't what?"

"Walk out of here by herself—perhaps she had *assistance*."

Jerrod's mind was spinning too rapidly to even begin to get a grasp on the various implications of the word *assistance*. He hung up the phone and called for Wanda.

Despite exhaustive searches by the authorities no sign of Courtney was found. It was as though she had disappeared into thin air, vanished—poof. Although Jerrod knew that Courtney was *someplace* alive and well, he feared that he would never see his daughter again. He prayed that she had finally found her peace and was in the loving hands of the Lord, and he also prayed that Maxwell Hall, the man who had caused all this, burned in the hottest flames of hell.

Though Jerrod had a pressing need to share Courtney's disappearance with Josh Ledbetter, the promised letters from Gambia did not arrive. A few phone calls revealed that the church had not heard from Josh since his arrival in Africa, and neither had his parents heard, who were frantic. Seemingly the doctor had vanished into the thick bush of Gambia. Jerrod often wondered who Josh Ledbetter really was, but one thing was clear; he was no ordinary, mortal man. Though Josh seemed lost forever, Jerrod knew in his heart that Josh was providing care for needy Gambian souls beyond the reach of primitive telephone lines. *Who else was he caring for?*

Jerrod smiled at Wanda as the *Sea Sprint* heeled over in the stiff breeze. A brief respite in early winter's cold had given the couple one last opportunity to take the sleek craft out for a sail before she was put away for winter. The distant, rolling hills to the north, that Courtney so loved in her innocent youth, sparkled in the golden sunlight. Jerrod was rewarded by the thought that even though *bad things happen, time heals*. His simple thought was replaced by the more poignant words of his hero, William Faulkner. *Memory believes before knowing remembers. Believes longer than recollects, longer than knowing even wonders.* Jerrod would remember Courtney in his own way.